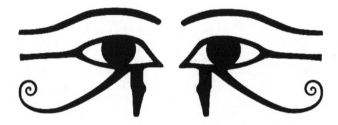

SONGS OF THE OSIRIAN

Christopher D. Abbott

ISBN: **1535166398**
ISBN-13: **978-1535166393**

Other titles by this author:

Sir Laurence Dies [The "Dies" Trilogy – Book 1]
Dr. Chandrix Dies [The "Dies" Trilogy – Book 2]
Beast: Revelations [Ethology] Songs of Beast
Revolting Tales: Christopher D. Abbott & Todd A. Curry

This book is dedicated to two people:

My best mate who also happens to be my dad, Phil Abbott, and my other best mate, who happens to be the older brother I never wanted, Todd A Curry.

Special thanks, in no particular order:

Chase Masterson, Todd A Curry, John & Amy Levine, Patti Geesey, Richard Sutton, Susan Munson, Carol Ann Swan, Rob Reddan, Phil Abbott, Shane Emery, Sally Rothenhaus, Jennifer Taylor, Joe Wolf, Laraine Richardson, Scott Charnick.

The Garcia Clan: Anthony, Tammy, Sam, Alexander, and Anthony Jr

Li Williams and all at Burgundy Books

Table of Contents

NEW AGE OF MAN

THE EVE OF WAR

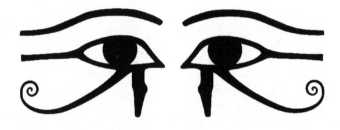

SONGS
OF THE
OSIRIAN

Foreword

By Chase Masterson

Imagine, if you will, a world in which people of all races and cultures coexist in harmony. Where people openly share their resources, and the acquisition of wealth no longer fuels their existence. Sounds fictional, right? Given the nature of the world we live in, it doesn't appear that humans are remotely capable of living that way. But it isn't just Science-Fiction or Fantasy that holds this desire to better the world we live in. My work has brought me in contact with many people who believe this type of enlightenment in action is within our reach on a local scale, and perhaps someday, globally. A desire for humankind to be more than the sum of our parts is not a lofty or unattainable goal. Take Star Trek for example, a series very close to my heart. The ideology Gene Roddenberry developed has endured for over 50 years. Fans and actors of the show continue to bring life to Roddenberry's concepts years after it disappeared from main stream television. Actors from the show have developed friendships with each other, and with our fans, based on this ideology, and through it we have clubs that support important causes, gender equality champions, anti-bullying coalitions, and many other charitable groups that follow the very essence of Gene's vision.

I first met Chris at TerrifiCon in 2015, and we immediately connected, discussing these concepts. He kept in touch with me through social media platforms. We met again at Long Island Who and spent time talking about the Pop Culture Hero Coalition. Chris expressed a desire to want to contribute. Then when he told me about the concept of this book, and asked me to write the foreword, I was more than happy to oblige, because the concepts of his work are in sync with the Coalition's crucial work.

Songs of the Osirian explores many present-day issues, through the Science-fiction and Fantasy genres. The story deals with real world problems such as greed, hate, and domination of the weak — but the message it delivers is of triumph through empathy, cooperation, and understanding. The story builds on the mythological concepts of Osirian Gods, and Chris deftly weaves a Science-Fiction element into their Pantheon. He gives vision to the idea that these beings have extraordinary abilities and are so far evolved; they are considered Gods by this understanding. Layered beneath a human tale of good vs evil are complex nuances of gray that delve into the desires and emotional conflicts each person faces on their respective quests; the story presents a dilemma, prompting deep introspection for characters and readers alike.

The predominant characters are human, and we experience a familiarity in the conflicted journeys of characters such as Mary Wilson, or the boy Ammon, who have opposing views for the world they find themselves in. And the message I truly cherish is that, despite adversity, compassionate strength in the midst of devastation leads to a world enjoying a previously unknown peace and harmony, without greed, where no one is hungry, and where preventable disease is almost entirely eradicated. And beside them through this adversity, protecting them from evil, live the Osirian. One of the more interesting aspects of the Osirian is their use of music as their power. Songs replace magic, and this musical element is woven throughout the story. With relatable concepts, *Songs of the Osirian* takes us on a fast-paced journey through both darkness and light, pain and joy. And even in moments of obscurity there is forged an enduring strength and optimism. It's a story where even the villains are sympathetic, which leads to philosophical reflection that makes for a rich and evocative read.

Roddenberry's influence is clear in Chris's vision for the future of humanity. And while there are elements reminiscent of classic Science Fiction, such as Tolkien's the Lord of the Rings and H.G. Well's The War of the Worlds, Chris has taken his optimism, sense of justice, and caring nature, and has developed a unique, allegorical world all his own. *Songs of the Osirian* is a story that will appeal to both Fantasy and Science-Fictions fans alike. I am pleased to be associated with it, and with him, and I hope you enjoy the story as much as I did. Given time, and perseverance, and boldly heroic imagination, humanity has an opportunity to make the iconic words "live long and prosper" into more than just a salutation. Inspired by stories such as *Songs of the Osirian*, we can create compassion amidst adversity and make those words a reality.

Enjoy!
Chase

About Chase Masterson

Chase Masterson has most recently been seen guest starring on CW's The Flash, which won the People's Choice Award for "Favorite New Drama." Best known for her break-out role on Star Trek: Deep Space Nine, one of the highest-rated syndicated shows of all time, Chase is loved by millions of fans worldwide.

Connect with Chase here:
www.chasemasterson.com

Introduction

By Christopher D. Abbott

This story was born from a love of fantasy. As a boy, I read J.R.R. Tolkien's The Hobbit and The Lord of the Rings and I was instantly transfixed by the power of the story, but more so, the richness of histories developed in writing it. It stayed with me for years, and I held desire to write something similar, but inspiration never fully came. Years later after I'd published a few short stories and a couple of books, I developed a keen interest in the mysteries of Ancient Egypt. I had a burning desire to blend fantasy with mythos. It was after I submitted a short story entitled Songs of Beast for an Ethology, that this book took full shape.

I created the world with its various characters, delving deep into rich histories of ancient mythology. I found scope in diverse and differing opinions within the mythology and cosmology of the Osirian myths, from there the bases of my story developed. I am passionate about music and I wanted this to be a key element to underline communication of my Osirian characters.

So, Songs of Beast developed into Songs of the Osirian.

I made minor changes and anyone who reads the short will find it embedded here as foundation.

I'd like to thank Chase Masterson for her enthusiastic involvement in this project. She has been an inspiration, and a good friend.

At the end of the book you'll find a short story, The Last of Us, by Rob James. Rob and I have been friends for many years, and I've been keen to get him noticed for a while. I hope you enjoy his story as much I did.

Thank you. My best wishes to you all!

CDA

The Music of Ardunadine: "The Vision of Arrandori"
Extract from the Book of Narrudeth
The Beginning of Song

"Arrandori gathered the nine Ardunadine and caused them to create a complex harmony of music. He called on each of them to bring their own powers and thoughts to bear on their part, and one in particular wove his own desire for mastery into the Great Song. After its ending, Arrandori created a Vision of the World that sprung from the Music, and then gave that Vision reality, thus bringing the universe into being."

Professor Arnold Darcorion
Transcript from "The Cult of Beast Society"
London, 1854

"A single thought can engender profound breaks in reality, and when this happens, anything might be possible. Precise cohesion and concentration of imagination brings with it a cause to effect. It can happen in the slithers of darkness, when an unnoticed malformed aberration sneaks up on you. It can be immeasurable, incalculable, and without doubt, often times, ephemeral. And when this darkness fills the fabric of our world, and the light of the waxing moon is hidden from the faithless, this manifestation will slip into the hollowness unseen and unheard. And ladies and gentlemen, this is the moment we seek, where a tendril of this unimaginable dreadfulness finds a pathway through the membrane of our reality, to touch us, to change us, to bridge the gap between those who are mortal and those who aren't. And when the moment comes, when the world seems still, those who are worthy will bear witness to the birth of a brand new world."

Prologue
The Creation of Beast

The Celestial Temple of Song

Beyond the reach of mortals, atop the highest mountain, the celestial temple of the Ardunadine shone with an angelic light that maintained the temporary equipoise of life. Inside, immense pillars of cryptocrystalline held aloft a dazzling, stunning sky. Rays of ruby-red shimmered and bounced off a protective miasma shroud, far above, exploding in noiseless flashes of purples, blues, and reds. Golden clouds of coalescing multi-coloured gases tumbled and fell along the maelstrom of an angry tempest. The depths of the sky itself, alight in vivid shifting turmoil. Just visible through a rhombohedral latticed floor were serene orange mountains, the inhospitable peaks swathed in purple snow, and at their base, sparkling turquoise rivers disappeared far off into the purple-blue mist of the horizon.

In the centre of the cavernous temple, a dais manifested without noise from within the trigonal-crystal floor. As it raised, ethereal wisp-like beings shimmered into existence, one after the other. Their manifestations concluded with a unified phonological chorus of celestial melody. Eight of them. Wraithlike. Each with their own distinct façade, different, yet the same, took up equidistant positions adjacent to each other, encircling the dais. Their transcendent idiolect was an incomprehensible blend of blissful symphonic chattering. The platform lit, and within its centre, a skeletal structure of incredible size manifested from swirls of multi-coloured smoke. When the skeletal structure had formed, internal organs filled the cavity, followed by muscle, sinew, skin, and fur. There, in the centre, stood a majestic lion-like creature. Translucent shackles flew from the dais, hardening around powerful legs and a colossal neck. Its penetrating eyes were emerald green. It raised its head and let loose a ferocious roar. It shook the very foundation of the world.

The ethereal beings continued their mutterings, as the creature tried in vain to release itself from the restraints. One of the beings, the perceived leader, spoke with the loudest voice, but his words were echoed by the others as if they were somehow connected in communal colloquy.

'You will not be able to release yourself from the restraints,' they said.

The creature growled but did not speak.

'We, the Righteous, keepers of the sacred Songs of Harmony, have decreed you are one of the most contemptable and corrupt beings this race has ever spawned. We name you Beast now and forever,' the choir continued.

'Your venalities, Beast, are so great we cannot begin to enumerate them. Your wickedness is beyond any dimension or calculable measurement seen since Arrandori's vision birthed life into our Songs.'

Beast laughed. At first soft, almost a titter; it concluded with a bellowed, thunderous roar. The wraiths continued their mutterings and with deliberate pause, he spoke. In comparison to their sainted chorus, his voice was an admixed unity of disharmonious malevolence.

'Why have you locked me in this form, brothers?'

There was a hiss of discontent as one of the eight spoke. 'You are no brother of ours.'

The leader continued his refrain. 'This appearance was chosen, Beast, to not only reflect the seriousness of your sins, but to ensure they can no longer continue. In this ... shape, you are barred from ever again using the power of your Song, a birth-right, lost, stripped by proclamation of Arrandori's symphonic judgement. Before the final ruling, Beast, we give you a moment to speak to the Righteous.'

Beast curled a lip displaying huge fangs. 'When I break free from these chains, I will leave nothing alive, brothers. I will devour you all and everything you have created through your self-appointed divine righteousness. I will swallow your pathetic construct and choke it in my darkness. The very fabric of you all will nourish me for eternity. I will tear this world apart, piece by precious piece, until I am all that is left.' A claw extended from a massive paw. It scrapped at the dais, causing a small scratch in the surface that resealed itself in an instant.

'Will this suffice, brothers?' Beast stared unblinking with huge, luminous, disc-like eyes.

The choral-voices went on.

'You leave us no choice then, Beast. It is the judgement of the Righteous you be banished to a place where you can do no further harm. Into a universe in infancy, where your cruel influence can never reach or hinder another sentient being; onto a planet where your existence can never affect its growth, and locked in this shape, you will live out a mortal life. You will perish the way of all things corporeal. Your flesh will age and your body decay. And when your finite form expires, the Righteous will come to displace your mortal remains across this world. Your essence will be lost in this wilderness and you will never again be made whole. This is our final Song.'

Beast roared, his massive bulk heaved and pulled.

'You cannot expel me, cursed brethren! I am eternal damnation. I am the foundation of darkness.' His words were deafening but gone was the confidence, in its place, panic and fear.

'I am constant, fools. I am foul. I am annihilation and ruin. Hear me, I will devastate this world. My tread will leave a path of dust and devastation, the Music of Ardunadine, the Righteous, Arrandori himself, will agonise in eternal suffering. ...'

The eight ignored his rambling and circled him. Their movement slow at first, but soon increased in speed. All the time he roared, cursed, spit, and screamed at them. His body strained, and muscles tore. Their movement became faster and faster, until it was no longer possible to see an individual entity. The heaving bulk lifted away from the dais. Huge eyes widened as an intensity of pain the likes of which he'd never before experienced ripped through his new form. Nerves screamed in outrage, sending signals of unimaginable agony to his brain, as he disassembled before them. Beast's howls filled the judicial chamber. No longer threats, they were the shrieks and cries of a being in anguished undulating torment. Unperturbed, the eight moved with rapidity turning them into a brilliant snake of ghost-light.

Beast's form fizzled from view in a roaring blaze and he ceased to be. His structure dissolved into a blending ripple of sparkling smoke-like vapour that funnelled into a towering and deafening tornado. It sped upwards and out through the protective miasma membrane above.

The Righteous slowed.

The dais melted and disappeared into the crystalline floor.

And, as their chorus continued long into the night, the swirling, twisting, vapoured whirlwind left the turbulent purple-blue-red sky, disappearing out into the stars beyond.

One
First Age of Beast

Ancient Egypt: Waset - circa 2000 BC.

The might of Pharaoh's army stood in silent apprehension, glistening in their uniforms of turquoise and gold. There were no clouds overhead but a heaviness was in the air. It was unnaturally hot for the season. Pharaoh squinted as he beheld the horizon, his eyes centred on the hazy rising sun. Just behind, following it slowly up to sky, he saw a growing darkness. His heart told him a storm was moving out to meet them. He knew the time had come. He felt the dark shadow slithering with malice across his land and he called to a priest, who was at his side in an instant.

'Tell me what your eyes see that mortal men's cannot, for I would know the darkness that blights my land.'

The priest's white eyes did not squint or blink as he leant hard on his golden staff. Blessed by the Osirian with a vision of things to come, he held out his free hand and said, 'Oh High King of Kings. I see the darkness. I see the festering shapes within, far on the horizon. But what these things are I cannot yet tell. It is not for the haziness of the sun, but rather a blackness forcing eyes to fail. A vast horde has come, Great King, war is at hand.'

'How much distance lies before them?'

'As the crow may fly, three days' march. But something gives unnatural speed to these foul fiends, I say unto thee, King of Kings, he should ready for battle within two days, maybe less.'

'I would have it so,' Pharaoh said and turned towards his men.

The thousand-strong army stood in wait for the horde of death to arrive. He saw their love and passion and it pleased him. He ordered water and food to pass lips, for he knew battle would soon be upon them. Men rested and well fed would fight better for it. He walked amongst them and took wine.

They sang and made merriment despite the oncoming doom.

On the eve of the second day, the sky fell utterly dark. The foreboded storm approached from the east. Their lines were many. Impish things crept and crawled, amongst them towering high, hideous winged beasts, their bodies alight in flame bound forth shaking the land with each step. Black shapes continued to slither in silence. Amid these giants, trumpets and cursed wicked shrieks filled the air. Pharaoh again called for his lector-priest.

'Battle is upon us, and it is not a pretty thing to behold. It is time for you to weave your magic,' he said.

The priest remained impassive as he opened arms and began incantations. He drew upon the secret names of the Osirian and called upon their Songs.

As the army of darkness neared closer, Pharaoh looked up at what should have been the sun rising, but bleak clouds stole the precious light, and he cursed them. What little sunlight penetrated sat behind advancing darkness, forming great silhouettes, hiding hideous truths from him.

'Priest, bring forth light, for I would have these foul things see my face, ere the morning is over.'

The lector-priest of the Osirian nodded, emanating calm radiance. He lifted his staff and flooded the land in bright illumination. It bathed the great king in warmth and strength, and reflected off his silent army, who sparkled and glowed under its supreme majestic power.

The enemy came ever closer, but the priest's light did not pierce their ranks, for they stopped at its boundary, fearful. Pharaoh held tight grip on the hilt of his sword, waiting. The priest sang sacred songs into the silence.

The great host parted leaving deep path into their ranks. The priest's light fought to break the darkness, but failed, so it wasn't possible for Pharaoh to see the fullness of his enemy or gauge their numbers. But the path revealed something of the depth of the legions of darkness and far worse; for at its heart amongst the fiery winged behemoths, a pair of luminous green eyes shone out of the gloom. As they moved closer, a colossal lion padded softly into view. When it reached the forward column the path closed and it roared. The sound so terrible all that heard it trembled.

But not Pharaoh. For in his veins flowed the power of the Songs of Light. He leant on his sword in quiet strength and waited for the Lord of the Darkness to stand before him. His army, iridescent and powerful, took comfort from the strength of their king and trembled no more.

At length the great lion and the king of kings met. Beast prowled before him and Pharaoh eyed his movement with calm.

'Little King of men,' Beast sang. *'How prodigious your army looks, shimmering in their love for you. I offer chance of surrender. Pledge yourself and your men to my will, for there is still a place in my new order for your delusional army, but not your cretinous Osirian deceivers. Come now, oh Mighty King. You know what foulness approaches. Shall I bring forth torment and cruelty upon thy men? For I will, my Lord King, and you know they will beg for a death that will never come. Is this what you desire, King of Kings? Speak as only a guileless ridiculous man can do, but choose those unsophisticated words with care.'*

'Oh Great Lord of the Dark, I did not come here to waste *any* words on you.'

Beast growled a great warning, but Pharaoh ignored him and continued.

'And let it be said for now that I see you, I admit to pitying you, ever more so than I was born to.'

Beast roared and lunged but the priest's light prevented his assault. He sat back down.

'You have chosen poorly. I shall show no pity, man-filth, when I turn your feeble form into an undying scavenging rat, as all men are bound to become, in my mercy.'

Pharaoh laughed till tears fell. Beast curled his lip, but his rage softened. Although the king insulted him, he admired the strength, even though it wouldn't save him from the worst possible punishment he could conceive. The king wiped his eyes and became serious.

'Very well, Great Lion of Darkness, let us pit swords, for maybe you are greater with them than you are with songs?'

Beast's fur rippled at the insult and before he could respond, Pharaoh turned his back and walked towards his men, leaving his priest in situ, maintaining the light.

Soon after, battle commenced.

*

The ground shook hard above and slithers of sand slipped through the cracks. A roar close by, along with screaming, confusion, and panic, startled them. Inside the beautiful temple, a group of ten beings dressed in flowing coloured robes, leant on their staffs. They towered above a group of priests. Each of them adorned with unusual animal headgear, gifts from Pharaoh and the men of the Realm. A ghostly light flowed through them as they called forth amazing songs. Outside the temple, the roaring and screaming grew louder and those who sat in reverence looked at each other, muttering in nervous apprehension.

They knew what was coming. They knew the horde of Beast was close and one by one, they writhed in shared terror. Osiris, King of the Osirian stood benevolent beside his beautiful sister-queen, Lady Isis. His skin held a tinge of green hue, upon his head sat an Atef crown of pure white.

He spread arms outwards, crook and flail in each hand, bathing them in strength, offering a serene smile. It calmed anxieties.

A man burst into the chamber bowing his head. King Osiris looked upon his face and read much. The messenger said, 'Oh Great King of All, Pharaoh's battle does go ill. Warriors of the mighty foul Beast will soon arrive, and thus I say, he too would soon find us.'

It was as he had foreseen. The king looked at his sister-wife and smiled. Turning back to the messenger and inclining his head, he sang deep chorus, 'Pharaoh's part is now complete then, it is time for us to do ours.'

He shone great light and those around, gods and man, prepared for the coming of darkness.

The priests of men lowered their faces to the sand.

One of the Osirian, a man with a white beard woven with neat complexity down to a point on his chest, held aloft his staff and sang a song causing his form to fuse with that of a great falcon. Light burst forth from the crystal at its top. It bathed mortal men in a soft glow, fuelling courage, and they were joyful.

There was a guttural grunt behind them, a heavy snort, and they turned. In the doorway, silhouetted by the brightness of a sun far younger than himself, stood the giant lion known only as Beast. He slipped into the vast room and bore teeth.

The Osirian, in conjoined forms of men and animal, powerful in faith, came before him whispering songs of capitulation. He snarled defiant response. They formed a semi-circle as he prowled to and fro, waiting. His tail flicked in the anticipation of the fight.

King of the Osirian, Lord Osiris stepped out to meet him. Eyes of each never left the other. Beast wondered much. His thought gave way to a deep hunger, and globs of drool fell in great splatters as he salivated. The dark lord fancied he could bequeath prolonged cruel death upon his enemy, but pondered if it was less fitting than he deserved. What might Osiris taste like? Would his earthly flesh quench desires? Ideas caused unconscious movement within him; his body tensed, he bent low, ready to strike. Repressed fury, excitement and craving boiled beyond control. He lunged, massive jaws biting down with a snap—on nothing—as Osiris was now standing behind him. He felt the sting of a great staff on his hind and turned in snarl.

'Silence, Beast,' he commanded. The other Osirian approached. He felt them as they closed around. His head turned a little, great green eyes took in the room. Isis whispered strength to devoted King. The priests of the Osirian now stood and filed in behind their masters, flanking him.

Beast rested before King of Light.

Tell me, Osiris, warrior farmer, what do you dream about when the darkness hits, hmm? My magnificence, maybe? Your impotence, perhaps? These things you seem bent on protecting are weakened by your failure to do so, for I have tasted many a man and rejoiced in their anguish. You know my power is beyond even your comprehension, withdraw now, go back to the Temple of Song, and inform my brothers that this world now belongs to me.'

Osiris laughed. 'Your song never changes, old one. Your power is potent. I acknowledge, and have healthy fear in it.'

'You should. For even you must know, I hold the power to crack apart this world and pull from its depth hideous things I wove into it, long before your light was birthed.'

Osiris said, 'The problem is, Dark One. Half of what you sing bears little to truths taught. I do not think even you could vanquish us all. Feel inside me, great son of our Maker. Within me you see my truth. Unlike you, conveyer of mistruths, I share knowledge free in hopes you will break from dark spells. Recognise now our power to banish you, forever.'

Beast laughed hard. *Foolishness. I see as if you were made of glass. You have nothing. You are barren. A sad flicker of an old failing song only. You and your harlot queen may have ensnared feeble men in bewitching spell, but I am beyond you. Far stronger than your elevated forms could ever realise. My brothers thought to banish me powerless upon this world, but here you see me? Am I bound? Am I powerless? No ... I am supreme. I wove the discord in Song that formed worlds like this one, underling. Let us not play games with one another. Relinquish your light and I will be merciful.'*

Osiris growled at him, his form grew in size, he raised his arms. 'Know this fallen son of Arrandori, your time here is done. I will smite thee into void, and banish thee into a darkness of no depth, into which you will fall now and forever.'

A great light flooded the room, emanating from all. Their Songs of Light encased him.

Beast roared a complex malevolent chorus. It beat back their light, disarming them.

'You have no such power. Puny thing, I am the foundation of this world. Nothing you possess can defeat me. I give you chance now to flee. Flee I say, before the foulest of my servants arrive to devour you all.'

And Isis came beside her devoted king and pronounced, 'Let it be known that we, Osirian keepers of the Songs of Light, will no longer stand idle and allow your domination of the will of mankind to continue. For we, in the might of our King, are the protectors of this world. Even if we are to be locked together for eternity, willingly we would endure it. For in your arrogance, Lord of Darkness and Corruption, you misread the truth of things. Look at where you stand, oh great blind Lord of Shadow. This assault on us was predestined. You think we unprepared, fool? Nay, we were ready for you. You walked into trap with eyes wide shut.'

Beast's confident swagger wavered.

King Osiris felt it.

Beast turned from him and padded away with a low growl. The great entrance was blocked by many. Osiris waved a hand and they parted. He saw the doorway blocked by an impenetrable wall of light, not of their design. Its power he could not perceive. It enraged him.

'Betrayers!'

King of the Osirian remained calm. 'Nay, Servant of Darkness, you can never leave. Your own kin, in their magnificence, made plan of your defeat. Our Song now flows in the land of men above, filling them with strength and majesty beyond their frail form. Your armies of foulness will be destroyed, and it is well.'

Osiris held Isis's hand as they came forward in joint power.

With a charge, they all attacked.

Beast cursed, roaring defences, throwing them into walls. They came at him, again and again, relentless and resolute. The Beast Lord swept them aside, and he felt no threat from them. He sang to his horde above, showing them the path, providing instruction to unblock the door. Silence answered his call. Cursing, he saw the truth of Isis's song. She had bound him to their temple, trapping him in light, cutting him off. He sang to the darkness with more power than they had understanding of, but found he could neither hear nor control his servants.

They came at him again, under renewed strength. King and Osirian brethren gave no quarter. Again, Beast thwarted them, over and over. They persisted. An irritation only, no more a danger to him than a fly against a hurricane, yet neither side could claim advantage.

For an age the stalemate continued.

*

Above ground, Pharaoh's grand army gathered for the final assault. Beast's legion bathed in the darkness he'd summoned, but the priests of the Osirian banished the clouds and new light from the sun fell upon the enemy, smiting them to dust. Swords ended blackness and shadows shrank. All but the Faulgoth remained. They shattered the land, uprooting sands, exposing the fires below. Pharaoh, however, laid prepared plan for their devastation. Catching them in crossfires of light and golden arrows they fell into well-hidden pits of blessed water with sizzling shrieks.

The battle lasted a few hours, the bulk of the horde easily vanquished when their master gave no further commands; in confusion and panic, as their master's song fell silent, they lost will to fight and fled. Even the mighty Faulgoth, still independent in their power, shrank, burrowing back into the Earth never to be seen again.

When the war was over and men reigned supreme, there was great rejoicing but also heavy burden of sorrow for those lost.

*

Deep beneath the Earth the battle raged on.

They fought with no ground given and none taken. The lector-priests of man were old and wasted. They were shrunken now, eyes white. Their wraithlike hands outstretched. They continued to maintain song, till their mortal vessels expired and they fell spent, with sigh.

Beast bellowed his fury. So hideous was his counter, the room itself feared and shook.

The bearded Osirian held up his staff and formed a barrier above the men. He called out in alarm. 'Father, he seeks to bring the temple down upon us. The men will not survive if the rocks fall on them.'

The Lord of Darkness ran his tongue over large white fangs as he took in this new development. The weakness of the Osirian exposed. His attacks shifted to the frail things giving strength to them. Through their discord, he found advantage. They turned in protections of man, and broke their defences, forcing retreat.

Beast waited for ripe opportunity and leapt upon Osiris, mauling him as they dropped to the ground. They grappled in violent struggle. Isis rushed forth and plunged the tip of her staff into the pit of Beast's left eye, and he howled leaping away, pawing at the wound in indignant agony. The Osirian formed a circle of light, protecting the king.

Lady Isis lifted her King from the ground. His wounds were severe but not fatal.

Beast prowled and hissed. His hateful good eye never leaving them.

'My love,' she whispered softly, 'we cannot win this fight. We wound, we heal, and so it goes on. You must take what I *know* is hidden. Use it. Would you not see battle's end?'

'No, my Queen, we have strength. Do not despair and stay on true path. Together we can overcome him. See? I am healed now, let us fight on.'

Another voice called to him. 'Father, do not doom us to spend eternity with this darkness, locked in the same useless philosophical debates of old! If we have advantage, use it.'

Osiris looked between them, jaw set firm.

'You cannot know what you ask, great son. Let a king do battle as he sees fit.'

Queen took his face into her hands, the touch softened features harder than rock.

'Son of our Light is right, my beautiful love. The time for debate is passed. Listen, husband, for although I grieve with heavy heart, I say this truly, you must call forth that which ends all.'

Osiris looked at the malevolence prowling before them. Turning back to his Queen, he said, 'Isis, sister-queen … no, you cannot ask this of me … I am weary with misery at thoughts of being gone from you.'

'My King, there is no other way.' She took his hand and flooded him with love. He felt burden of misery at her tight hold, it both energised and destroyed him. Their eyes met in tears, forming as truths were communicated as one.

Osiris grabbed her hard and kissed her more passionately than he had ever done before.

'Farewell, my Queen.' He looked to bearded Osirian. 'Farewell, faithful son. May knowledge and wisdom bring good council, to any who are fortunate to sit at your feet.'

The Osirian son flooded the room with pride. 'Farewell, brother-father. I will listen out for your great song in difficult times.'

'You shall have it.'

Isis's tears fell as she sang, 'While I can still see, I will call to you, crying out to heaven's height. I know you may not come, although I am your sister, whom you have loved on this Earth, I will grieve and weave spell to bring you unto my own. Go now, my love above all things, become the storm and banish this foul thing forever. It is the only thing worth the sacrifice of my heart.'

With a grief-burdened smile he turned, bursting into grey-shadow through the hidden power he alone possessed, and Isis choked on her tears.

Grey-shadow stepped forward, voicing song bursting in immeasurable power of dark and light, his ethereal form shifted through beasts and kings, a multitude of bodies conjoined and hundreds of different arms seem to fly from the shapeless cloud, and he flashed as bright as a supernova. His robes fluttered to the ground as he no longer held form on Earth. His great wind roared dreadful assault and Monster King howled in pain. The grey-light burnt and scarred and he recoiled.

The Osirian tapped into their king's new power, joining songs. They advanced. He bit at them but jaws found nothing but smoke.

They shimmered in and out of earthly form, their light as bright as a sun, surrounding the swirling greyness of their king.

Beast shrieked in pain and rage and the room shook. Rocks fell, hitting old corpse-like priests, knocking a few to the ground. Sand, rock, and stone fell, turning temple to ruin which then froze, floating in mid-air as time stopped.

Beast rested fury and retreated from cutting latent energy assaulting him. Before its supremacy, he was not fearful, but powerless. He now heard the Songs of the Ardunadine, betrayers and usurpers alike, as they gave Osiris more power than was just.

Bleeding, wounded, scarred, and half blind, Beast submitted and lay before the greyness of neither light nor dark, in impotent rage.

The Osirian reverted to earthly form, but Osiris remained metamorphosed wraithlike, shimmering.

Beast sneered at him. The Osirian king was no longer the Servant of the Light; he was the light itself.

Osiris ceased the hurt laid upon him, and in defeat, he stood brooding, when a faint whisper of something familiar caught his attention.

He was standing away from them, dripping in blood. He breathed hard but made no move to battle. Instead, he lifted ears to hear faint melody resurfacing. Trace undertones, hidden in the score of their conjoined harmonies. He recognised faint notes of underpinning complex subtle disharmony; overlapping here and there within their loathsome virtuous melody, likely to murder him.

Deep he went, down into the very notes and there he found trace of *his* original Song. It called to him, the arrangement comprehendible to him alone, offering aid. He didn't recognise the one who gave it voice, so he followed its path in secret as the evil-tendril showed him the way. Within a chorus inside chorus, there was expression of admiration, but more than that, there was warnings and whispered instructions.

The Osirian, oblivious, maintained their unified song. The subtle mingling of discordant sounds was evident, yet they failed to hear. Beast's eyes found the one who offered silent homage and plans for escape. He communicated appreciation. The meaning of the secret melody was clear: his banishment into the void was inevitable. From it he would never find exit. He must trust in the tune, submit to them, and leave evil, twisted songs to do their work.

So he obeyed.

Paying close attention to instructions within the mellifluous arrangement, he let saintly chanting wash over him, played along to the phrasing of their song.

He writhed and screamed. He cursed and spat blood at them.

And when the song instructed him to do so, he yielded and rolled over. The flesh upon his hideous form shrank, withered, and fell to dust, leaving only a skeletal frame that collapsed in a great heap. His immortal spirit leapt into the air, a vast black spectre, and Isis called to it, locking it within a ball of crystal, held tight between her palms.

The Osirian returned to earthly form and Isis came forth to her king, who was nothing but an empty cloak and Atef upon the ground. Weeping, she picked up his crook and flail, and gave intake of breath. A crystal heart, alight with fire, sat in the pile. She picked it up and turned to the others in agony of grief but also in joy. Above her, his grey-white form shimmered and pulsed.

'Behold, the heart of our King, destroyer of Beast,' she said. 'Through my magic, I will summon him back. But I know he may never take on the form of my beloved again. My heart cannot bear to be parted from his touch, so I choose to perform the conjoining.'

They sang for hours and the form of Isis turned ghostly and beautiful. The two of them came together in melding. When the ritual was complete, a new earthly form appeared and stood before them.

They observed a confused old woman who leant heavy on her staff. Though her features were unknown to them, they could see the blending of both their king and queen within her. She looked upon the faces of them all and smiled.

'Do not feel sorrow, for I am reborn into merged form,' she said. 'Isis and Osiris no longer. Together we share power in our love, and I am now born Sister-Daughter. Lady of Light shall I be known, or Etheria as some might choose, and always Osiris, whose will dominates greater than my mother's inside me.'

*

Pharaoh surveyed the destruction of his bittersweet victory and a tear fell from him. They had lost so much. The land burnt and a little over half of his once grand city lay in ruin. It had taken days to clear it of the filth of his enemy, but he was proud of the people who came together in comradery to clear it. His contemplations were disturbed by a soft cough behind. He did not turn. A voice he knew well spoke to his thoughts.

'Do not wallow in grief for what was. Look now to the future.'

The king turned in wrath. 'What future? This was not the fight of men, Great Horus. This was a battle of gods, and we are wrecked by it.'

His words stung. 'What you say is true, my Lord King. Yet we all suffered loss.'

'Loss?' He reached out with his hand. 'Look at this place.'

Horus came beside him. 'I grieve at it.'

Pharaoh sighed. 'I do not seek to lay the failings of the heart of men at your feet. But truly, this is no victory.'

'I would argue otherwise.'

He turned and smiled through his sorrow. 'I know. You of all heavenly kin have stood proud amongst worshipers, and I thank you for that. But my people have seen too much of your war and I know more than they about the nature of Osirian. Gods they say, yet knowledge within me tells different stories. From another world you sprang, even though I do not understand how. But whatever they know or choose to think, I wonder how they will see you now that their children are dead, their lands washed red with the blood of innocents?'

Horus leant heavy on his staff. 'The Osirian myths and legends attributed to us by your people are syncretistic of the complex nature of beliefs and knowledge. I choose not to use the term *God*. But others of my kind are less precise with words.'

'Above all, I choose to think on you as friend.'

'As I do you.' He put a hand on his shoulder. 'You have been gifted above all men. They need strength in their King. Cast aside doubts and fears.'

'Do you fear anything, Horus?'

He nodded. 'I fear, King. Far too much.'

'I draw strength from the fact that even you feel as mortal men.'

'Many people through the ages have considered themselves fearless, but it is a thing inside you that cannot be completely extinguished.'

'Then I will tell you my fear. The battle is won. The great beast destroyed by your sorcery. Yet … something dark stirs still.'

Horus sagged. 'I know, I have the same foreboding. Others of my kind disagree.'

Pharaoh set his jaw firm. 'And there is another reason to fear, my friend.'

The Osirian said nothing, his eyes fixed on the horizon.

They stood in the small, decorated chamber, a sarcophagus open before them. Osiris placed the crystal sphere inside and laid a cloth of fine silk over it. She called forth a song of strength and a slab of granite lifted and sealed it within. Horus breathed easier.

'It is done.'

They left the tomb and the native workers began the work of sealing it.

Together they ambled through the chamber, an array of golden items were piled inside, ready to be placed for the burial ceremony.

She frowned. 'It is strange they would treat such a thing as he, with reverence and fine offerings.'

'It is their way, Etheria.'

She raised an eyebrow. 'I will go, there is a gathering called, and it may be the last before we enter our great sleep.'

'I will stay and oversee the entombment. I won't rest easy until I know this place can never be found again.'

She put a hand on his face. 'I look forward to seeing you soon, brother-son.' And her light came forth, and she faded from his view.

The last brick was pushed into place and they covered the wall. A priest then sealed it in cartouche. They then began constructing the second wall as Horus had instructed. A swirl of mist appeared inside the room and they dropped to their knees, burying faces into the sand, as Seth manifested before them. He strode with purpose and walked through the wall into the sealed chamber. In the dark, his amber eyes burnt symbol upon the casket. When he completed, he lowered his head.

'Purpose is revealed at last, brother.'

Seth lifted his eyes and turned. Behind him stood Horus. For the longest time neither spoke, then Seth smiled.

'You always were good at hiding in shadows, little brother.'

'And you have become the shadow.' He sighed. 'Why?'

'Become? I was always a shadow.'

Horus shone bright, gripping his staff hard. 'Step away from the casket, brother.'

Seth put a clawed hand on the granite. 'Of course.'

'What have you done?'

Seth's eyes shone. 'Done? I have done nothing.'

'Lies. I read things much clearer now.'

Seth's anger turned his form into mixture of human and unidentifiable animal. 'Let me tell you what has been read. Nothing. I have set a thing in motion even you, with all your cleverness, have failed to realise.'

'What have you done?'

Seth boomed dreadful laughter and flew forward.

And a battle of Osirian brothers began.

*

Priests entering the tomb found all the workers dead. Tradition swept away, only fear compelled them to seal it before it was finished. They called for others. In haste they buried it beneath the sand and rock. All trace of knowledge removed from records.

*

Of the Osirian and Beast, neither were ever seen nor heard of again.

Pharaoh commissioned priests to write great stories and songs in their honour. But he was careful to guide them, so history would remember things in a way that pleased his mind. The evil of the world now vanquished. Life trickled along to the sands of time. The power of the Osirian Songs, the gifts of their magic and powers, diminished. Truths became tales. Tales turned into legends, and legends became myths lost in time.

* * *

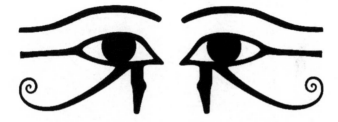

NEW AGE
OF MAN

Two
The Hidden Tomb

Egypt: Cairo - 1923

Former Professor of Cambridge, Albert Kartz, sat perched on a high chair in an open bar in Cairo. Deep in thought, he nursed a second glass of gin. A shift in light broke his melancholy. He looked up and smiled as a man in a white-linen suit slipped into a seat beside him, calling for a drink.

'Howard Carter,' Kartz said, lifting his glass. 'Don't you have a tomb to excavate?'

Carter took a sip and savoured it before swallowing.

'If the Antiquities Service didn't keep adding new layers of bureaucracy every time I woke up, I'd be doing just that. Honestly, Albert, it's becoming impossible.'

Kartz hummed. 'You're simply not a diplomat, Howard.'

'Well, that's true enough.' He laughed. 'Ah ... Sorry. Didn't mean to bother you with all that.'

'No, it's fine. I wish I could help.'

Carter nodded. 'I know. Me too, but it's out of my hands.'

'Now that you've had time to start studying the artefacts, what is your impression?'

'Astonishing. The beauty and refinement of the art displayed by the objects surpasses anything I have ever encountered. It's overwhelming, still.'

'I saw some photographs, they didn't do justice to the headlines, but I'd love to view them if you could sneak me in?'

Carter sighed. 'You know I can't do that, Albert.'

'I know, but it doesn't hurt to ask.'

'If Carnarvon were to ever find out ...'

'Say no more, Howard. His Lordship and I aren't ever likely to resolve our differences.'

Howard Carter pulled something small wrapped in cloth from out of his pocket, and placed it down on the table. He pushed it towards Kartz and sat back into his chair.

Albert stared at the celebrated archaeologist, who smiled through his cigarette as smoke drifted up over his head.

Albert's hand shook a little as he reached for it. He turned his head. 'What is it?'

'A gift, Albert. I found it this morning. It's something in your line.'

He picked up the small object, unwrapping it with care. Inside was a figurine. Albert pulled a magnifying glass from his coat pocket and examined it.

'It's Osiris,' he muttered and then frowned.

'Yes. You notice the unusual thing about it?'

Albert nodded, his frown deepened. 'It's a fake, Howard.' He put it on the table in disgust and picked up his glass of gin, swallowing it in one gulp. It was refilled in an instant.

Carter picked it up and turned it over a few times. 'Fake?'

'Yes, it's fake, has to be. Probably made by one of those fellows out there to fool a tourist. Doesn't fool me.'

Carter raised an eyebrow and put it back on the table. 'You think it would fool me, also?'

Albert hesitated. 'I didn't mean–'

Carter waved at him. 'Albert, look again. I wouldn't have come here if I thought it was a fake.'

'Where was it found?'

'Inside the tomb, mixed in with other antiquities. Carnarvon pocketed a few when he thought I wasn't looking. Damn fool. This one I found and thought of you. But if it's fake then there's an end to it.' He reached out but Kartz picked it up.

Carter smiled.

'You realise what this means, Howard?'

'No. Why don't you tell me?'

'This figurine has the head of Osiris but the body of a woman.'

'You don't say.' Carter lit another cigarette.

'Everything we know about Osiris says he was *father* to Horus, not mother!'

Howard Carter laughed. 'Or maybe sister? Or a hybrid Osiris and Isis? What we know is small in comparison to what we don't.'

'True, but no one will accept it.'

'It's just a figurine, Albert, nothing more. Maybe a child's toy, we really can't know anything for certain.'

'It could turn our understanding of the Osirian history on its head.'

'Or, it could just as easily be a deliberate insult to Osiris made by a disgruntled priest. Anyway, I knew it'd keep you thinking, better for you than gin.'

Kartz turned it over a few more times then wrapped it in the cloth and dropped it into his pocket. 'Has to have been some kind of joke, that's all.' The spark Carter saw in his eye pleased him.

'Well, maybe, but it's a three-thousand-year-old joke. Perhaps it will bring you luck?'

'Perhaps.' He looked up with genuine affection. 'Thank you, Howard.'

He stood and dropped enough coin to cover his and Albert's tab.

'Well, I'd better be off. I've made reports, filed paperwork, so now it's back to digging. I have a burial chamber to catalogue. Take care of yourself, Albert.'

'You also, Howard. You also.'

Albert sat for some time in contemplation. He turned over the figurine a number of times, mesmerised by its intricacy. A soft cough behind caused him to pocket it and turn. An elegant man stood smiling at him. He was holding an unusual black cane. Long, with a snake wrapped around it to a gargoyle head of some description, its jewelled-like ruby eyes glinting in the light.

'Professor Albert Kartz?'

'Never heard of him, unless of course you're here to hand him a fortune from some dead relative?' He chuckled.

The man seemed bemused.

Albert smiled and came forward. 'I'm Kartz, sorry, you are?'

'Arnold,' he said, 'Professor Arnold Darcorion, British Museum.'

'Well. You had to go and ruin it.'

'I'm sorry?'

Kartz put his hands on his hips. 'Now look here. Whatever it is this time, I had nothing to do with it. I thank you for your visit, and I bid you good day!'

He turned away and headed back to his seat.

'I think you might have confused me with someone else, Professor.'

'Stop calling me that. I'm no longer able to claim the title.'

'Doctor, then? I understand you have two doctorates, or are you a different Albert Kartz?'

Kartz turned to the man and frowned. 'Who are you?'

'Arnold Darcorion, I just told you?'

'Darcorion? Never heard of you. I do like the name though. Want a drink, Darcorion?'

He shook his head. 'I wonder if we could talk in private somewhere.'

'About what?'

Arnold leant a little forward. 'About making all your dreams and wishes come true.'

Kartz laughed. 'What a curious fellow you are.'

'Will you hear me out?'

Kartz swallowed his drink. 'Why not. Beats sitting here all day, I suppose. Come on then, my rooms aren't far, follow me.'

Arnold held out a hand and allowed Kartz to pass. He scanned the room once and made eye contact with a man on the opposite side of the bar. They exchanged a look and the other left. Arnold followed Albert outside.

Arnold and Albert chatted amiably as they walked along the dusty, crowded streets.

'You say British Museum?'

'Yes, a special department. I'm part of a … well, you could say … team. We're working on a number of sites across the world.'

'You're a representative of the Antiquities Service?'

'No, no. A field operative of the Department of Antiquities and Strange Artefacts.'

'Operative? Sounds clandestine. Never heard of your department, either.'

'Few have, Albert.'

'So clandestine operatives in the BM now, eh? Things have definitely changed.'

'Certainly, since the war.'

'Makes sense I suppose. Sites around the world? Not specific to Egypt?'

'No, not specific.' A few local children bustled around Arnold. His elegant and rich look attracted them. Albert shooed them away in their own tongue.

'Well, unless it's Egyptian, it's not my area of expertise.'

They pushed their way through crowded streets, Albert making disconnected conversation as they walked. He failed to notice the natives giving them a wide berth, as if they had seen or felt something making them afraid.

'What is it you're digging for, anyway?'

'Bones, mainly.'

Kartz nodded and then seemed lost. In thought, he turned a few times and put a hand over his mouth.

Arnold leant against his cane and tried his best not to look out of place.

'You have to forgive me.' Albert smiled apologetically. 'These streets look very much alike. I need to get my bearings.'

Arnold waved at a fly and took in the neighbourhood and people while Albert did his best to remember where he lived.

'Ah ... there we are, up here. Come along, old chap.'

Arnold followed and they ascended stone stairs into an apartment full of boxes and miscellaneous items. It looked as though Albert had just arrived.

'I see you're still unpacking.'

He laughed. 'Sorry, no. This is how it always is. Now let me make a space.' He picked up some boxes and shuffled papers until a chair was exposed. He pointed to it, and Arnold sat.

'Would you care for a drink?'

'Yes, thank you.'

He came out with two glasses and a bottle of sherry.

'It's a little dry, but I find it helps with the sand in my throat.' He poured and handed him one of the glasses, dropping into the opposite seat with a thump.

'BM sent you to find me, eh?'

Arnold nodded.

'Bones you said?'

'Very much so.'

'Well, what's that to do with me?' Kartz frowned in confusion.

'Ah, a good question, Professor Kartz.'

'Albert, titles … so pompous.'

Arnold inclined his head. 'Albert, I'll be frank. I'm looking for something and as Howard Carter is busy doing other things, you're probably the only other person that can help.'

'I see.' He chuckled. 'You realise that isn't very flattering.'

'I'm looking for a tomb.'

Albert blinked a few times. 'You're serious?'

'I've never been more so.'

'Well, flavour of the month, all these tombs, isn't it?'

'It would seem so. But I can see you're excited by it?'

Arnold sipped at his drink.

'Well, of course I am, but let me be honest with you. I fell out of favour with some people, and I'm not in a good position right now.'

'I know who you fell out of favour with. I also know all about the incidents at Cambridge.'

Albert sighed. 'It was never a secret, old boy.'

'Let me start by saying I am not concerned with your past, Albert. I'm interested in the future.'

'I'm a liability now. No one takes my work seriously anymore, not since Cambridge.'

'Nonsense. Gaston Maspero and Howard Carter both spoke very highly of you.'

Albert's shoulders lifted at the compliments. 'That's gratifying.'

Arnold watched the conflict pass over his lined face. 'Albert, your knowledge of Egyptian antiquity is second to none. And those fools in Cambridge understand little of modern progressive viewpoints. If I'd been there, you'd be elevated to the Deanship by now. The article you published on the history of the Osirian, was simply inspired. Sadly, and I do mean this sincerely, foolish and unyielding attitudes are far too common in the intellectual community. Albert, I *much* prefer to work with those, like yourself, who approach work with an open mind and not be restricted in their thinking by commonly held beliefs.'

Albert beamed.

Arnold's calculations had paid off. It was obvious from the start he should appeal to his intellect to gain his support. He heard it in the reply.

'I sincerely appreciate that, Arnold.'

'I meant it.' Over the rim of his glass, Arnold observed the effect his words had on the man. He'd said enough to win him over.

Albert organised his thoughts and at length asked, 'Where exactly are you planning to look?'

'Same place Carter is.'

Albert sank into his chair. 'Well, then you're out of luck. You can't go digging around in the valley. Lord Carnarvon is the only one with the permit and Howard has dug most of it up already.'

'I'm not interested in Lord Carnarvon.' He pulled a rolled papyrus from out of his jacket. 'Anyway, I know exactly where to look. I have a map.' He handed it over.

Albert carefully unrolled it on his lap and began a thorough examination. 'This is extraordinary, how did you come by it?'

'It's a ... family heirloom.'

'*Ta-sekhet-ma'at*,' Albert muttered.

Arnold swallowed his drink and placed the glass on a box beside him. He leant forward. 'Yes ... the great field. The Royal Necropolis.'

Albert looked up, his eyes shone bright. 'The tomb is closer to *Ta-Set-Neferu*, the Valley of the Queens, according to your map.'

'Midway between them, to be precise.'

Albert was in awe. 'Arnold, this is worth a king's ransom.'

'Several, no doubt.' He placed both hands together, centring them to his lips. 'You're interested then?'

Albert continued to read. 'You're sure of the maps authenticity?'

'I'm no expert, Albert. That's why I came to you. You tell me?'

'Well, I mean ... ah, the parchment is certainly authentic as is the text. What I meant was, the detail of the map and text.'

'I don't follow you?'

'Well, the text seems to imply the tomb is a ... prison?'

'That's my understanding as well.'

Albert frowned. 'Built in the Great and Majestic Necropolis of the Millions of Years of the Pharaoh? Doesn't that seem odd to you?'

'I have no opinion either way. I can only tell you what has been passed down to me. It's a tomb for a very powerful king amongst kings. But until we go in and look, we won't know.'

Albert shrugged. 'Why haven't you excavated it before now? You said it was a family heirloom.'

'That's a very good question. The honest answer is the time was not right.'

'And it is now?'

'No, not yet. I'm gathering the people necessary for *when* the time is right.'

'You're being very mysterious, Arnold.'

'Will you help me?'

'I'm in no position to turn you down. You see how it is with me. I'd be glad of a paying job, but ...'

'Don't concern yourself over permits and other mundanities. I'll take care of everything. You can see the tomb is located in a remote area far removed from Carter and his legions of press.'

'It looks like it will be a difficult excavation. I'll study the map, maybe even travel to the site.'

'Albert, ours will be a subtle intrusion, in and out. No one can know.' He looked hard at the older man.

'Of course, I'll say nothing to anyone.'

'Not even Howard Carter.'

'As you wish.'

Arnold seemed satisfied. 'There's something there, Albert, something of value beyond measure.'

'Treasure, is that it?' Albert frowned a little.

'No, Albert, knowledge. I'm sorry. I can't let you have the map, not yet.' Arnold held out his hand and Albert reluctantly handed it over.

'What should I do, then?'

'I have some tasks for you in preparation for the work.'

'Excavating this tomb will be costly.'

Arnold shook his head. 'You needn't concern yourself over money either. I'll organise everything.' He stood and Albert did likewise.

'I'll call for you when I am ready.'

Albert nodded. He looked around the room and then back at Arnold. 'I hate to ask this, but–'

'Of course.' He opened his pocket and pulled out a bundle of notes. 'This should get you a better room and some furniture. I'm staying nearby when the moment is right, I'll contact you.'

'How will you know where I am?'

'I found you, remember? I'll find you again.'

Albert looked down at the money in his hand and his eyes widened. 'Arnold, this is far too much. I wouldn't need half of this.'

Arnold retrieved his cane.

'There are things you will need to do before I call for you. The money will become necessary.' He paused. 'Did I not tell you I would make your dreams and wishes come true?'

'You did, I admit the excitement is boiling within me.'

'Excellent, Albert. There's just one final thing we must do before we seal the deal.'

'A contract?'

'Something like that. The details we will work out later. Albert, the people I choose to lead these tasks become … family, of sorts.'

'I don't understand.'

Arnold put a hand on his shoulder. 'In time you will, but first … well, you can't walk around like that anymore.'

Albert looked down at his shabby garments. 'I'll buy new clothes immediately.'

Arnold flashed a smile. 'That's not quite what I meant.' He grabbed Albert's throat with a swiftness that belied his physique, lifted him up and snapped his neck in quick succession, dropping his body to the floor.

'You can't walk around in that mortal frame, Albert. It's time for you to arise anew, my brother.'

Arnold began to sing. His eyes turned black as night. He pointed his cane at Albert's face. The gargoyle head came alive and blinked ruby-red eyes. From out of its tiny mouth, a black mollusc-like creature wriggled then flopped onto Albert's cheek. As Arnold continued to sing the creature made slow progress towards Albert's half open mouth.

*

In the crowded Cairo streets, the people stopped in confusion and fear. Thick, bleak, black-grey clouds began manifesting. The clouds seemed to distort into a huge lion-like face. It roared in thunder. The sky darkened to the point of night and the clouds burst, unleashing a burning downpour, scorching the skin of anyone who'd failed to find shelter.

Three
Destiny

Somewhere in the Syrian Desert: 1926

Doctor Mary Wilson perched in rigid apprehension as the light dusting she was employing to the ancient bone, just visible under the surface of the sand, took shape. A trickle of sweat fell down her dirty neck, and with repetitive monotony, she wiped it clear, further irritating the inflammation she'd yet to address. Her work on the prehistoric site had turned up gold, but not without its measure of disappointment. Three members of her team had surrendered to the operoseness of their tasks, and although she understood why, their defeatist attitude left a foul taste in her attractive mouth.

The brush strokes she employed with precision, unearthed the entire bone within a few short hours. It took less time than she'd calculated. Sometimes, she mused, the sands gave up their secrets quicker than expected. Other times, they remained as stubborn as her Shih Tzu refusing to go out when it rained.

Mary inched the trowel under the visible crevice. With the precision of someone who spent thirty years failing to unearth anything of value, she took great care in coaxing the monstrous bone from its resting place. The lack of decomposition surprised her. It made a hollow in the pit of her stomach. It looked clean and un-prehistoric. She knew it was too large for an animal of the region, but the fact it had none of the characteristic markers of a fossil gave her considerable pause. Against all her training, she took the tip of the trowel and made a light score along its side. The mark remained visible for a brief moment and then it fixed itself and her exhilaration resumed — whatever it was, it shouldn't have done *that*. Examining it with authority, she recognised at once it was a femur. And whilst she couldn't determine its age, she knew ... *knew* ... it wasn't the femur of any animal on Earth.

My Maryosaurus.

Laying it with repressed excitement into the container beside her, Mary looked down at the void and was thoughtful. Deciding an impression would be useful, she reached for the bucket to her right and pulled a small packet of plaster from her kit. Mary emptied it along with water and slowly mixed until it formed a thick paste. Tipping the plaster into the void, careful not to upset its shape, she continued until the cavity was engulfed. The dry-heat sped up hardening and when it was tacky she placed a small net on top. Mary picked up her find and tool-kit, and after a brief moment of contemplation, she headed back to the canvas makeshift-home to examine it further.

In the marked-off sand dune, a misty smoke wisped from the rectangular hole. It curled up and twisted. The initial intensity was light, but it soon thickened, forming a coalescing ball. It looked like smoke in a bubble, and when it finalised, melded into a horrifying visage. It was a devilish mixture of lion and man, and it laughed, in a wicked and exaggerated way.

'Excuse me?'

Mary looked up with astonishment at the elegant middle-aged man resting upon a cane, just outside the door to her tent. His dress was out of place and unsuitable. The suit he wore befitted a cold London morning, rather than the oppressive heat of Syria. He waved at a fly as it buzzed around his face. Mary's eyes fixed on his cane. She was mesmerised by its elaborate design. Elegant, like the man holding it, black with a twisted snake-like stem and a gargoyle head with ruby-red eyes seemed to follow her movements. All the time she stared, he made no move to enter.

'I'm so sorry to intrude on your work, Doctor Wilson, but I understand you just uncovered something of, well, value?'

Mary lifted her eyes to meet his and smiled.

'I'm sorry, you are?'

The man lifted his cane and pointed inside.

'May I?'

'Of course, please.'

Mary set down tools and indicated towards the make-shift chairs on a worn sand-covered rug. Her temporary home wasn't extravagant.

'Most kind.'

Pulling out a card from his waistcoat pocket, he entered, handing it to her.

'My name is Professor Arnold Darcorion.'

His smile was charming and she found herself responding to it.

'I am from the British Museum, the Department of Antiquities and Strange Artefacts to be precise.'

'I've never heard of it, or you.' Mary noted his slight disappointment with mild interest. 'Won't you sit?'

'Thank you.'

Professor Darcorion slipped with grace into the chair. He pushed his cane deep into the sand and crossed his legs.

'I'm not surprised you've never heard of me,' he said, running a finger and thumb along the crease in his trouser leg. 'I tend to stay out of the limelight and as for my department,' he shrugged, 'it isn't well-known outside of … certain circles.' Professor Darcorion locked eyes with her. 'Nevertheless, I do take a particular interest in specific finds, like the one you uncovered today.'

Mary frowned. 'I'm not sure I understand. Are you talking about the bone I uncovered this morning?'

He nodded.

'Well, we're just studying it now. It isn't ordinary, but it's not extraordinary either.'

'You don't think so?' His penetrating gaze saw through her story.

'Clearly you do, or you wouldn't be here. So, why are you?'

'Ah, an extremely important question.'

He seemed pleased, but she couldn't understand why.

'Doctor, before I go into detail, I have to say I'm disappointed. Your reputation isn't exaggerated. You're guarded, and I think that's because you've grasped the implications your finding might bring. Or perhaps you simply aren't sure of its authenticity?'

Mary shrugged. 'Well, I haven't confirmed anything yet.'

'You can be frank with me, Mary.'

She smiled. 'You're right, I am guarded. But I'll say this. My suspicion is it's prehistoric. That's all I'm giving you. Drink?' She pointed to a clear dusty bottle on an untidy shelf. It looked like one of the relics. 'It's a local brew, pretty horrible, but it's the best I can get this far into the desert.'

'Please.'

She filled two glasses.

He took a sip, grimaced, and raised an eyebrow. 'You were correct. This is horrible.'

She chuckled and took a long drink. 'I'm used to it. So, tell me, Professor–'

'Arnold.'

'Tell me, Arnold, seeing as we're both just chatting. What do your observations tell you about this fossil?'

He took another sip and contemplated his answer. 'I suspect any number of things, Doctor.' At a look he said, 'Ostensibly, I can tell you this: it isn't a fossil, at least not in the traditional sense, but I think you already know this.'

Mary remained impassive.

'You can't possibly know what I know. I haven't even finished matching it to established reference materials. Just from *my* observations I can say it is old–'

'Old, yes.' He nodded.

She bristled at his interruption.

'Look, Professor …'

'Arnold, please.'

'I'm not dismissing anything at this stage, Arnold, so let me be straight with you. The simple truth is, until it's positively identified, it *stays* an unspecified fossilised relic. Anything else is just pure speculation.'

'Your repressed excitement tells me you don't really believe that, Doctor.'

'Really?' She could not hide the scorn in her voice.

'Your eyes … they tell a *very* different story.'

She let out a short laugh.

'I think you're assuming far too much, *Professor*.'

He looked at her over the rim of the glass. 'I never make assumptions about anything.'

'Did you even examine it?'

He gave a slight nod. 'Yes. Remarkable and so well preserved, so beautifully … *unfossilised*.' He raised an eyebrow and she softened her stance.

'Yes, you have me there. Its lack of decomposition *is* remarkable, considering its final resting place and how long it's been buried. Arnold, you're right. I *am* excited. More than excited. But I just can't let it override my duty to properly evaluate it. Until I know more, until I can formally identify it, I have to remain objective. There's also a financial situation that must be satisfied in order for my dig to continue to be funded. Look, Arnold, I've been digging up false hopes for almost thirty years and the people who fund me know this very well. This could be the one, you know? But they'll want more than my gut feeling. They'll want proof. If this is what I hope it is, I'll be fully sponsored. Hell, they might name it after me: *Maryosaurus*. I'm sorry if it appears my enthusiasm isn't—'

He sighed and leant forward. 'It's not from a dinosaur, Mary.'

She rubbed her eyes. 'Clearly you're more versed in archaeological osteology than I am.'

He acquiesced. 'Let's just say on this particular subject I have considerable knowledge. Doesn't the lack of decomposition strike you as odd? Even if it *was* a dinosaur relic, which it isn't, a million-plus-year-old bone should be *fossilised*. The actual organic structure lost to time, correct?'

'True, but—'

He raised a finger.

'Let me ask you this. Why do you think I'm here?'

Mary shrugged. 'I have no idea. I'm not in the "circle". As I said before, your department and its goals are unknown to me. Frankly, Arnold, *I* spend all my time digging about in harsh locations rather than sitting behind a comfortable, warm desk in London.'

'Your honesty is refreshing.' He finished the drink with a grimace. 'Terrible.'

He handed her the glass.

'Another?'

'Please.'

As she stood, he brushed a few grains of sand off his trousers.

'Let me be equally as candid. I'm not in this region by chance. And I'm *not* interested in dinosaur bones, Mary. They're just ... dull. I'm working on the singular, the remarkable, the exceptional, the unique. Can you imagine the reaction in the civilised world to a centuries old bone with no observable evidence of the type of decomposition it ought to have? It's a paradoxical find and it defies science, you do see my point? Somehow this relic miraculously retained its original organic structure. And, just so you understand where I'm coming from, it's not the first to be discovered. You do, of course, recognise what this bone is?'

'It appears to be a femur.'

'Have you calculated the size of the animal?'

'I haven't, no.'

He sat rigid. His expression said, *I know you're lying.*

'Fine, of course I have. It's an approximate size, but I'd say equivalent to a mammoth.'

Arnold relaxed, nodding.

'I agree. Mary, neither of us has to be an expert in osteology to recognise the truth. There isn't an animal alive on Earth that this bone could have come from.'

She knew he was correct. Her expression must have told him so because he relaxed back into his chair.

'Good. Now let me get to the reason I'm here; to the reality of your situation. I'm about to make all your dreams and wishes come true.'

She handed him another glass, but didn't sit down.

'I've heard *that* before.'

'I assure you, I wouldn't have said it, if I didn't mean it.'

Her face reddened as her irritation increased. 'Right … I dig up a remarkable find and out of nowhere you turn up and offer me the world … please … the next thing you'll do is take ownership of everything and I'll lose any claim. I'll probably end up as a footnote in some archaeological magazine, the woman who unearthed the mysterious bone for the misogynistic fools at the British Museum. Sorry, not going to happen. Didn't they tell you, Arnold? They don't allow women to be members.'

'Your reputation does you justice, Doctor.'

She sighed and rubbed her eyes again. 'Look, I'm enjoying a well-earned break and sharing a drink with you, because I know you've come a long way … you've said what you wanted to say, and I'm not being rude, but I'm tired.'

'Doctor … Mary, I completely understand your feelings. I'm not here to steal a claim from you. I'm sorry if I gave you that impression. It's far more complex.' He emphasised his point by leaning forward. 'I'm here to claim *you.*'

Mary put her free hand on her hip.

'You're not making any sense. What are you talking about?'

When he answered, the response was so unexpected she failed to catch the truth of it.

'I'm here to kill you.'

With inhuman speed and strength he was on her, a hand around her throat. He snapped her neck so rapidly she didn't even have time to drop her drink. Mary turned deadweight and he caught the glass as it fell. He released her and she crumpled to the ground. With one gulp, he finished her drink and dropped the glass.

'It's time you were freed your mortal constraint, Mary,' he murmured. 'It's time for you to rise anew.'

Arnold reached out, and his cane flew to his hand. He pointed it head down, and started a lyrical monotone chant, causing the gargoyle's ruby-red eyes to brighten. After a few minutes it came alive and the tiny mouth opened. A thick-black viscous tar-like liquid emerged with the slowness of a mollusc. It flopped out onto the sand and slithered towards her, leaving a slick trail in its wake, forcing itself through the lips of her closed mouth. After a moment or two, a scream broke the stillness and Mary's arm shot outwards. The flexing and bone breaking rotation was unnatural, suggestive of a marionette whose strings were tangled. The broken cervical vertebrae pushed against the taut skin, as her head twisted, causing odd bulges and irregular bends. Her head flopped backwards and the abnormal protuberance disappeared with a sickening crack. Mary's body convulsed, shook, and arched upwards. Her eyes fluttered open, blackening for the briefest moment, and then closed tight. She continued to gurgle and thrash, emanating peculiar noises. When the sound stopped, Mary spluttered a discharge of white-red froth from her nose and mouth, and became still.

Arnold stopped muttering and the gargoyle cane reset.

Sometime later, Mary took a loud intake of breath and her eyes snapped open. She blinked a few times in disorientation. Focusing on the concerned face of Arnold, she lifted herself with his help. Groggy but otherwise cognisant, she made it to a chair.

'What happened?' She rubbed absentmindedly at her throat.

'You had some kind of … fit.'

He knelt beside her. 'I'll call a doctor.'

'I *am* a doctor.'

She was weak, but colour returned to her face.

'Don't look so worried, Arnold. I've been epileptic since childhood, although I haven't had an episode for years. Get me some water, will you?'

Arnold handed her a canteen and she took a long drink; the water seemed to revive her.

'Are you sure you don't need medical attention? You did drop rather quickly.'

'Into soft sand, Arnold.' She placed a hand on his shoulder. 'I'll be fine. I … I just need to sleep it off. It's sweet of you, but I'm okay.'

Nodding, he said, 'I'll leave you to rest, then. We can talk later, Mary. I'm staying close by.'

'I'd like that.'

Mary felt different. Her eyes unfocused, her mind raced with ideas, possibilities, new knowledge, and strange images. It was overwhelming. New facts flooded her mental pathways. She knew Arnold now. She knew *everything* about him. It terrified and excited her. The onslaught to her senses took their toll, and Mary's eyes closed as she lost the fight to stay awake.

Arnold Darcorion paused at the entrance. He looked back into the room and smiled. The planning of thousands of years was at long last coming to fruition. A whisper in the air caught his attention and his eyes burned a kaleidoscope of yellow-red as he disappeared out into the sand.

Four
Powers of Ancient Balderdash

Egypt: The Valley of the Kings – 1927

The heat from the midday sun had not hindered the work as much as she'd expected it to. Mary Wilson was busy labelling the labours of their work. Wooden boxes of all sizes, sorted by content, walled an entire tent. The range of artefacts found weren't exciting in number, but the quality of some of the pottery, considering the age, was remarkable. She continued her inventory for a few more hours. She stretched to ease the static-tension in her neck and then stepped outside. So far they hadn't found what had been hoped for, but she knew digging in the sand required significant patience. She was nevertheless pleased with their progress even if she didn't voice it.

The sun, relentless in its onslaught, made everything around her shimmer. But Mary had a new way of looking at the world. Since Syria, since meeting Arnold, she had changed. She didn't seem to ever get tired, and sleep never came—she had never spoken about the changes, but in quiet moments, which were few, she would often wonder what had happened to cause that fateful seizure. Mary required little food to sustain her. In fact, she often went days without food at all. Arnold had recruited her, along with a number of others of similar experience, and the mission had changed. Her thoughts drifted back to simpler times. The reflection was less negative as time went on. She had to admit, with money being no object, her successes, and those of her colleagues, had been quite remarkable.

One hundred different sites around the world had given up the secrets they had searched for. Each one a single bone as remarkable as the one she'd discovered in Syria. They were ancient, majestic even, but untouched by the natural decomposition of time. And when a bone had been discovered matching the characteristics of the others, Arnold had taken it away in haste, stopping any further work. Mary had no idea where he was taking them. She knew they were of personal value and he spared no expense in their retrieval. In Egypt, however, they were given a different set of instructions.

'Doctor Wilson!'

The frantic call made her look up and squint. She shaded her eyes and looked amongst the many natives who might have called her name. She saw a boy, Ahmed, running towards her, his foot caught the edge of a rock and he pitched face first into the sand.

'Ahmed, are you all right?'

'You must come. Come, quickly. Come, come.' He was already up by the time she reached him. He grabbed her jacket and she quickly followed in the direction of his tugging.

'Okay, I'm coming. What is it?'

'Come. Yes, come.'

She followed Ahmed into the Anti-Chamber of the unnamed tomb they were excavating. It was an enigma of sorts because the tomb, whilst robbed of most of its primary value thousands of years before, bore no identification of the occupant. As she reached the third chamber, the Egyptian workers stood waiting, along with one of her new colleagues, Professor Albert Kartz. He was a small man, tanned, the lines on his face a roadmap of age and experiences. His grizzled grey hair always stuck up on one side. He had a genuine aura, a soft demeanour, and a kind approach. He'd earnt great respect from the natives. Albert smiled at her approach.

'Mary, come and see.'

He took her by the hand, careful to hold the burning torch in front of him. With no air movement, when he stopped, the flame remained steady. The chamber didn't appear any different to how she'd left it just a few hours earlier.

'I don't see anything different, Albert.' Mary sighed but Albert Kartz had lost nothing of his enthusiasm, despite her obvious disappointment.

'Ah, Mary, Mary.' His voice was soft, fatherly. 'You will see. Now, stand here. Good, yes … now just watch.'

He circled the chamber in a shuffle, the torch ahead of him.

She sighed. 'Really, Albert?'

'Just watch.'

As he reached the second of the four walls, he stopped. Moving forward he brought the torch upwards. She noticed the well-trodden ground. But the wall remained as she had last seen it. Frowning, she was about to say something when the flame of the torch shifted. A slight flicker was all, but it was significant because it shouldn't have been possible.

'There! You see it?'

She felt the excitement rise and was beside him in an instant.

'What's causing it?'

'Air flow, my dear. Air flow.'

'But that's impossible, unless …'

He nodded sagely. His look of praise a natural one, formed from years spent teaching at Cambridge.

'Unless … there's another chamber *behind* this wall.'

He left the torch in place and the flame flickered once more. Reaching forward, she ran a hand along the rough surface of the wall, and as she did so, the ancient sands crumbled away and new hieroglyphics manifested, illuminated somehow, like phosphorus, bright blue-white. The brilliance intensified at her touch.

Exclamations and anxious chattering from the natives broke the stillness. It was a repetition of articulated dread uttered in local and ancient dialects. Fright caused most of them to run from the spot, torches dropping, tools discarded. Mary and Albert turned towards them, and Mary scolded them.

Albert put a hand on her arm and shook his head.

'Panic and superstition is far too powerful to be overcome with threats, Mary.'

He was right, of course. Mary made eye contact with those remaining, assuring them in their own tongue they had nothing to fear. Sand-swept faces nodded, but their eyes told her they weren't convinced. Some muttered a superstitious chorus; she chose to ignore it.

Albert, for his part, just continued his observation of the mysterious symbols as their manifestations resumed to Mary's touch. Each symbol appeared so bright the room took on an unusual, eerie aspect. Instinct told Mary when a line was ended and she was soon able to trace out where the symbols would next appear without pause. Her fingers didn't leave the sandstone once. It was soon apparent to her that *she* was responsible for their appearances. When she stopped, they did too.

Albert looked at her for a brief moment then turned back to the wall. Unlike the natives and their ideological superstitions, he was a staunch scientist, grounded in facts. But the reality before him couldn't easily be answered. Even with his great intellect, his lifetime of study and knowledge, he could find no precedent. He knew his science might not have all the answers but it didn't follow, by definition, the cause must be supernatural.

One of the workers voiced a cry translating to: *Protect us from the powers of the Ancient Ones.*

He didn't respond, but muttered, 'Powers of ancient balderdash. Science and knowledge, no ghosts or magic need apply.'

Still he had to admit, there was no denying he couldn't find a logical reason to explain how the symbols were forming. As he watched the last of them take shape and finish, Mary stepped back. Each illuminated pictogram flashed bright white in unison, and then the room plunged back into the soft-yellow shadowed lighting of a flaming torch. The new text looked as ancient as the tomb, as if it had always been there.

For a moment they just stood in wonder, then the inquisitive nature of the two scientists took over, as their examination started.

Mary's eyes followed the hieroglyphs and found one she didn't recognise. It was different to the others. Conceding that Albert was the more skilled at ancient texts, she pointed at it.

'Albert, what is this symbol here?'

He handed her the torch and put on his spectacles. 'It's a cartouche. A royal seal. Fourth dynasty. I'm sure of it, well, mostly sure. It's not always easy to pinpoint. I'll need my reference books to be positive. What's interesting is the name.'

'How so?'

'Well, ah, the vernacular of this specific dialect doesn't match with the rest. It's entirely unfamiliar to me, in fact ...' he traced it out with an aged finger, 'this seems more like an expression of an abstract idea, not what I'd expect in a cartouche of this significance, especially since its purpose here would seem to indicate or reference a person or singular form of great authority.'

'Are names usually this abstract?'

'Well, no, they typically aren't, with perhaps minor exceptions. Thank goodness for the Rosetta stone, is all I can say.'

'I remember you once said, "Thank God it was a French officer and not a British officer who stumbled upon it."'

'Ah, yes.' He chuckled. 'I seem to recall my observation about the fact the French were slightly more intellectually minded caused rather a stir.'

'I can't imagine why.'

He continued to make notes. 'The Rosetta stone was a very clever bit of political propaganda on Ptolemy's side. He commissioned it to bridge the gap and ease resentments between the elite and the commoners.'

'It's not really my area of expertise, the politics of Ancient Egypt.'

Albert chuckled. 'Well here's the interesting thing. The governing elite could neither speak the language of the common folk, nor read their hieroglyphs. They only spoke Greek. The stone provided a mechanism for Ptolemy to foster connection with the people. It allowed him to proclaim *his* right, publically, as the only true Pharaoh of Egypt. A practice of political manoeuvring which doesn't appear to have lessened over the years. '

Concentration stopped his lecture, as frequent checks to his notepad distracted him. His features turned from excitement to perplexity and back again, and the crease in his brow, though deeper than usual, hadn't seemed to dampen his excitement. In truth, they had heightened by degrees.

'It's not ancient Greek, or Demotic. This might not be the same language at all.'

'You're the expert, Albert.'

He smiled at her. 'The basic premise of the writing is a story, of sorts. But it isn't what you might expect in a tomb of this kind. No celebrations, no stories of the life on the occupant, or the journey on to the afterlife. It's the tale of a great battle between Horus and Sutekh. No ... It's not between them ...'

He turned to her with a light in his grey-mottled eyes.

'Mary, this is extraordinary, if I'm reading this correctly, they put their irreconcilable differences aside and joined forces to fight against ... ah, wait, what's this? Oh, yes, a common threat or enemy. I suspect this enemy is the one named in the cartouche. There are many references to "Beast", but not "a beast". The word Beast is written in the way of name, rather than definition. It's difficult to explain.'

'I think we've found what we've been looking for.'

'I believe you're correct. This must be what Arnold was anticipating when he said, "You'll know it when you find it."'

Mary rubbed at her lip. 'I think it's time we call him.'

Professor Kartz agreed.

'Should we consider breaking through?' He could barely contain his excitement.

'No, not until Arnold arrives. I want him to see this first. He may know more, and we need the name of this unknown enemy, this Beast? I think it's significant. The inexplicability of it seems linked to what we've discovered elsewhere, although how I can't say for certain.'

'Is this a theory, or do you have tangible evidence to back it up?'

'It's a feeling, Albert.'

'Bah ...' He waved at her in mock indignation. 'Intuition cannot be measured scientifically.'

'That doesn't mean I should ignore it either. My insight has served me well, as you well know.'

'Well, I don't like the idea of it, but I do acknowledge it.'

She put a hand on his shoulder and then turned to the few remaining loyal workers. Mary barked orders in their own tongue. One man made a quick cross of his arms and lowered his head before leaving. Mary observed as Albert continued to copy down the hieroglyphics. She was pleased because they might hold the key to what Arnold was searching for. And, she deliberated, might also just as quickly disappear.

Albert paused his writing and leant forward.

'Mary, I'm finding it hard to translate all of it, but it does seem as though Horus and Sutekh were in an immense battle—again the references to Beast.'

'I suppose they were fighting a beast.' Mary shrugged.

'No, It isn't written "They were in a battle with a beast", it says "with *Beast*". Like I said before, it's a specific reference: A name.'

'Did they win?'

'Yes, the story does end with a victory, of sorts.'

'Is there any indication of what Beast was?'

Albert nodded. He turned to her and removed his spectacles.

'It would appear this Beast was a colossal lion.' He returned to the wall. 'This last line, here, tells us the battle was fought for well over one-hundred years.'

Mary was deep in thought.

A colossal lion?

She suddenly processed what Albert had just said. 'Hold on, what did you mean by "a victory of sorts"?'

'It's difficult to translate most of these last five lines, but from what I can make out, Beast was referred to as either the "Under-Immortal", "Undying-One", or "The Forgotten".'

'Priests were obsessed with the notion of immortality, it's not unusual.'

'True, but this text seems to imply the enemy *was* immortal, and not just seeking it. Hence the battle for a hundred years, I suppose.' He put his notebook in his pocket. 'The ambiguous victory appears to come when Beast ... now this is very interesting ... it says here that it voluntarily allows itself to be ... I think the word is "displaced", but I'm not certain.'

'Voluntarily. Are you certain?'

'Well, no, not exactly. I mean ... those appear to be the words, and I admit, my translation might be off, but history is replete with rewrites by victorious leaders and priests for Ancient Egyptian pharaohs. It doesn't seem credible an intelligent being allowed itself to be "displaced", if that is even the correct terminology, but it's more a matter of interpretation, than a clear definition.'

Mary held her chin and thought for a moment.

'Displaced,' she said. 'I wonder what it might mean.'

'Well, that's the question, Mary, isn't it? But it must occur to you with all this new information, and if you add the bones we've been harvesting from across the world, then all of this is—as you earlier suggested—intrinsically linked. Arnold has been very quiet about what these bones represent, or even what they are from. Want to wager they're a colossal lion-like beast?'

Mary and Albert exchanged looks.

'Perhaps, my dear, I should pay better attention to your intuition in the future.'

Five
Animated Human Cadaver

Egypt: The Valley of the Kings – 1927

The entity calling himself Professor Arnold Darcorion stared in wonder at the strange hybrid language Mary and Albert had discovered just a few days previous. Both he and Mary had cultivated a very special relationship since their first meeting. Arnold had always considered her a potential recruit. His work started by many others, centuries before he was born. Descendant from a long line of people who, like himself, were part of a heritage cult, he'd been imbued with certain powers, transcending the over-wise frail human confines.

Arnold had forgotten what it was like to feel hunger. To feel pain. To feel, well, normal. Since his death over one-hundred years previous, he had been born anew with one objective. It had driven him for far longer than his outward middle-age suggested. His cult had grown and the work moved far quicker as a result. Money was no object. Greed and the impiety of man, stretching back thousands of years, gained him wealth beyond most people's comprehension.

A few very special individuals, like Mary, had come into his life. Most of the recruits had no real understanding of him, but her proximity and attachment had allowed a fleeting touch of his erstwhile humanity to surface. The animated human cadaver named Arnold Darcorion lifted his gargoyle cane launching into an expressive chant. Its eyes lit red, bathing the chamber in an esoteric ambiance.

Albert and Mary both stood behind him. Their eyes black, their features devoid of emotion or life. In a way, he felt sorry for Albert. The man had no idea what was coming and even if he could comprehend it, he'd never understand, embrace, or accept it. Mary, in contrast had come to terms with her transformation. It had taken some months and her powers had grown with Arnold's subtle tutelage. Her initial reactions were hatred, aggressiveness, and torment; but she had come to realise her life, whilst over in the traditional sense, was now exclusively devoted to the work she had always enjoyed, with none of the old distractions. No fear of financial worries or uncomfortable pious interactions. No lecherous male colleagues with invitations of work laden with lascivious intent.

As Arnold's incantation increased, so Mary and Albert followed suit in a disharmonious chorus of melodic luridness. A blending of yellow and red lights cast eerie shadows around the room. Their incantations shifted the ambiance; it made the walls whisper and the stones sigh. Ancient hieroglyphs awoke in rhythmic pulsing, bright white-blue, to an unbroken monotone chanting; and then they moved. Sluggish at first, but the constant dissonance seemed to influence them. Their unified voices fuelled by the exigent circumstance, increased in pitch, fostering an accelerated impetus.

Wisps of smoky vapours rolled from the sand and curled aloft, grotesque and unspeakable. Unable to grip, they swirled around ankles. As time passed, their misty states solidified into unnatural outlines, the light from the torches casting hideous silhouettes. Unaware, the three of them continued their discordant unity. With growing haste, the glyphs repositioned, shifting left to right, reorganising their sequence and with matching energy, the dreadful malformed spirits gathered in strength. Voiceless perverted aberrations, both mutated and wretched with partial disfigurements and deformities hidden behind unnatural bends in the light. Their anomalous forms appeared radiant and terrifying; they were beautiful and monstrous. As they neared full maturation and became their most dreadful, the ancient glyphs slowed their reorganisation, the gradual change left a large void between them. They settled and became still. The orderless shaped nightmares stopped their scuttling and in unison uttered a horrifying, gurgling shriek. In an instant, they dropped and dissipated back into the sand.

The room was bathed in an abnormal fusion of flame-yellows and ruby-red, as it returned to its previous state. The reorganised hieroglyphic layout now had a door-shaped space between them. Wisps of vapours, curling into the air, were the last remnants of the nebulous and vague embryonic-like creatures.

Arnold paused for a moment and allowed the transformation to wash over his senses. He then tapped his cane into the sand and Mary and Albert regained their humanity with a jolt. As if stepping out from a dream, Mary smiled at Arnold as the blackness in her eyes disappeared and transformed back to piercing blue. Albert didn't miss a beat.

'Ah, Arnold, there you are ... what the devil!' Albert examined the new layout of the text whilst Mary stood transfixed and lost in Arnold's eyes.

'How did this happen?' Albert asked.

Arnold broke eye contact and turned to him. Mary came up beside them both.

'It's an Ancient Egyptian puzzle, Albert. I just happen to know the secret of it.'

'It's a doorway now.' Mary used a light touch on the stone void. 'Well, doorway shaped, at any rate.'

Arnold's eyes scanned the symbols. He smiled and said, 'And here is the door handle.'

He reached forward and placed a palm on one of the pictograms. There was a hollow grinding sound from deep underground, it shook the room a little, and dust dropped from the ceiling. Arnold gestured for the two of them to step back and as they did, the stone void sunk inwards and swung to the left. A hiss of musty trapped air escaped into the room. Arnold grabbed a torch and peered into the darkness. There was an immediate glint of gold.

Mary and Albert found their own torches, and they all stepped forward. Arnold took the lead.

As they passed into the new chamber, Albert was quick to voice his observations: 'This is a fourth ante-chamber, but it appears as though they stocked it with all the treasures supposed to be in the third. Perhaps they were intending to move the treasures later on?'

Mary was more interested in the skeletal forms strewn haphazardly along the inner pathway. Most were close to the doorway and they were still holding crude tools.

'Looks like these people died right here.'

Albert and Arnold stopped to examine one.

Arnold moved dust-webs away from a skull. 'What's your opinion, Albert?'

'I suspect these people were sealing the tomb and got trapped by that mechanical doorway. The air in here would have been thin. With the doorway sealed they must have died of suffocation.'

Mary pulled a rudimentary hammer from the skeletal hand. 'Still holding their tools?'

Albert shrugged.

Arnold sniffed the air and stood.

'I believe we'll have better answers after a more thorough examination. Come on.'

They continued into the chamber and Mary and Albert placed their torches into the sand. They were chatting together, excited by the treasures, when Arnold beckoned to them.

'Look at this. They were building another wall across this room.'

'Curious, partially finished at that,' Albert said, leaning into the opening. 'There's another wall about four feet in parallel with this one, Arnold, and more of those poor people seemed to have died in here, too.'

Mary frowned. 'Doesn't it seem odd there would be people just left to die here?' She turned and spread her hands wide. 'And look at this treasure, it's undisturbed, but it's almost as if it was all just thrown in, dumped ... untidy ... disrespectful. Don't you think this is all just a little unusual?'

Albert nodded sagely. 'Mary's right. Priest and the common folk were highly superstitious. To leave a tomb in this way, would certainly invite the wrath of the occupant from the underworld.' He rubbed at his chin as he ran an eye around the corpses of the room. 'Whatever happened here must have transcended tradition. Something frightened someone enough to abandon centuries of procedure, and seal these poor fellows in.'

Arnold stepped into the space between both walls.

'What we are looking for is behind this wall. I can feel it. Our long search is almost over.'

Albert put his head in. 'It must be the burial chamber.'

Arnold didn't look back. 'Of sorts ...'

Mary examined the incomplete inner wall.

'Why would you need a second wall at all?' she muttered.

Arnold turned to her.

'I should think the answer was obvious to you both.'

At a look from each of them he said: 'I'm sorry, perhaps it's obvious to me. This entire structure and its layout, the rooms, the additional wall and the unnecessary elaborate hidden doorway, not to mention the evidence of these workers left here to die—and the fact it's *unfinished*. Don't you see? It all points to a single purpose, to an inescapable conclusion.'

'To keep people out,' Albert said with confidence.

'No, Albert, to keep something from getting out. ...'

Six
The Ungodly One

Egypt: *The Treasure Chamber*

The room was dark. A dull sound of tools against stone increased in volume, along with muffled exclamations of excitement, as the work to break through continued. In due course, the sound of hammering sharpened as they breached the ancient sandstone. A shaft of light penetrated the gloom for the first time in thousands of years. Fresh air was sucked into the chamber with a sigh. Sand trickled inwards from the thin opening. It widened enough to allow for tools to be pushed through. A rhythmic chorus of counting and physical exertion heaved in even intervals at the chiselled out stone, ending with a violent crash on the opposite side. Whispers and shuffling followed then hushed as Arnold peered inside. The space within was far smaller than he'd expected. The torch shone a ray of light that hit an ornate oblong stone plinth; it was typical of the kind of housing a sarcophagus might have. In excitement, he barked orders to the natives. They worked with greater intensity and some hours later, the opening in the outer wall was large enough to allow Arnold, Albert, and Mary to enter.

They were cautious, suspecting traps of some kind, and where they could, hung torches around the small chamber. It was free of decoration. Glyphs and symbols covered the plinth. Albert dropped to his knees, examining them.

Arnold knelt beside the older man.

'What do you make of it, Albert?'

'Warnings of dire consequences if this casket is opened, all the usual curses and messages from the gods, unimaginable horror bestowed on those who disturb it ... you get the idea.' He looked perplexed. 'It's a mixture of languages, Arnold. What I can read doesn't make much sense.'

Arnold put a hand on his shoulder.

'What it does or doesn't say is irrelevant. This is it, Albert. The moment has come. *This* is what we have all worked so hard for.' He turned to Mary. 'We need to open this. Go and get some of your local friends.'

She nodded and hurried out.

They waited for her return in silence, each enthralled by the box but for very different reasons.

A few minutes passed and four men, followed by Mary, entered the chamber. Arnold had already assuaged the fears of most of them with his hypnotic charm, and those remaining were offered as much treasure as they could carry. Albert had made a public outcry, but Arnold reiterated *their* treasure was knowledge, and ignorant illiterate natives would never understand it. He ended any further talk on the subject with nonchalant suggestion that a few gold trinkets lost to some delusory common folk, were of no consequence in their grand schemes. With antipathy Arnold had said, 'Look at them ... these fearful, principled, superstitious, self-righteous men. All tempted and bought through the lure of gold.'

Mary had sided with Arnold so the subject was dropped.

Four men took up corner positions around the stone casket, and with a nod from Arnold, pushed with all their might at the heavy stone. It took massive effort, but the cover moved enough for the men to be able to grip it. With back-breaking work, the four men lifted the massive stone and lay it down. The natives exited before further orders were given, and Arnold came forward, inspecting the contents. There was no sarcophagus, as he'd expected, but a simple layer of dusty cloth which covered a bulge in its centre. He peeled back the layers with suppressed excitement, feeling energised by the fact *his* hand was the first to touch it since it was laid inside.

There, in the heart of the casket, sat on a pedestal of gold was a perfect glass sphere.

Arnold reached out and took it. As his hands made contact, a swirl of gas deep within tumbled and twisted. He lifted it up and was transfixed by what he saw. The gas fused and separated in flashes of reds, purples, and blues and then to his absolute astonishment, three-dimensional images came into focus, like a silent motion picture, but with a difference; these images had clarity and depth overwhelming his senses and they were in colour.

He saw ethereal beings, flashes of alien landscapes, whirlwinds leaving a strange crystal palace. There were flickers of deep blackness; it shifted again to volcanoes erupting, lava pooling creating landmass.

And then there were pools of mud, with weird looking amphibious-type creatures. The gas swirled and churned again and again, and with each shift, new images flashed into focus. He lost count of the number of changes. It was clear now he was watching history unfold. Huge green landscapes appeared along with enormous creatures: dinosaurs. He was joined by Albert and Mary who both gaped in wonder at the strange artefact Arnold held aloft.

'It's some sort of motion-picture crystal ball ... it's incredible,' Albert said.

Mary's mouth opened in awe.

The turbulent tumultuous gas switched from one stunning scene to another. All three unable to comprehend its illogical absurdity, captured and hypnotised, they gave in to the power of it and continued to look on in wonder.

The image shifted again, this time to a huge lion standing on a precipice. It looked at them through the gas, seeming to make eye contact with each of them, and then, it looked away and roared in silence.

Seven
The Second Age of Beast

Mount Vesuvius: The Coming of Beast - 1944

The monotone chant resonated in echo around the depths of the cavern, reverberating off the igneous rock walls. A group of nine, black-robed, formed a semi-circle around a heap of bones. Their chanting increased in volume, mixing with the occasional hiss of gusts of gas through pits and holes in the pumice. One of them stepped forward holding a black gargoyle-headed cane. The eyes alight, flame red, it washed over the disconnected bones and when the light reached its brightest, they moved.

Mary Wilson pulled her hood down whilst continuing to illuminate the ancient skeleton. She intensified her chant, the others followed. Soon the bones miraculously snapped together and it wasn't long before a giant skeletal creature assembled before them. Bound by her song, its form remained still, when all of a sudden the gargoyle's eyes flashed bright red-white. The ruby-crystalline gemstones detached from the cane's head, tumbling along an invisible path, settling with a snap into the sockets of the titanic skull. Mary's exertion exhausted her and she fell backwards, the light from the cane extinguished. The skeletal form twitched; its movement clumsy, uncertain. Glowing red eyes now absorbed the light in the room, penetrating the souls of them all. The group maintained their chant, parting in unison, as another figure came forward holding a crystal-orb sphere. The gigantic skull head turned towards him.

Throwing back his hood, Arnold Darcorion spoke in song. It was a melody of whispers and strange aberrant animal-like chattering, which captured the skeletal creature's attention. Arnold's eyes, a metallic hybrid of conjoining colours and shapes burning and shining, reflected the fluctuating light and energy of the cavern's luminosity. His reciting was echoed by the others, except Mary, who held the black, snake-like cane high above her head. A hole cracked open in the pumice, wide enough to see the inferno below. His incantations concluded and he released the orb, it fell into the fires far below.

The magical sphere landed with a soft thud. For a brief time it lay there devoid of any change, untouched by the extremes in temperature. The chanting ceased. The rumble of the mountain replaced the hushed silence. Vesuvius shook at the intrusion in outrage. Arnold ignored the warning, and continued to stare at the orb, unblinking, waiting for something to happen. Time passed and the orb remained stubbornly intact … and then, it turned green.

As it brightened, spider-web like fractures spread across its hemisphere. It became opaque, shuddered and collapsed, melting into the fire. A fractional crystallisation within the melt occurred, affronting the somnolent magma far under the mountain, angering Vesuvius further. A wrathful molten lake of liquid death churned and spewed upwards. From deep within the heart of the mountain, a vapoured plume shot high into the cavern. Upwards it went, hitting the igneous rock ceiling, twisting into an angry winged beast of smoke and fire. The giant skull followed its upward cycle. Gemstone eyes turned into beacon-like rays; they engulfed the burning-winged nebulous creature, coaxing it towards them. It changed shape in swift reaction, becoming a spinning, tumultuous gasiform ball. It didn't budge.

'What's happening?' Mary shouted to be heard.

Arnold looked back at her. 'Two parts of the same. Spirit and body.'

The light intensified. The great fiery ball juddered and struggled against the pull.

'Why are they fighting?'

'Dominance. The creature needs to be whole, but the spirit doesn't want to be locked in.'

The light grew in strength. A muted scream of outrage shook the cavern as it shuddered and twisted, but the great beams of light consumed it; the giant swirling gaseous ball gave up its fight, yielding to the light and it collapsed with a sigh. In an instant, it was pulled downwards through skeletal eye sockets, filling and surrounding it.

'It's beautiful,' Arnold intoned.

Mary stepped back in fear.

When the roaring whirlwind stopped and the bright white-blue majestic glow dimmed, there stood a fully formed majestic lion. It looked around the cavern and blinked its huge luminous, disc-like eyes.

It shook its mane, adopting an intimidating pose. Then, as his mouth opened wide and took breath for the first time in centuries, the ancient immortal lion roared in song. *'Free!'*

His thunderous voice a torrent of energy echoed around the fissure, causing Vesuvius to shake, exhale, and scream in anger and fear, expelling through the air her molten tears.

Beast and man locked eyes. Neither blinked nor moved. The volcano rumbled, lava boiled and pulsed. Visible now beneath the pumice, it overflowed, seeping out of cracks and holes. Superheated gases and smoke burst through, choking the cavern. The great fire-filled mountain reached out with brimstone smoking hands for the monster seated proudly upon her belly. Beast's eyes shone green and a bubble manifested around himself and his followers.

Nothing penetrated it, but she never stopped trying.

Arnold opened his mouth and bestowed lyrical worship.

'Oh, Great One, we your servants welcome you back into the world.'

Beast's quick forward movement startled the others, but not Arnold. His voice-song, pure malevolence, tinged with pride. *'Little things,'* he sang, *'I find you worthy. Your heroic deeds will not be unrewarded, for I bestow upon thee the Song of Knowledge.'*

Each of them jerked as their minds were suddenly assaulted with new information, images, knowledge, secrets, histories, more than they could process. When the assault stopped, they fell back breathing hard.

'Your primitive minds will need time to comprehend my gift. You are clerics, my Nurrunadine, for I have imbued you all with powers and knowledge beyond the limits of your mortal brothers and sisters.'

'Divine Majesty,' Arnold bowed deeply, 'we are most grateful. We wish only to fulfil the oaths of our forefathers in bringing your mighty powers and rule back to a world in desperate need of it.'

'So shall it be, Son of Man.'

Magma splattered off the protective bubble, the ground shook and cracked, gas and liquid death flooded the cavern.

'The volcano erupts,' Mary shouted in horror. 'Arnold, we must go!'

The giant lion turned to her, his lips curled back in smile, then looked upwards. *'She has always been ireful, this great and beautiful mountain of old.'*

Vesuvius thundered her response by hurling chunks of extrusive igneous rocks at them.

Beast turned away from Arnold. *'I am immune to her wrath, she knows this, but your frail forms will be consumed. Come.'*

He strode towards a tunnel, his black clad servants in procession. He led them out into the hospitable brightness of a beautiful Mediterranean afternoon, far away from the angry mountain. When they were at a safe distance, he lay and watched with his followers beside him.

'See how she spews her malice onto the world.'

Arnold and Mary sat together taking in the terrifying eruption. His hand found hers and their fingers locked together.

Beast smiled, emitting a contented purr. *'Isn't she magnificent?'*

'You speak as if the mountain were alive?' Mary's eyes didn't leave the spectacle.

'In a way. There are many hidden things deep beneath the surface of this world, treacherous, wonderful, and malign. You will come to understand in time, Daughter of man.'

Arnold turned to Beast. 'What is your decree, Master?'

'I need your experiences, your history. Come. Open your minds to me.'

Beast closed his eyes and the nine did likewise. He took in their knowledge and when he was done, he sighed.

'This world has become stolid. Small. The age of man an infestation. It shall be great once again. I will awaken it with my Song. We must replace what has hitherto been the dominion of the weak and primitive. Ageless servants, hidden beneath the surface, will once again come forth to walk this world and rout the vile blight of mankind. But we must take care. Other things have slept along with me, the accursed Osirian, servants of the Righteous. They will also awaken and fill the world with Songs of Light. They will seek out our ruin, as they did before. We must be mindful of their power. We must be ready.'

Arnold frowned. 'Who are the Righteous?'

'My brothers. It was they who banished me onto this world. The power of their Song is formidable but not without weakness. My brethren, a reckoning is coming, we shall be the victorious.'

A voice from the nine spoke up. 'It's war, then?'

'Yes,' Beast purred in wicked pleasure, *'a great battle of old.'*

'There is a war being fought across Europe now. Thousands are dying,' Albert voiced sad concern.

Beast laughed.

'You understand little of war, Albert-Nurrunadine. A nascent new age begins. The time of man is ended. ...'

Extract from the Book of Narrudeth–Appendix A

"… The realm known as Earth endured through many ages of beast and man. The Last Age–as it was written, since its ending was born through hardship, destruction, pain and suffering, where the dominion shifted to others in place of mankind–became the foundation for the darkest time on Earth.

The Beast Lord–one of nine Ardunadine immortals, banished from the Heavens in the form of a giant Lion–forged the word anew, passing it into shadow and ruin. As Man was engaged in a struggle for its own survival in one of the bloodiest wars of its era, so the Beast Lord struck. He called forth hideous beings from beneath the bowels of the world. Twisted, shapeless, nebulous creatures, named the Faulgoth, capable of changing forms at a whim, able to withstand fire, ice, wind, and mortal weapon. They took what was known to be the land of Europe and of the Americas and emptied it of its population. The war with man lasted a few short years for the Faulgoth were swift in their devastating destruction, and the dominion of the Beast Lord was such, he held sway over everything, and everyone.

But he did not eradicate mankind entirely, for within their limited primitive minds, he found a beauty in things that surprised him. For not always was he so black of heart. And so the nine celebrants, known only as the Nurrunadine, were given dominion over much of the land. And Beast encouraged them to build the world of men and their technologies towards single purpose that was never revealed to any, but the Nurrunadine, who kept the secrets of their master's plan. And so the Last Age of Man came to an end.

And in this new age, no man ever went without food and no child ever died of curable sickness; where the driving forces of the world was not for wealth, but peaceful coexistence. And so the rout of mankind ended, the Faulgoth withdrew, and Beast was once again Lord of all, and there followed a period of peace across the world. A peace that would have remained had the Osirian stayed asleep. …"

Eight
A New Age of Man

The Awakening of the Faulgoth

When the moment came, it was so swift the people of the world had no time to react. The battle for Europe was in full force, unyielding, devastating. But no one was prepared for the battle that would follow. In Normandy on the morning of 7th June 1944, fighting along provinces was at its most destructive. Those that survived the landings the previous day continued their push through the Atlantic Wall. In an opened field where German and British troops occupied both sides, a most ferocious battle unfolded. Shells hit random targets churning up ground, as both sides intensified their forward momentum. As fierce firing continued, no one noticed a mound of mud and stone growing larger. It pulsated and lifted as dirt rose into giant hillock. Something trapped underneath was burrowing out. The movement caught the eye of a few men. They faltered and stopped their assault, confused by it. The mud mass grew larger and larger in slow surging pulses. The fighting stopped. The guns on both sides fell silent. Stillness filled the air. A few men on both sides moved forward, exchanging glances. Despite their differences, they shared a common inquisitiveness, they shared confusion, and fear.

One by one they moved inwards, quiet, apprehensive. The mound had stopped its growth, trickles of dirt and stones the only movement. An eerie quietness lingered, and those who'd unconsciously held breaths exhaled in quiet relief. The advancing soldiers reached the foot of the mound and stopped. The ground shuddered, they looked at each other in terror, and some began to run. The shuddering intensified, and with explosive ferocity, the ground erupted high into the air, raining earth, mud, and stone down upon them all. Those closest were instantly buried. When the dust cleared, the mound was gone, replaced by an enormous pit. In its core, something stirred. Gasps of horror mixed with cries of dread, as a monstrous creature awkwardly heaved itself out of the burning crater.

Screams in various languages said the same thing: a demon was escaping from Hell.

The incubus came to full height, its body a mixture of molten lava and blackened gnarled scales. It stretched itself and vast wings unfurled, covering the land in shadow. It opened its eyes for the first time in an age, and watched the little things fleeing. Its mouth opened and fire burst forth in a screeching roar, compelling them to fall to the ground, grabbing their ears, screaming in terror. It took a first step into the world, shaking the ground, and then … it destroyed every living thing in its path.

Similar creatures, across the world, pushed themselves out from beneath the surface and started their master's rampage.

From country to country, through rivers and streets, in forests and deserts, the war between man and Beast raged on. It was no longer a fight for man's supremacy. It was the beginning of the end of civilisation. With one goal in mind: the massacre of mankind. Putting aside differences, faiths, irreconcilable divisions, the men and women of Europe stood shoulder to shoulder, brave, resolute, unwavering. Powerful in their determination, they marched on the enemy with every tool of warfare at their disposal. But it wasn't enough. Caught off guard by the dreadfulness of beings immune to everything thrown at them, they soon realised there was no hope left in fighting, and retreated.

City after city fell to ruin. The people crushed, annihilated, routed. The Faulgoth pulled apart the land. They brought forth fires from the underworld in boiling, screaming lakes of malice and hate. The earth split open and bubbling rivers of molten fire spewed onto the world, ruthless, torrid, and inescapable. Wading through rivers, towering above peaks, nothing and no one affected them. Terrifying giant behemoths foul and unimaginable, unrelenting in sheer ferocity, swept across the land uprooting mountains, transforming landmass, and felling forests with a single look from their hideous eyes.

Against this enemy the people had no chance. The Faulgoth continued their relentless storm. Nothing survived their wrath. Beautiful architecture fell into the earth. Powerful ancient seats of man's supremacy now reduced to rubble. The last vestiges, desperate to escape, made for shores in hopes of a boat to ferry them out of France. Without discipline or order, defenceless and emptyhanded, they stampeded towards this goal. Thousands of men, women, and children;

dirty, malnourished, and frightened, overwhelmed the frantic demoralised British soldiers. Class divisions gone, rich or poor, a boat was a boat and no amount of barter secured a place. It was first come, first served, and the inconsolable terrified soldiers shot anyone trying to climb aboard once launched. A vast crowd forced their way onto an already packed landing craft, it listed and capsized.

Borders were no longer maintained. The mass exodus left thousands trapped; there were not enough vessels to save them all. Those lucky enough to find passage away, escaped in relative safety, but for every safe vessel launched five overfilled and burst, committing refugees to watery graves–or worse–to be floating victims of the Faulgoth.

The last boat filled to the brink. The refugees and soldiers managed to huddle close as it powered away from the shore. A soldier looked up at a man and woman, carrying an infant, as they burst across the shoreline frantic in their screaming and waving. He called for the captain to slow down but the request was ignored. They splashed into the water, faces stained with blood and tears. The soldier clambered aft shouting encouragement. From out of nowhere along the top of the cliff face, one of the Faulgoth screeched its fire and thundered towards them. The soldier continued his shouts, along with others, who were all hanging over the side ready to haul them in. The man edged towards the boat, desperate to reach them, pulling his exhausted wife with one arm whilst struggling to swim holding his child in the other. The monster reached the water's edge and bellowed at them. The man was still not close enough to the boat to get to the waiting arms. His exertion left him too exhausted to continue on. The nightmare waded out towards them. He looked up at the soldier, an artilleryman, and communicated his intention with a look. The artilleryman nodded once, and the man threw the infant up into his arms. He stopped, and watched the steamer slip away. The man remained in eye contact with his daughter's saviour, until the Faulgoth reached him. He smiled, mouthed a thank you, and was pulled out of the water along with his wife and ripped apart. Their muted-screams etched into the memories of all those aboard. The young artilleryman still holding the sobbing infant, watched the nightmare creature as it feasted on the two of them, as the steamer made it to safety.

Never before had such a mass of boats advanced towards the White Cliffs of Dover. It was soon to be the greatest beacon of hope.

The land of Europe lay in utter ruin, the shape of the continent unrecognisable and forever changed.

The boats continued in haste towards the shoreline, screams and whimpers were now a massive collective as the Faulgoth entered the channel, wading after them. And when it seemed as if all hope was lost, they stopped midway and went no further.

The Last Days of Man

The battle for supremacy was lost within days although the American people put up organised resistance. The vastness of their land allowed for many men to coordinate and build defensive groups in regions that hid them from the enemy. One of the largest groups to amass was successful in escaping the devastation. Knowing their weapons to have little effect, they retreated into large, abandoned underground facilities, coexisting in secret. Law and order maintained, for a time, but when hunger and greed took hold, it wasn't long before coexistence gave way to anarchy, as they attacked each other with stockpiles of weapons. Before long, half of them were either dead or dying. Those that survived did not rejoice for long, as the sound and energy of the fighting attracted the Faulgoth, and they tore apart the rocks and the land, pouring venom into caves and tunnels.

And it soon followed that America, like Europe, fell to Beast.

Man's opposition in America ended as they stood beaten and withdrawn, surrendering on the lawn of the smouldering ruins of the White House. Fires across the city had long since self-extinguished, but left destructive marks on the monuments the American people had once built and revered. Law and order long since abandoned where state and federal governments and their armies fell silent. A ragtag group of men and women stood in huddles, some armed, most resolute, and all terrified.

Beast stood before them, proud amongst his Faulgoth servants and the Nurrunadine. His song burst forth.

The world is ending. Man's dominion is over. Come. Bring forth the one who leads these broken things, let the leader of man see my might and feel my justice.'

The mix of men and women moved aside to allow a ragged individual to come forth; flanked by groups in varying uniforms adorned with medals they wore with pride. Their protection and adulation of him was fierce, and Beast noted the defiant undefeated expression, even in the face of utter ruin, with respect. He moved with measured pace ahead of his followers. Remaining steadfast, head held high.

'You are the leader of man?'

'I am the freely elected President of the United States of America,' he intoned.

'Little thing, you cannot claim ownership of a realm that no longer exists. There is no freedom upon which you can claim title, in case you were unaware,' Beast reminded him.

'How should I address you, mighty lion?'

'With care.'

The President remained impassive. 'You may have destroyed our cities, great lion, with your unnatural monsters. Our way of life, our very world, may be over, but our hearts remain strong. The American people will resist. We have fought for our freedom before and we will do so again.'

Beast prowled as he sang. *'Know this, Man called President. There is a new age now, my age. The time of men is at an end. You will pledge yourself and your followers to my will.'*

'And if we do not?'

'Your world is in ruin, President of naught. Your cities burned, your offspring dead, your civilisation at an end. Do not ask me questions you already know the answers to.'

'We are proud, mighty lion. We would rather die fighting for our freedom than be subjugated to slavery. We are Americans, sir. Your immoral war with mankind is iniquitous, without honour, without justice, without foundation. We, the freemen of America—'

'Death is easy. Do you choose it so willingly? Do the people you lead wish it? Do they follow you, and resist, even though they are powerless in the face of what will come if they do?'

'They are not powerless, great lion, so long as they have hope.'

'What hope do they have?'

'That God is on our side.'

'God? Where is this God who allows His world to be so utterly devastated?'

'Faith will keep our hopes alive.'

'Faith in what? Would all mankind lay down their lives so needlessly? Is the promise of what might follow so alluring?'

The first seeds of irritation crept across a defeated face. 'I will not bandy words over my beliefs with you, faithless lion.' He felt the shifting of those behind and recognised he'd allowed his feelings to better him. He calmed his inner fears. Beast laughed in roar.

'Son of man, for thousands of years I've watched as you've fought your own brothers and sisters for lands upon which you've laid specious claim. You have slain one another over primitive paradigms, over Delphic abstruse beliefs and spiritless objects, valueless things … for what is life's worth when compared to gold, or land, or anything else? You wrap yourself in abstract blankets of values and deceitful well-meaning principle, engorging in cornucopia as your own kin writhe and die in wretched penury, and you do nothing but fatten in response. You are fleshed in falsehoods, men of dishonoured mendacities and corruption … you dare preach to me about morality? President of the crushed. President of degeneracy.'

The president licked his dry lips. 'You're right, great lion, we *are* flawed. But I do not wish to see further conflict between us. I cannot speak for the world, but I can speak for my people. You are powerful, mighty lion. Let us have dialogue to end this destructive conflict. Will you allow that?'

'Ah … you seek conciliation?'

'I do, yes, I do. Can there not be discourse between us? Can we not find common ground? Is there chance of peace?'

Beast stopped his prowl and sat. *'But what of your people, President of the overcome? Do you speak for all, or just this horde behind you?'*

'I speak for the free people of this proud country.'

'The earth is no longer free. You speak for no one.'

'While I draw breath, there can be—'

The fallen son of Arrandori leapt forward and in swift roar, bit down on the President of the United States of America, tearing him in half. Blood and entrails splashed across the men and women close by. There was screaming, crying, outrage, panic. Some dropped their weapons and ran. Others stood their ground and fired. Beast laughed, his song disarming them, he leapt from one to the other, biting, clawing, eviscerating—his fur matted with blood—until there was nothing left but lumps of flesh and a river of bloody entrails.

'Now you no longer draw breath, President of sustenance.' His giant green eyes followed those running, and then he sat and cleaned his face. When he'd finished, he turned to the nearest hooded Nurrunadine, who stepped forward.

'What is your bidding?'

'Arnold-Nurrunadine, this structure, what is its name?'

'The White House, my Lord.'

'Ah…It is, was, a symbol of hope?'

'Yes, it was the seat of power in America.'

'A palace?'

'Yes, and no.'

Beast turned his head and frowned.

'This nation had a presidency, a democratically elected leadership of the people. Only a few nations have a royal head of state, one passed down through blood and birth-right. Someone of royal lineage would have a palace … but, well, it really is the same thing in the end.'

This nation, you say? The president of the dead called it, United States of America. When I took your memories, I saw many names like this. You and Mary-Nurrunadine are from … Great … Britain. This is on the other side of this world?'

'The same hemisphere, Lord.'

'And are you still proud of this Britain of Greatness?'

'I have been in your service all my life, Lord. That, and only that, I am proud of. I have devoted my existence to your will.'

Beast lowered his head. *'You are truly worthy, Arnold-Nurrunadine. These senseless things will learn much from your teaching.'*

Arnold bowed.

'Each has their own part to play, once the world is secure, the Faulgoth will retire and we will rebuild anew. During the last great battle for dominance, the lines of royal bloodlines became formidable, powerful. Of these we must be weary. This president of man had no power in his blood. Thus he was easily vanquished.'

'That used to be so, but not anymore. Most of the remaining royals are simply figureheads now, their bloodlines mixed many times over. They have no real power, not like the days of old.'

'You mistake my meaning, Arnold-Nurrunadine. The power flows in their blood, imbued by Songs of Light, a gift from the accursed Osirian. There may yet still be some who have the power of Song, but they must surely be few and far between. …'

Arnold rubbed his chin in thought, but said nothing.

Beast continued to stare at the White House. *'It is of no consequence. Have the Faulgoth raze it to the ground, then build a temple atop, so these sons and daughters of man may see my greatness and rejoice. Have all such places treated so.'*

'It shall be done.'

There is something festering within your mind. I would hear your concern.'

'It's Albert, my Lord.'

'Ah. You are unsure of the direction of his loyalty?'

'No. He is loyal.'

'Then what?'

'He is also a good man.'

'I see.' Beast contemplated the exchange with eyes closed. *'You believe this goodness to be a liability?'*

'Frankly, yes … if it pleases you, I would like to address it myself.'

'Let it be so. Your loyalty to me will not go unrewarded, Arnold-Nurrunadine.'

Beast turned, paused, looked back at the White House and then walked away.

Nine
The Osirian Return

The Untouched Land - 12th Year of Beast

The tanned little boy sat with stones and sticks, building a fort in the sand, humming to himself. An old, bearded man approached dressed in flowing robes of turquoise and white, lined with symbols of gold. He rested on a long white staff, woven into the top, a jagged crystal ablaze with multi-coloured fire. The boy looked up and smiled. The old man said nothing for the longest time. When he did speak, the voice was pure, calming.

'Do those things you set before you bring you comfort?' he asked.

The boy shrugged.

The old man continued to watch and the boy stopped his playing and said, 'You are very old, aren't you?'

The man laughed. 'Why yes, I am old, as old as the stars. Does that bother you?'

'No.'

'Good. Age is no indicator of wisdom, young man.'

The boy frowned. 'What is wisdom?'

The old man bent forward. 'Wisdom is the quality of having experience, knowledge, and good judgement; the quality of being wise.'

'You are wise?'

'A good question. I used to think so. Now, I fear, I'm not as wise as I once was.'

'You are afraid?'

'Oh yes. Fear is another indication of wisdom, young man. Fear brings with it judgement, and knowledge, understanding. Fear allows us to think and to act accordingly. I am very much afraid, but experience has taught me to embrace those worries. Are you afraid?'

'No. I'm not.'

'Why?'

'Because the monsters have not come, they dare not come.'

'How can you know that for certain?'

'I feel it, inside.' The boy pointed to his chest.

The old man smiled. 'Ah ... intuition. What men call gut feeling ...' An unearthly screech in the wind caught his attention and he looked away, his eyes narrowing. 'You may have been mistaken.'

The boy continued to play with the objects before him. 'The noises scare, the wings flutter, but they don't reach us here. We are safe.'

'For a time,' the old man agreed. 'But fate can often be cruel.'

The boy looked up and frowned. He asked, 'What is fate?'

'That is a question you must ask those that are wiser than man.'

'I asked you. You said you were wise.'

The old man laughed. 'You are perceptive, young one. Wise I may be. That doesn't mean I have all the answers you seek.'

'Maybe, but you haven't answered my question. What is fate?'

'I suppose the best answer might be, fate is the universal principle or ultimate agency by which the order of things is prescribed.'

'By God?'

'By everyone.'

The old man straightened, his grey-blue eyes observed the symbols being drawn unconsciously by the boy. Without looking up, the boy continued his questioning. The wanderer eyed his drawings with interest. The boy's questions were spoken with a voice far older than his youthfulness suggested.

'Has the world always been so horrible? Are we always to suffer the curse of beasts and monsters?'

'I don't know. A darkness lies behind us, and out of it few stories have come.'

'I like stories. Please tell me one.'

'Very well. Long ago before the time of Great Kings, before this world was formed, there was a mighty celestial being named Arrandori. He was the fairest and wisest of all and he and his beloved sons, the Ardunadine, sang great songs that gave life to this universe, as it is known. Their harmonies were so magnificent they gave rise to entire worlds, ecosystems, life. He imbued his sons with different gifts, and they each sang songs that conferred knowledge to lesser beings. They came from a universe old beyond measure. You see, young man, every race has philosophies and concepts of God, or gods, and the Ardunadine were perceived as divine, but really, they were simply evolved beyond understanding.

'Each of these beings wove differing music, but one of them, the oldest, whose true name I will not speak, gifted with songs superior to those of his brothers, wove in threads of disharmony, creating flaws no one saw. He was inquisitive and reckless. He tired of a simple life and sought to bring his own mark upon the worlds he and his brothers sang into existence. They had shed their mortal confines, existing as ethereal beings and for millennia, sat in the majestic Celestial Temple of Song just outside the reach of any mortal man.

'When the disharmony was discovered, Arrandori rebuked his oldest son. So mighty was his anger, he set decree he be named Beast, formed into mortal creature, and banished to this world, doomed to live out a mortal life. But the Ardunadine failed to fully understand the songs he had woven into each world, so that when he arrived, despite the limitations of his earthly form, he brought forth armies of darkness and set on course an evolution that resulted in his supreme dominance of the world.

'The Ardunadine named the Righteous saw this, but did not act, as their Songs would always be more powerful, now that Beast was cut off from the power of the Celestial Temple of Song.

'But Beast was not so powerless as they'd imagined, and when the world was dominated, the people so repressed and subjugated–for Man had sprung from the earth far earlier than intended–one of the Ardunadine, the fairest and wisest of the eight, sent servants of the Songs of Light to assist man, and a great battle ensued. It lasted generations. Finally, Beast, knowing he could not hope to defeat the Light, accepted the hand fate had drawn and was cast out of the world, his mortal remains disbanded and sent to its farthest reaches. For thousands of years the world calmed, the ancient monsters fell back into shadow and slept. And for a time, all was right. But Beast, who was far more cunning than they realised, had not been vanquished, for his life's Song remained ever-present, and his treacherous desires fuelled all that is evil in the world. And so, a little before your birth, the world of man once again felt his mighty wrath and this time, one by one, they fell.'

The boy looked gloomy. 'I don't like that story. It's too sad.'

'Nevertheless,' the old man responded. He smiled with kindness. 'The story isn't over. Your part in it is about to begin. Tell me, what is your name?'

'Ammon,' the boy replied.

'Do you know the meaning of your name in the language of the ancients?'

'I don't, no.'

'It means: unseen, concealed or hidden.' He leant forward. 'It's fitting. ...'

He became old and bent clutching his staff in support. 'Man stands on the precipice. The fate we just spoke of will be decided soon enough.'

The boy looked up and they locked eyes. 'I have to leave this place, don't I?'

He gave a solemn nod. 'Your fate has also been decided, Ammon, although you are scarcely aware of it.'

'You've come to take me away from here, from my family, from my friends. I do understand that. Are you a Malakh?'

The old man laughed hard. 'No ... no, not the way you think of it. It's true, by definition, I am a messenger, but I'm not a divine messenger, although perhaps from your perception you may think otherwise. Ammon, I'm just an old man who has seen much of this world. I've walked through many ages of man. And I've slept long. Now I am awakened, and so will you be, young King. For it is the time for monsters to fear. It is time we rouse the gifts in your blood, so that you may hear and understand the Songs of Light. Right now, Beast holds dominance over this beautiful world, and it is time to set things right.'

The boy stood, dropping his stones and sighing. The old man scanned the horizon. Far into the distance the silhouetted peaks of the Pyramids of Giza stood proud and untouched; he found that comforting. The boy took his aged hand and he looked down into innocent brown eyes. 'Where do we go now, old man?'

'To the seat of your ancestors, Ammon, to the home of your great, great grandfather's fathers.'

'What is your name?'

The wanderer paused in frown. 'My name? Do you know ... I've quite forgotten?'

'Well, I can't call you old man, that's not very polite.'

'No, I suppose it isn't.' He caressed his beard in thought for a moment. Eventually he shrugged.

'I suspect it will come to me. For the time being I will tell you this: I am one of the servants of the Songs of Light, Little King Ammon. It is time my own light shone anew and ...' he tapped Ammon's nose, '... yours to shine as well. Come, we must go.'

They walked towards the horizon hand in hand.

'I think I will call you, Akhet.'

'If it pleases you, Ammon.' The old man snorted, but he seemed quite happy with it.

Ten
Lady of Light

The United Kingdom of Great Britain: 14th Year of Beast

Mary-Nurrunadine stood on the bow of the giant black boat moving with swiftness through the channel towards Great Britain. Her black robe flowed in the breeze. The flags and banners, along with the men and women of her entourage, were each adorned with symbols of the Temple of Beast. The great ship reached the shores of her old home and she disembarked with measured pace. Holding aloft Arnold's old cane, she stepped out onto the dock, her entourage solemnly followed.

A huge crowd of people gathered around the dock. They parted as she moved through them. She felt their fear and loathing; it poured from them in waves. She continued her slow pace, ignoring insults and jeers. No one had the courage to come close, except one. The man standing in her path had a handsome, rugged face. His rifle lowered but ready. She looked into his eyes, and stopped her advance, her followers mirrored her.

He spat at her feet. 'You are not welcome on these shores, Lady of Death.'

'We will speak with your king,' she said.

'Did you not hear me?' He growled.

'I heard your words, Man,' she said without emotion. 'You will take me to your king. Now.'

Their eyes never left one another. His fierceness matched hers, she found it alluring, but showed no outward sign. He lowered his head and stepped aside, with a gesture he said, 'He expects you, follow me.'

She glided forward without further words and exited the dock, following him through the old boatyard. She noted with mild interest they had maintained it despite the lack of resources. They passed out into a small enclosed circle, with long since abandoned shops, into a battalion of red-tunic soldiers, who poured in behind, baring their escape. Her blackened eyes did not blink. When the area was secured, two Standard Bearers holding the pennants of the king came forward. They marched towards her, stopping midway and halting. They turned so they now faced each other and waited. The courtyard was quiet. When the king entered, the soldiers instantly responded to voiced command, stamping in unison, the sound reverberating like the crack of a rifle. Dressed in the same regalia, he was flanked by a group of guardsmen. He came forward with them but unlike his army, he looked awkward in a uniform. His guards halted behind the Standard Bearers, they remained ready at all times. She found herself enamoured by the ceremonial display. Even after everything that had happened, she mused, they still maintained it. The King of England approached and stood before her, neither spoke for the longest time. The king broke the stalemate.

'You were once a British citizen?'

'Once,' she responded.

'That is why he sent you?' The king crossed his arms over his medalled chest. 'If this is an attempt to ingratiating yourself with us, you, and he, have made grievous errors in judgement.'

'I am not here to curry favour with the king of nothing,' she responded.

'The entire world stands in ruins yet here we are, alive, *not* defeated, Lady of Lies, nor are we king of *nothing*. Save your puerility for others. We, and I mean everyone in this courtyard, are *not* amused.'

'My Lord sent me to offer you terms of surrender. He is not without mercy.'

The king laughed. 'Your Lord has laid waste to the entire planet and he could do so here with ease. There is no one here that can challenge him, so why hasn't he?'

'He does not seek to eradicate man; he reimages the world. Men, like you, are needed to reign over those that still draw breath.'

Again the king laughed. 'Really? He destroys all of Europe, the Americas and Lord knows where else, but he stops at the border of England because he needs me to lead the remnants of the human race? Come now, my Lady, we both know the truth, so I ask you again. Why has your master not destroyed this country?'

A voice from nowhere said, 'She will not answer you, Highness, and even if she does, it will be a voice of lies.'

Mary-Nurrunadine turned her gaze to a dishevelled old woman, in flowing robes of emerald green, red, and silver. She hobbled slowly through the armed guards, her hands clasping her staff for support. A jagged green crystal, at its top, glowed bright as she approached.

'You, Nurrunadine, have nothing to barter with, for I know that your master's power cannot reach inside the borders of this sacred land. My power prevents it.'

'Who are you, old woman, who address me so?'

'We call her Lady of Light,' the king said. 'And by contrast, we call you, Lady of Darkness.'

Mary-Nurrunadine laughed. 'Your appellations are fitting, if superfluous.'

The ancient woman stood beside the king. 'Know this, daughter of this land, we allowed this meeting so you could send message back to your master, who festers in his iniquitous temple.' She raised her staff and a blinding light burst forth. Mary-Nurrunadine's entourage screamed in terror, falling to the ground, but she was unable to move, caught in the powerful light, and the old woman called Lady of Light sang a euphonious tune, filling her mind.

'Beast, hear me!'

In his lair, Beast growled at the intrusion. Above Mary-Nurrunadine a huge ghostly lion head shimmered into existence. It roared and the soldiers and king himself stepped back in terror. But Lady of Light held out her hand and comforted them with a smile. 'Fear him not, for he has no power here.'

I hear your Song, Osirian witch. We will see who has no power.' He roared and broke Mary-Nurrunadine of her trance. She lifted her cane at his command, the head of it grew and red light flashed from ruby eyes. The Osirian blazed in sweet song, and the cane shattered and fell to the ground, broken beyond repair. Mary-Nurrunadine staggered backwards, Lady of Light fixed her in place with another tune.

'You feel my power, old one, you feel the Song of Light. You remember it was *I* who warned you of the consequences if you were ever to return.'

Beast roared. *'Curse you, Osirian hag. You should have remained asleep along with your brothers and sisters. This is my world now.'*

She pointed the light of her staff at him and he flinched. 'We have awoken anew. We come now to reclaim that which you have polluted with iniquity.'

Beast chuckled. *'Poor ancient old hag, you've awakened too late. What will you reclaim? Broken empty lands? For I have turned this world into images of darkness. Rivers of human blood and seas of their corpses nourish my armies and feed their wanton desires. They will do my will and sweep the last of mankind, and the accursed Osirian aside; a fitting end for you, creature of Light, to be extinguished into shadow. You cannot hold Song against the dark, hag. My Faulgoth will swallow you all in their maleficent wantonness.'*

'The powers of the ageless are awakened, Beast of Lies. Your own sister gives me life. The kings of old will unite the people of this world and we Osirian servants of the Songs of Light, keepers of the bloodlines of old, will vanquish you from this land along with your acts of turpitude, your vile creatures, and your putrescent essence.'

Beast sang Songs of laughter that shook the world.

'Not even the power of my brothers and sisters combined could vanquish me, hag, crone. You have nothing. There are no powers in this world upon which you can call that give credence to those idiotic and foolhardy notions. How small you have become.'

'We will show you how powerless we are, son of beauty and wondrousness.'

He hissed at her insult.

'Despite all your dark enchantments, despite your ramblings, there are rules. You know of what I speak.'

Beast snarled.

Lady of Light stepped forward, touched her staff to Mary-Nurrunadine's head and said: 'I release you from the fowl thing that sits in your belly.'

Beast's eyes widened. *'No! Curse you, hag. I'll tear you apart—'* and then, for the first time in millennia, he fell and howled in agony.

Mary-Nurrunadine grabbed at her throat and let out an inhuman cry.

Around the world the eight other Nurrunadine suddenly dropped and writhed in agony.

Mary-Nurrunadine fell to the floor, kicked and thrashed, arched her back in agony. Beast howled and cursed, as Lady of Light held out her hands and sang a sweet chorus that eased Mary-Nurrunadine's pain. She turned over, coughed, convulsed, retched, and heaved. With effort, she finally vomited out the black slug-like creature that had entered her years previous, and she was Mary Wilson, once again.

The Osirian watched on as Beast writhed. She sang and he cursed. The slug-like-being shuddered, squealed and flipped, as it became nothing more than ash; and Beast screamed so hard he was heard across the entire world. Her entourage continued to writhe and scream. The soldiers looked on in concern, but she hushed them. They flailed and gurgled, and then fire burst from within them, through mouths, ears, eye sockets. And it was over. They screamed no more.

The Osirian and Beast locked eyes for the longest time, then she lifted her staff and thrust it into the ground, and the ethereal head of Beast vanished in a howl of swirling smoke. She knelt down and picked Mary up from the ground as if she had no weight. She cradled and sang, and Mary's eyes fluttered open. She looked up at the angelic face, no longer old, but young and vibrant, and then sobbed.

Lady of Light caressed Mary's cheek. 'There, child, do not despair. You are free of it. You are back into the world of men and it is good. Allow your tears to fall. I will take away the burden of your grief with my Song. Sleep, sleep, beautiful daughter of this land. I have freed you. You have come home and you are safe here amongst these brave, brave men.'

Mary awoke in a luxurious room decorated with heavy ornate fabrics and regal pictures. At the foot of her bed, a young woman sat embroidering. She looked up and smiled.

'You're awake.'

Mary coughed and rubbed at her throat. The woman put down her sewing and filled a glass of water from a crystal jug. She handed it to her and Mary took a long drink.

'Thank you,' she said, placing the glass on the bedside cabinet. The young woman sat down on the edge of the bed.

'How are you feeling, Mary?'

'Unsure. Like I just came out of a terrible nightmare. I'm not sure where I am.'

'It's understandable, given what you've been through.'

An echoed roar went through her mind and she jumped. The woman put a hand on her arm, and Mary found odd comfort in her touch. 'Lady of Light said you may still get flashbacks. A part of you will always remain connected to him, even though you're free of his control.'

'I have no memories of you or this place. Where am I?'

'You are in my bedroom, Mary. My name is Elizabeth.'

'How long have I been asleep?'

'Perhaps a month, maybe longer.'

Mary rubbed her eyes. She didn't recognise the woman. Time had flown by and whilst she hadn't aged, the world had grown around her. 'Oh, dear Lord, I feel like I should know who you are, but I don't, I'm sorry. I'm suspecting you're royalty, by the decoration in this room, by the pictures on the wall, by your posture, by the ...'

Elizabeth threw her head back and laughed.

'You are a refreshing companion to talk with, Mary.'

'I can't have been that talkative, asleep in your bed.'

'You were ... a comfort to me.' Elizabeth smiled, but there was something hidden behind her eyes.

'I'm so sorry,' Mary stammered. 'The last time I was ... was ... *me*, it was 1926. What is the date now? The real date? Our date.' She tried to get out of the bed.

Elizabeth said, 'Stay in the bed, Mary. You've earnt the rest, take it. I assure you, if I need sleep, I will crawl right in beside you. To answer your question, the date is 15th February, 1958.'

'1958? Thirty-two years ...' She sank into the bed.

Elizabeth took her hand and looked into her eyes. 'We are not so beaten that a few years would force us back into despair, are we?'

'No, no. You're quite right. It's ... well, the last time I remember being normal, I was digging in Syria.'

'You were an archaeologist?'

'I still am. I know things I'm not supposed to. I have knowledge still in my head that shouldn't be there. I ... I don't even know what to call you?'

Elizabeth nodded. 'Right now, you can call me Elizabeth. As to your knowledge, we might need that, Mary, if the day comes that we lead our forces into battle against this vile Beast that has taken our world.'

'We? You? Wait, you're a little young to be a leader of men, aren't you?'

Elizabeth sighed. 'It's true, but we have to accept those great responsibilities thrust upon us, Mary. When my father died it fell to me to lead my people.'

Mary knew her father's death was recent. But her sorrow ran deeper than that, Mary read it in her eyes. She had lost more than just her father, much more.

'I'm ... I'm so sorry for your loss, my Queen.'

Elizabeth nodded, tucked her back into the bed, kissed her forehead and said, 'Sleep now, Mary. When you are fit, we will have the kitchens prepare you a meal.'

Mary sank back against the pillows and fell into a deep, dreamless sleep.

Eleven
The Gathering

The Earthly Temple of Song

The crystal room etched into the hidden mountain housed nine men, women, and children. An equal number of Osirian stood before them dressed in flowing robes of all different colours. All ages, a mixture of men and women, they stood serene, resting on similar staffs.

'Welcome kings and queens of the earth,' they said in unison. 'You are all that is left of the ancient bloodlines of old. Each of you has a part to play, but there is one here whose blood is purest of all. Ammon, please come forward.'

The boy looked nervously out from behind Akhet's robe. He held the old man's hand, and they both came forward together.

Akhet said, 'My young king is a little nervous in such royal company.'

Lady of Light laughed and knelt down. 'Come to me, Little King,' she said, and he sat on her knee. She placed a hand on his chest and felt his rapid heartbeat. 'Calm,' she said and he felt her power course through him. 'There is no need to fear, for you are the strongest of all your kin.'

'I am not scared,' he said, and smiled at her. 'I'm just nervous.'

The room erupted in laughter.

'Well, King Ammon, you need not be nervous either.'

Akhet lifted him off her knee, and sat him onto a chair that had appeared from nowhere.

Lady of Light said: 'Kings and queens, you all know this world is in ruins. Beast has devastated the lands, killed and murdered your people, and taken possession with help of the foul creatures from the shadows. You are all stained in grief and despair, you are wearisome, and you are defeated. But let your hearts be untroubled this day, for although the past is unchangeable, the future is not so.

'We have awoken from our long sleep and we are here to guide. However, we do not have the power to challenge Beast directly. Our Songs did not finish him before, despite our self-congratulation. The battle between us ended in stalemate, we know now only by man's hand can Beast be vanquished, for the Songs of Light and the grace of Arrandori has so decreed. You and you alone hold sway over lands untouched by the blight.'

'Lady of Light', one man spoke up. 'How are we to face this Beast when no weapon we possess can harm him or his demon servants?'

There was a murmur. She smiled at them. 'Each of you has the gift of the Songs of Light, which we will awaken in you, and so you will have power to command, and to fight, and we will teach you how to forge weapons that will fell the servants of Beast, but, we also have something else. We have Ammon. The young, nervous, little Ammon. Whose destiny is written in the great Songs of my people. He, the boy of pure blood, will vanquish the undying spirit and banish him back into the shadows forever.'

Akhet came forward. 'We also know that Beast made a grievous error. He poured too much of his essence into the foul things that turn men into servants. That turns rock and stone into monsters. With each one destroyed he is weakened. When Mary was released and the part of him that expelled was destroyed, he screamed. We all *heard* it. We all *felt* it. It was a scream of agony. The other eight Nurrunadine must be released from the spell he has cast over them, and that should make him vulnerable.'

A man of Indian descent leant forward. 'Should?'

Akhet smiled. 'Yes, with a lot of hope, I believe it to be so.'

The Indian king looked around him.

Another Osirian came forward. 'The language of men is imprecise. Know this, when we, holders of the sacred Songs of the Righteous, fought Beast, no power in our possession made him scream, as he did when Mary was freed.'

Akhet smiled, nodding. 'You see? He has a vulnerability that he made himself. But he will understand this now, he will make it difficult for us to get to his servants, and he is likely to step up his campaign to destroy us all, but let us not worry about that now!'

Lady of Light smirked at him. 'You are upsetting the kings and queens, brother, perhaps you should stop talking for a while.'

Akhet nodded apologetically. 'Yes, yes, quite right, Etheria.'

She stood before them, in all her beauty, and smiled. 'Kings and queens of the earth, you start a new chapter in the age of man. Today, we must all be in agreement. To do nothing invites death, for we cannot simply linger indefinitely. With your combined strengths, with the powers at your disposal, with the people of this great world at your command, you must rise up and take it back. Rescue it from monsters and beasts, from creatures that belong in shadow. What say you, sons and daughters of man? Will you fight to win back your world?'

Each of them stood and in unison they voiced a resounding yes. ...

Extract from the Book of Narrudeth–Appendix B

"… And so, the Osirian awakened and with them the great Songs of Light roused those whose blood had been imbued with kingly gifts. Beast had been dealt a significant blow by the loss of his Nurrunadine servant. When the part of him that was connected to her was destroyed by the Osirian, his weakened physical form felt the loss and pain of it and he locked himself away in his fortress, calling his servants to him.

The kings and queens of men found new courage in their alliance with the Osirian; they, who taught wisdom and grace, helped forge weapons that could fell the mightiest of monsters. For the first time in ages, man was no longer weak. Man had purpose and guidance, and with the strength of the ancients, they forged a union the likes of which the world had never known.

With the coming of the unions of man, the world was peaceful in its devastation, and the Osirian kept the monsters at bay. Any of these foul things that strayed too close to the protected lands, were vanquished by their Light, and soon, even the Faulgoth stayed clear for they too were afraid. And the men learnt how to build again. Science, music, art, literature, history, and all that the Osirian had to offer, was once again taught in the Schools of Light. Their education in the corruptions Beast had woven into them was taught at the earliest age, so that the generations would know not to fall into the same traps as their forefathers. Industries were once again alive, but this time, out of mutual desire to better all mankind. Hunger eradicated, as man farmed protected lands, distributing overstock through trade of commodity, not for gold."

Twelve
The Gift of Arrandori

The Earthly Temple of Song - 15ᵗʰ Year of Beast

The gathering continued and much was learnt and shared. The map of the world had changed. No longer bordered by known continents, only a few of the original lands were left intact. Some of those countries, once the economic centres of the old world, still stood. Most were devastated wastelands, blackened by ash, fire, and death. As the discussions continued, the Osirian sang imparting knowledge. Their teachings awakened old wisdom dormant in their blood. Imbued with Songs of Light, memories stretching back years were now at their disposal. When the summit concluded they ate and drank in their new found comradery.

The kings and queens shared knowledge and experiences. But more than that, they found they now had a communal link to one another's thoughts. And with this newfound ability, they were able to comprehend much with sagacity, for each could now communicate by the power of Song as well as vocalised speech. Etheria, known as Lady of Light, or Osiris, bathed them in serenity.

Testing these abilities plunged the room into silence; they were now capable of understanding the world of Beast. Insights grew, allowing higher perception, their minds began to restructure as neural pathways reorganised. When they focused together at peace they felt strong … they felt powerful. New perspectives granted sense beyond the range of mortal man, and as they attuned to one another, the Osirian fed them more. Little by little they assimilated the flow of information. The knowledge caused laughter, song, and weeping.

The Osirian teachers shifted their song, moving them to a newfound level of understanding, and then the flow of knowledge stopped, as a booming trumpeting noise filled the world.

The room shook but they knew not to be afraid, although they weren't sure what was happening, they perceived no danger. The Osirian lifted their arms and lost their earthly forms, becoming ghost-like, ethereal. The resounding noise gave way to a beautiful and majestic Song, the likes of which no one alive had ever heard. It filled everything and all heard, or felt, its magnificent symphony.

The vile creatures of Beast patrolling the undying lands also heard it, but they did not rejoice. Instead, they fell to the ground shrieking dreadful curses. Beast cowered into the darkest corner of his lair. He recognised it, as only one of his power could, and was deathly afraid. Nurrunadine dropped into foetal balls, recoiling in terror. In contrast the men, women, and children of the earth felt joyous as they looked up into the sky. Kings and queens rejoiced in their new found abilities. They were able to comprehend some of its meaning, and felt the benevolent power radiating from it, but they weren't able to discern the source.

In the darkest part of the world, where thick, black-grey thunderous clouds crawled across sky at Beast's command, a ray of angelic light pierced through causing them to shrink outwards. Where the shaft of light touched, ash and barren rock became fertile. Long dead fauna sprang to life. Flora sprouted and flourished.

A lone Faulgoth, who hadn't managed to escape, found itself imperilled and exposed. It bellowed malice as it became suffused, bursting into ash in roaring scream; the ash sparkling into seeds as a warm breeze carried them across the utopia. Where they settled, vegetation sprang, filling the air with sweet scents, expunging the fetid stench of darkness. Beast howled in rage and pain at the loss of his servant and at his own impotence.

The light increased in radiance, washing away everything foul caught in its wake. Its energy flowed outwards in all directions, like ripples from a rock fallen into a pond. It spread out restructuring, terraforming blighted black lands into picturesque paradise. When it dispersed, a perfect one-hundred mile span of flourishing new terrain stood anew. Beast pushed himself deeper into his lair and snarled. He understood its meaning, like the Osirian and their awakened pet humans; he could see the effect the powerful Song had on his black kingdom.

From the hypocentre, a magnificent bubbling mass of liquid crystal burst out of the earth. It grew and grew, high onto the world, solidifying as it slowed into an incredible diamond fortress. The sun, visible in the land for the first time in many years, bathed the tower in its warmth. An aura of angelic purple-blue energy burst from the fortress. Where it touched, rock formations pushed out from the soil, riverbeds formed and filled with clear water.

When the work was done and the powerful energy retracted, the pure Song faded into memory. There in the midmost point of the inhospitable, dangerous, and fiercely guarded besmirched area on Earth, stood a veritable garden of life.

The Osirian lowered their arms, shining bright as they reverted back to earthly form. For some time they stood unspeaking, swept away by the nature of the Song. A young woman, regal and beautiful, stood and broke the silence.

'We all recognised the wondrous nature of that sound. It filled our hearts and minds with joy and beauty. Tell me, Etheria, by what name do you give this Divine Song?'

Etheria smiled, and her aged lined face reflected both wisdom and youthful beauty. 'That dear Queen Elizabeth of the England Realm was the voice-song of Arrandori.'

King Ammon then stood and came forward. A bright light flowed from his young body. He appeared to grow as he approached. When he opened his mouth to speak, it was neither his voice nor in speech, but a unified symphonic phonological choir that surged outwards, so that all could hear.

The Osirian fell to their faces.

The others sensing the majestic nature of the power knelt in dignified response.

And the bright light of King Ammon sang:

'Oh most beautiful and joyous children of Earth, I grant thee aid, noble providence, and erudition. Heavy hast been thy burden of late, but if thou hast eyes to see, and will, thou will knowest by which path thou must walk, albeit thorny by labour and arduous of mind. For thy pain we grieve in anguish and as restitution, we bequeath unto thee thy Servants of Light. May thy Songs strengthen thee, sons and daughters of man, for now I bid thee farewell. ...'

Ammon fell to the ground, breathing hard, Akhet beside him in an instant, holding him to his chest, tears of joy streaming down his face.

Then Lady of Light held out her hands. 'The magnificent, wise, and benevolent Arrandori has given us much needed hope, sons and daughters of man. You do now know what privilege you've witnessed today, for His Songs have not been heard in millennia, and never by man. He sings us the means to rid the world of Beast. He shows us with His perfect Songs of creation, love, and grief through Ammon, the chosen amongst all men, a path to victory. For young King Ammon has held the spirit of the Creator and we can rejoice for we know above all things King Ammon will lead us to triumph. Rejoice!'

They cheered.

Ammon's eyes fluttered open and Akhet could not hide his fondness.

'Welcome back, my King. You have been filled with the Song of Light. You are now High King of all the earth. How do you feel?'

Ammon looked around him. He saw the faces of kings and queens and those of the Osirian, but now through new eyes they looked different somehow. Although they were before him, he understood and perceived their true forms.

'I feel strange. Powerful ... humble, and–'

'Yes?'

'Thirsty.'

They all laughed.

'Ah ... it would seem you have become wise, after all?'

Ammon rubbed his eyes.

'I see you now, Akhet, as you truly are. Not old or young, and far beyond wise. You're known to me and I sense our bond, but I also sense more. I ... I have something in my mind, a vision, a place. But ... but I can't tell you where it is.'

Akhet nodded and placed a hand on the boy's head. 'Let me see with you.'

They closed eyes and shared memories.

In unison they sang, *'We see a fortress of crystal, a temple, sprung from ruined earth. We see soil once barren now teeming with new life; a majestic sanctuary, one the servants of Beast will not enter, for fear of the light. But we also see great peril as this Temple of Song is hidden deep inside Beast's most foul kingdom.'*

They disconnected and Ammon and Akhet stood.

A tall man arose from a chair and came forward. He exchanged a quiet smile with Queen Elizabeth and asked, 'Are we witnessing the hand of God at work, Akhet?'

Akhet pulled at his beard. 'I suppose you might consider it so, King Philip of the Greek Realm, but in reality, an area of land has simply been cleansed of the putrescence of Beast's darkness. A mighty power, certainly, but from a being so old and so beyond the understanding of man, you would be quite justified in considering him godlike, yet to beings such as He, I suspect, less so.'

'Yet you say he transformed dead land anew. How is this possible, if not by the hand of God himself?'

'Well, reorganising matter must seem like magic to you, I grant that. But listen, if you were to travel back to a time before man had developed language and used your everyday technologies before them, such as a flashlight or one of your projectile weapons, would that not also seem like magic?'

King Philip inclined his head. 'I understand that, but some things are unexplainable by science alone.'

'Yet your definition of science is an intellectual and practical activity, encompassing the systematic study of the structure and behaviour of the physical and natural world, through observation and experiment. Now if you were to become so enlightened, so far evolved intellectually, then isn't it just possible that along with this evolution your understanding of science might be elevated also?

'When I first walked this earth, those men were driven by science, too. But even with their imagination and intelligence, they would consider something like breaking the sound barrier impossible, and the machines capable of it, magical. I understand that this has occurred quite recently? So with each innovation, your boundaries change, and when that happens, you become a little further enlightened. Much like your new found knowledge today. '

Queen Elizabeth touched Philip's arm and he took the hint and sat.

Etheria chuckled. 'You always had a fondness for exposition, brother, a little too fond perhaps?'

Akhet took the criticism with self-effacement. 'I like their inquisitiveness, sister. I enjoy helping them to understand the universe they live in, especially their perception of it. I do not apologise for that.'

'Nor should you, and maybe in time you will bring further enlightenment, but less so for today.'

He bowed and she inclined her head. Turning her eyes back to Ammon, she said, 'You understand your task, Little King?'

He nodded. 'I know I must travel to this land and enter the fortress at its centre. But I don't really know what I'm going to find, do you?'

Akhet touched his nose. 'We will learn that together, for I am pledged to you, my King. I will travel to the undying lands with you so long as there is life in this old body of mine, together we will discover the secrets.'

Ammon threw his arms around Akhet's neck and hugged tightly.

Lady of Light then said, 'Let it be so. The rest of you must start to infuse your people with our Light. It will take time to raise and train them. It will also take time to forge weapons we need and teachings needed to wield them. Until you are ready, each of my brothers and sisters will stand as protector of your lands. Today we have hope. Today we see a new future. For it is bright and full of the Light of Arrandori's Song. Let Beast know this ...' and she sang loud enough so he would hear, '...*we, the sons and daughters of man, Osirian servants of the Ardunadine, will never rest until he is driven from this earth.*'

Thirteen
The Coming of the Dark King

The Lair of Beast: Undying Lands

Beast contemplated much in his hidden lair beneath the earth. The world was born of new vision, and he took pleasure by what he saw. A mixture of burnt land and foul creatures subjugated man, cleansing the world in his darkness. The recent intervention of Arrandori had been a set-back but despite His ultimate power, He'd followed His original rule of balance. It was true a part of the world could never again feel Beast's touch. But surrounded as it was by the foulest of his servants, he saw no way for man or Osirian to navigate through with success. Still, he mused, it might be prudent to reinforce it.

When his servants arrived, he gave orders to safeguard his lands. The Faulgoth already patrolled much and their numbers were many, but Beast considered calling forth fouler things—then paused—there was one that might help, but controlling him would be difficult. He would also be a challenge to reach, imprisoned in a place of Light, where Beast dare not enter. Even the Faulgoth would be hard pressed by the task. There was yet another possibility.

Beast called out to his chief servant and Arnold-Nurrunadine knelt before him.

'You are the most cherished of my servants. Stand before me. No longer will I ask you to kneel.'

Arnold-Nurrunadine stood. 'What would you have me do, Lord?'

'A quest. Perilous but necessary. It will cost you many men, but if you succeed, you bring back a mighty trophy.'

'I am willing.'

'Let it be so. There is one whom I would find. It was he who wove escape into my expulsion from the world of man, from which you delivered me. I seek him, for his power added to my own, will bring a change in fortunes.'

Arnold-Nurrunadine nodded. 'Has he a name?'

'I suspect, Bane of the Osirian, but other than that I know not, nor do I care. I will feed you the knowledge needed and you will set out upon the task.'

'There is one other matter I should like to address with you.'

Beast lowered his massive head. *'Time is short.'*

'I ask this about the greatness of the essence filling our bodies with your magnificence. What was given can be removed without damage, yes?'

Beast blinked a few times then leant forward with a glare. *'Choose your next words with care, Arnold-Nurrunadine. You stand on the precipice with your blasphemy.'*

'Lord, I speak of transference.'

Beast contemplated for a moment. *'You seek to take a gift already bestowed and move it to another?'*

Arnold-Nurrunadine nodded and then with care said, 'A gift that might be wasted on the wrong person. By your leave, I would seek to bring it to one who is truly worthy of it.'

'With whom do you suggest this transference?'

'Mary.'

'Ah … your thoughts dwell on this Daughter of man.'

'I believe we can save her.'

'Do you? Why?'

'I love her.'

'I see. Is this love you have for her greater than the one you have for me?'

'It pales in comparison, Lord.'

'Well answered. Speak your mind.'

'If it pleases you, I would seek to bring her back to the fold.'

'Because she can be of value to me, or is it out of love only?'

'Both. She has knowledge, my Lord, the Osirian scourge are strengthened by. It's in our best interests.'

'You speak wisely. But come, how do you propose to achieve this? Not easily does my greatness part from me. What was lost is gone, curse their Light. I have no parts left to give.'

'There is one who possesses it I would be willing to lose, my Lord.'

'Of Albert-Nurrunadine you speak?'

'Yes, Great One. I feel his conflict, his desire to break free. It ripples beneath the surface, minute, quiet, but there.'

Beast closed his eyes and lifted his head. His great nostrils squeezed shut as he took in air. After pause, he exhaled a snort. Two huge puffs of foul air rippled his servant's black cloak.

'I also feel this. Again you demonstrate your loyalty. Much surprise I find in you, son of man, I would not have expected. Know this, Arnold-Nurrunadine.

Hence forth, you shall be known as King of my Nurrunadine. The trust I place in thee is unrecorded in your history, I give you leave to do what you feel is just for our cause. Go, do thy bidding, seek your love and bring her home.'

He bowed low. 'You will never have cause to regret your trust in me.'

'See that I don't, my loyal Arnold-King.'

Beast trilled and a staff as black as night manifested before him. Like the cane he once held, destroyed by the Osirian, it too had a serpent wrapped around to its top, but unlike the cane, the serpent at the head of the staff merged into a lion's head, its mouth open in mid-roar. Inside, anchored between giant teeth, perched a crystal of blood-red.

'A gift, loyal servant King, may its power protect you from the Light.'

King-Arnold took the staff in hand and power surged through him.

'And reward ...'

King-Arnold bent double and screamed. A pain coursed his entire body, and he thrust arms wide and grew in might and in form, as his body altered, becoming wraithlike, eyes sunk back into skull, shining dark ruby-red. The features of his human face slipped away until only dreadful darkness remained. He became shadow and death. Then he shrank and was King-Arnold once more.

'Thank you, Oh mighty Lord of the Dark.'

Beast revelled in King-Arnold's worship. *'I have filled your being with all that you require. You are elevated beyond your original form, born of black shadow in my magnificence. There is none, save me, to equal your new power, for even the mighty Faulgoth will fear you now, as they should, oh monster King-Arnold of Dark and Shadow. Never again will you bow to any being over me. Go now, travel light in your haste, for I would see the blight of man and Osirian gone from my world.'*

'I will not fail you.'

With a bow he left, setting out on his quest, in new earnt sovereignty.

King-Arnold and his entourage rode on horseback across the scorched earth for many days. They crossed vast distance at unnatural speed. At the border between Bethworth and Nelandrith–the lands formally known as Colombia and Brazil–they stopped and rested.

A shadow covered the sky in darkness. Here and there soft light from the sun passed through breaks in clouds. It shone brightest over distant mountains, raised of Faulgoth wrath. The mist was an impenetrable defence never drawn up. The men of his company fell exhausted into deep sleep.

King-Arnold considered his journey. His riders would need strength to continue his pace. He woke them and brought water. Before they drank he sang to them, when he finished they felt rested. He gave them enchanted bread and cured meat. After eating, his men were stronger, faster, and less frail in form.

'Lord,' a man said between mouthfuls, his deep southern American accent a reminder of an older world. 'You've said nothing since we left. It's been a week. We're full of questions. Can you tell us anything?'

The monster King was thoughtful. 'We have a quest for our Lord, Sam.'

'Yes, we know. What is it, though?'

'A test, I suspect. One of loyalty, perhaps?'

'With no reward?'

King-Arnold chuckled. 'Reward? This isn't the old world anymore, Sam. Rewards are knowledge and power, we've transcended wealth and gain.'

'Unless you're a king, of course?'

The Dark King flashed red eyes at him and his form changed as he grew in anger. Sam held palms out in parley, but not in fear. 'I misspoke, Lord.'

Then he shrank. 'No, Sam, you didn't. You shouldn't be fearful to speak your mind.'

Sam inclined his head. 'Then I'll say it. We're loyal to you, we always will be. But we aren't powerful enough to protect you. Honestly, we don't think we could protect you from other men.'

'You ask for something, Sam?'

'Yes. To be a feared guard of Arnold, King of the Darkness.' The other men nodded in agreement. He looked at their faces and felt their resolve, their devotion.

'Feared by whom?'

Sam threw the crust of his bread into the fire and looked around at the men. He met his king's eyes with firmness. 'Everyone, my Lord.'

King-Arnold smiled then stood. They followed likewise. 'Kneel then, feared guard of the king.' He called forth the staff by his side, bathing them in darkness. They held firm despite the pain as their bodies changed. The pain led to shrieks and screams as flesh scorched and blistered, hideous rips in flaky-burnt flesh brought forth demons, pushing out of the human carcasses, to be born anew. They writhed until the pain left them and strength filled their veins. Wounds healed in quick succession. They breathed hard, looking down at the remains of their former identities. And Sam looked up, his eyes black, a piercing blue dot at their centre. He ran a tongue over his teeth that were sharp as points. Sam looked down at his hands and clenched them, he felt power flowing through him, and as he looked amongst the others in his company, they each in turn howled in delight.

King-Arnold released them from the power of his dark and they remained kneeling, heads bowed low.

'Stand before me, mighty guard of the king.'

They obeyed.

'How do you feel now, Sam?'

When he answered, his voice was deep, guttural. 'Like I can now protect my king.'

'Good. I name you my captain. Lord of the King's Guard.'

They roared in cheer and broke wine in celebration.

Captain and King surveyed the heavy-mist that fell from the mountains. The soft glow of yellow light seen seeping into the world was sinking behind the long western arm of the horizon, while his company broke camp. They watched as the hateful light of the sun slipped away, and the clouds parted to show the beautiful white-blue light of a full moon. The darkness following it up into the sky brought them comfort.

'We make for the port of Nelandrith, Captain. Our journey will take many days. Then we secure boat, travel east for many weeks, until we hit land.'

Sam surveyed the camp. 'Our journey will be faster since we no longer need any of this equipment.'

King rested hand on Captain's muscular shoulder. 'Then let's set out at once, loyal Captain.'

King and Guard sprang forward on horse. They galloped as never before–with the shadow of darkness fuelling them–as if no power on Earth could stop them.

Fourteen
The Procrastination of King Ammon

New Egypt: 15ᵗʰ Year of Beast

Osirian guardian and King shared water perched on a rock under shadow of the great Sphinx. Behind them the ancient pyramids sparkled in the kind light of the mid-morning sun. Akhet took in the splendour of the ancient kingdom and his thoughts drifted. Past, present, and future all conjoined. He mused over possibilities and saw many futures, many paths. They were at a tipping point, Osiris had shown him. Similar to the one they'd faced thousands of years previous, when monuments like the Great Pyramids were new. Life's struggle against inevitable entropy notwithstanding, it was testament to the workmanship of the time they remained intact. He found odd comfort in that.

His mind focused on the present. He looked over at Ammon and smiled. The boy had grown much in the three years they'd spent together. Akhet had become attached to the boy. So fierce was his protection of the young king, it was difficult to separate them. Akhet taught him many things. The power of Ammon's Song was great, but his application and concentration of it often left the old man exasperated. When they first came together, Ammon was but a child with a will to do childish things. Soon after, he was thrust in new destiny as a king amongst kings, with little time to play with toys. Osiris had made that very clear. But in secret, Akhet had allowed the boy a few hours a day to develop his imagination. It was an important part of his development and their bond.

Ammon spent time every day in the old library in Giza. He immersed himself in the pages of those Akhet chose, but secretly–when Akhet fell asleep–Ammon pulled out books on Ancient Egypt and adsorbed much of the culture of his ancestors with passion. His ability and understanding grew and he retained vast knowledge. Ammon excelled in linguistics. After a year, he could speak many languages with ease, although his power of Song wasn't where Akhet wished it to be. He'd often rebuked misplaced labours, and Ammon reminded him man didn't communicate in Song. As king, he'd said, his time would be better served learning the nuances of discourse first. Akhet had–as he often did–snorted his irritation. Ammon often rolled his eyes, but he was never annoyed for long. He saw past the old man's bluster at the pride and love he held inside.

Ammon found politics and religion difficult concepts to understand, which he often avoided, and Akhet understood but urged him to persevere. Akhet was pleased with his pupil's aptitude in sociology, albeit focused a little too much on ancient cultures rather than the ones unfolding around him.

Three years on, Ammon was now a young man with knowledge, both old and new, with wisdom of generations of kings before him. No longer a boy, yet still childlike, he saw the path Akhet guided him towards, and it couldn't be put off much longer. Today though, he was content to read in the shadow of the Sphinx.

'What is that you are reading from, young King?'

'It's the Christian Bible.'

'Bible? Bible of what?'

'The word of God.'

'Never heard of it.'

Ammon laughed. 'In all the time we've spent together in the library, you never once came across this book?'

Akhet looked sideways at him. 'I didn't. Why does that surprise you?'

'Because it's probably the most known book in the world.'

'Is it?'

'You know it is, old man.'

Akhet raised an eyebrow. 'I beg the king's forgiveness then.'

'You are forgiven, loyal guardian of Light.'

Akhet looked up at the sun again and thought for a moment. In truth, he'd known for some time about the little book and Ammon's emotional connection to it. However, he also understood it was an association to his past, his family. The subject would often cause the young king to shut up like an oyster if approached. Akhet decided to probe a little.

'Did you take it from the library?'

'No.' Ammon paused, reading the old man's intention. He cleared his mind before answering. 'It belonged to my father.'

Akhet smiled at the sand. 'A subject you're not often willing to discuss.'

'True.'

Akhet drew symbols in the sand with his staff. He looked over at the boy and asked, 'Will you tell me something about your parents, Ammon?'

Ammon folded the page he was reading. 'It is a hard subject for me.'

'I know.' Akhet shifted his eyes back to the sand. 'But if it makes you uncomfortable—'

'No, no … I'm ready to tell you. You've been as a father to me for three years. I know in my heart he would be pleased I had such a strong teacher in you. He too liked to take me to the library.'

Akhet beamed. There was a long pause, and then Ammon spoke.

'My father was British, my mother Egyptian. I don't remember much about them, but they were happy. My father was a strong man. He loved to read and tell stories. He had an important job at the Museum of Cairo where he'd often take me. My mother was always kind …' A tear ran down his tanned face. He wiped it with the back of his hand and continued.

'I was four, I think, when the monsters came. My parents took me and we left our home and joined with the many others who fled the city. I remember that my father was strong. He kept telling me we were going on an adventure and he carried me on his shoulders, like he always did. We moved around a lot. He would hide me and my mother when we needed rest. When I was frightened he read to me from this book. I never saw him show any fear. Never did he show less than love to me, or my mother, even when I did things that might deserve it. Although my memories are hazy, I still feel their love for me, inside.

'I remember my father guided us to the Nile. He put the little book into my bag. Told me to keep it safe. Made me promise to read from it every day, and that through the words of the book, I would find peace. Then a monster burst out of the ground and everyone panicked. I was separated from them. I heard my mother and father calling my name, I tried to find them, but more monsters came. Then a man pulled me by the hair into the Nile. He carried me kicking and screaming into the river and got me to the other side, but he never came out. I waited for a long time, hungry, scared, alone. I never saw them again. A woman found me on the bank. She took me into her family and became my new mother.'

Akhet was moved. 'I'm sorry, Ammon. Yours is a story of love and grief, but you tell it with great strength. Your parents would be proud of that.'

Tears streamed from Ammon's eyes. 'My memories of them make me sad. I still miss them. But I honour my father's words, and read from this book every day. It doesn't bring me the peace I hope for.'

Akhet came beside the boy and hugged him. 'Grief can overwhelm but it can also fortify. Not all the memories you hold inside are sad ones. Think of those times when you were most happy, think of the love of your mother, your father. These will allow you to visit memories that are hard to bare, and give them context. Ammon, you mustn't avoid memories because they make you feel sadness. Emotion, good or bad, is the key to developing balance. It will make you fair and wise.'

Ammon wiped the tears from his eyes and smiled.

'You found comfort in my words?'

'Yes.'

'Then I am pleased. You're wrong you know, about the book, I mean.'

'I am? How so?'

'You said it doesn't bring you the peace you hope for, that may be true, but your father's words were specific. Through the words of the book, you will find peace. I think you did find it, and strength as well.'

Ammon contemplated for a moment. He wiped his nose on his sleeve. 'You always know the right things to say to make someone feel better, I love you for that.'

The old man was moved. 'And I love you too, as a son, as a king, as a friend. Thank you for sharing your beautiful story with me. One day, I will teach you how to sing it and through this great song, you'll heal those whose suffering was as great as yours.'

'I look forward to it.' Ammon opened the book again and then said, 'May I read you something, Akhet?'

'By all means.'

Ammon said, 'And it came to pass, that at midnight the Lord smote all the firstborn in the land of Egypt, from the firstborn of the Pharaoh that sat on the throne unto the firstborn of the captive that was in the dungeon; and all the firstborn of cattle. And Pharaoh rose up in the night, he, and all his servants, and all the Egyptians; and there was a great cry in Egypt; for there was not a house where there was not one death.'

'Why should you ever want to read me that?' Akhet said with astonishment.

'You lived in those times. I wondered if you might have been there when this happened.'

Akhet laughed. 'I don't remember anything like that, although, there was a lot of smiting done during my time, far too much. I mean no disrespect, but my understanding of the religious beliefs of man is limited. In my time, men worshiped me as a god, but look at me? I'm old and bent, I have power, without doubt, but I am not, and have never been, a god amongst men.

'As to the passage you just read. I suspect it's not meant to be taken literally, like all works of man there's interpretation and context to be considered, and perhaps a little poetry. But whatever your thoughts, little things like this book—the value you place on it and the power it gives you—is what makes man unique from other races I've walked amongst.'

Ammon read for a little while longer and it was nearly midday when he put down the book. He looked up at the Sphinx in contemplation.

'Tell me something, Akhet. Is it coincidence this monument has the body of a lion?'

Akhet looked up at the ancient wonder and shrugged.

'Who knows what thoughts go through a man's mind when they build statues to idolise or worship? There is possible relationship or maybe there's none. Myth may have forged unconscious links to Beast's appearance, or, it might simply be just a very large lion. I don't answer with any confidence on the matter.'

'It is hard to believe there wasn't some influence in the design.'

'Then for me, the matter is settled.'

Ammon smiled.

A scorpion scuttled from under a rock and disappeared into a hole in the sand. Ammon frowned. 'I wonder where they go.'

Akhet turned to him. 'Go?'

'Yes, the creatures of the sand. They pop out, run around, and then they disappear again. I wonder where they go.'

'They go to where they are most comfortable. Natural enough. You are full of questions today, Little King. Come, we've sat idle for far too long. We must go to the city and speak with the people, your procrastination is noticeable.'

Ammon sighed. 'Must we? A little while longer will harm no one. Besides, I prefer it here, in the sand, next to the monuments of my ancestors. The city is full of those who cling to the old world. I don't like them.'

Akhet stood.

'That's not a very kingly thing to say,' he scolded. 'They need your guidance now, more than ever.'

'But they don't listen. They stick to the notion that the old world technologies will save them. What if the leaders don't take my counsel, or yours? They fight over things and hurt each other. It's as if they don't realise the world is changed at all.'

'Well, for some perhaps that is so and you must understand something. It may be so for some time yet. It is up to you and your generation, to guide them in new wisdom. Many have never even left this place. They do not see the damage done to their world, nor do they see much change in their circumstances. Their technologies shouldn't be discounted. The science of man is still critical to the success of this world. Beast and his servants may be immune to gun powder, but other things are needed, if we are to build a brave, new world.'

King Ammon sighed. 'Will they take my counsel, Akhet?'

'If they know what's good for them.' He chuckled. 'Come on, it's time. Let's go.'

Ammon reluctantly slipped off the stone. He reached out for Akhet's hand, and they walked the path down to the city.

They journeyed through ruins down to the road named Al Haram and travelled along it into Giza. It took them a few hours to finish. Hand in hand they continued, and at length, they made it to the old Cairo University building, where a large group of men and women were gathered. As he and Akhet entered, they parted, hushing into whisper. Akhet smiled and nodded as they passed by, up great steps into a packed hall. Cairo itself had been devastated. Those who'd escaped into Giza found sanctuary there for the Faulgoth would not cross the Nile.

King Ammon walked through their centre, feeling questioning glances on his back, attuning to their whispers. As they approached the front, Akhet turned and leant against his staff. Ammon came beside him. He looked over the few hundred faces from all walks of life with fear in his belly. Teachers, scientists, doctors, politicians, tradesmen, and uniformed military leaders whose armies had long since turned to dust, all waited for Ammon to speak. Akhet sang a sweet refrain and the room was bathed in the light from his staff.

'People of Egypt,' Ammon said softly.

Shouts from the back made him wince. He looked up at Akhet, fearful, who leant down and whispered into his ear. 'You must show strength, my King. These people need you. They may not realise it, but they will soon come to rely upon your wisdom. Be strong for them, and for yourself. You have the power of Song, call it forth.'

King Ammon began to sing.

Shouts echoed around the rooms. Whispers became full conversations. People laughed and cursed. And Akhet raised his staff. Ammon, however, stepped forward. With one word they stopped and took notice. Every living thing in the vicinity heard it.

'Peace,' he sang.

When the room was still, he spoke. 'Know this, my people. I will lead you out of darkness.'

The room erupted in laughter.

Overlapping shouts of, "He's just a boy", "We don't need you to lead us", "Where were you when the creatures came", "Silly boy, go back to your mother's womb".

And then Ammon threw his arms wide and power burst from within him as he called forth the Songs of Light. The people were humbled by what they heard.

'Hear me, my people. You see perhaps a boy, but a boy with power that you cannot understand. I am here. I am your salvation. I am High King Ammon imbued with the Songs of Light, born of sacred bloodline dating back to pharaohs of old. You all understand now. My light is within you. You hear my voice yet my mouth remains closed.

'I do not seek your worship, unlike he who lives in caves and darkness. I seek your guidance. I seek your skills. I request your teachings. I hold the power of the Songs of Light, but you hold the key to our salvation. Will you not hear my song? Will you let me grant you the wisdom and knowledge to save the people of our world, so that we may fight common enemy in Beast, Lord of Lies and Shadow? Have we not suffered enough already? Or do you cling to the old world with such passion, you'd rather fight brothers and sisters over things that no longer have any meaning?'

The silence grew until even Akhet felt it. The breathing of those sitting before them was all that could be heard.

'The world you knew is gone. Burnt away by greed and evil. Manifested through giant creatures who fear the light. This is our reality. What say you, sons and daughters of the New Age of man? Will you pledge your support and loyalty to me? Will you allow my lead? Or do you wish to wander the burnt cinders of our world and live in fear of those foul things which seek our annihilation? I would hear your answer. I would hear your hearts.'

Akhet smiled in pride.

One by one, they stood. Clapping broke out amongst some of the scholars at the front, soon the sound rippled throughout the entire hall, until everyone was cheering. High King Ammon shrunk back to a boy. His light diminished. He held out his hands and silence filled the hall.

'There is much we must do in order to rebuild our society.' He turned to the old man beside him. 'This bent old man is my priest, he is of the Osirian.'

There was a collective intake of breath.

'Yes, in our darkest hour, the Ancient Ones come to our aid. He is so old,' he smiled wide, 'that he cannot remember his own name. I call him Akhet.'

There was laughter in the hall and Akhet laughed with them.

'I look to you all, leaders in your fields, specialists of industry, scientists, teachers, and warriors. We have a duty to rebuild our civilisation, and yet, we can no longer afford to cling to old-world values. This I sense you realise now.

'We will not make the same mistakes of our fathers' fathers. The evil that has uprooted our lands and slain everything in its path cannot be defeated conventionally. It is to my friend, Akhet, we must look to learn from. Together we will teach new generations of man the secrets of the Songs of Light. Alongside this, we must share the history of the old generations, so that we learn never to repeat their mistakes. When we achieve our goals, a great choice will be set before us, one which will decide the fate of all mankind.'

Some hours later, Akhet, King Ammon, and twelve men and women stood together in an ornate conference room. Akhet had separated each of them, based on knowledge and skills. Not necessarily leaders, they were of good character and sound judgement. Akhet tapped his staff and they all turned to him.

'You twelve men and women of New Egypt have agreed to take on the sacred tasks bestowed upon thee, by His Majesty, High King Ammon.'

Akhet bowed before the boy-king and they followed. He nodded at each in turn.

'Will you pledge your life to his service and swear allegiance to him, above all else? Will you swear to uphold his rule, his law, and obey commands he would set out in his wisdom, and those of his servants, the Osirian?'

They each lowered their head and answered, 'We will.'

King Ammon, who wore no crown, smiled and bowed to them. He sang a song and the men and women felt power flowing through them. They gained knowledge of the world, understanding of the power of song, and they saw this boy-king now anew. They recognised his power and saw with it his love, innocence, and above all–in their view–his divinity.

'Each of you know what must be done. Farmers must be united and taught; doctors must start to pass on their knowledge. Every one of you here will lead a group, and will pass what has been learnt on to the next. Our society will build on knowledge and understanding.

'No one shall go hungry. The sick will be treated. There is nothing of value left in this world but that of each other. Every life is precious, since Beast and his servants consider man a blight. Everything they hate and curse we will love and pay homage to. It is time to build on what we have.'

Akhet waited until the king had finished before adding, 'Use your knowledge of infrastructure to determine what technologies can be harnessed to greater use. Look to irrigation, sanitation, food production, and medicine. These, first and foremost, must be your priorities.'

One of the young men said, 'What about our protection, Akhet?'

Before an answer could be given, Ammon asked, 'Dalyn, isn't it?'

He bowed. 'Yes, my King.'

'Stay with me when the others leave. I would like to discuss things with you.'

'As you wish, sire.'

Akhet then said, 'You can look to me for your protection, until that is, you have an army of your own with the power to replace me. Today is a joyful day. We have understanding now, knowledge, power.

'The Nile is our boundary. It borders that which is most foul. And the creatures that lurk east of it dare not step in, even in places they might step over. They know what sits on the fair side and they would not be so foolish to do so. The land westward is protected. But we must be cautious. The servants of the enemy may send lesser things to cross the border–your kin who are corrupted or worse–may try to infiltrate and cause discord amongst you and the Songs of the king.'

'What should we do with them if we catch them?'

'Like all rabid things, in my view, they should be put down. However,' he looked at Ammon, 'the king in his wisdom has decreed no living *man* should be harmed in his land. That is now law and I cannot undo it. So, corrupted and vile though they may be, if they are still men, and no evil other than their own lurks in their bodies, they will not be harmed.'

'What if they should seek harm to us?'

Akhet leant forward. 'They will undoubtedly seek harm to you, Palash.'

'So, we are to let them harm us and not strike back in response?'

Akhet tapped the tip of his staff on Palash's head. He yelped in response.

King Ammon laughed.

Akhet replied, 'I was just checking to see if there was anything inside your head, Palash. For someone so clever, you ask stupid questions.'

Palash rubbed his head in frown, but Akhet's smile fixed his injured pride.

'Perhaps, I should think harder before asking them.'

'Now, there's a better response,' Akhet agreed.

'Still, for fear of having my head bashed again, I do wonder how we stop someone with murderous intent, without harming them.'

Akhet rolled his eyes. 'Maybe you should build a big net, Palash, and throw yourself in it while you're at it.'

Palash bowed to the Ancient Osirian.

'Thou art most wise, old man.'

And again, the room erupted in laughter.

Fifteen
Mary's Request

The United Kingdom of Great Britain: 15ᵗʰ Year of Beast

Mary Wilson stood at the control centre in the large plant and looked over the blueprints the chief engineer had given her. The design was simple and efficient. She studied them for a while then with a sigh, dropped them onto the table and stood by an observation window. Outside, some distance away, stood a giant hydro-electric plant. Its simplicity was pleasing even if its elegance was not.

The project had taken time, been arduous, and challenging. Now the monstrous construction was complete, the test results fuelled excitement. Electricity had been restored in some areas, where fossil fuels were still abundant, but infrastructure problems and lack of cohesion amongst power companies meant the reach was sporadic. The queen and her newly appointed prime minister picked the project leaders, Mary now an advisor to the queen, served as liaison.

It was a slow march to enlightenment as leaders refused to cooperate. They failed to listen to the people. Dismissing notions of knowledge and peaceful coexistence over financial or political gain, and carried on regardless; secure in their knowledge of what was right. Safe in the haven protected by Osirian, they refused to change, maintaining philosophies, politics, greed, and ineffectiveness. The bickering amongst the elite was unending, leading to vacuum at the heart of the political spectrum. Some men joined the proletariats in questioning the unequal status-quo. So Osiris stepped in and sang a song to influence the change they'd refused to admit and the incumbent government fell.

The queen then took control, ending centuries of royal non-interference. She stripped parliament of its power, redistributing it to those the Osirian found worthy. The new government was then born. Senior officials became advisors. The queen, with her own power of song, calmed fears. Through her new advisors she had organised food distributed. It became one of the many things she was praised for.

The hydro-electric plant, the first of this new age, would supply an entire population with power, but more than that, it was the first joint venture, where politics and economics of old were no longer a driving force of such innovation. For the first time, the people had access to commodities and services with nothing asked of in return. Most willingly offered their skills to whatever tasks were necessary, and the queen rewarded them with humble gratitude.

Not everyone shared in the delight of the new world, however. Those men and women, who'd held influence over others they could no longer coerce, were difficult to pacify. Such people, Mary mused, would find other ways to gain position. It was their nature. Despite the benefits of a society free from the underpinning vices driven by wealth alone, Mary like many of the elite yearned for old times. As the months passed it grew, and she felt lost in this new world.

A shift in the ambiance cleared her mind. She turned as Osiris shimmered into being. Mary offered practiced smile. 'You're just in time. We're nearly ready to start the first of the tests. With any luck, in a week, we'll be running electricity into the grid. Things should be up and running in no time at all after that.'

'I'm sure the queen will be happy to hear that, as well as everyone else. This will give your people the much needed moral boost they've been looking for.'

Marry nodded. 'The construction took a little more time than we'd first thought. We had to scavenge most of the materials from disused factories and shipyards in the area, but these people have worked tirelessly.'

Osiris looked out the window. 'I understand its design is based on the waterwheels of old. I see why they asked you for help to build it.'

'I'd recommend them all for a bonus, but we don't do that kind of thing in this new world.' Mary spat the words with more anger than she'd meant to.

Osiris was thoughtful for a moment.

'Their reward will be the results of their labour, Mary.'

Mary turned and sighed, rubbing her eyes. 'Sorry, it's been a long day. I'm tired.'

'Are you?' Osiris's lined face frowned a little.

'No. I'm not.' Mary's supressed irritation boiled to the surface.

'Your mind is full of anger, ill directed and misplaced.' Osiris put a hand on her shoulder. 'I understand it and would seek to take the burden away ...'

Mary turned from her. 'No, please. I need my anger. I need my pain. It defines what I am, what I was ... whatever I am now.' She turned back. 'It's so difficult to explain.'

Osiris flashed white. 'Then sing it to me, Mary, as I know you can.'

Mary closed her eyes and projected her song. 'I'm finding it difficult. I see no place for me in this world. I miss my old life.'

'You are powerful, Mary, released from blackness. You have much you can teach these men and women. The queen values your counsel, and I also would learn much from you.'

'From my knowledge of Beast, you mean?'

Osiris inclined her head. 'I do mean that, but why should that anger you?'

'I don't know. I'm angry all the time and I don't seem to be able to control it.'

'Then let me show you wisdom. I don't propose to take your pain away, Mary, but rather to guide you in control of it. You saw much of the evil of this world, and although I delivered you from the foul essence that dominated you, you still have connection to the Songs of Darkness. That knowledge and power imbued within you is still accessible. I can teach you, but you should know of the dangers in our undertaking. If we connect minds, I will share in your experiences. I will attempt to localise the anger, but you are in control. However, should the bonding break, or should your emotions separate us, there could be damage to the centres of your brain where these memories are held. I would not have you do this lightly. '

Mary smiled. 'I understand. I'm ready.'

'Very well.'

Mary felt Osiris slip through her barriers and enter her mind. As they connected, she shared the power of the Osirian, and her anger dissolved. It was an odd sensation and she felt giddy as Osiris's light pushed away the remnant residue of the evil that was once within her. Mary found new control at Osiris's subtle guidance. She heard the ancient being whispering. As the neural pathways altered to accept her intrusion, Mary had the sense of being in a number of places at once. She was able to look at her own face, as well as Osiris's. When they were joined together, the world shifted in a fizzle, and they stood in a black void.

Mary looked around at the dark. Even Osiris's light could not penetrate it. Here and there, flashes of bright white-blue electrical-like sparks zipped across the void. They made her jump.

'What is this place?'

'This is the darkness in your mind, Mary. This is the last vestiges of your connection to Beast. We will not enter these memories, look to your right.'

There was a path that uncurled and shaped itself into a sandy brick road that went off away from the dark.

Mary beamed. 'Follow the yellow brick road, Osiris?'

The old woman frowned. 'I do not understand you.'

'It's from the *Wizard of Oz*.'

Mary laughed at Osiris's blank look. She put an arm around her. 'It's a story about a young girl, named Dorothy, who finds herself swept up in a tornado and deposited into the enchanted Land of Oz. She spends her time looking for a way to escape. She follows a yellow brick road into a rather magical adventure with a tinman, lion, and scarecrow. Along the way she has confrontation with a wicked witch. Eventually they reach the emerald city, where the wizard lives, who of course turns out to be a charlatan and therefore can't actually grant their wishes at all. '

'It sounds quite absurd.'

'Oh, it is, really, but I always found it comforting to read. It brings back a lot of good childhood memories. I was just reading it again the other day; it still has the same effect on me, even now. You should really take the time to read it, Osiris. It's a beautiful story, despite its absurdity.'

'Perhaps I will.' She raised an eyebrow. 'Tinmen and scarecrows, eh?'

Mary felt alive. 'Oh yes,' she spun in a circle on the bricks, 'and a cowardly lion, munchkins, wicked witches, and did I mention the flying monkeys?'

'Flying monkeys as well? Goodness, the power of the imagination of man is something to behold. Your mind is using these images. It has chosen something you find peaceful.' She smiled then said, 'Well then, let us follow this brick road together. Who knows, maybe along the way we might find our own scarecrow or tinman?'

They linked arms and walked away from the dark, deep into the centres of her mind, out into the brightness of happier memories. Behind them, in the void, a pair of disc-like green eyes blinked as they faded from view.

They were standing in the desert now, a small team of people working around dug out pits, and tents. Mary watched the scene unfolding before her and smiled.

'Where are we?' Osiris asked.

'Syria. That's me over there. Are we visible?'

'No, we are not part of these events, so our presence here will go unnoticed.'

Mary frowned. 'Why is the view so distorted?'

'We are in your memories, Mary. Anything you didn't witness or perceive isn't visible to us, so the world will seem as it is, missing parts. We can't walk outside its boundaries.'

Mary observed her counterpart digging carefully in the sand. It flooded her with emotion. Osiris put a hand on the back of her neck. Their eyes met.

'This is it.' Mary sighed. 'The moment everything changed.'

Osiris looked into tearful eyes then back at the scene before her. 'Yes … I feel it. This is a catalyst. It will soon lead to a turning point and these shape the things that come.'

'I'm about to uncover a bone.'

'The first of many we scattered around this world.'

Mary crossed her arms. 'Not long afterwards, Arnold came to me and offered me the world. And like a fool, I took him at face value.'

'You have a strong connection, I sense that.'

Mary said nothing. She simply watched the digging continue whilst cursing her younger self. Mary observed the excitement in her; she remembered the feeling. Then her counterpart extracted the thing that caused the world she knew to end.

'I wish I could talk to her.'

Osiris released Mary's neck. 'What would you say?'

'I'd stop her, cover the thing up, and tell her to run.'

'This would change the outcome?'

'Of course, if I don't find the bone, Beast can't be whole. It's logical.'

'It's fanciful. You might delay things, but the coming was foretold thousands of years before you were born. I sense you understand that, too.'

Mary sighed and nodded.

'Come, we've seen enough. We must move onwards.'

The view changed and they were now in a tomb and Mary's heart missed a beat. This was the moment they had discovered the ancient symbols she now knew were Osirian. The mystical doorway had just been opened and they were entering the room beyond.

Osiris and Mary watched from a corner as Arnold and Albert were studying a body. She looked at them and smiled. Osiris noted her affection.

'You love these men?'

'One of them, very much.'

'What are we seeing here, Mary?'

'This is the place Beast's essence was hidden in. There's another room just beyond that half-built wall. Arnold found it inside a small burial chamber. At the time, we had no idea what it was or what would happen next.'

'Yes ... I know this place now. It looked different back when we had it constructed. I am surprised you were able to find it at all. Beast's servants are powerful indeed.'

They stood watching the interactions; Arnold and Albert's conversation flowed over them.

"What's your opinion, Albert?"

"I suspect these people were sealing the tomb and got trapped by that mechanical doorway the air ..."

The conversation went on and Osiris said to Mary, 'The affection you feel for these men is connected to your anger, you understand that now?'

"... They must have died of suffocation."

"Still holding their tools?"

Mary shuddered. 'I've seen enough. I think it's time we moved on again.'

Osiris nodded then they both gasped as great darkness penetrated them.

Arnold turned eyes black as night on the pair. He saw them standing in the corner and he snarled. 'Mary ...'

Osiris's eyes widened. She held hold of Mary's arm. 'Quickly, my dear, break the bond between us.'

'How can he see us?'

'Mary, I will answer your questions another time, please, we must go.'

Arnold growled and grew in size. His body shifted into a massive black creature, face distorted into nothing but void. Only two great red eyes were visible, and they burnt with hatred. In the background, the other Mary and Albert continued along their linear progression as if nothing was different.

Osiris sang a song and her majestic light burst forth, but the shadow slapped it aside with ease. He became wispy black smoke, evading her every attempt to stop him.

'What's happening?' Mary asked, confused.

'I do not know, Mary. Try to calm your fear. It's feeding into his power and weakening my own.'

The room shook. Dust and rocks fell around them.

'Osiris, do something!' Mary screamed.

The ageless woman threw a shining bubble of energy around him. The monster thrashed as he pushed against it, his form altered into smoke and flame, but for now he was contained.

Osiris sighed and dropped her shoulders, drained by her exertion. The hideous apparition howled and the magical energy shield turned black as night. Osiris saw Mary's fear and sang a calming verse. 'Mary, he is somehow able to draw power from your fear. I'm not as strong here. Locked within your mind, I may not have the strength to–'

Arnold burst the bubble with a hideous score. Out he flew, his ethereal arms reaching for them, but each time he got close, his dark was defeated by the Osirian's light. With every defeat, he angered further and in this anger he found greater strength. Lady Osiris remained calm, weaving her song, calling upon every melody she could. Then, he spat venom into her face, blinding her. She stumbled backwards in surprise, and he pressed his attack. Lady of Light threw out her arms. A shockwave of sound hit him. The intensity knocked him hard into the far wall, and he grunted in pain.

Mary backed away as her fear consumed her.

Osiris continued her songs of protection. Realising they might not be enough, she pleaded with Mary one more time.

'Mary, you must break the bond, or he will consume us.'

As if sensing his advantage, he came forward with smoke and flame. Lady Osiris engulfed and extinguished his fire. They grappled together but, at least for the moment, she was the stronger and he fell back with a hiss. He shifted again, from smoke, into a vague nebulous man-like being.

And Osiris saw what she fought and was aghast. Black-hooded robes fluttered as he elevated into the air. Within them nothing but shadows; he flung back his hood revealing a twisted, jagged kingly crown and yet, there was no head visible upon which it rested. A void sat between it and the darkness engulfed her. Red eyes of fire beneath the crown, unblinking, fixed on Osiris. From an unseen mouth came a deadly laughter.

His voice-song hissed in screech. 'See the truth of me, witch. See my form and fear my wrath, for I am the bringer of Osirian death.'

'You cannot expel me from this place, foul thing.'

'I feel your power diminish with each passing moment. It is only a matter of time before I consume you.'

He turned to Mary, cowering in the corner. 'Mary, my love, feed me your power. You and I are destined to be together. It was always meant to be. I sense in you the power this foolish creature has fed from. Only together can we destroy the Osirian. I am coming to rescue you, release your fear!'

Lady of Light shook her head. There was no anger, in her song, just pity.

'See his true self. He'd promise you the moon, Mary, if he thought it would give him what he desires most.' She turned on him. 'You think you have your master's power? Truly you are betrayed. A slither of your master's darkness and unlike we Osirian, who would share our power and knowledge, he dare not. I pity you, poor wretched man. Go back to the darkness and think on that.'

Mary looked between them. Her mind raced. King-Arnold turned; his voice-song reached her, soft, soothing.

'Don't listen to her lies. The Lord Beast is not as she says. His darkness blesses all who embrace it. Come, be all that you desire and more, Mary, Queen of Darkness. Use my knowledge, I beg you. Choose between light and dark.'

Osiris brightened. 'Silence your foul song, we've heard enough.'

King-Arnold laughed. 'See how she forces your hand, Mary? How she denies you the choice I offered you?'

Osiris bathed him in truthful light, and he cowered from it.

'Choice? Blight of darkness. Your master destroyed this world and upon the throne of the merciful dead, claims benevolence? I've heard enough of your foul song.'

The darkness and light locked in battle of wills ended when the ageless Osirian reached for inner reserve. She flooded the room with a song of enormous potency. King-Arnold fell back with roared defence. His rage drove him to new strength. She staggered under the assault, clutching Mary's arm for support as she was thrown into the wall beside her.

Mary was lost in her indecision. She looked at Arnold, then back at Osiris. She looked down at the hand now clasping her arm, and felt warmth, love, and beauty, flow from the touch. It surged through her, awakening her spirit, her courage.

Mary stepped away from the wall in confidence and King-Arnold read new purpose in her eyes. He snarled at Osiris. 'No! You cannot have her, she's mine!'

'You speak of choices, Arnold? What choice did I have in Syria, eh? When you forced me down a path of your own? I hate you, I hate everything about what you've become. You aren't a man anymore; you're just an evil, twisted abhorrent thing,' Mary bellowed.

He cowered back as she walked towards him.

'Choices? You disgust me. Look at you? Your power's gone, you crawl away in fear. I choose neither dark nor light. Here's my choice, Arnold. I choose *me*.'

King-Arnold cried out as her words drove him away. He shrivelled back to a man as her power left him. She stepped towards him feeling the Osirian by her side. He lashed at her, but she pushed him back with a wave of her hand. His power slipping away, only a snarl came out of his shadow.

Osiris glided forward. She sang sweet songs, lifting the shroud of darkness.

'You are beaten, worm. Feel the might of our light as you crawl upon your belly. Go, go back to the shadows.'

She turned to Mary. 'Release this thing to its foul master. Break the bond.'

The darkness screamed as Mary closed her eyes and released her fear.

The last vestiges of Arnold's voice whispered into echo in her mind. 'I'm coming ...'

They staggered back into the control room.

The Osirian guardian caught Mary as she collapsed.

Osiris, visibly relieved, held Mary in tight embrace.

'We are safe. You did well.'

'I'm sorry I let my fear consume me.'

'What matters is you found the strength in the end to bring us out of it, and your timing couldn't have been better.'

Mary noticed a wound on Osiris's neck.

'You're injured!'

Lady of Light smiled. 'It will heal, Mary. Do not worry about such things.'

In response, the wound closed.

'You see? It is gone.'

'How could Arnold see us? And what the *hell* has he become?'

Osiris looked uncertain. 'Hell may be right. He is not as he once was, that much I know. His power was as strong as mine, maybe stronger. How he saw us, I cannot say with any confidence, but your bond with him is strong. He professed his love for you. That along with his power ...' Osiris frowned and touched her neck. '... We have new enemy in this Nurrunadine, far greater than we realised. It would appear he has been made anew, dark to our light ...'

'You're saying Arnold is now, what? A dark Osirian?'

Osiris helped Mary to stand. 'I believe it to be so, yes. He is like us now with power of Song at his disposal. I must consult my brothers and sister. '

She shifted into ethereal being.

'Wait, I need to ask you something, before you go.'

She shifted her form back. 'Of course, although the matter is pressing, delay may harm us.'

'I understand, but you were right about my feelings, Osiris, and you were right about my bond and connections fuelling my anger.'

Osiris held Mary's cheek for a moment. 'I wish there was something we could do.'

'I think there is.'

'Explain yourself, Mary, but use haste.'

'I mean for you to do what you did for me.'

Osiris dropped her shoulders. 'Oh, sweet Mary. If only that were possible.'

'You couldn't do it again?'

'Yes, but we would find no easy way to do it.'

'Why? If you can release someone from Beast's grasp a second time and rescue them from their imprisonment, from everlasting torment, you must, please. I insist you try. Please understand, I was aware of everything whilst under his control. I saw what I did, the things I was made to do, through the eyes of someone else. I know he is trapped, too.'

Osiris sighed. 'What you ask is perfectly reasonable, but impossible–for good reason–because Beast understands this vulnerability now. Mary, last time we had the element of surprise. He never assumed we'd rescue you from him. That was his arrogance, for I knew above all things his overconfidence would be a huge weakness to exploit. But our enemy isn't witless. We cannot possibly hope to fool him in that way a second time.'

Mary tried a different tact. 'But we don't have to do it the same way. They want to get me back, there's our advantage, Osiris. You heard Arnold. He wants to rescue me. We use it as a trap.'

'You put yourself in far too much danger, I cannot allow it.'

Mary stood defiant, desperate for Osiris to understand.

'It's my life to put in as much danger as I choose. No one tries to stop you from protecting us from the same dangers and I'm not weak, like those you aim to protect. You know this and you know I'm right.'

The ageless Osirian looked down upon her pupil with grace. 'You have the strength of an Osirian, Mary. I admire you for it. Let me ask you this. If I refuse your request, will you heed it?'

'You already know my answer.'

'I do and I grieve. This man you seek to rescue, your love for him is strong enough to defy my wishes?'

Mary lowered her eyes and sobbed. 'Yes, it is.'

Osiris looked on her with a sad smile and lifted her face, wiping away the tears with her thumbs. 'Love, in any universe, is power beyond even the Songs of Light and Darkness.'

Mary smiled through her crying. 'I would save him, Osiris, above all others. I alone know how gentle and wonderful a man he is. I feel his desperate struggle. His unyielding screams in the darkness. They keep me awake at night, they flood my soul. If I cannot rescue him, then *I* will end his nightmares, so that he may be in peace, free of the dark.'

Osiris stood in quiet thought. Mary's arguments were persuasive, but she still held onto her reservations. Mary continued on through sobs.

'We know if we kill the thing inside him, Beast becomes vulnerable. When you rescued me, I felt his pain.'

Osiris nodded. 'He is down one part, it is true. How more vulnerable he'll become with the loss of another is uncertain.'

Mary nodded. 'I know, but please, you must help me do this, Osiris. Not just for me, although I admit my motives are purely selfish, but for mankind.'

Osiris made up her mind and conceded with a nod.

'Very well, Mary. I have cautioned you against this action but for the good of mankind, I will not stand in your way. I will ask my sister, Neith, to aid your request. She is powerful. There is much she can teach you and you should learn all that she has to offer. But be warned, she is not like my other brothers and sisters. She wields the flames of war. Neith is not a peaceful soul and I would have you understand that before you embark on any training. You have your own power, Mary, but nothing like Neith's. You are forewarned.'

'Thank you. I will learn all I can from her. I have a plan. It might not work, obviously there is danger involved, but it's a starting point. There's something else ...' She hesitated.

'What is it?'

'I feel him.'

'What do you feel? His power?'

'Yes, along with his desires and ideas.'

Osiris frowned. 'You banished him, that connection shouldn't be possible.'

Mary smiled. 'No, I didn't. I kept him. Don't look so concerned, Osiris. It's all part of my plan, you understand?'

Osiris nodded, her face broke the calm and doubt flooded her.

'Mary, I do, and it worries me enormously.'

'Why?'

'If you are connected and can read him, he may be able to reciprocate. Any plans you make might be thwarted by it. You are strong and I trust in your choice, but I beg you, wait for Neith to guide you. Will you do that for me?'

'I will. You have given me new life, Osiris. I won't forget what you've done for me, thank you.'

The old Osirian beamed. 'You showed me something I did not expect, and I will not easily forget the choices you made today. Neith will arrive in her own time. She follows no path but her own.'

Osiris began to shift from existence; her form almost gone, just a lingering song echoing in the air.

'You must be careful, Mary. There is great danger in Arnold. He is not like you or the others. Your love may be strong enough to hold the slither you trapped in your mind, but I do not think his earthly being will come to the light willingly. Neith will teach you how to prepare for that.'

'You've misunderstood. I was never ...'

But Osiris did not hear what she had to say, as she had already departed.

Mary turned to the observation window, folding her arms across her chest. She took a breath and closed her eyes. She looked deep into the darkness, navigating its currents and eddies, and found him, lost in the shadows.

'Hold on, Albert.' She whispered. 'I'm coming.'

Sixteen
The Warrior Goddess Returns

New Egypt: City of Giza

King Ammon, Palash, Dalyn, and Akhet enjoyed a light meal at the base of the Great Pyramid. The long conversations slipped from frivolous philosophical debates—as they often did when Akhet was involved—to the serious topics worthy of a king's attention. Ammon enjoyed the discourse. He listened to Palash and Dalyn spar whilst sipping at his tea. They were both strong willed. Palash had tendency to use humour in serious conversation to great effect, whereas Dalyn would stand his ground in defence of a principle, oftentimes aggressive in response. Ammon observed their conflict and remained thoughtful.

Palash's particular conversation was interspaced by mouthfuls of food.

'The leader you appointed to run the food ministry reported huge uptake in contributions. They've had to open up new rooms in the university because of the number of donations. They really weren't prepared for the generosity. Minister Ibrahim has set up a committee, with local farmers and businessmen, to find more appropriate accommodation for the food bank. They are also trying to see if they can locate some land where they can build, what he called, crop zones. A few of the old big estate owners were receptive he said, and they've offered assistance. It was felt that their willingness came from worry, by what you might decide to take from them, if they didn't. Still, it's very positive. There's huge excitement in the community right now. Many people are involving themselves freely, and I understand the local hospitals have pooled their resources and are staffed to the max as well.'

Ammon finished the last of his meal and pushed his empty plate away.

'That is excellent news, Palash. The key to improving morale and well-being is keeping the people engaged and involved. We need to get the entrepreneurs of our society involved in maximum ways. Scientists, teachers, people of vision and innovation will help build bonds and bridges. We'll have a flourishing society soon enough.'

'Not everyone is keen to give up what they once held, my King,' Dalyn remarked, with a note of caution.

'That will not always be so, Dalyn, but you're right, we shouldn't force the issue,' Ammon agreed, 'at least not yet. We need their support first. The material things they hold so dear are not our primary concern.'

Akhet hadn't said much during their meal. His lack of interaction hadn't gone unnoticed. Ammon observed him as he reached down taking a handful of sand, letting it slip away through his fingers. His eyes were unfocused and his whispering and muttering gave him cause for concern.

'There's no fertile land here, nothing but ancient sands, older then monuments sat in shadow of what will or won't be. Where can evolution spring? We must be cautious. There are no answers to the illusive things hidden beneath the morning air ...' He continued on unaware Ammon was watching. When he broke from his trance, he noted their conversations ceased. Akhet looked up at the sun setting atop the tip of the pyramid. He felt Ammon's eyes upon him and ceased his mutterings, releasing the last of the sand.

Palash and Dalyn caught up in discussion failed to notice the subtle shift in Akhet's body language, but Ammon saw and was troubled. He decided to voice concern.

'You've been mumbling incoherent things for hours, old man. What's wrong with you?'

Akhet snorted and turned. 'I do not mumble, young King. You mistook it for murmur.'

Palash and Dalyn chuckled.

King Ammon wasn't convinced. 'Akhet, you forget murmur or mumble, I see into you as none can. I know something is wrong, even if I can't determine the reason.'

Akhet let out a great sigh. 'How far you've come, and how long I've walked to see it. You're correct something *is* wrong. I feel the changes in the songs; illusive, like whispers on the wind just out of reach, on the edge of my perception. Our enemy is growing. In strength and in scheme but hitherto, his legions are still in infancy. No, his plans are far from set, but ...' He grunted exasperation.

Seeing the look of concern on his young charge's face, he waved a hand and softened the frown. He offered practiced smile. Ammon recognised it and was not comforted.

Akhet saw the confusion and worry in the young king's eyes, and said, 'Do not worry unnecessarily. I cannot say with any certainty what it is that vexes me. It's an old man's foolishness, pay it no heed. It's probably nothing.'

'Probably nothing you say.' Ammon wasn't persuaded. 'Meaning it may be something?'

Akhet raised an eyebrow. 'Your wisdom increases daily, little one. It won't be long before I am seeking answers from you. And I would see it so ere my long life passes into oblivion.'

Palash belched loudly after finishing a second small loaf of bread and Akhet turned scowl upon him. 'Or perhaps it's just Palash's stomach crying out to me, complaining about all the things he continually stuffs inside. Tell me, how does someone so small fit so much within, hmm?'

Palash stopped for a moment, mouth full, shrugged, and finished the rest of his plate.

They laughed and Akhet, grateful of the levity, felt it begin to quash deep anxiety festering within. He stood and put gentle hand on Palash's head.

'You bring light to my dark thoughts, little Palash. May your stomach be ever empty.'

They shared a moment and Akhet turned to Dalyn. 'And what of you? Have you accepted your king's command?'

Dalyn nodded. 'Yes, Lord Akhet. I have accepted the duty as captain of his Majesty's Medjay. I am humbled by the appointment.' He bowed his head to the king.

'Dalyn will need guidance and song, before he can give the power of protection.'

Akhet seemed pleased. 'It will be one of my first duties, then. A captain of Medjay? This I haven't seen in an age. Where did you learn such things?'

'I read, Akhet.'

He grunted and turned to Palash. 'Well, what position did we find for you? King's jester, perhaps?'

The three of them laughed hard, and even Akhet's frown faded through smile. Ammon, wiping away tears, said. 'I was thinking chief advisor. You have skills and knowledge, Palash, as well as fair mind and joy in life. I would not put you into a hole, but rather, allow you to develop your own position over time. What do you think?'

'Chief advisor to the king? It has a nice ring to it, Majesty. I'm proud to serve you in anyway.' Palash tipped his head in acknowledgement of the king's trust and friendship.

'*Chef* advisor would be more suitable!' Akhet snorted in amusement, leaning on his staff, allowing comradery to wash over senses, quelling thoughts of doom.

'Despite my fears, for the moment at least, I am pleased the three of you are aligned so. It brings joy and comfort to an old man's heart.'

A whisper on the wind caught his attention. He looked to the horizon. When he turned back, the three of them noticed the frown reappeared upon his aged face, as if some new burden weighed heavy upon him.

Dalyn was alert. 'What is it, Lord Akhet?'

'A shift in song, Captain. My sister seeks gathering. I must leave.'

Ammon stood. 'How long must you be gone?'

'I cannot say. For a time. I suspect, at least I hope, answer for my fears would be its purpose.' He shook away his concern. 'Be together. Continue your labours. Oh, and do *not* start any wars until I return, understood?'

Ammon's face dropped. 'I should be sad to see you go from my side, Akhet. But I hope you find your answers.'

The old man fell to his knee. 'Hope? Yes, that is powerful. Hope is what I cling to. My sister will know more, she has deeper connection to this world. Ammon, I cannot know how long I will be gone. Time is measured differently by us. The blink of an eye, maybe, or longer, but I will return. Keep to your learning and your reading. These things are important and necessary. You can discover a great deal from words of those who came before you, even in the books you read in secret when you think I am asleep.' He tapped the king's nose. 'Stay close to these two. The bond growing between you is powerful. When I return, we will make preparations. Do not be downcast, Ammon-son. I will come to you as soon as I can. Wait for my return.' He hugged the boy with love, stood, glowed bright white and faded into nothing.

The Earthly Temple of Song

Osiris took in the overlapping songs of the assembled Osirian for a short time, and then held out her hand. A calm quiet filled the air. Akhet bent over his staff in silent contemplation. The others turned, waiting for her song.

At length she said, 'Our enemy lays new plans, worse than before. He has fashioned men into corruptions of our Light. I have encountered one and he is powerful. I've called you all to determine our next course of action. I sense vile purpose in his neoteric wickedness. Beast has never been so strong, we are in grave danger.'

Akhet nodded. 'I too have felt it, on the edge of my mind, a growing darkness matching our Light. You faced it?'

Osiris nodded. 'Yes. It was strong. I battled with this Arnold … King of Darkness; for he is no longer as man, fashioned into weapon with our destruction his target. The nucleus of his might is in infancy but growing steadily. Had Mary not chosen to fight alongside me, I would not be here to sing verse.'

There were mutterings of shock around the temple. Then great song shook the room and they stopped.

A woman's voice resonated deep in the air around them.

'Perhaps the pacifism you developed during your long sleep has simply weakened you, little brother?'

Wisps of smoke twisted around ankles and rolled across the floor. They swirled through unsourced light, shaping in slow pulses, until a vague and blurred nondescript approximation of earthly form manifested. When it sharpened, a scantily clad dark-skinned woman, the Osirian Warrior Goddess Neith, stood proud before them.

There was no match for her beauty. Her presence radiated sovereign grandeur and unlike her Osirian brethren, she did not cover herself from head to toe in long ornate robes. A simple purple silk covered her breasts, fixed via an elaborate multi-layered golden necklace, ornamented with gems of various shapes and sizes. A golden cobra armband wound from her left bicep to her shoulder. The length of her, painted in gold cobra motifs. Prominent above her striking painted face, sat a gilded bejewelled diadem with a blue-gold uraeus as its centrepiece. Her dark hair was woven into tight braids, each weighed heavy by jewelled clasps at their tips. An ostentatious belt was slung loose across her hips, and from it an array of weapons hung, each decorated in delicate carved scene. Fixed upon her naked back sat a shield of magnificent design.

Osiris smiled at her. 'Welcome home, older sister.'

The warrior goddess raised an eyebrow. 'Greetings–brother no longer–sister now, it would seem?'

Akhet chuckled. 'I am pleased to see you, Neith. And your timing couldn't be better.'

'Little sister-son.' Neith inclined her head. 'I see you are more bent than usual. Perhaps it is time for you to trim your beard?'

She turned to Osiris, dark purpose in her dangerous eyes. 'I would know this King of Darkness who dares lay hand upon my sister. Sing to me, for I would learn much. I wield the Sacred Flame of Arrandori, and I will rain the desolation of the void upon any dark thing crossing my path.'

When many suns had settled on the world of man, the Songs of the Osirian ended. Neith stood in thoughtful composure. The others bathed in her golden hue.

'Truly this age is darker than foretold.'

Osiris agreed. 'We cannot hope to defeat Beast without your help, Neith.'

'Then you will feel deep sadness by my refusal.'

Lady of Light lowered her eyes. 'More than you can know.'

Neith came forward and placed a shimmering golden hand on her shoulder. 'You knew answer, yet you asked anyway, why?'

'I was hopeful, nothing more.'

Akhet banged his staff upon the ground. Neith turned to him, eyebrow raised.

'More to say have you on the subject, sister-son?'

'You cannot fail to understand the consequences of your choice, for without your power, we may be lost.'

'I cannot help you vanquish him. You know why, or have you slept too long to remember?'

They said nothing.

She angered. 'Do not make requests upon me you know I will not fulfil.'

'Very well, sister.' Osiris's light washed away the lingering mood. 'I will make one you can. Teach Mary how to harness her power.'

'Why?'

'I've seen a time where her choice might save us all.'

Akhet nodded. 'Yes, and Ammon too, they are linked, I feel the truth of it.'

Neith closed her eyes. 'Along with this Arnold thing.'

'Yes,' Osiris said nodding. 'Mary is in love with him.'

Neith said nothing for the longest time. When thoughts were organised she came to decision.

'I will see if she is worthy of my attention, but I make you no promise either way.'

Osiris inclined her head. 'Let it be thus.'

'I sense another corrupted man in this web of destiny.'

Osiris nodded. 'Albert.'

'Yes ... you are wrong about Mary, sister.'

'How so?'

'She has no love for this Arnold of Darkness.'

Osiris frowned at her.

'Did you not know this? Her love is directed at the other, Albert.'

Neith then looked upon them all with reverence, glowed bright gold and faded from the temple.

Akhet sighed deeply. 'I have grave misgivings, Etheria. Neith's conceit may upset our balance. I love her, as kin should, but I do not see things as clearly as I would like.'

The others sang agreement.

'Do not concern yourself. Neith has her part to play. Her presence will, if nothing else, foster fear in our enemy. That fear will give us advantage.' She turned to them and raised her arms. 'Go back now and begin the preparations. It's time for armies to rise, and men to bring peace and prosperity within their much smaller world.' She watched the others fade till only Akhet remained.

'What is it, brother-son? I feel the heaviness of the burden weighing upon you. Tell me what troubles you?'

'You will not like what I have to say.'

Osiris beamed. 'That has never stopped you before, my son.'

He chuckled. 'Perhaps not ... *he* stirs.'

Osiris's face dropped. 'You're sure of that?'

'I felt it, only slight, but it was unmistakable.'

'This is dark news indeed, that void is sealed. It cannot be opened.'

'There's more.' Akhet rubbed at his chin. 'I sense a deeper sinister plot afoot. If Beast were to set him loose—'

'Even he could not do such a thing, the locks of the void were designed with his intervention in mind, or did you forget who forged it?'

Akhet harrumphed. 'I know this. I was there. I believe he may have found a way we didn't conceive of.'

Osiris pondered and then her eyes widened. 'You think this is the reason he elevates humans beyond their boundaries?'

'Why else would he? He doesn't share power.'

'I have been so blind. We cannot allow this. I must mediate and seek answers in places no one dares ask questions. I will call for you when I know the truth of things. Go now. Be with Ammon and at peace. You must not let fear control you, brother.'

'It has always been my weakness.'

She put a hand to his cheek. 'It's your strength too, son of vision.'

He took her hand and kissed it. 'May Arrandori's light ever guide you.'

They faded from the temple.

Seventeen
The Brutal Lesson of Neith

United Kingdom: The North Yorkshire Moors

Doctor Mary Wilson sat alone in the picturesque meadow, soaking in the warm summer sun. At times like this, when she was alone and able to relax, she felt almost as if the world was as it once was. Birds flew from the treetops, warm breeze carried their song. Mary closed her eyes and took a breath, filling her lungs with the sweet scent of the day. A woman's voice from nowhere startled her and she was quick to stand.

'I cannot abide the sun in these parts,' the disembodied voice said.

Mary couldn't discern its source and looked around in concern, a deep frown etched across her face.

The voice continued, 'It is timid and shallow with a heat that never quite soothes, or warms.'

'Who are you?' Mary asked. 'And more to the point, where are you?'

'Perhaps you are not the Mary I have been burdened with. I understand *she* has some power worthy of my attention, yet I find nothing of value in *you*, who cannot see beyond primitive sight.'

Mary smiled. 'Then I am sorry to disappoint, Neith?'

There was a flash of golden light as the Osirian Warrior Goddess Neith took earthly form. She was striking in beauty, heavy in adornment, lacking clothes as well as humility.

Mary raised eyebrow. 'Well, you certainly like to make an entrance.'

The warrior goddess placed her hands upon her hips. 'Are you worthy of my attention, of my grace, woman-child of man?'

Mary shrugged. 'That's really up to you. Look, I only need your training. It is really a matter of indifference to me, whether you consider me worthy or not.'

The goddess Neith was quick to rile. Her form shifted so that she now stood tall enough to cast Mary under great shadow. Her voice became heavy, baritone, and unlike the other Osirian, her song had a tone of condescension.

'Do not presume to speak to the Warrior Goddess Neith in that tone, Mary underling, for I am not so like my younger brethren who genuflect to man as servant. I serve but one and *He* is the greatest of all things in this and other universes. I am older than your creation. A power beyond your primitive understanding, matched to lesser Lords of Ardunadine. I will have your respect, woman-child, or your head. Choose now.'

Mary felt wrath penetrate her and instinctively dropped to a knee and lowered her head. 'I sincerely apologise. Forgive me. I'm old and stubborn and not at all used to idle conversation with a goddess.'

Neith shrank back and crossed her arms. 'Better. But a little more flare next time. Do get up from the ground, child.'

Mary did as instructed. 'I don't even know how to address you?'

Neith seemed genuinely surprised by the question. 'In the same way you would address any goddess, surely?'

'I'm sorry, but I don't have any experience with that kind of thing, I'm a scientist. I have never been particularly religious,' then added, 'Majesty?' She held her breath, hopeful of her choice in words.

Neith, however, rolled her eyes. 'I have surely slept for far too long. Very well, since you appear to have no notion of righteousness, I will allow Neith.'

She turned to the meadow and looked out. She was not charmed by the mixture of green colours and scents others found uplifting.

'You find comfort in this place?'

Mary shrugged. 'No, not really.'

'Then why bother coming?'

'I like to be alone.'

Neith looked upon her with annoyance. 'Poor answer. Be truthful and be precise. Think and try your answer again.'

Mary frowned in thought for a time. At length she said, 'I don't like to be around other people anymore.'

'Better. Why?'

'I don't know.'

'Again your answer is poorly chosen. You *do* know. At this moment I find you undeserving of my interest and conversation. I would have you unfiltered and plain of speech. Answer.'

Mary supressed her irritation. 'It's not easy to articulate. I'm not like them.'

'You bandy your words like grotesque poems people would rather cut off their ears, than hear. Be more precise with your detail.'

'I don't know. It's hard. I suppose it could be I consider myself different, or maybe the others different … it just feels like I'm no longer fully human. I don't always connect with them, but then I haven't always been easily able to connect with anyone. I think it stems from my mother–'

'Stop your senseless babbling. I am ready to cut my *own* ears off. Your answer is imprecise and the indecision within it, weakness. Try again.'

Mary allowed her irritation to surface. 'Fine! I *am* different. I don't fit in. I don't *want* to fit in. I miss my old life, my old world.'

Neith seemed pleased. 'There now, child, much better; plainly spoken at last. Now the truth of you is exposed, explain this longing.'

'I miss the world I was born into, where I came from. Before Beast, before everything that happened afterwards. I miss the things I understand or understood. Even though there was great unfairness and discouragement in my world, I miss those things, too. This new world, with its gods, songs of magic, along with foul creatures from nightmare and books, is not mine. I hate it. And I would do anything to put it back as it was.'

Neith was thoughtful for a moment then came forward, placing her hand on Mary's chest.

'Good, child. Good. I sensed this from the moment I first observed you. You have great desire to slip backwards, to find ways to undo what was done, but I tell you, it is no use thinking that way. What has been will always be.' Her voice softened and there was empathy in it. 'I am plain spoken, Mary, I prefer it that way. Be straightforward with me, always.'

'I would use all the powers of the Osirian to find a way back.'

Neith removed her hand. 'Back? Back where?'

'In time.'

'I see. What would you do, if this were possible?'

'I would find a way to stop Arnold, before we met.'

Neith nodded in understanding. 'You would do harm to him?'

'I would. If it meant restoring my world.'

Neith grinned. 'You would kill, to bring about this restoration?'

Mary met ancient eyes unflinching. 'If I had too, yes.'

'When?'

'I'm sorry?'

'When would you do it? When he is a man? Or perhaps a child? An unborn, then? Still kicking inside his mother's womb? When?'

She grew angry. 'I don't know! Early maybe, as a child, perhaps. I hadn't given it much thought.'

'Do not tell falsehoods to one who can read your every thought and intention. You *have* thought about it, in great detail. But you could never do it. You are too weak. To kill a child and undo what has been done would make you worse than he, and you know it.'

Mary sighed in frustration. 'As a man then, when his choices are already made.'

Neith said, 'But by then it is too late. Things are set in motion. Kill him before the task is complete, others would pick up his mantle. You have shared connection with this man? You know of what I speak?'

'Yes.'

Neith tired of the discourse. 'In any event, it is fruitless. Even if it were possible, the power of the Osirian could never be used in this way. I tell you, even with all the knowledge in your world, you could never go back far enough to affect this change you so desperately seek. Enough of this nonsense.'

'Of course you're right. Neith, will you teach me to understand my power?'

Neith looked blank. 'What powers do you speak of? You have strength of character, that I perceive, and acknowledge, but as to any power, I say, nay. You are mistaken. There is nothing in you at all.'

Mary lowered her eyes. 'Osiris saw it. She is alive because of it.'

Neith circled her, like a prowling lion. 'She was mistaken. Her age-addled mind confused. No. There is nothing in you. Like most of you kin you are a disappointment.'

'Osiris promised me you would help.' She was confused.

'It was not her promise to give.'

'You're wrong. I do have power. I just don't know how to use it yet.'

Neith snorted. 'Then you have no power, if you cannot wield it.' She continued her circling. When she was behind, she leant towards Mary's right ear. 'Lack of knowledge renders any power you *think* you have useless and pathetic, much like you.'

'Tell me how to call it forth,' she asked through gritted teeth, 'and I will show you I'm not as you think.'

'It is too late for that, child.' Neith stood before her and sneered. 'In three-thousand years amongst men, I have never yet met anyone as pitiable and weak as you. You should be ashamed.'

Mary felt her anger bubble inside of her but forced it down. 'I'm not ashamed of a lack of knowledge.'

Goddess Neith laughed hard at her.

'You should be, child. I would be. I cannot find words in your basic tongue to describe the contempt I have for you.'

Neith stood with back to the treeline. When Mary turned to her the anger welled deep from inside. She fought to maintain control because she recognised she was being manipulated, and she would not allow herself to be coerced.

'I have seen insects with more strength. Your weakness will affect more than just you. The one you love will never be free. You can thank only yourself as he wallows and chokes on unyielding dark until his body becomes flame and ash; his eternal screams forever to fill your mind, till you burst in the sorrow of your inaction. Poor Albert ...'

Mary's anger hit a tipping point. 'I'll cut that tongue from your foul mouth, you vicious cow.'

Neith's eyes widened. 'How dare you, underling.'

'I'll say whatever the hell I want, you loathsome bitch!' And she exploded in voice-song sending shockwaves of dark energy so vast they destroyed trees and flora in front of her, in an arc of one-hundred feet. When her anger had subsided, she stood panting hard. For some time, she was unable to see anything through the dust storm. When it cleared, standing unharmed at the centre of the crater was Neith, wearing a wide smile.

Mary fell to her knees and wept.

'Now *that* was something worthy of my attention.'

Neith approached and lifted her from the ground and her misery.

'Finally, child, you reach inside and silence the viciousness of my voice-song. Your self-control is extraordinary.' She wiped away a tear from Mary's face. 'Come, I will teach you how to reach deeper, but also how to focus. The strength of you is something to behold, truly.'

Mary wiped away the rest of her tears. 'You deliberately caused my anger with your cruelty. Why?'

Neith paused. 'Why? Because your strength *lies* in the darkness you hide from.' She again put a hand on Mary's chest. They connected for a brief moment. Mary became overwhelmed by her power. When they disconnected, Neith softened her features, changed the pitch of her voice, and her words were never as harsh again.

'I do not apologise for my method, child. You do not yet realise your potential. My little sister saw something of it, but I see much deeper. The essence living within your mind is power beyond Osirian, maybe even beyond mine. I wonder … do you even understand what it is, festering in the deepest parts of you?'

Mary nodded. 'I know what it is. I've seen it in my dreams; in waking moments, too.' She sniffed and wiped her nose with her sleeve.

Neith put an arm around her. 'I sense you do understand, but in limited ways. I can help you with that as well. I will show you some history in this world. I know much of you, and I understand you spend your time digging around for ancient relics. Well, we shall seek some together. Your training will be hard and it will be relentless–but not without enjoyment–and once you understand how to use what is within, perhaps you will know something of my power too, for it is birthed of same source.'

Mary opened her mouth but Neith put a cobra-ringed finger to her lips.

'You have many questions. Now is not the time. We must go, for I would find myself warm again. Let us depart this dank land, and walk naked beneath a sun that bakes the skin. Come, child, take my hand. We walk in providence towards conjoined destiny.'

Joined in hands, the power of Neith's touch filled Mary with joy unknown. Her mind was clear for the first time since she'd been freed of Beast's control. She felt something new in Neith. Goddess and warrior she may be but in their connection, Mary saw kindred spirit. They smiled at each other as the unnatural whirlwind twirled mists around them. Mary watched as the meadow turned hazy. In the blink of an eye, it was replaced by sand as far as her eyes could see.

Neith looked up at the sun and her skin turned a golden hue.

'I am home at last,' she declared.

The contentment in her voice made Warrior Goddess sparkle.

Eighteen
The Taming of Melrah

Blackenridge: The realm formally known as Africa –
16ᵗʰ Year of Beast

With only a few hours of what passed for daylight in the heart of the blackest lands, they rested. The dark chased away light, bringing with it heavy, unnatural noise. At length they set out on horseback over the eastward arm of a hardened slag covering a once fertile terrain. They were always more comfortable at night, their hearts lighter for the dark enveloping them. For many miles the white-blue eye of the moon seemed to gaze upon them as they continued onwards. The craft of men from previous times could be seen embedded in mounds of metallic-like rock, jutting out from murky pools of water. Here and there, they observed grotesque twisted crumbling masonry in nondescript stonework, along with vast heaps of barely distinguishable misshapen metal carcasses, unnatural and artificial by design. The immense towers of scrap could only have been gathered and erected by Faulgoth. Possible shrines to their devastation of the land, the king mused as they passed by.

His company named them "The Pillars of Faulgoth Wrath".

As the long journey unfolded, the king's captain pondered their brief respite in the river town they'd disembarked from six days previous. He thought back to the filthy desolate men attempting to waylay them with tales of dreadful carnivorous dog-like creatures. At the time, the only thing of consequence to him was procuring horses for king and company. But now as they trotted further in, Sam became aware of a growing presence just on the edge of his perception. Not for the first time, he wondered if he'd erred in dismissing those tales out of hand.

For many miles they rode. Horses steaming, their bits covered with foam. They traversed roads cloven through felled cities, deeper and deeper into territory that was unknown and undiscovered, except to the Faulgoth who henceforth strode. In the deepest part of Blackenridge, two-hundred miles east of the port, the land was plagued with lurking unnatural things. They were aware of hideous monstrous animals, tortured and disfigured, mutilated by foulness and filth choking the land, hateful viscous ooze they named Shadow-Venom or Faulgoth-Blood. It followed alongside terrors unseen emerging from pits under the earth. Its slow, progressing touch tainted everything as it leached and crept through ruptures in the membrane of the earth. They avoided contact with it, which often meant long detours.

With each night's ride, their senses attuned to skittering things hidden deep within the dark. They knew them by sounds of whispered chatter along with shrill hoots, low grunts, and a constant rancid corpse-like smell. Occasional luminous eyes pierced the dark. Not always in pairs, at times threes. Appearing and disappearing at random intervals, seeming close and afar at the same time. Hunger kept them nearby, but the powerful Songs of Darkness emanating from the king, and to a lesser degree, his entourage, caused courage to fail and kept plans hidden. But the captain had good understanding of them, creeping alongside the company night after night, so remained vigilant. They knew him also, and varied their game. With the ray of morning's light over the horizon, the black lands became more horrendous to behold. Daylight halted the company and they rested once again.

The days passed by easy enough. King-Arnold spent the time testing his powers and in turn, so did his company. When the king sat in meditation, the feared King's Guard stood ready in their protection of him.

Captain of the Dark King's Guard, Sam, made a careful examination of the petrified trees and flora he'd discovered near the camp. The trees seemed in perfect shape; frozen at the moment of their endings. It was nothing Sam had ever experienced before. Expecting nothing but rock and the viscous black venom that scarred the land, it was with great surprise he found himself face to face with strange stout flora, sprouting from within the desolation. Even the mighty Faulgoth had failed to eradicate all life in this part of Beast's new kingdom. He reached down and pulled out an entire thicket, root and all. Pulling off a leaf, he tasted it and was astonished by its sweetness. Born of fire and death as he was, this strange plant seemed fitting as food. He brought it to the king.

'Majesty,' he said, and King-Arnold turned.

'What *is* that, Sam?'

'I thought to ask you since you are most powerful. It tasted fine, energising my muscle and thought. I have no idea what to call it.'

King-Arnold took a leaf and the plant seemed to recoil from him. He tasted it and raised an eyebrow. 'How odd. One would never expect such sweet tasting vegetable to be born here of all places. It's good. Gather more of this and make a stew. There is no meat here I would dare try, for as powerful as we are, I suspect even we'd be hard pressed to digest anything caught here.'

Sam laughed. 'I agree, my Lord. These strange creatures lurking in shadow might try to feast on us when the day passes to night. I've set eager men on watch. I don't imagine anything would be stupid enough to attack us, but a stomach might override sense, so I say we take precaution.'

King-Arnold put a firm hand on Sam's shoulder. 'Wise, loyal Captain, but unnecessary, for I would test my guard against these things and wipe them from our path.'

Sam was thoughtful for a moment. King-Arnold didn't miss it. 'You have another idea?'

'My Lord, you are the wisest of us all, what I think is hardly of any consequence …'

Dark King laughed. 'But?'

'Well, I was just wondering if killing them might be counter-productive. We are deep in our own lands, these things might serve you a better purpose, if you would but wish it. I do have an idea and I would be happy to share, if my Lord is willing to hear?'

'I said it before, Sam, and I'll say it again. You and you alone may speak freely without concern on any subject. Let me hear this idea.'

Sam inclined his head. 'If we could command these things under your banner, they might prove valuable. And the arsenal of Arnold, King, would be greatly enhanced by their obedience.'

King-Arnold thought hard.

Sam said, 'Imagine, a horde of spies able to move swifter than man, melding into shadow, capable of going into places we might never find or return from. I'd risk the men on any errand you'd command, and willingly they'd die in attempt, or suffer my wrath—but with numbers as small as ours—we might be hard pressed to complete our quest, if most of us were dead before we arrived. Send in these things, Lord. I count thirty or so shadowing us. They are pack animals similar to dogs.

Larger, faster, and hungry. Their minds are underdeveloped but they hunt well.'

'Your senses are growing, Sam. I noticed the numbers increasing each night we rode. When we were at the dock I heard men talk of great warrior dog-like beasts roaming the land to the east. When we first ventured from port, I'd not travelled long within to give it much thought. Now I see the truth to it. There is one thing I fear in this world and dog beasts are not it, but caution is no weakness, Captain. There are many things here to threaten us.'

'They are directed, my King. Each time I sensed purpose in them, they changed tact. It appears they are well organised as hunters.'

'Not easy are we traced, Captain. We are hidden from normal eyes, with the exception of the mighty Faulgoth, whose number we have yet to meet on our journey.'

Sam grimaced. 'That goes well with me, Lord.'

'Why? Do you still fear them?'

'Not since you gave me strength. But still, I admit, they unnerve me.'

'That is their purpose.' King-Arnold closed his eyes. 'I've been aware of this larger presence for some time. I perceived it five days hence, remaining on the edge of my awareness ever since. It followed us from the west gates of Blackenridge harbour, leaving us at the great scrap towers, the plains being too open. I thought it gone, but a day after, it shadowed us again. For the last three days, his servants have crept closer.' His eyes reopened and he leant heavy against his staff. 'At the dock, when we met those less-worthy men, I heard tell of a beast three or four times larger than any dog, yet dog-like in figure.'

'I heard the same tales, my Lord. They said he has only one good eye, the other white as snow.'

'They,' Arnold scoffed, 'who couldn't have seen such a beast, for if he is all they say, how come they're alive to retell tale of it?'

Sam chuckled. 'True enough.'

'Still,' Dark King narrowed eyes, 'I sense now, deep within this torrid land, we are hunted. I get fleeting glances of its–no–*his* mind. He isn't sure what to make of us, I read that well enough. Hunger must be driving them.'

Sam shook his head. 'We haven't seen a man since the port city, at least not one who wasn't stripped of meat. And those men who talked tale were largely cowards I paid no attention to. It's doubtful any of those men would venture this far, or be seen again if they were stupid enough to try. So why has this thing followed us, for food? Surely he could stay close to the port and pick foolish men off as they leave? Why bother with us at all?'

Arnold rubbed his chin. 'You make a good point, and your wisdom excels, whereas mine diminishes. I have been too quick to judge motives. There's been many an opportunity to attack, yet he stays back, hidden. We can't be like any prey his pack has hunted. If there were easier targets this far out, we'd be off the menu. I sense now greater intelligence. You were right to question my first thoughts and to point out my idiocy.'

'My Lord gives me more credit than I deserve.'

'It's time I found this beast.' King-Arnold scanned the darkness, his eyes closed, surfing ripples of thought. After an hour passed, a slow smile spread across his face.

'There … I've found him. Lurking just beyond our border … yes, he is far closer now, I can almost smell him.'

Sam sniffed the air. He ran a tongue along the sharp points of his teeth. 'His pack surrounds the camp.' He hissed, 'We've forced hand, and here must be where he makes plan for ambush.'

Dangerous voice said, 'He has no comprehension of what he faces, or my might.'

Sam put his hand on the hilt of his sword. 'Then I will drag him before you so he may see it, and despair.'

'No, stay your hand. I have a better way.'

There was no mistaking the hideous malice in his lord's face, and Sam backed away, as the truth of his terror immerged.

King-Arnold turned black as night, his body shimmered and grew. The hazy red eyes under a ghastly jagged crown burnt with intensity and shot beams that penetrated deep into the gloom. They found their mark, a huge black-blue beast. He snarled but remained still. The Shadow King elevated into the air and gave a call that compelled the monstrous dog into his presence.

Slowly it padded forward, its one good eye taking in the lay of the camp. In the blackness surrounding them, howls, hoots, and sharp barks emanated, and they were closing in.

The great leader of the horde barked command and there was stillness in the dark.

King-Arnold, wrapped in darkness, called him forth with threatening song.

'Come to me, leader of the pack, for I summon you into my presence and you shall not refuse. Feel my majesty and know my terror. For I would unleash upon you and your pack, such torment the likes of which you could never conceive of. Come forth at my feet for I would hold dominion over you and those who follow you.'

The great dog growled. His swagger was almost a warning, his power over all lesser creatures, complete. To those who could understand barks and yelps he said,

What say you, Blackness? Your number small, we number more. I fight, I win, we eat. I lose, we go hungry. That is how it is with me.

The dog offered low growl, eyes narrowing, teeth flared.

'I would know why you track us. What are your intentions? Speak, or be flayed and remade into formless pulp.'

Not like others, you. Powerful. Melrah's land, this. Can only be one king.

The Shadow laughed. 'I find you worthy, Lord of beasts. Come, sit beside me and do thy bidding.'

Never. Melrah will rip out your throat and drink from you.

And he leapt high into the air, before Sam or any other member of the guard could react.

In response, the Shadow offered terrifying screech into the air. The mammoth dog fell from mid-flight with heavy thump, screaming at the unrelenting pain and anguish. He rolled and howled under the ruthless and unforgiving assault. But that was not enough for the Shadow and he intensified his song, reaching out to all those hidden in the impenetrable darkness. Around them, at varying positions, great shrieks, whimpers, and yelps were heard. They were much closer than before.

Stop the pain.

Free us.

Save us from hurt.

Help us!

Mercy, mercy.

They cried.

Then Melrah, through torment, cursed and praised him. Before the last breath was forced from his body, he capitulated, offering the Great Shadow King his obedience in exchange for the life of his pack.

The Shadow King ceased his torment. His faceless void bent downwards to the giant dog cowering in dread some distance away. He lowered to ground, the subjugated animal cautious in movement, sliding forward inch by inch on his belly. Arnold remained dark; blood-red eyes commanding the submission, the dog's fight gone, he gave over his life to a new master. He continued to edge closer. When Melrah reached the heavy armoured shin, he closed his eyes, expecting swift end.

Shadow became man. He knelt and reached towards a conquered giant, who did not flinch, but met hard gaze with steel of his own. It was not pity that stayed his hand, for King-Arnold had none. The great dog had been altered and mutilated by the world. He'd grown strong, a leader amongst his flock. A warrior. It wasn't just a blind eye this brute had suffered. His entire body was covered in scars.

Something passed between them, and the great dog lifted onto his paws, bowed his massive head and waited. Arnold scratched behind his ear.

'Great warrior, do not fear, I shall not harm you. I see you now and feel your truth and I find you magnificent.'

The giant dog lifted his head and licked at King-Arnold's hand.

'I shall call you, Melrah, most loyal.'

Melrah gave soft whine.

'I'm glad you like it.'

Sam came forward and Melrah growled.

'Be nice, great warrior Melrah. This is my captain. It was he who suggested I tame rather than destroy you. Perhaps you should show him your appreciation?'

Without warning, the giant dog pounced, knocking him to the ground. Sam reached for the knife in his boot but saw something in Melrah's good eye and stopped. The mammoth dog-like warrior pinned him to the ground and licked at his face in gratitude.

The king and men laughed.

It was not long afterwards that the area was full of the wild dog-like creatures. Melrah, leader of the pack, sat proud beside King-Arnold. Where he went his loyal pet followed. Arnold had never been much of an animal lover as a man, and less so now, but there was connection forged between them.

'You command yours and I'll command you. That is the order of things.'

Melrah barked.

'Good. I would have you send them east towards the great river. They are to watch and report back any movements, foul or otherwise, to you then you to me. Is that understood?'

Melrah put his giant head onto Arnold's lap.

'I'll take that as a yes.'

When orders were given and the group departed, a number of the larger animals remained behind.

The Guard looked bemused, but Melrah gave a sharp bark.

'They are Melrah's lieutenants. They will stay and watch over us, so we may rest.'

When the sun lifted up through the haze of the day, they slept under guard.

King-Arnold sat and stroked Melrah to sleep, lost in deep thought.

It seemed to Sam, as he lay between wakefulness and sleep, his great king had two personalities matching both earthly and dark form; each terrible to behold, yet the latter more so. Sam held healthy fear in his master, for with one look from his dreadful gaze, his wrath could strike the heart from a man. And yet there was still some humanity left within, at least when he wasn't wrapped in the sheath of ireful terror. But Sam was under no illusion. King-Arnold was horrendous, vengeful, and most of all, terrifying in his new found dark sovereignty. As he fell into sleep, his last thoughts centred on their quest. Were they strong enough to walk deep into enemy's camp and steal the precious things the Dark Lord Beast claimed absolute control over? He saw no answer. One thing was clear. It would not go well with them to fail, for if Sam feared King-Arnold's wrath, then surely Beast's would be one-hundred fold more severe. He shuddered. His resolve was set: succeed or be thankful to die trying.

The march east was lighter the following evening as cloud parted, allowing the watchful light of the moon to glisten across fetid pools of murky water, dotted in haphazard path before them. King-Arnold took lead, followed by Sam and the rest of the guard. Melrah ran ahead, his speed far greater than a stallion. He took in the lay of the land and called quick change, lest they be swallowed up by unseen bog, into nothingness. Some hours later, they reached the bank of the great river. It was vast, and its opposite bank could barely be seen.

Sam came alongside his master. 'This is the Nile, yes?'

'Yes. We've travelled deep into Blackenridge. We are in what was once called Sudan. We can follow its path north from here to where things will be a little more challenging.'

'We ride into Egypt, Lord?'

King-Arnold's eyes sparkled under moonlight. 'New Egypt, yes. We ride to the ancient seat of man's power, where the last great battle took place three-thousand years before our births. It is here we will find quest's end, one way or another. Most of it is ours, but a fraction is protected by Osirian filth. We must become ever vigilant. Our enemy cannot discover us or our quest's purpose. We must ride in secret, until we are at their door. Their arrogance blinds them to truth. Our Lord has given me the secrets of them and we must succeed at all costs.'

'This thing we seek. It will bring good fortune to our Great Lord?'

'More than that, it could tip the balance of power in our favour.'

'And if we should fail?' Sam recognised he'd spoken before thinking.

King-Arnold took on a hideous look, but Sam didn't feel it was directed at him. 'You know what answer I would give, Captain, and it would not please either of us to witness the truth of it.'

Captain of the guard remained impassive, looking north.

'Aye, my Lord. I seek to win all battles or die trying. I feel that would be better than the alternative.'

King of Darkness followed his gaze but said nothing.

Sam contemplated the distance. The dark king said, 'Curious. You've never asked me what it is we seek.'

'And I never will.'

He turned to his loyal captain. 'Most men would, but not you. Why?'

Sam shrugged. 'Sometimes it's better not to know. You'll tell me when I need knowledge of it, until then, I follow you as Lord and will die proud in your service.'

'Know that I would not allow such a thing to happen, so long as I hold power enough to prevent it.'

Sam gave tight smile. 'You honour me, my Lord.'

King-Arnold turned to him and put a hand on his shoulder. 'You are like family to me, my Captain. I do not say these things lightly. You know what power I hold over this world, and whilst you do not yet see it, there is great peril ahead. A war will soon be upon us, and I would spend ten-thousand lives before I let death claim yours.'

'My vengeful Lord of Malice and Darkness, I shall die happy today just for knowing that.'

They exchanged a rare moment, and then Sam looked north. 'How far do we ride?'

'It's around two-hundred miles to the original border, give or take.'

Sam stroked his steed's neck. 'Even for us, my Lord, with few stops, it will be a hard six days' ride.'

King-Arnold looked over the western horizon and frowned at the first rays of morning's light as it pierced the dark.

'You may be right. Let us find shelter and make camp. We can discuss our journey over food and rest. Perhaps loyal steed may not be the best choice. I do have another thought, but it might turn ill if handled poorly. Come. We must rest. My bones and seat ache.'

Sam turned his horse and gathered the men. They found a deep ravine at the shores of the Nile. It ran less murky than any other source of water and the company stripped naked, washing themselves and their garments free of grit and grime. When they were less foul smelling, they came to sit around one of two large fires the king had made. They hung wet clothing on sticks around the other.

Melrah came from the water in a great splash and shook himself dry. He placed three large fish, still flipping, before his master then bounded back. After six more trips, there was enough to feed them all. He came and lay beside the fire and yawned with a gentle squeak.

King-Arnold bent low and whispered into Melrah's ear. The great Lord of dogs grunted as his dark master stroked his massive head. The king left him and retook his seat beside the roaring fire.

Melrah yawned again and, as if his head had suddenly become too heavy, he dropped it to the ground and let out a slow sigh.

Sam chuckled. 'Poor Melrah,' he said, sitting beside him. 'Our long journey has been tough, but we are grateful you kept us on straight path. Mighty Lord of dogs, sleep now. We will stand as guard for you this night.'

The giant dog blinked a few times then fell deep into sleep.

Nineteen
A Prince and his Blade

The Nile: Blackenridge East

Sam, roused by sudden movement, sat up and stared. He looked around the camp, his men slept soundless. His gaze shifted to the king, eyes closed, arms folded across his chest. Shaking the grogginess from his head, he sighed. He wasn't sure what caused him to wake, but alert to some new sense of danger, he rose and put a kettle on the fire. Melrah raised his head, huffed, then dropped it and closed his eyes.

It was late afternoon. The sun was westering when the king opened his eyes. He regarded Sam and stirred. Melrah stretched and yawned. Sam poured a warm, sweet smelling drink for him, and he took it and sat. The great dog skulked off to find food.

'Difficulty sleeping, Sam?'

He nodded. 'My dreams are slow to come and then so full of images, they force me awake. I've not slept well for the last two days.' He stretched and rubbed his neck.

Arnold sipped from the cup, hypnotised by a dying flame. 'What images do you see?'

Sam contemplated his answer. 'They fade too quickly after I wake to remember. Whatever it was that broke my sleep didn't feel like a bad dream, it seemed real.'

'Your senses are developing, with them comes a period of transition. The acclimation of mind and body is difficult, unpredictable. In time you'll become accustomed, as I did.'

'If I may ask, how long have you been in our Lord's service?'

Arnold cradled his cup and shrunk into himself. 'I've always been in service, Sam, from birth till now. I was first inducted into the Cult of Beast at an early age, ten or maybe eleven, I don't remember now. I went through a similar transformation, and had moments of confusion. I come from a long line of loyal advisors. We date back to the earliest recorded time.' He chuckled. 'It all seems like a lifetime ago.'

'I'm curious. What will be our place, when our Lord shapes this world into his dream?'

King-Arnold looked thoughtful. 'Lord Beast isn't interested in managing the affairs of man, Sam. He sits above, founding visions in song, defining destiny, as gods should. It is to us the most loyal and trusted of servants he looks at, to bring focus to this vision. Our Lord was forged in a great song and it is a privilege for men like us, to dance to its tune.

'The world we knew is gone. Those, like the men sheltering within the light, who cling to such thoughts, are doomed to despair. I've not seen the future, but I know enough of what went before, to see destiny in the making. We stand on the crossroads. All men will eventually seek our guidance, once final wars are fought and won and Osirian are banished into void.'

'Their light will be choked from them, and darkness will fall across the land, Mighty King.'

Arnold smiled. 'I don't choose to live in darkness, Sam. I love the sun's warmth like anyone else. It's easy to think because we're born of shadow, we might shun its comfort, but our Lord understands the wonder of things no mortal has ever seen. There are fouler things dwelling beneath the world, who would cry at the sun's touch, but when it bathes my skin, I feel content, not contempt.'

Sam sighed. 'I miss daylight at times, but my eyes prefer dark.'

Arnold put his empty cup down. 'We have strength of purpose. We are shades of grey within this world. Unlike our enemy, we move unhindered by either. Their weakness lies in the fact they see light as the only strength, but the two are not diametrically opposed. Our victory is ensured because we are not foolish enough to give credence to this stereotype.'

Sam nodded and looked up at the sun. 'Still, I find its great yellow face irritating. If I had the power, I would pull cloud across it, and feel comfortable again in the dark.'

As if to answer his prayer, a heavy cloud did fall across the sun, plunging them into shadow. The two men looked around, each sensing much. A hideous trumpeting chorus filled the air, and Melrah howled and cowered away. Both men turned, bearing witness to the spectre of their Great Master, and dropped to knee, lowering their eyes, as he manifested before them.

They felt his song. *'Truly, you are both worthy. Such loyalty will be rewarded beyond imaginations of even you, my Dark Servant King. Stand, become shadow and hear Song, for I would convey new quest upon thee.'*

Sam did not once look upon the Lord Beast. He felt the change in his king. It was as if he was able to increase his strength by pulling life from anything in darkness; sheathing him deep within it, using its power to boost and amplify his own dreadfulness. When he formed into shadow he was more terrifying than a second spent in the fires of Hell.

The men did not stir and that was well, for if they did, it might go badly for them if they weren't immediately on their faces in reverence. The world was silent and dark for many minutes. Then a song filtered into his mind.

'Look upon thy face, Loyal Captain.'

'Lord, I dare not, for my fear overwhelms me.'

Beast was pleased. *'Yet I command it.'*

With huge courage, he did as instructed. Beast came forward and sat before him. Sam had never seen him up close. The face he met was dreadful, beyond a worst possible nightmare. His great luminous eyes bore deep into him. They were terrifying to behold. In them, Sam found every fear he'd ever known, multiplied by a thousand. Lost in this dreadfulness, he shook in paralysed terror. Beast sang a malevolent chorus. Under frightful gaze, something unknown stirred, his blood burned. Tendrils of unimaginable pain pulsed, lancing his mind with knowledge, images, thoughts, and a power he'd never known. The Songs of Darkness coursed every cell, mutating them. In the pain of it he found new ability to realise the world. And from those very same eyes he perceived wicked benevolence. It gave strange comfort. Sam shook, breathing hard. He'd filtered the screams of his pain deep into himself, proud that no sound had left his lips. Beast roared his songs conclusion.

'You are reborn. Be in good cheer.'

Sam felt new power. When he turned to the king, he saw him in both forms at once, conjoined and overlapping. His eyes opened him to truths he was yet to fully comprehend. He turned back to Beast and dropped low before him.

'There are no songs I could sing, or words I could utter, that would do justice to the smallest fraction of expression, gratitude, and love I feel for you, oh, High Lord of Darkness and Shadow.'

Beast growled in delight.

'Yet you found a way and it pleases me, Man no longer. You serve your king and thus I, with princely character now repaid with reward. I bestow further gift, such is my will. Behold, I fashion weapon only you may wield, born of despair and foul purpose. I name it: Underblade. Any other hand placed upon hilt, will find unimaginable burden of torment. In its wrath, single graze will turn victim to ash. I sing henceforth, you shall be known throughout as Sam, Prince of Shadow. Your enemies, who have eyes to see the truth of you, will despair and beg for swift end.'

A mist swirled around him and formed into a blackened sword, its intricate hilt decorated in serpent design. Sam stayed low.

'Great Lord, your gift honours.'

Beast said, *'Arise, Sam-Prince. Feel strength wash over you. Know my foulness and rejoice. Your destiny is written. You two shall become the power in darkness, bringers of strength to man, peace to those in need of our direction, alongside Osirian torment and death.'*

He turned his head to the other.

'Arnold-King, Chief Servant, bringer of fates and power beyond any, I leave you now. Your path is clear of obstacle. Go. Bring back the prize I covet, and come home to me whole.' And with no further song he vanished.

Sam took Underblade and found it light in his grip.

'We are brothers now, Prince amongst all men.'

Sam dropped and wept before his king. Arnold knelt low and took his face into his hands. 'Tears, my Prince?'

'Yes, of joy, Brother-King.'

Arnold kissed his forehead then lifted him from the ground. 'Come let us make preparation to leave. Sun sets and we have a detour to make.'

Prince woke the men.

It was dark when they gathered around the remade fire and ate. Sam was the topic of conversation. They showed their love for him in song and stories of great deeds.

Arnold finished the broth and stood, addressing them.

'Loyal Guard, tonight we stay in this camp, at least you do. The prince and I have task for our master. It can only be accomplished alone.'

The look of concern in their eyes was comforting.

Aaron stood. 'My Lords, I would feel less anxious if I were to ride beside you.'

Prince Sam gave a broad smile. 'Aaron, lieutenant of the guard, your men need you here. We will be back tomorrow, so rest and be watchful. Look out for us by the coming of the sun. You see how it is with us? Our king's power will protect me from anything we may face, and in turn I and loyal Melrah, who is never far from the king's side, will watch over him. Be at peace. We will soon be together.'

Aaron nodded. 'We will keep flame ready for your return. Safe journey, oh, and if you find any more of that root, bring it back with you, my Captain!'

King and Prince mounted horses and bade them farewell.

With Melrah beside them, they headed north. King-Arnold made swift change in direction north-west and they followed. Horses rode hard and Melrah followed for three hours straight. When the king put up his hand, they slowed. Melrah trotted alongside, panting from exertion.

Ahead in the gloom the path bent down to rock, disappearing inside a great black entrance under massive piles of slag. The coming of the Faulgoth made holes in the world and this fissure led to forgotten darkness, cracked open in their awakening, many years previous.

Arnold dismounted and tied his horse to a tree.

Sam followed his lead. He peered into darkness but saw nothing, even with new sight. 'This is our destination?'

'No. This is *your* destination, Sam.'

The Prince frowned. 'I do not understand.'

Arnold smiled at him. 'Our Lord has in his wisdom devised a test for you and you alone.'

'Why? Am I not loyal? Trustworthy? Did I make some error?'

Arnold was hard with him. 'How could you think these things? He, who fashions sword only you can handle, imbues you with powers almost equal to mine and makes you prince amongst men, would now decide to seek test of your character?'

'Forgive me.' He reddened in shame.

The king softened. 'There is nothing to forgive. Your task is set. Go deep into this place. Inside you will find creatures guarding a hammer of crystal. It's vital we have it, or our quest will fail. Bring it out of the dark, but be wary. Your sword will not be enough to protect you. Listen, Sam, you must find a way to unlock your inner power. Keep your wits about you, though. If you hope to overcome all obstacles in your path now and in the future, you must learn to manifest and draw on this power. Only then will the prince you're destined to be, surface.'

Sam looked unsure, daunted.

'But … I don't know how to become shadow as you do. Will you not teach me first?'

He shook his head. 'I am bound by oath not to, brother.'

Sam was downcast. 'What if I am unable to learn in time?'

Arnold-King took on a hard face. 'I will then grieve and avenge your death in great disappointment.'

'It's like that then.' Sam lifted slumped shoulders and met the eyes of the king. To contemplate a decision as if he had a choice was pointless.

'Then, my Lord, as man I go into darkness and out I shall come as shadow.'

Arnold showed his pleasure by drawing him into tight embrace. He put mouth to ear, whispering, 'Draw from the fire,' and let him go.

Sam looked down at Melrah with fondness in his eyes. The dog lord barked twice.

'I guess that was good luck?'

Arnold put a hand on his shoulder. 'Something like that, brother. I'll await you here. I wish you success and good fortune. My faith is strong. I know you will not fail.'

Sam pulled out Underblade and ran eye along its edge. Under the light of the moon, its blackness tinted purple. 'No,' he said with confidence, 'I shall not fail, for I would not dare to come back without prize. Farewell, Brother-King, and to you also, Great Lord of the Pack. Look for my shadow or avenge my death without mercy.' With a nod he turned, heading towards the cave.

King and loyal watchdog followed his back until he disappeared into the darkness of the entrance. Arnold sunk deep within himself. Reaching out with his mind, he attempted to get a sense of what Sam may encounter. He felt them now, great beasts, older than anything he'd seen first-hand, but somehow hidden from vision. He sent out projection, and was now able to see from both positions. His concentration was exact.

Melrah howled in question.

It broke Arnold's concentration and he lost the image. Irritation crept into his response.

'What?'

Greatness. You know what lies at cave's heart?

'Yes.'

There was a pause before a growled response.

Hideous, they are.

'Indeed.'

Worse than others, foul, old.

'I know.'

Melrah looked up at his master with sad eyes. Arnold paid him little attention. He attempted to reach out in projection again.

Poor Sam?

Arnold looked down in annoyance. 'Shush.'

Melrah whined and lay flat.

Twenty
The Prince of Shadow

Blackenridge: The Cave of the Beborreath

The path sank deep into the darkest tunnel he'd ever walked. Down it went, for the longest time, deeper and deeper. The atmosphere became dank, cold, and the smell of the air was rancid. At some point, it opened into a cavern. His vision did not avail him and he was soon unable to see his hand in front of his face. In this disorientation, he could not find the original path. His intention to go back and get a torch was now thwarted.

Sam did not fear. He realised if he was unable to find a way to perceive what was around him, he would not be able to see any crystal hammers to collect. He stopped and closed his eyes, slowing his breathing. Blind, he spent great energy focusing his other senses to assist him. He strained to listen but heard only his breathing. It didn't help.

One thing that was working, and working far too well, was his sense of smell. The rancid odours that assaulted him were strong. They increased with each step forward. Sam used the wall for guide and shuffled forward.

'Poor thing, lost in shadow,' a voice hissed from around him.

Sam froze.

He searched for the source in his mind, finding nothing but void. He held out his sword, but his reaction was of little use, as he was not sure in which direction he should point it.

Loud cackles reverberated around the cavern.

'Lost and senseless, that's just how I like them.'

A different high-pitched voice said, 'Is it juicy, sister? Will it be sweet?'

Then the first voice said, 'It is much stronger than a man, I can feel that. It smells sweet. Perhaps it will taste that way, too? I suspect it's not quite as putrid as the babbling things we caught last night.'

High-Pitch hissed. 'Shall we not try it, and find out?'

Sam cleared his throat and in a steady voice said, 'I am neither sweet nor wholesome, vile creatures of rancid odour. You would not want to eat me, for if you were somehow able, Underblade would render you ash before you were able to swallow.'

'Ah, it speaks.'

'Very sure of itself it is, too,' High-Pitch remarked.

The first voice asked, 'What is Underblade?'

Sam put his back to the wall.

'You'll know its sting soon enough. Tell me, what are you?'

'What are *you*?' An indignant voice responded.

'My apologies,' Sam said, and meant it. 'I am the Prince of Shadow, wielder of Underblade bestowed upon me by Beast, lord of all things dark. Brother and servant to Arnold, King of Darkness. I am your destruction, and you shall fear me.'

They laughed.

'That was a very nice introduction, truly, and such wonderful accolades and titles, Sam of Lies. But I will tell you, since you mention it so, that I know nothing of any beast ruling my darkness, teller of fantasy. Come now, if you are all you say, why do you not see us?'

'Yes … stand before us, if you can, Prince of Blindness.' High-Pitch hissed a cackle.

Sam was thoughtful. 'Oh Mighty Ones, I dare not stand before your grace, for then our eyes would meet, and my Lord was most insistent I bring back the head of anything seen. You seem violent and foul, and I do not wish to appear rude by chopping off your heads, so I choose to keep my sight to myself.'

They hooted and gurgled in delight.

'You have a good tongue, young one. It flaps like a banner in the wind. It's a long time since anything caught was so courteous. I like the cut of you, and I shall enjoy eating you enormously.'

High-Pitch said, 'You say Prince of Shadow? You need no eyes to perceive us, foolish thing.'

'Well,' Sam continued, 'I spent time on *my* introduction maybe you would grace me with yours?'

There was a dreadful unnerving silence. Odd feelings rose up from the pit of his stomach, into his mouth as bile. Sam spat out the bitter taste. Fear had now frozen him to the spot and he could no longer function. He remained still, his back firm against the wall. Although his courage was gone the ability to reason was still intact, and he fought a hard battle over his mind.

Sam considered possibilities. If he were to exit in failure, having fought hard in attempt, his master *might* be merciful. But if he were to flee in terror and come before that same master, what might be his response? Sam knew there would be no mercy, for King would deal torment upon him, the likes of which Sam couldn't conceive of, and that was a far more terrifying thing to fear.

It helped. The shame of weakness boiled into anger, like fire in a cold boiler. Slow, at first to warm, it cascaded through frozen veins melting fears, allowing limbs to move. It didn't stop there. A chain-reaction within sent strange sensations throughout; they made the skin of his entire body tingle. Fear of unknown voices in darkness no longer held him. The strange warmth of his anger spread through nerves until it reached into his head, stabbing hard behind his eyes.

Sam took a sharp intake of breath. Instinct forced his hand to rub away the pain, and when he removed it, the cavern immerged into focus as new sight filled him with courage once again.

He could see them now; their truth visible in hideous terror. He was deep inside a cavern littered with centuries of waste and filth. The things he saw made him–almost–wish his sight had not been returned. The dread he felt before was nothing compared to the horror now standing in front him: Two giant spider-like creatures with rows of black eyes and sharp teeth. Both as large as houses, they sat on plump bellies.

Rotten unidentifiable remains of previous victims were strewn in heaps and piles. High above from the crown of the cave hung great pods in their hundreds. He knew them for what they were. Food sacks. Sam shivered. He recognised his fear was being amplified. He was convinced it was part of some spell. It had almost succeeded in destroying him. Now he recognised it, he would not give in to its paralysing effect.

'We are Beborreath,' a bloated brown-yellow spider thing said.

'Long have we lived and never into the light have we stepped. Introduction, say you? We are from the deepest place in this world. We have grown through feeding on the delights that fall through cracks we sit beneath.'

Knowledge flooded Sam's mind. Whether it was fear or the mention of their name triggering it, Sam could not tell. He knew these things now. They were old and dangerous. They were able to amplify fears likely through pheromones of something similar, so Sam's inherent dread of spiders was multiplied tenfold. He was paralysed, again, unable to do anything but stare.

The second of them, a red-blue spider shifted her many eyes to him.

'It's a senseless thing, sister. It resists our spells.'

'Yes … I told you he was strong. Oh he will be a delightful meal.'

Red-Blue salivated. 'Less chatter, more eating.'

They scuttled forward and Sam backed further up against the wall.

Brown-Yellow halted and hissed. 'Oh … It has opened eyes, sister. When light touch of us is made, no man can hear it, you see? It knows enough to back away, it sees us. We are betrayed.'

Blue-Red cursed and they continued to advance.

Sam's terror had almost overcome him. He fought against it, reminding his mind it was spell, not his own. Then he remembered how he'd broken it before, and he reached inside for the anger and shame. He tore at it, in terror and horror, as he watched the creatures advance, almost upon him. And then he found it, a thing, inside his body. Alien. He reached for it in his mind and it recoiled and slipped away.

Closer they came, putrescent stench overpowering senses. Sam gagged.

Stuck against the wall in a fright never known, he willed his stubborn muscles, but they would not budge. He screamed in outrage, but they ignored him. The fight went on, and the alien thing inside grew. He cursed legs for refusing to obey commands. He strained and strained, till blood vessels burst in his eyes, along with the thing inside him. Black liquid penetrated his overbeating heart, diluting with blood, pumping through his cardiovascular system. He doubled over in excruciating, crippling agony. Sam howled in torment. Vomit erupted in waves and pulses matching the rhythm of his pain.

The two fat spiders ceased advancing and looked at each other.

'What is its game?' Blue-Red said.

'I do not know.' Brown-Yellow gurgled at her. 'No matter, let us put it out of its misery. Let us kill it and be done.'

Sam choked through tears as the torture of pain took away ability to breath. He was barely conscious of them. His eyes blurred. Then pain subsided and his eyes turned black as night. A power flowed through him, filling his senses, and this time, his eyes saw different things.

The monster spider creatures took on different aspect. They were bathed in an ethereal green glow; it flickered like a great fire around them.

And with a snarl, Sam broke their spell. Wiping the residue from his mouth, he spat and met the advancing spiders head on. His anger turned face sour. They faltered, many eyes staring. The look of him was terrible, but they had overcome worse and were masters of it. Sam held sword tip outwards and scowled.

The two great monsters attacked.

Sam fought with strength unprepared for. Yet even though he was strong, they were more so. He rained blow after blow upon them until his muscles screamed and his eyes were blind with the sting of his sweat. But in deep frustration he backed away. Underblade could not penetrate the pitted age-old layers of thick growth on their hides. Every blow he unleashed, just bounced off. All he could do was defend until he could figure a way of hurting one of them. Underblade was magnificent as sword, and to its credit, it did not recoil or vibrate so as to send shock into his hands. He continued to parry and sidestep, keeping mental note of each of their attacks, and last positions.

The two bloated spiders were formidable working well in pairs. He wiped sweat from brow, focusing on anything but the sour smell. It left him on permanent verge of gagging. *'If the claws and stings didn't kill me, their fetid stench surely will.'*

He dodged under legs, fended off blows from claws, surprised by the speed of their attacks. His advantage, he knew, was size. He used it to good effect. Sam twisted, turned, bobbed, weaved and the two cumbersome and awkward creatures collided into one another with a curse. Sam stepped in between them hoping to use the same tactic, but they were too shrewd and his strategy failed.

A lifted section of encrusted hide had caught his eye, exposing vulnerable flesh on one of Blue-Red's eight legs. Without thought, he took the provided opportunity and drove Underblade down into it, with all his strength. Its bite went deep into soft flesh. A spurt of green-black blood hit him. For the first time in an age forgotten, the agony of pain befell her. She shrieked. It caused the other to falter. Her utterance was so loud, food sacks loosened and fell from above and bounced onto the cavern floor.

'Help me, sister. It hurts. It hurts, oh, spare me the pain!'

Brown-Yellow withdrew to sister's side.

Blue-Red recoiled and crouched, shuddering and spinning on the floor, beating the air with her forelegs. He advanced upon her, and she turned and fell back into a ball, whimpering as her injured leg turned hard as stone becoming nothing but ash. They looked at him anew and Red-Blue cursed. Her ethereal flame grew strength as she staggered up. Her anger made the hairs on her seven remaining legs stick out. With fire in the rows of her terrible black eyes, she came at him.

Sam stood breathing hard, sword pointing down as he turned to defensive posture. His mind sent messages to him, warnings, images, strategies, and then King-Arnold's whispered message surfaced. '*Draw from the fire.*'

The epiphany came. With renewed purpose he understood meaning in his words. A great intake of breath caused ethereal flames to leap towards him, surrounding and enveloping him. They coalesced and conjoined within, imbuing him in ireful malice, bolstering strength, causing transformation within cells. It exhilarated and charged him. With great song he burst into shadow form, and pulled life from the darkness of the world and wrapped himself in dreadfulness; and those ancient creatures of the old world recoiled in alarm as he elevated himself high into the air above them. Inside his cloaked form, they saw no face or mouth, yet heard his song in their minds. They pushed themselves away and shook in their terror.

'I am Prince of Shadow. You will suffer my wrath, creatures of old.'

'Spare us. Spare us,' they cried in unison.

In dreadful song the Prince replied, 'Give me what I seek, and I will consider showing clemency, and leave you to your filth. But should you choose not to comply with my command, I will engulf you without any mercy and drop you out into the light above.'

'That would kill us. That would kill us.'

'Then give me what I seek.'

'Tell us. Tell us what it is you seek?'

'A hammer.'

'Mercy. There are no things like that here.'

'Do not test me. I say you know. Give it to me, and I will be merciful.'

'But it should know. We have no need for crystal hammers.'

The prince glided forward with snarl. 'I didn't say it was crystal, cretinous thing.' Without any further song he unleashed a shriek so terrible, the giant spiders wailed themselves into balls, rolling and cursing in their anguish.

'Save us. We will show you. We will show you! No more. Please. No more!'

He ceased and Brown-Yellow staggered to a chest, flipping it open with her forelegs and backing away with speed that belied her bloated form.

'Take everything. Take everything, Great Lord Prince of Shadow and Pain. Now he has what he sought, will he go, as he promised to?'

The prince and his sword saw the object of his task and claimed it. He heard whispers from the hundreds of beings wrapped and hung above. He sensed them; neither alive nor dead. It sickened him and he turned dreadfulness upon them in rage never before felt.

'Will he go now, yes? Will he go and leave us in peace as he promised?'

'Enough!' Prince of Wrath turned and engulfed them. He gathered the screeching things in tight squeeze. They shrieked, yelped, and pleaded, but he continued to crush them until the sounds of gruesome snapping and popping of legs and joints could be heard alongside undulating cries of unrelenting agony. He continued until they found no voice to scream with, till whimpers and gurgles and squeals were all they had left.

The shadow released them to the ground with a squelching thud. Legs broken, eyes half put out, green-black goo spurting and seeping from ruptured hides. They flipped, rolled, and flopped as they dragged themselves as far from him as they could, but he was still locked upon them in a terrible fury.

'Mercy.'

But there was none.

'Leave us ... we beg ... Will you leave us in peace?' they gurgled in utter panic.

Prince of Shadow paused, pointing Underblade towards them. He sung a chorus filling the cavern, and purple flame leapt from the hilt to its tip. In the void where a head was no longer visible, in a voice dripping in malevolent scorn, he said, 'I will leave you ...'

'In peace?' They squealed hopeful and in surrender.

'In pieces,' the Great Prince of Darkness responded in deadly song. 'MERCY ...'

Great Melrah prowled in wait and then stopped and grunted back at the king. He turned to the tunnel entrance, his eyes seeing things men could not. Arnold had perceived most of what transpired in the cave. He smiled in delight as Sam—with explosive force— thundered out of the entrance to the tempo of a triumphant song. Prince of Shadow advanced and was terrible to behold.

Melrah barked and his great tail wagged.

King of Darkness stroked his head.

Prince of Shadow hovered before the king and dog, Underblade held in one hand, a crystal hammer in the other. He lowered to the ground, shifting back to earthly form. Sam now stood breathing hard before the king. He held out the hammer and lowered his head.

'Quest's goal is found and claimed, my Lord. My test complete and I am grateful. I have strength now unequalled in man, except you, Lord. Will you now teach me new things?'

'You have my word, Sam.'

Arnold-King took the crystal hammer from his hand and placed it with care into the saddle bag of his horse. He turned to Sam, holding him in tight embrace.

'Sam, you overcame much in your task. It was hard on you, but I do not apologise for that.'

Sam smiled. 'Nor should you.'

'You amaze me, your strength is enormous, brother-prince. Now we can go head-to-head with the worst this world can throw at us. We are shadows together.'

'It was hard fought ... what a battle it was.'

'How do you feel?'

Sam rubbed his stomach. 'Powerful and ... hungry?'

King laughed. 'Yes, it does affect that way. You learn to find ways of nourishing yourself whilst in shadow form and I will show you different ways to focus your strength. But not tonight, for we have hard ride before we can eat, and our men await our return. But be of good cheer. I gathered more of those vegetables things while you were gone.'

Melrah growled low.

Arnold laughed. 'Very well. Melrah wanted you to know that it was he who found them.'

Sam knelt and smiled at him. 'You are truly magnificent. Maybe in my new found power, I will finally be able to understand what you say?'

Melrah barked and Sam sighed.

'I guess not.'

King of Darkness asked, 'Sam, I have a question. Those things in the cave, you offered them mercy and then reneged, why?'

He mounted his horse.

'It's simple, my King. I don't like spiders.' With a smirk, he turned his horse and rode away.

'Well,' Arnold said, looking down at Melrah, 'that's fair enough, then.'

Melrah howled and chased after Sam.

Arnold was thoughtful for a time, watching his new prince speed ahead of him. He kicked his own horse hard and followed.

Weary of their journey, they arrived back at camp just as the sun lifted to sky.

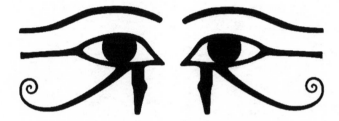

THE EVE
OF WAR

Twenty-One
The Army of Light

New Egypt: 17th Year of Beast

Mary looked out upon the bleakness of the sand, rocks, and collections of dusty incomplete ancient ruin temples, and gave a huge smile. She had spent a number of weeks travelling around Egypt in the company of her formidable teacher, Neith, and today she was on her own for her first test. Mary consulted her map and turned her attention towards the ruins.

The structure of the temple had largely fallen away, robbed of its material. The floor remained, along with some pillars, faceless statues, and other unidentifiable blocks of sandstone. Mary approached one of the pillars still upright and observed the hieroglyphs. She ran her fingers along the inscriptions. It reminded her of the past. It made her think of Albert.

The sun was high, free of clouds. She shaded her eyes from its brightness.

Crouching, she put a hand onto the floor and closed her eyes. Images flashed through her mind. Flickers of warriors, battle ready, or in battle. People, beautiful faces, children, flashes in dark, swirls of clouds. Then she heard overlapping voices; whispering, shouting, cursing, crying, and laughing. It happened fast and she released the sand, a tingle in her skin seemed to electrify her senses.

'This is it,' she muttered. 'This is the lost temple of the Osirian. I did it.' She laughed.

'And you did it well, child.'

Mary turned to see Neith standing beside her in all her glory. Her smile was broad.

'You improve daily.'

'This is it, isn't it? The last battle between Osirian and Beast occurred here.' She stood and brushed the sand off her hands.

Neith nodded. 'Yes, this is the place. The last stand between my brother, Osiris, and Beast, so I heard it sung.'

Mary frowned. 'You weren't there?'

Neith shook her head. 'I was not.'

'I've been meaning to ask ...'

'Why is my brother now my sister?'

'Neith, you have to stop asking my questions for me, it's very annoying.'

Goddess laughed. 'Very well, I will wait for them to be proposed, before I consider answering them. However, I have no patience for the length of time you take. This question has been on your mind since we first met, and that was many weeks past.'

'I know, I'm sorry. I haven't a good grasp of the Osirian Pantheon. The records on the subject often come with huge inconsistencies and variations in the accounts of their, well your, mythology and I suppose, history. It's not really my field. What was written back then was very subjective and heavily censored. Even the Greeks rewrote a number of the stories, years later ...' Mary smiled at Neith's look.

'I'm babbling, aren't I?'

'I am ready to cut off my ears, yes.'

'Sorry. Now it's all rather immaterial, isn't it? I can just ask you. So, why is the Great God Osiris an old woman and not a man?'

'I will tell you but not here. I do not trust this place. There is somewhere we need to go. There I will discuss any topic because I can be assured privacy. The spies of Beast are everywhere.' She slapped a mosquito off her neck and scrutinised it. She offered Mary the tiny squashed body. 'You see?'

Mary nodded. 'I understand. Where do we go, now?'

Neith looked up at the sun and back at the horizon. 'We are in the City of the Sceptre.'

Mary frowned. 'City of the Sceptre? Waset?'

'Yes, I believe that is what we called it.'

'Thebes, Luxor, right. I know where we are now.'

'Good. So, we must travel a short distance west and then we can raise my temple from the sand.'

Mary smiled. 'You, Neith? You have a temple? I'm so surprised.'

Neith look sideways at her. 'This is sarcasm and not a ... joke, I am correct?'

'Yes, exactly.' Mary beamed.

'I see.' Neith pushed the knife back into its scabbard.

'I'm so proud of you, Great Goddess.'

Neith grunted. 'This new-age language is difficult to get habit of. Now with newfound sarcasm and jokes, why, it is becoming ever more difficult to recognise the moment when head may be parted from its body. Come.'

The Prison of Light – Nubia Region

Lady of Light stood before the ancient doorway and was thoughtful. Its location was a secret known only to a few. Not even all her brothers and sisters knew of it. It was well hidden. Just outside the boundaries of the world, deep within hundreds of feet of solid rock and stone. Holding up her staff, the Osirian glided forward, whispering song, waiting as crack in stone appeared. A huge section of the rock face sunk inwards and parted, without noise, revealing an expansive ancient opening.

Within the depths came unison of approaching footfalls. Closer and closer they marched, until ten jackal-headed male warriors—three metres in height dressed in loincloths that hung from golden belts—marched into the light. Each had perfect physique. Sculptured, as if the muscle defining their masculinity had have been carved from stone. They formed impenetrable guard. Holding great staffs with curved blade atop, they bared her entry. Lady of Light put out a hand and their posture relaxed, ready, in military fashion.

Another figure approached, like the others, but more heavily adorned. A great crystal set in a pendant hung around his neck. He came before her and dropped to a knee. His jackal-head lowered. She reached out and stroked between his ears.

'Lethor, loyal Captain, stand before me.'

'My Lady,' he mouthed, gruff of voice. 'You called and we awaken. What is thy bidding?'

'I seek assurance our prisoner is safely locked within.'

'I give that assurance, then.'

'It is well. But, we must bolster defences, Lethor. There is grave danger.'

'Here? I say nay. We are the ancient guardians of this prison, with no fear of primitives or wild beast roaming the land.'

'You have slept long. Much has changed. This world is devastated. Beast rules nearly all of it, curse his name.'

'You bring ill tidings, Great Lady. It saddens heart to know he lives free again, considering your personal sacrifice.'

She put a hand on his arm as they walked. 'We were tricked by one of our own. Too late did we see the truth of it, and now it seems, even greater purpose may lay in its foundation. I fear, as before, we've made yet further error.'

'But come now. Our borders may not be breached by him, this you know well. He can neither step upon this ground nor come within miles of it. It was the Lords on High above your greatness who built this place and he is ever barred entry.'

She nodded. 'You speak truth.'

'Then what is this fear in you?'

She looked up, her smile thin. 'That he may have found another way.'

'What other way?'

'I believe he has created servants to act for him. I do not see it all clearly, but my heart tells me some truths. I'm wary.'

The jackal-headed captain laughed. 'But I am relieved, then.'

'Lethor?'

'Yes, I am. My Lady, I do not possess an ounce of your greatness, but of mine and loyal guardians, though limited, we can repel most things dreadful or otherwise with ease. Even vile Faulgoth dare not walk here, for I have smote many in my long life and yet still live to tell tale of it. Even you, great Osirian would find difficult task in it, not that we would fear you doing so. What then have we to fear from servants of things that can be smote by your grace, and by my sword?'

She smiled. 'I wish I could be as confident. Take caution, great warrior. The pride you display in your abilities is handsome, but you are no fool. My fears are not the whims of an old woman.'

'Never have I seen you thus conflicted, Lady. It alarms.'

'I fought one of these dark servants, human-shadow hybrid. He was formidable, this King of Darkness. Remember this well. Beast *is* one of the Lords on High. He has power beyond either of us. We underestimated him once. We cannot afford to do so again.'

Lethor inclined his head. 'I agree. Come, let us walk the borders to ensure securities and quash concerns, perceived or otherwise. You will see all is well. I will double guard until you say threat is no longer felt. Might that make confidences grow?'

'Perhaps.'

Lethor nodded. 'Good.'

He matched her slow pace. She held onto his muscled forearm as they walked. Together they entered, guard followed behind, and the rock face resealed.

The Sands, West of Waset

'We arrive at last,' Neith said.

Mary came alongside her, panting. 'Here? Unless I've gone blind, I see nothing but sand.'

'Yes here.' Her eyes sparked. 'All eyes are blind to it.'

'It's cloaked from vision in some way?'

'Yes, in the best way possible. It remains where I left it, hidden and untouched beneath the sand. I buried it when I last walked this world. Now I shall bring it back to sunlight. I expect you to marvel at how glorious it is, child.'

Mary chuckled.

Goddess Neith raised her arms and her semi-naked body made swift change to golden glow. She called forth majestic song. For the longest time nothing happened. Mary watched her and felt their connection as she also reached into herself, as Neith had taught her, summoning her own song. The power emanating from the goddess was beyond anything Mary experienced to date.

The world around them shook. Sands trickled down dunes. Neith intoned great volumes of song and the rumble beneath grew in intensity. Sink holes appeared, swallowing sands into void. The dunes flattened and disappeared. A huge oblong of white marble began to slowly surface. It cleared dunes, lifting through them and up. The effect of the surfacing displaced and restructured the land. The building began to shape. As it lifted–growing into a huge platform of white marbled pillars–the giant colourful statues and murals depicting great battles dazzled splendour on Mary's eyes. Its elevation almost complete, the temple slowed.

Mary stood amazed at its beauty. Unlike the temple ruins filling most of the land, Neith's was bright, new, as they had once been. The Ancient Egyptian temple of the Goddess Neith stood proud. The sunlight bathed it for the first time in thousands of years. Its extravagance once more visible, beautiful, full of vibrant colour, and when it finished its ascent, Mary stared in awe.

'Did I not say it was magnificent?'

Mary nodded. 'I'm ... I'm ... lost for words.'

Neith laughed hard and slapped her back. 'Then that is also something to cheer. Come, let us go within. We may speak free here. There are things I would tell you, things you need knowledge of for coming days.'

Neith took her by the hand before she could ask the questions forming in her mind, and led her into the majestic temple.

City of Giza

King Ammon sat in deep concentration behind a desk in the old library, reading through documents Palash had handed him. They were a collection of reports on agricultural initiatives, construction projects, and a few scholarly programmes he'd personally endorsed. He looked at the growing pile and sighed. Administration was really not his forte.

'How am I supposed to know which of these things are of more or less importance? I really should get an assistant.'

A voice said, 'Muttering to yourself now, my King? I wonder where you could possibly have learnt that.'

Ammon swung from his chair in delight and threw himself at the old Osirian, who caught him in a great laugh. The boy hugged him tight.

'Teacher, I'm so happy to see you.'

'I am too, my young friend. I see young Palash has been feeding you more and more paper. One wonders how many trees have suffered since I was gone.' He looked hard. 'Please tell me you didn't start a war with the trees?'

Ammon laughed. 'Oh how I missed that dry sense of humour. But, you do make a very good point. I shall make it law: Henceforth, by order of the King. It is forbidden on pain of death for any tree, in my land, to ever be made into paper.'

Akhet said, 'Pain of death? Didn't you make it law already that no man would be harmed?'

'True. Hmm, well, what should be the punishment, then? Because I do feel quite justified to make exception here, then I won't have to suffer this.' He pointed to the pile.

Akhet laughed. 'You have grown so much, but joking aside. Trees are life baring things. With so few left, I would seriously consider an alternative to paper.'

Ammon picked up a document. 'Here, this is a report from Palash on that very subject. We've had agricultural meetings all morning.' He yawned. 'But enough of this. Take me into the sun and tell me what happened while you were gone. These nine months have been long without you. Oh, and it had better be a good story.'

'Nine months, you say? Goodness. You've grown at least five inches since I saw you.'

'And you've shrivelled and your beard is longer. Won't you tell me the story?'

'Yes. I will tell it and we will need good time to hear. But let us go out to a place free of the chatter of men.'

Ammon looked into him and frowned. 'Something is wrong, I see it inside you.'

Akhet shook his head. 'No, no, not at all. I have things I would say that I do not want overheard, that's all. Come, boy no longer, take my hand.'

Palash entered the king's chamber reading a new report. 'I have another one for you, my Lord. It's more of the same, I'm afraid. It's time–' A whisper made him look up, just in time to see King Ammon and Akhet fading into nothing.

Palash smiled. 'Welcome back, Akhet.'

The Temple of Neith

As Mary entered the first hall of the majestic temple, she found herself charged with its power. The design was extravagant, luminous, and stunning in ornate luxury. From arched empty windows white silk drapes fluttered in a warm breeze. Lined along the walls were many statues she recognised as Osirian. Mary came to one, larger than the rest. It was centred proud between them, a crook and flail across his chest. Unmistakable by giant Atef: Osiris, Lord of the Osirian. Neith came beside her.

'My brother no longer, as he once was.'

Mary nodded. 'This likeness is how we've always known him.'

Neith smiled. 'A Great King, formidable in power. The last high-born of my kind. I am the only one now lingering in this world.'

'The other Osirian have less power?'

'Truly. Etheria known now as Osiris is a blending of both king and queen. Her power is formidable, but the strength of both within diminished in her rebirth. My brother was a force in this world. He had no equal along with my sister, Isis, his queen. Her magic imbued the men of this world to become greater than they were. It is what still resides within kings and queens of today. Smaller perhaps and less potent.' Sadness crept across her face.

'I was not here when my brother sacrificed his form in the last battle with Beast. Had I been, things would have been different.'

Mary continued her wandering. 'This is a magnificent temple. It's smaller than I would have thought, certainly from the outside.'

Neith was pleased. 'Ah, but then appearances can be deceptive, can they not?'

Mary nodded. 'Yes.'

Neith's eyes never left those of her brother's statue.

'It was built by my loyal protectors. When I was first birthed onto this plane, I had no need of such places and rarely would I stay in this form long. I preferred to wander as spirit. Worshipers fashioned this temple and guarded it with fierceness and love I had never before experienced. But I had no real understanding nor did I choose to seek any.

'In this form, Osirian are able to feel and express the range of emotions defining humanity. I felt cursed by them, thus I stayed true to myself, refusing to form as I appear now. It was my brother who convinced me to accept it as gift. He challenged me in a way he knew I could not deny him. So with challenge accepted, I began frequenting this form more. I lived amongst men, experiencing concepts such as love, joy, sadness, and anger.' Neith touched the statue. A tear fell from her eye.

'I lost.'

'Lost?'

'Yes, my brother sang about the reward of being amongst humanity. I cursed him and threw his Songs down. I ground them into dust under my foot, but he did not flinch nor anger at my actions.'

"'Come let us make challenge, then.'"

"'What challenge would you make?' I asked him.'

"'Why for you to spend one rotation of this planet's course around sun, as one of them. I say opinions will be changed by it, or are you too afraid to try, noble sister?'"

'He was clever, for I was not gifted with the greyness of words. I replied, "I fear nothing as well you know."'

"'Then where is the harm in it?' He knew me too well and I cursed him. But I could not appear weak by refusing such dare. "Very well, brother-king, I accept. Be warned, I will show you the folly of your song" and he laughed hard at me, curse and bless him.'

"'One entire rotation, sister. If you win, or rather, if opinion remains, I will never broker subject again.'"

"'And if I lose, and change opinion, what then?' He came forward. He had a way of expressing his love without songs. He put his beautiful strong hand upon my shoulder. His touch always made me weak and would soften foul mood. "Then, beautiful warrior-sister, you win."'

Neith removed her hand from the stone, eyes moist.

'I miss those days, child. My heart is weary, heavy. It fails to leap with any joy at this new world of yours.'

Mary frowned. 'This isn't my world either, Neith. I've no love for it. You know that.'

'I do, child. We are much alike.' Goddess turned to mortal. 'More so, perhaps now, than first meeting?'

Mary released her frown. 'Where's your shrine?'

A wide smile flashed across her golden face, and she wiped the vestiges of tears away. 'It is beneath us, in the sanctuary. Come, let me show you.'

They descended spiral stairs carved from sandstone. It was not ornate, like the upper chambers. It opened up into a cavern that defied belief.

'Behold. My sanctuary.'

The cavern was enormous. The walls were mixings of rock and sculptures. Four identical statues of Neith, around fifty-feet high, held the crown of the cavern between their enormous hands. The source of light was not discernible. Along the skirt of the walls, sculpted in the typical art of Ancient Egyptian masculinity, were rows of men in loincloth, each holding a mixture of spears, swords, and daggers. Expressionless eyes on chiselled faces were turned in direction of the closest statue. Their heads adorned with crest bands, a uraeus centre most.

'This … this is absolutely stunning, Neith.' Her heart dropped as another thought invaded her mind. Neith caught the change.

'What is it, child?'

'I was … I was thinking of Albert. He'd be tickled pink to see this.'

Neith frowned. 'Tickled … pink?'

Mary laughed. 'Excited.'

'This is another way of expressing admiration? Being tickled by this pink?'

'Something like that, yes.'

'One of the first things I will do, when I am Goddess on High again, is to wipe all men of this language and make them learn the old tongue so I may understand words again.' They stared at each other, and then the corner of Mary's mouth lifted.

'Why Neith, I do believe that was your first joke.'

The goddess threw her head back in laugh and slipped a bangled arm around her. 'You will soon be ready to claim your love. I understand this longing within you.'

'Thank you.' Her gratified expression said much. She hesitated in question.

'You have more to say on this subject?'

'I have a plan, but I suspect you've already read it.'

'You speak truth. I have sensed the purpose of it.'

'Yet you said nothing?'

Neith raised an eyebrow. 'Was it not you who said *not* to ask your questions for you?'

Mary grinned. 'Well, what do you think?'

'About your idea to rescue your love?'

'Yes. Please. I'd really like you to tell me what you think.'

'Then I will do so. I think it dangerous, foolhardy, and without any doubt, almost certain to fail.'

Mary's heart sank.

The Great Goddess Neith spread a smile from ear to ear. 'In other words, child, it sounds like fun.'

'Oh Neith, I adore you.' Mary cried in joy.

'As well you should. Now come, let us walk these floors and perhaps you can be tickled with this pink, as well. I have one last thing to do to astound you.'

'I don't think you could do anything more today to astound me.'

Goddess shone golden, her eyes flashed along with a toothy grin. 'Is that a challenge?'

The Wastes of the East

Within the dust and devastation of what once held thriving city, about a mile from the east bank of the Nile, King Ammon and Akhet stood alone.

The boy looked outward with sadness. He found the deafening silence of desolation hard to bear. 'Why have you brought me to this horrible place?'

'It is time you saw something other than sand. It's time for you to grow up.'

'I see. Are we safe?'

'Safe?' Akhet looked hard at him. 'Good grief, no.'

The young king was thoughtful. 'Tell me something of the men that live in the darkness, Akhet.'

'Now is not the time for stories.'

Ammon sat on the black ground and smiled up at him. 'Yet I would hear one anyway.'

The old Osirian raised an eyebrow and smirked. 'Very well, then.'

He leant on his staff. 'The men here live in fear and oppression. The blight rising from the depth of the world has tainted and corrupted them. No longer as they once were. Now bitter, twisted, and hateful of everything and each other. The industries of the enemy, born within the borders of darkness, are turned to things other than the basic needs of man. They are tormented, incapable now of free thought, completely dominated by the black will of their master. The fate destined for all men who stray from the sanctuary of light.'

The king frowned. 'I do not think they are *all* evil.'

In mild irritation, Akhet said, 'Did you not hear my words?'

'I heard your interpretation of things, yes. But I refuse to believe all men have succumbed as you suggest. We are stronger than you give credit.'

Akhet grunted. 'You've read far too many books, young one.'

'At your suggestion, old man.'

A smile spread across his face. 'Indeed. Please do not dismiss my words as folly or fantasy. I have not dressed them up or down for your ears. What I say, I see in my mind, I feel its truth in my heart.'

'You have never been this difficult in conversation with me before. I begin to wonder what happened to you, while you were gone.'

The old man huffed and turned from him.

King Ammon stood. 'Have you walked amongst them?'

'Well, of course not! The very idea—'

'Then how can you truly know there aren't nomad groups lost in the wilderness? Untainted by the land? Desperate to find peace, with no idea how to? Tell me that, great Osirian. Tell me with certainty that all men in this darkness are unredeemable and I will believe you, and never speak of it again.'

He grunted a curse. 'I cannot speak with certainty about anything, but I know something of the world that boys don't. And they would do better for trusting in the wisdom of my judgement, above the foolishness of their books!' The irritation in his voice was uncharacteristic.

'Why are you so angry? It is not like you.'

Akhet's shoulders dropped. 'I'm sorry, my King. It's this place. We shouldn't have come. Yet now perhaps you see some sense of what this land does to a person? Even I am affected by it.'

'I don't feel affected.'

The old man looked hard. 'No, you don't.'

Lowering eyes, Ammon said, 'I feel great sorrow for their suffering.'

Akhet knelt before him. 'I know you do. And your altruism does you credit, but there is nothing to be done now to save them. Your own people need strength. Waste no more thoughts on unattainable goals.'

'They are my people, too.'

He let out an exasperated sigh. 'What is this idea festering in your mind?'

'I would seek to save all men. Not just the lucky ones, like me, who survived the destruction of the world, but the ones out there, too. Alone. Without hope. Desperate. Unloved.'

Akhet put a hand on the boy's forehead. 'Have you fever?'

Ammon's resolve was set firm. 'Why do you dismiss me so?'

'I do not dismiss you, my charge.' He stood and animated his response with great strides around him. 'I seek to dismiss the ideas from your mind. They are foolish. What you suggest … is impossible.'

'I do not believe anything is impossible, so long as hope remains. The Akhet who left me nine months ago would have said the same.' His response was calm and considered.

'It's out of the question.'

'Why?'

Akhet lifted his arms in exasperation. 'Because I say it is!'

In thought, the boy looked to the ground. He reached down and scooped up a handful of the ash at his feet. 'This is what man in this land lives on?'

'Yes, a blight of ash and dust, like most of this land, stark and lifeless.'

'You're wrong. There is life.'

'Life? If vile accursed creatures can claim that title, then yes, life there is. However cursed, unnatural, tainted, or distorted it may be. Like their views of the world. The life they knew is gone, washed away beyond reach.'

'I sense more than that.'

'What? Hmm? What do you sense that I do not?' Akhet flared in irritation.

'Above all? Courage.'

'Nonsense. There's nothing here but lies and deceit.'

The young king remained in a calm repose. 'I consider it my duty to free them. Is that such an unworthy goal?'

Now Akhet seemed to grow in size and a great sharpness laced his words.

'You filled your mind with ludicrous and romantic notions whilst I was away, foolish king, and they will lead you to crushing defeat. No I say, no, and thrice no! I forbid you to speak on this foolhardy topic again. You have predefined quest already. *That* is the goal you should set your mind upon, not this nonsense. Bah! Now I should leave before anger overcomes me.'

But the young king remained calm at the rebuke. He closed his hand and a light enveloped it. Akhet opened his mouth to say more, and then felt the power the boy employed. It wasn't from any song he had taught, and he could not discern its source.

'I bring life,' the young king said. He opened the hand and offered it up to his teacher. The ash once held was now gone. Sat upon his palm was a fine brown soil. Akhet stared in disbelief, his eyes widened.

'How have you done this?'

The boy smiled at him. 'I don't know how, I just knew I could.'

Osirian looked deep into calm young eyes. His uncertain hand reached out, taking a pinch of the soil, rubbing it between his fingers.

'This … this is impossible. Even I cannot turn slag and ash into soil, as you just have.'

'Impossible, Akhet? Twice now, you've said it, but perhaps you will stop. Nothing is impossible.'

Akhet opened his mouth, but the boy cut him off. 'There is more, see.'

King Ammon bent low placing soil on top of ash, and watched as it dissolved into fertile ground. From within, new vegetation curled and opened.

Both of them felt new life teeming in waves from it. Akhet looked between King and the land, his mouth hung open. For the first time in an age, a thing occurred before him he had no ability to explain.

The boy then said, 'I will tell *you* a story now. Years ago a great heavenly spirit took form through a boy, who was destined to become a king. When it left him, a trace of its grace remained. The boy could feel it, just out of reach. While his teacher was away doing other things, this boy figured out how to unlock its secret and learnt to commune with it. A melding of insights and knowledge occurred; it imbued the boy with a power beyond the understanding of even his old teacher, who stands now with his jaw slack in the most comical fashion.'

Akhet dropped to the ground, bowing as low as he could, and wept.

'Forgive this ancient and foolish old man who knows nothing. I will never question you again.'

The Sanctuary beneath the Temple of Neith

The great goddess elevated high into the air as her song wove incantations of complex design. The intensity of them created ripples around her, forming into a bubble of energy, growing in size. Her golden glow filled the cavern and Mary shielded her eyes. As the bubble coalesced, she became obscured by colourful swirls of mist bouncing around its confines. Her song was beautiful to behold and then, as the melody came to crescendo, the bubble burst outwards, filling the cavern with a magnitude of light and energy, knocking Mary off her feet.

The room plunged back to an unsourced illumination. Mary looked up to see Neith touch down to the sand with grace. Her skin tingled. Her eyes saw the goddess's shining aura as she came forward, helping her up from the ground. The room shook a little. Dust and sand fell from stone.

'Prepare yourself, child.' She smiled into the room.

'What's happening?'

'Did I not promise to astound you? Witness my last marvel of this day. See? My Army of Light awakens.'

Along the skirts of the wall, the sculptured statues burst from rock and stone. They filled the room in silent march. One by one, they came to formation before her, until there were too many to count. Warriors all. Golden, armed, and beautiful. When ranks were formed and no more came forth, they dropped to knee in perfect timing.

Mary looked over them and shook her head in amazement. The room rumbled once more. A crack appeared on one of the statues, and with a burst of sand and stone, a warrior– much larger and adorned in similar fashion to the goddess–stepped out.

He marched towards them, his eyes fixed on the goddess. Mary noticed the anticipation in his eyes, a wanton longing she'd not seen in a man for a long time. Neith revelled in his gaze. There was odd anticipation flowing from him and from Neith.

When he was before them both, he came to knee and lowered his handsome face. He exuded masculinity. Mary's heart fluttered at his proximity.

'My Queen,' he said in deep, rich voice. 'Too long have we been apart. Now, I despair no longer. I am overjoyed to feel your presence wash over me.'

Neith lifted his fine chin and their eyes met. 'Arise, beautiful husband. Take me, for I would taste your kiss upon my lips.'

He stood.

She, Great Warrior Goddess of Old, melted into muscular arms of her beloved husband, as he took her into his hard embrace.

Twenty-Two
The Scouts of Melrah

Blackenridge-North: Border of New Egypt

Melrah's pack of servant dogs reached the border between Blackenridge-North and New Egypt, and filtered out along it, merging into shadows. To other ears, their communication along the breeze sounded like any other calls from the wild. Sharp barks and howls echoed along lines of around one mile. The runners briefed, they ran back to each point and passed messages at set intervals. One of the lookouts from the King's Guard caught movement and sent call back to the camp. Melrah bounded forward and received his lieutenant.

The two shadows sovereigns of Beast bent over a rough map discussing their next moves. Melrah came beside them. The king stopped his discussion with Sam, and turned.

'You have news?'

Border is watched. No sign of enemy.

'Excellent. We are so far undetected?'

So far.

'Tell your lieutenants the pack must remain in shadow. You must forbid their engaging the enemy, even if hunger takes them.'

Already done. Loyal pack will wait for commands, or Melrah feasts well on them.

Shadow King laughed. 'Good. They will be rewarded with more flesh than they can consume.'

Close we are. The light there is strong.

'Yes, we must maintain cover in darkness. This is our best chance of surprise.'

I am to stay with King?

'No, my friend. Once we reach the border, I have another task for you.'

Send me away, you would?'

'I do not send you away easily, loyal companion. You will provide diversion only. You and your brethren are our best chance of drawing enough fighters out. You are faster, agile, and small. They are warriors of old. But not dull of sense. Pride will be their undoing. Once drawn, they will pursue until true intention is realised, but by then, it will be too late. Once their lines are thinned we will come forth unhindered, attacking from the front. You have the rear, and they will find themselves flanked. You understand this strategy?'

Understand, yes. Pleased by it? No.

The king raised an eyebrow. 'Why?'

Would not leave Great King. Melrah fears for his safety.

Arnold smiled. 'I am blessed by your loyalty, my friend. Go, instruct as I have commanded. We will meet at the border, and then new commands will be given. Once our task is complete, and the object safely collected, we regroup and head home to our Lord.'

Home?

'Yes, unless you have no desire to follow me further?'

Melrah bound to King. Where he goes, Melrah follows, until death.

Arnold-King knelt before him, stroking his massive head. 'Thank you, my friend.'

The Great Lord of dogs howled. Arnold took his head into his hands, planting a kiss on its crown. 'Be fierce, but above all, be safe.'

To Prince Sam, their conversation seemed one sided but he got the gist of it. He bade Melrah farewell and the giant dog licked his face. With that he left, disappearing into the night.

'The time draws ever near, I sense that much?'

Arnold nodded. 'Yes, closer we come to quest's end. I have you to thank for the smooth way it unfolds.'

'How so, Lord?'

'Wasn't it you who suggested turning these things to our advantage? And you were right. Melrah has become a great asset, one I would not lose easily.'

'Fond of him we have all become. His love for you is evident.'

'I also feel the same love for him, although I would never have thought it possible.'

Sam considered his next questions carefully. 'It is to love I would speak, my King.'

'A subject you've never raised before, speak your thoughts to me.'

'I would speak of the other quest I see upon your mind.'

The king flashed a dark look but Prince Sam remained expressionless. 'I read your purpose right enough? You would seek to rescue Mary and bring her back to us?'

'You read that from me?'

'Am I wrong?'

'No ...'

'You're annoyed by my foresight?'

Arnold contemplated his response. 'Perhaps.'

'I apologise for my intrusion into thoughts.'

King shook his anger away, and put hand on his shoulder. 'You meant well, Sam. The subject should be aired between us. Let me hear what you know and I will fill in the rest.'

'She is your soul mate, your queen. This I see, your purpose is to redeem her, but I do not see a clear outcome to it. Is it a wise quest?'

'I would have her back, and nothing will stop it. She will be the dark queen of all, and everyone will bow before her majesty.'

Sam put a hand on the king's arm. 'My Lord. My Captain. Know that I will bow before her majesty and be joyful. You have Underblade added to your arsenal now. I would lay ruin on anything standing between you when the time comes.'

'Thank you, brother. You are the only one I trust. Together, the three of us, will rule this world under our Lord's banner. I have love beyond words for you, and more so for her. But for now, we must concentrate discussion on this mission.'

Sam released him and felt the shadow inside him calling. 'That is well. I am in haste to do battle.'

'Then let us get to it. Here's what I know. ...'

The Prison of Light – Nubia Region

Lady of Light and Captain Lethor finished reviewing security of the Prison, and she felt better assured of its strength. A song erupted around them and Lethor's ears twitched. The Osirian sensed recognition as Lethor said, 'Another comes.'

'Yes, my brother-son Akhet.'

'Akhet? This is not a name I recognise.'

'You knew him as Horus, but he doesn't go by that name anymore.'

'Horus, you say? Mighty Horus?'

'The very same, but I wouldn't mention it. Akhet is the name taken from a boy's mouth, born on high, and loved as son. Until such time as it is revealed, I wouldn't say the old name aloud.'

'Well, now I feel strength and happiness. I do not care for reasons why he chooses a new one. Horus? Akhet? Whatever he decides to be called changes nothing. I will look upon the face of my old friend and smile.'

Her smile was tight. 'I will remain for a while longer.'

Lethor bowed.

The jackal warrior captain strode through chambers and hallways until he found himself out in the desert before Akhet and, to his surprise, a boy, who viewed him in quizzical fashion.

Lethor studied him, and turned head with smirk at Akhet who, like always, leant heavy upon his staff.

In an ancient tongue few knew, Lethor said: *'So, I'm told I must refer to you as Akhet now, is that so?'*

'It is the name I travel by, yes.'

'This name was given thee, by this boy?'

'I see your skills haven't diminished, nor your eyes, old friend.'

Lethor shifted those same eyes to Ammon. *'What is this, then? You bring a man-child here, of all places? This is no place for men and you know better than most why.'*

Akhet didn't hide his amusement. *'Do not fear him, old warrior friend. This is no ordinary child of man. He is a bloodline descendant to the true Pharaoh. He is also more than even I can see, but enough of that, I say, what happened to your manners while you slept, eh?'*

Lethor came forward and grabbed the Osirian in warm embrace. For a moment they held each other by the arms and the long friendship between them could be read in their eyes.

Lethor said, *'If you weren't Osirian, and my friend, I would cut off aging head for bringing this boy here. My lunch was larger.'*

'Trust me when I say, appearances should not be underestimated. And, old friend Lethor, your sword would dull, rust, and wither to ash before head departs and falls from its cut, or have you forgotten our last sparring match?'

'Aye, truer words have never been spoken. As for the match, I concede you as victor, but only by a hair.'

Akhet laughed.

'*Well*,' Lethor said observing Ammon again, '*it seems harmless enough. Why is it here?*'

'*Harmless he is not, I assure you. Here? Because I choose that he should be and that is enough for jackal captains.*'

'*It is not safe for something so small and frail, where large feet may squash it without ever knowing it was underneath.*'

Ammon then said, '*I would suggest you look where you are walking then. You certainly have large enough eyes for the task.*'

They both stared in shock.

Ammon smirked. '*What? You thought this boy wouldn't know your ancient tongue? Wiser men would consider their audience before engaging in secret conversations they assume I would not hear or understand.*'

Lethor said to Akhet, '*You taught this boy our words?*'

Akhet shook his head. '*No, I did not.*'

'*Akhet forgets I excel in linguistics. But the Servant of the Light did teach me one thing: manners. I would consider it courtesy, if you neither referred to me as "it", nor continue a conversation regarding me, as if I wasn't standing right before you. Surely even Captain of the Guard of Songs should acknowledge a king of man, when he stands some feet before him? If he would but greet, I would say hail, I am Ammon, honoured to meet him.*'

Akhet smiled wide.

Lethor stared for a moment. Something in the calm way he put things, in the old tongue, gave the boy age and wisdom beyond his youth. Lethor knelt down in front of him.

'Oh, wise King called Ammon. You speak as few have since last I was awake in this world. I am pleased to greet thee, Little King of men. I would ask him, how come he speaks the language of old? And I would beg he grants old warriors forgiveness, for stubborn and impolite ways.'

Ammon smiled at him. 'You are forgiven, magnificent warrior.'

Lethor bowed head low, and then stood. He looked sideways at Akhet. 'Are you sure you taught this boy? He is well-spoken and wiser than you ever were.'

Akhet was again humbled by the king. 'You speak much truth, old friend. Ammon, this is Lethor, the Captain of the Prison of Light Guard.'

Ammon inclined his head. 'It is my pleasure, again, Lethor. As to your question about language, I study hard. I like to read, but languages are something I find very easy to pick up. It only took a little time.'

Lethor reached out and was amazed by the power emanating from him. 'You have power within, young King. I read some of it, but I am not as skilled as others. A sword I would choose, over words and songs. In my friend here, a better teacher you could not find. So, I call you friend, too. Friend of Lethor.'

The boy reached out and stroked his greying fur. 'You are hard warrior, ageless … a soft heart beats within you and something more. Illusive. I sense you are the holder of many secrets. I also sense you don't like me probing you.'

He narrowed his eyes. 'I guard and hold knowledge of much, little one. Yes, there are things in me I would not share, until I am certain of loyalty. You understand?'

'I do. I hope, in the fullness of time, where friendships transcend secrets, we can share in knowledge. But for now, I am proud to call you friend. But my teacher is not friend alone. He is like a father and I love him beyond the world itself.'

Akhet beamed at Ammon's love for him.

'Aye, that much I read.'

The Osirian said, 'Lethor, you must show him the Library of Song within these walls. There is knowledge here, Ammon, I know you will find useful and insightful, would you not agree, Lethor?'

'Why yes, he shall be welcome. But to other matters I sense you would turn conversation?'

'I would. Where is my sister?'

'She is inside. I will tell her you seek her counsel, as I take my new friend, most noble king of little men, to the Library of Song.' He turned to Ammon. 'There are great texts within no eyes of man have seen in thousands of years. Books, you say? I will show you books!'

King Ammon took Lethor's hand. Lethor chatted as they sauntered towards the entranceway. Akhet followed their backs with a smile. A whisper on the wind caught his attention. He narrowed his eyes and scanned the unscalable walls.

Two Osirian stood alone in the shade of the high craggy rocks. Osiris put a hand through the crook in his arm and they ambled around the stone perimeter.

'What troubles you? I felt your brooding long before you arrived.'

'I cannot say for certain, but we must discuss Ammon.'

'Very well, I am listening.'

He stopped and disengaged from her. She saw the turmoil within him and frowned. 'Sing to me. What is it that worries you so?'

'Ammon is no longer human.'

Osiris blinked a few times. 'I have not seen any change inside him, why do you say this?'

'Because whilst I was acting more foolish than usual in the blackest lands this world now possesses, he reached down before me and took a handful of ash and slag, and made it fertile by his touch alone.'

Osiris set her jaw firm. 'No songs? Just touch?'

Akhet said, 'No song. Just three words. "I bring life".'

Her eyes widened. 'You sensed nothing?'

'Oh, I sensed the power when the boy employed it. *Greth'nnia Delfor'sona.*'

'The Great Song ... how?'

'He told me. There is trace of our Great Maker's grace left within him. Apparently he learnt to commune with it. For emphasis, grew selections of carrots afore old eyes, in the black ash of desolation. We must tell the others. Our plans need to be altered.'

'Explain.'

'He would seek quest to rescue all men.'

She frowned. 'Impossible.'

'I know. Nevertheless, he won't be put off. Believe me, I've tried.'

Osiris pondered a while. 'He cannot make this quest alone.'

'He wouldn't be alone, Etheria. His people are loyal, his servants even more so.'

'Meaning you?'

'Meaning me, yes.'

'Brother-son, he has quest. The importance of it cannot be over emphasised. Through our Great Maker he is shown wisdom, and now he would abandon it for his own desires? And you would not re-steer his course?' She shook her head. 'I should never have paired you two. I should have foreseen this turn of events.'

'You misunderstand things. I would do whatever this boy commands. He is conjoined now, the spirit of our Great Maker at his call. You think the boy's choices are his alone? You would put your faith in what is right, above his? Above the boy who can bring life where neither of us could? Above the Songs of the Ardunadine themselves? Come, sister-mother, I know you better. Conjoined mother and father, do not dismiss what I say as fantasy. This boy is developing into something more than anticipated, greater than even we foresaw. It is of destiny I speak. The boy no longer has clear path.'

'What do you mean?'

'That is why I came to you. I cannot see beyond today, with him. I'm cut off to his fate, no longer do I see the various facets his choices would lead him. It's as though I were as blind as a child still within womb. But you, Etheria? You are better at such things. I would ask you to assuage fears, and show me, I'm not losing my mind.'

Osiris understood. 'I will look into the boy and see if I can find a touch of this power. Truly he is blessed, but if he is what you say, and I do not doubt you, he is *not* safe here.'

'For the time being, he is safer here, with us and the Guard, than alone in his library of books.'

She looked up into the sky and closed her eyes. 'We must convene gathering, but now is not the time.' She turned back. 'When the danger is passed, we can address all these issues and fears together.'

He sighed, relieved. 'Thank you. The heaviness upon me is lifted.'

'Because you care for him?'

'Yes.'

'Because you love him?'

'Yes.'

She smiled. 'Oh brother-son, it is not—' Danger overwhelmed her.

Osiris burst into light, turning faster than thought. Throwing out her arms, she issued great shrieks in chorus, sending arcs of light outwards. When the wave hit, a number of giant black-blue dogs were revealed. At being discovered, they squealed and yelped, running away as fast as they could. Akhet raised his staff, banging it hard on the ground. A shockwave chased after them. It caught one or two in their escape and they fell to the ground. The others made it away, safe.

Lethor and his guard emptied the prison and gathered around them.

'What are these things?' Lethor said, poking one.

'Servants of the enemy,' Lady of Light replied.

Akhet looked around him. 'Where is Ammon?'

'He is safe, reading the books.' Again Lethor poked at the body. 'Is it dead?'

Akhet shook his head. 'No, stunned only.'

He pointed the sword tip of his staff at the ground. 'Then I will cut its head off.'

The old Osirian grabbed his staff. 'Do no such thing, foolish jackal! I will learn more if it is still able to think! Once I am done, you may do as you please.'

'Very well, Lord Akhet, but I will stand here with sword ready and no further words from you will cease hand, if this thing does but twitch a whisker. Nothing dark has entered this far into my keep, and I would be ready for more invisible things who dare to try.'

Akhet knelt beside the giant animal. 'These dog-like creatures were shielded from our Light in the Songs of Shadows and Darkness. How they breached our defences in daylight I could not say, but we have knowledge of it now and therefore, we can form defence. It is highly unlikely they will try this tactic again.'

Osiris came beside him. 'This boldness, it is from him, Arnold Shadow King. He has become a shining black light in their wicked darkness. Never before have servants of the enemy been able to get this far into the light without our knowing. His power is growing by the day.' She leant down and touched the dog with her staff. 'Brother, these things hold limited intelligence. What do you hope to learn from them?'

'The path by which they came. At the very least, it will give us clues.'

Lethor said, 'Clues? To what they eat? '

'To their master's intentions, of course. These are scouts. They pose no danger at all. No, they were sent to see the lay of things and report it back. Well, that is just what they are doing. It would help to know how far they came. I should be able to gain images from this thing's mind and determine its path. Then we have some indication of the length of time we have to make ready for their attack.'

Lethor growled. 'You are certain attack would be made upon this place?'

'I am, and so is Etheria, or have you forgotten why she came?'

Osiris said, 'You are wiser than I.'

'I know, now let me do my work.'

He laid hand over the head of the stunned dog. A light shone from him. Even paralysed, the dog writhed from the Osirian's probing. Akhet took in as much as the creature's mind would give up and then sighed.

'There wasn't much, but I do at least know from what direction they come. The dark lands to the south, what man once called Sudan.' Osirian stood and walked towards the entrance. Lethor remained.

Akhet continued. 'Once dog legs carry news, maybe a day, depending on their numbers. We should assume our enemy would be upon us inside three days. This may be shortened as they are discovered. The news isn't all negative.'

'How so?' Lethor leant on his staff, as the two of them drifted away.

'They were hoping to catch us unaware, Lethor. It suggests a small group only. Now we are alerted, and have time to mount defence, their attack will be less certain.'

Lethor turned back to the dog lying on the ground. 'These things,' he called over his shoulder, 'you've learnt all you can from them?'

'Yes,' Akhet said without looking back.

'Good.'

Lethor lifted his sword-staff. With a roar, he swung down hard.

The guards set up in defensive positions.

'I will remain to defend this place, you must go,' Osiris said.

Akhet shook his head. 'No. You go back and convene gathering.'

Osiris hit staff on the ground in protest. 'Now is not the time for argument, brother-son.'

'Do as I say!'

She recoiled from his sharpness, as did Lethor.

He softened his tone. 'I will stay and protect this place, Etheria. I will stop them from freeing my brother, for that must surely be the intention? If they are somehow able, *I* will put them down. If my brother is freed, I will put him to rest, permanently. I know you, Etheria. You would never be able to do it, so stop your protests and heed my counsel.

'You are my sister. You are my father and my mother also. I love you. But know this. I am father today and I say, as he once said, "Bring me back an army." Now go. Do not argue. Just go.'

Osiris nodded and felt deep pride at his nobleness. 'What of Ammon, should I leave him here with stubborn master?'

Akhet laughed and broke tensions. She saw warmth in his fearful eyes.

'Yes, leave him with me. I sense he will serve better by my side, although why, I cannot yet tell.'

She put a hand on his face. 'Be careful, brother-son. Do not let fear imprison you.'

'I would be less fearful if you could persuade Neith to aid us.'

'I will do what I can, but you know how it is with her?'

'Play to her vanity, get to Mary. You still have link? Mary will help us, and through her, Neith will not refuse. They have grown in companionship. You know Neith's weakness, or at least my father in you knew it. Use it. She could never refuse him, so become his power.'

'I do not know if I can.'

'Now I say; you must put aside *your* fear. We will hold off the attacks as best we can, until you are able to reinforce us.'

She became ethereal. 'I will do as you say.' She turned to Lethor. 'Be well. Guard my brother-son and his charge.'

'With my life, my Lady.'

She smiled at them. 'I command neither of you to leave this world before me.'

With a twinkle in her eyes, she faded from view.

Blackenridge-North - Border of New Egypt

The shadow-dogs ran as fast as legs would carry them. They stopped at checkpoints, found brothers who switched, taking with them news to the next. This continued until they arrived at border's camp. Melrah took reports and grunted orders to them. He bound over to the king, who sat with his eyes closed, taking in everything Melrah said. Sam saw a great anger pass over him, and even Melrah cowered away. They talked for a long time, the king commanded him to repeat things, over and over. When he had learnt all he could, he dismissed him, and Melrah all but ran from his side.

Arnold-King closed his eyes and surfed waves of darkness for answers. He remained deep within his wrath for the longest time.

In the distance, the men heard great roars; it chilled them. A violent exchange of whining and yelping followed. The ferocious battle came to abrupt end in a horrifying series of screams. Not much time passed before Melrah strutted back into the camp, his head high, fur matted with blood. He made eye contact with his master, whose fury then subsided.

The King stood and marched. He stroked Melrah's head as he passed and continued on towards the men. Sam moved beside him as he launched into voice.

'Loyal guard, we are close to destination. You should know, for I would never lie to you. This battle will be hard fought. The risk taken to gather information was not successful and this failure has, as you just heard, been rewarded with swift justice from their master. Our enemy is now aware of us and possibly our intentions. They have no doubt also discerned the timetable for our attack. So, I will adjust the plans, but this is where I need your courage.

'We will go in two groups. Sam will lead one, I the other. We will call upon allies to create new diversions, alongside our canine friends; for they have done at least one good deed tonight. We know there are two Osirian and we also know they've woken the old prison guardians. Do not be under any illusion. The Osirian, for the moment, are beyond any of you.

'The prince and I will handle the Osirian. The prison guard, we will leave to you. Their captain is formidable, with little weakness I know of. I will ponder strategy along the way. We set out in one hour. Be ready to ride. Victory is at hand. Victory will be ours! Curse the Light, victory brings darkness, darkness is life.'

They cheered and hooted in their agreement.

Twenty-Three
A King is Lost

New Egypt: The Border of Nubia

His eyes never left the single path leading into the hidden sanctuary. The night was long, and the darkness deep. But his light was so bright and so fierce the night could find no hold on him. He remained as he had for many hours, standing in unwearied watch, sensing any changes in the land around. There was whisper of movement. Akhet felt Lethor's approach.

'Anything?'

'Yes,' he whispered. 'Eyes. Eyes in the dark; the servants of our enemy surround us. We are watched from all sides.'

Lethor looked up and noticed them. 'More of these dog-things?'

Akhet nodded. 'And others. It won't be long now.'

The warrior growled. 'We will be ready. Let them come, and they will fall upon our swords. Their vile nature will stain the rocks of my keep.'

'What of my charge?'

'He is restless, weary, but I have guard watching him. We will keep him safe. You can count on that, old friend.'

Akhet was relieved, but he seemed more bent than usual.

'I fear this night might be the last we have.'

'Do not say such things. We have lived through many dark times, and we will sing songs of these, too. If you would seek rest, I am ready to stand watch?'

'Thank you, but no. I am better choice, for I see far more than you, great friend. In time, your sword will be added to my staff, until then, I command you rest.'

Lethor bowed his head. 'As you wish.' He turned and marched back into the light. Akhet waited until the secret doorway closed behind him.

He turned back his vigil, aware of many eyes upon him. He stood now, a beacon within the darkness. His powerful eyes did not blink as he continued watching.

Ammon was plagued by vivid dreams. He opened his eyes. The call he felt was still heard, deep inside his mind. Throwing off the linen sheet covering his naked body, he dressed and found his shoes. The giant guard at the door to his room barred entry or exit. He approached. The guard turned.

'Young King, you should be sleeping.'

Ammon yawned. 'Yes, but I'm not finding sleep easy. I'd like to get a book from the library.'

The guard lowered his head, and stepped aside. Ammon moved past and guard followed. He stopped, turning around sighing.

'There really is no need to follow me. I know the way.'

The warrior tilted his head and frowned. 'I am commanded to never leave your side, Little King. Your words may not change commands given.'

'I understand.'

Ammon was thoughtful. 'Then take my hand. We will walk the halls together.'

The warrior did as instructed and as he took the small hand, Ammon turned into golden hue.

His voice was slow and modulated. 'Hear me, warrior of old.'

'I hear you,' he said in a calm voice.

Ammon commanded, 'Go back to your post at my door. There you will remain, and remember nothing of what transpired.'

The warrior released his hand, and marched away.

Ammon reached inside for power he knew lay dormant, and with a smile, faded from view.

He rounded corners and passed unseen through chambers, amazed at the complex's size. He could understand how the builders of the ancient temples of his people had been influenced by these designs. He passed by warriors who rested in bunks of cots. They seemed in the same state of readiness as those who were on guard. There was something magical about them. They were anatomically human except for jackal heads and their giant size. Ammon peered into them and discovered he could understand the complexity of their design, too.

Bred on Earth, their abilities enhanced making them formidable opponents, almost godlike.

Ammon continued to slip unnoticed through corridors, finding himself in a maze of small sepulchres. Each had a cartouche naming the occupant. The walls were filled with paintings and pictograms. Within the warren of hallways he somehow knew which paths to take. The young king kept himself hidden from all who would sense him. It was a trick recently discovered, thanks to Lethor.

The boy had found many books in the Library of Song, all with ancient texts and forgotten knowledge. Lethor had no idea what half the books contained, but Ammon knew. He'd found books of spells, the incantations of which he memorised and took their secrets for his own. Insight had helped source specific books necessary for him to develop a deeper understanding of the Great Spirit within him. And develop it, he did.

Just out of phase with the world around him, he moved with supressed excitement. He felt Captain Lethor approach and froze. If anyone might see through his cloak, it would be him. The old warrior, however, trudged through the corridor oblivious of him. Ammon waited until he'd passed by before he let out a held breath. Lethor reached the end of the corridor and hesitated in his turn. Something made him pause. His eyes narrowed as he scanned along the path he'd just trod. The boy did not wait to see what happened next. He skirted around and down a smaller passage. It opened into a cavernous chamber.

What he saw within made his young eyes widen.

The hall was bare except for an enormous upright slab of glass-like crystal. No more than an inch thick, at least fifty feet in height and ten feet across. At its corners, golden brackets fixed it in place above and below. He looked in. At first, Ammon thought he saw the opposite side of the cavern, but it soon became evident it was another room, existing inside the giant crystal slab. A doorway of some kind, he conjectured.

A strange whisper in his senses alerted him to something. He walked around the crystal mirror and saw the object the unknown voices guided him towards. At the far end of the room sat an enormous uncut gemstone on a pedestal of gold encrusted with gems, and decorated in ornate alien carvings. Ammon felt its power and knew what it represented. With caution he went towards it. When he neared, a radiant power emitted, calling to him. Ammon was close enough to touch it, a nervous hand came forward, when a beam of light captured and enveloped him. Ammon, in terror, found he was powerless to move.

A voice entered his mind, quashing fears.

'Welcome, son of man. You were expected,' it said.

Ammon's eyes then burnt and his vision disappeared.

When sight was returned he found himself on his back looking up at an alien sky. He stood, transfixed by the wonder of the place. He was within a huge temple made entirely of crystal.

Ammon watched as rays of ruby-red shimmered and bounced off some form of invisible shield. With no understanding of anything and deep sense of wonder, he stared at the sky. It was alive with exploding flashes of purples, blues, and reds. He saw magnificent clouds of gold–not white–shifting, growing, and shrinking. The sky exploded with colours he'd never seen. They reflected off his eyes.

A great fear of heights was one of Ammon's secrets. The floor was clear and he swallowed, cast eyes downwards, and his fear melted to awe. Below him–far below him–mountains coloured orange sat in a crooked line, their peaks covered in purple snow. Large birds flew underneath, occasionally diving into sparkling turquoise rivers, running as far as his eyes could see. It was a beautiful, wonderful world.

With courage, he took tentative steps on the crystal floor. He came to examine a colossal see-through pillar. It appeared to be holding up the sky. His confidence increasing, he ventured forward. He soon became aware of strange musical whispers. His eyes drawn to rolling, smoky mist manifesting in front of him, and from within, ethereal wisp-like beings shimmered into existence, one after the other. Their whispered songs grew louder in strength until a unified phonological chorus of cosmic melody erupted, as eight wraithlike beings began to manifest. They shimmered in soft glow, taking solid, yet also gaseous ghost-like form. It was nothing like Akhet or any of the other Osirian's true shape. These were not spirits or ghosts. He felt their heavenly chorus cleanse his fears.

At first, Ammon found it difficult to understand their lexis. They whispered incomprehensible blends of symphonic chatter, but as it went on, his mind began translating them. It took time but odd words came into focus, whole phrases then followed. Their superior alien dialect was a blend of many languages he'd learnt on Earth and from Osirian. But their complex lexicon and delivery was so evolved, it was impossible for a human brain to comprehend them. The changes within him somehow adjusted the ability to process and comprehend them. The wraiths perceived the change as they encircled him.

Ammon felt no ill purpose from them.

One glided forward as spokesperson.

'We are Ardunadine, Lords of Songs named the Righteous. Welcome!'

Ammon bowed. 'I'm no longer on Earth, am I?'

'You stand in the Celestial Temple of Song, young one.'

'How did I get here?'

'You traversed the Destorian Travestial entryway.'

'That large crystal thing, that's a doorway to here?'

'Yes. Every world in our network has such a link. Few are able to find them. Those who stumble upon them have no understanding of what they represent. They connect to the Temple of Songs, and within, the power of Songs derives. Beings, who are thus worthy, are able to draw on them through this same network.'

'Like the Osirian?'

'Yes, the Servants of Light draw strength from our Songs.'

'But not all of their power comes from here?'

'No, they are our children. We gave them life so that they could wander out into the universe.'

Ammon said, 'If I may ask, can they die?'

The notes of the song shifted. 'They are not as mortal men.'

'If their earthly form is bound to one place, and that form ends, will their spirit remain, or be lost?'

'We see your meaning now. The spirit of the Children of Light will return through the gateway.'

'But I am not like them. How was I able to come here?'

'You were granted the necessary molecular changes when Arrandori communed with the people of your world, through your form.'

'Am I the first from my world to come?'

'Yes, Ammon, your song is part of the Ardunadine chorus, now. We will sing to you and you will have answers to the many questions forming in your mind.'

For an age they sang. Ammon had no comprehension of how much time passed. The song's power was overwhelming, his earthly being lifted, bursting into light. Knowledge filled him as they conjoined. Ammon lost physical form, floating amongst and within them. He somehow retained his identity, but his body had long since ceased to exist. He saw things in a way he could now process. They filled him with wisdom, history, and a deeper understanding and connection to the universe around him.

He saw them for what they were. He knew a year in normal words could be spent, and still he'd be unable to explain them. They were beyond human concepts, but no longer beyond him. They existed as blending of intellect, knowledge, and life creating abilities, passed down through one-hundred-thousand generations of evolution.

Inside his mind he heard Akhet's voice. 'As a sun ripens fruits and gives its life and warmth to all living things, so shines the Songs of Light on all– black of heart or otherwise–filling them with the fire of love and great understanding.'

The Temple of Neith

Mary sat brushing her hair in front of the mirror. Since her life had been turned upside down, she retained a few things of normality. One of them was the long process of making ready for bed. The nights in the temple were often warm. When she finished, she stood and sat in the archway of her window, allowing the breeze to wash over her; she closed off senses and reached into the dark.

She found him, as she always did, in despair and agony. The power within her was impatient, holding longing, wanting action. Mary calmed it with new techniques.

A cough behind brought her back within her bedroom. She turned and found one of the attractive young warriors standing behind her.

He was completely naked.

'My Lady,' he said. 'My goddess declared you restless and unable to sleep. She thought I might help relieve tensions?'

Despite everything she had seen and been through; despite the destruction of her world, and the ridiculousness of what came after, Mary was still embarrassed by nudity. She turned her eyes from him. He looked confused.

'My Lady? If I do not please, I will summon another?'

Mary chuckled. Then the absurdity of Neith's simple thinking took hold and she laughed. She laughed so hard she cried. The naked warrior was unsure how to react.

At length, Mary asked, 'Do you do this often?'

She felt him puff his chest. 'I am a warrior in the bed as well as the battlefield. I have not lost a fight yet.'

Turning, she looked him up and down, pushing through embarrassment.

'You are a very attractive man.'

He was pleased by her words.

'What is your name, great warrior?'

He looked stunned. 'I … my Lady, I do not have a name.'

'That's ridiculous.' She put her hands on her hips. 'Everyone has a name.'

For the first time since he'd stepped into the room he seemed unsure.

'You are testing me?'

'Testing you?' Mary did not hide her confusion. 'No, I'm not testing you. Look, I'm called Mary, what was your name, at birth?'

Again he faltered. 'I cannot say it.'

'Why?'

His expression changed now. She noticed his turmoil. He was sweating. She had somehow broken him of his strength, his courage. And she didn't understand how. Mary watched his shoulders hunch, and hands carefully covered his pride. His eyes were cast to the floor.

'It is forbidden.'

'What is? To say your name?'

He looked at her, frightened. 'Please, my Lady. I must not. I cannot. I will not. Now … I will go. I have not succeeded in winning you. May my goddess's strike upon me be merciful.'

'Wait. Stay, please.'

'I dare not, Lady.' He moved towards the doorway.

The impatient power within her burst forth and took control. Mary, who had desires and longing of her own but could never express them, allowed it.

'Stop,' she commanded in a voice dripping in power. 'Turn around and face me.'

Unable to disobey, he turned as commanded. When their eyes met, he saw her new form—beautiful and terrible—and dropped to his knees.

'Forgive me, my Lady.'

Mary shone in a golden glow—yet also tinged with black—eyes blackened also, with thin golden slits in their centre. He was lost in her radiant power, her strength, and it excited her. She beckoned him.

'Come to me, warrior.'

Powerless to refuse, he came forward transfixed.

'I would have you confident again.'

She touched his chest and felt the change in him. His confidence and bravado returned. He stood before her proud, striking in his masculinity. She pushed him hard onto the bed.

Mary had given in to her power now, channelling it from the depths of darkness, manifesting it as Neith instructed. A sense of the goddess's nature bolstered alongside her own, levying controls she was either unwilling, or unable to. She took the young warrior in a way she would never have done as plain Mary Wilson.

He looked up at her with passion in his blue eyes, and Mary noted, a little fear.

In her chamber, the Goddess Neith lay awake within her own sheets. She felt the change in Mary and smiled. She sat up, closed her eyes, taking in all she could.

'Finally,' she breathed happy, 'you unleash the hidden power and take something you do not need, yet want. Sweet Mary, you are now ready for my next lessons.'

Neith fell back into her bed and laughed. The man beside her stirred and she stroked his hair in silent thought.

New Egypt – The Border of Nubia

The morning light crept over the western wall and the shadow of night was lifted. Akhet came back within himself and sighed. There was no sign of the enemy now, even his scouts and spies had slithered away from the sun. He turned to the entrance, weary, and a group of guardians met his approach.

'Put watch on the path, two forward, two back. And have three on compass points above. Our enemy may not attack in daylight, but his spies may still lurk. Go.'

They marched out as ordered. Akhet trudged into the complex and allowed the power within to rejuvenate him. He came to the guard outside the king's room, who moved aside and allowed him to enter.

Akhet flew into a rage never before heard. The guardian trembled at his wrath.

'Lord, he did not leave this room. I swear on my oath and my life.'

Captain Lethor along with a number of his men came forth in a hurry.

'What is it?'

Akhet turned to him, face a mix of anger and fear. 'Ammon is missing. Search the entire complex!'

Lethor barked at the guards that followed him; they ran to command.

The warrior, who guarded the room, lowered eyes at Lethor's stern gaze.

'I do not understand how he could have passed me? I stayed at my post until morning's call. Never have I failed as I have this night, Lord. My life is yours to take.'

Lethor grimaced. 'It is true, Lord. This man is one of my best. I vouch for his integrity and honour.'

'Your best, you say? Well with best like this we are *all* doomed!'

Captain of the Guardians of Light said nothing.

Akhet swallowed his anger and turned to the guard, whose head was bowed low. He reached out and put his hand between the warrior's great ears. Akhet reached deep within his warrior mind. What he found there made him curse aloud. He heaved a sigh.

'There will be no taking of lives this day, loyal warrior. The boy bewitched you. It was not of your doing.'

The guard lifted his head, relieved yet confused. 'Bewitched? How so?'

'He used an old Osirian trick of persuasion. He must have learnt it in the books.' He flashed a look at Lethor who shrugged.

The warrior snapped his fingers. 'Books? Yes, he wanted to go to the library ...' He looked aghast.

Akhet smiled in sympathy and put a comforting hand on his shoulder.

'You see? You're remembering.'

Lethor then cursed.

Akhet said, 'What is it?'

'I had sense of something, last night, in the corridors to the old catacombs. But as my eyes did not see anything, I dismissed it.'

Akhet pushed aside the guard. 'Show me!'

Twenty-Four
Dawn of Darkness

New Egypt: The Prison Shard

Lethor followed the agile old Osirian down weaving paths until they found themselves at the opening to the great Shard. Akhet paused before entering; his eyes never leaving the giant crystal slab. Lethor bent down surveyed the ground.

'He came through here. His prints are easy to spot, such small feet.'

Akhet nodded. 'Yes, and he didn't come out, either.'

Lethor followed his gaze. 'The Shard is undisturbed, his trail leads around.'

He made a move to enter, but Akhet stopped him. 'No, he is for the moment, lost. I would not enter this chamber till I knew more about why Ammon was compelled to. Let us leave. I do not sense he was pulled against his will, and no darkness has penetrated my thoughts on the subject. It would be wise for us to continue getting ready for our inevitable battle.'

The warrior captain agreed. 'Come, then. There is something I would show you. It might aid us in our fight.'

'Unless it is a great sword that can cleave shadow without songs, I fear whatever it is, will be of little use.'

'Fair point. Then shall we make ready?'

Akhet grunted.

He walked away, and Akhet stood staring at the portal for a while longer, then turned and followed.

Inside the great Shard a mist stirred. In silence, it formed into a dark-skinned man in a filthy white robe. Burnt-amber eyes stared out from an old-looking hybrid animal face.

*

The Temple of Neith

Mary.

A voice woke her with a start. Beside her lay the sleeping warrior. The sheets twisted. Nightdress now torn and shredded. She rubbed her face, eyes locked upon the sleeping vulnerable man who purred gently to the rhythm of his breathing. Mary got out of bed and found another nightdress. She replayed the events of the previous night, thinking to find herself ashamed but wasn't. In contemplations, she poured a glass of water from the crystal jug that wasn't there the night before.

Mary.

That voice again, calling. She moved to the arched window and looked out. It was now dawn. The first rays of the morning's sun peeking above the horizon. In the courtyard below a flicker of something white move behind a column. Mary looked back at her bed, then tip-toed out. She took a straight quiet path, down corridors, through royal chambers, emerging into the mild warmth of the morning's air.

Mary found her sitting on a low wall, and smiled.

'What are you doing skulking around out here, Osiris?'

'I have good reason why I don't want to be seen or overheard.'

'Neith?'

Osiris gave a slow nod. 'Let us go where we can talk, you permit this?'

Mary looked down at her thin nightgown, and then shrugged. 'Okay, but somewhere private.'

Osiris took her hand. Moments later, they stood upon a horseshoe cliff. Mary saw an arc of three-hundred feet of unscalable rock. It surrounded a single path leading in and out of a great cavern. It looked artificial. Osiris came beside her.

'Below us is the Prison of Song.'

'Prison? What do you need a prison for?'

'What does anyone need prisons for, Mary? To keep something locked away from those who need protection from it.'

'But, why do *you* need one?'

Osiris sighed. 'For the very reason I have just explained.'

Mary gave an exasperated exclaim. 'You Osirian! I'm sure you deliberately misinterpret our words. You know exactly what I mean.'

Osiris lowered her eyes. 'Yes. I'm sorry. The habit of only answering direct questions is old. I apologise. Yes, I know what you meant.'

Mary accepted her apology and looked hard at her.

A tear fell from Osiris's eye.

'What's wrong?'

'So much, Mary, I hardly know where to start. Let me first start by telling you that inside this prison is a fallen Osirian.'

Mary didn't seem surprised. 'Let me guess, Seth? Sutekh?'

Osiris nodded. 'Yes, even the history of your world records his terrible deeds.'

'You have him contained in there, and well-guarded, I presume?'

'For the moment.' Osiris seemed to grow. 'But he cannot be freed. He mustn't be free! I sacrificed too much and now, everything is unwinding.'

'You're talking about the conjoining?'

'Yes. Neith explained this to you?'

'There isn't much we don't discuss.' Mary crossed her arms. 'Out with it, you wanted me away from Neith to ask something. I have a pretty good idea what. And I know her well enough to say she runs on her own timetable.'

'I've come to beg your assistance.'

'Go on.'

'Mary, the darkness comes, and it comes here, this night.'

'Arnold?'

Osiris nodded. 'I fear so. Along with many of his followers.'

'He seeks to free Seth?'

'I fear that also.'

'A fallen Osirian in the camp of the enemy would be a hard blow.'

Osiris agreed. 'More than that, it would make things truly difficult for man, and for us. For no Osirian can harm another.'

'That would make things difficult. Is this a code, or can you physically not harm each other?'

Osiris turned from her. 'It is forbidden.'

She raised an eyebrow. 'Not the first time I heard that today.' She was thoughtful. 'What defences do you have?'

Osiris turned and leant heavy on her staff. 'My brother, Akhet, stands ready to defend this place, as does Captain Lethor and his loyal guardians. That is fourteen in total.'

'Fourteen? Against Arnold and whatever he might bring with him, that's crazy.'

Osiris smiled. 'They count as many, it is a formidable army.'

'You don't fully understand Arnold, Osiris. He will have scoped this place out. He'll know the defence of it, and he'll know your numbers, or at least have a good understanding of them. I know how he thinks, and what he's capable of. Trust me, Osiris, if he is chief of Beast's servants, the entire horde of darkness is now his to command.'

Osiris dropped her head. 'You speak truth. And he already sent in his shadow-dogs to gauge numbers.'

'When?'

'Two days previous.'

'Two days?' Mary put a hand to her mouth. 'Why are we just talking about it, then?'

Osiris frowned. 'We had a gathering, Mary, it only just concluded.'

Mary laughed despite herself. 'Seriously. You are enlightened and evolved beyond measure, you'd think a sense of time and urgency would come with it.'

Osiris cast her eyes downwards. 'Truly, this time, we are out manoeuvred. The old ways must be adjusted. Everything acts with more speed than I remember.'

'Well, there's no sense brooding over it. What do you need me to do?'

'Persuade Neith to bring her army. I will assist my brother in the fight when I am able, but Lethor and his Guard may not be enough … formidable though they are. If you can do this, I will be forever grateful.'

Mary thought hard. She saw opportunity, the power within whispering terms. 'It won't be an easy thing to accomplish, but I think I may have a way.' Osiris beamed. Mary let her inner strength guide her. 'However, it will cost you more than just gratitude.'

'Cost me? I do not understand.'

'Don't play coy, Osiris. You're using me to get what you need and this time, I require a payment.'

Osiris blinked. 'I … I have nothing to give you.'

'Yes, you have.'

'Name it.'

'Albert, free of the thing inside him. That is my payment.'

Osiris's face turned dark. 'An unfair request, you already know my answer.'

'True, but that was before you came begging for help, the situation is different now.'

'How far you've come.' Osiris sighed.

'You can thank Neith, she trained me.'

'Another mistake,' she spat.

'These are my terms.'

Osiris exhaled irritation. 'I do not know if I am able to deliver upon them.'

Mary shrugged. 'Then I guess we have nothing further to talk about.'

Osiris stood quiet for the longest time. She reached out and took in the measure of her power. Mary resisted, erecting a mental barrier, it was enough to stop her, and Osiris smiled.

'I sense your power and your strength. You have learnt Neith's lessons well, Mary. A little too well, perhaps?' She smiled, but not with the usual warmth. 'Very well, I will uphold my end of the bargain, if you agree to do your part?'

'Of course, Osiris. You may count on my help.'

'Now that you have something to gain? Disappointing. I won't be able to deliver Albert before this battle, you understand that?'

'Yes, I do and that's fine. I know you won't break your word.'

'Never.'

'It's part of the reason I enjoy spending time with Neith. As simple in thought as she is, her word is her bond. I like her straight talking no nonsense approach.'

'Yes, I see that in you now.'

Mary smiled. 'I hope there are no hard feelings between us?'

Osiris shook her head. 'None. In fact, I admire you for it.'

'Thank you, Great Lady of Light. Please take me back. I will do all I can.'

Mary sat in the arched window contemplating the choices before her. Her transformation into hybrid of old-self and new, had increased knowledge and understanding of the world around. It had taken less time to come to terms with it, and new power gave her command over things she'd never had before. She looked over as the man in her bed sighed and yawned awake, rubbing his eyes.

'Good morning, my Lady,' he said as he sat up. She sat beside him. 'You slept well?'

'Aye, like a baby. Is there anything I can get for you?'

Mary thought for a moment. 'No, just stay and talk with me for a while.'

'Of course. What would you like to hear?'

The archaeologist in her awoke. 'Tell me about life in your time.'

He was thoughtful. 'It was different than now; this world seems larger. And there are things in it I do not understand, nor care for.'

'Such as?'

'Well, for example, lights that do not need flame or oil to burn?'

'You surprise me. With all the wonders of Osirian magic, a simple thing like electricity should hardly raise an eyebrow.'

'True, our goddess has power, but that is expected. For man to have developed such wonders without their aid, that is a strange thing in itself.'

'It's called evolution. Do you know how long you have slept in the walls beneath the sand?'

'No, for me it seems as though it were only yesterday.'

'At least three-thousand years.'

He looked downhearted. 'Aye, that is the number I heard.'

'Why are you sad?'

'My family are dust, my people gone, my world a distant memory in books and etchings on walls.'

She put a hand on his face. 'I know how you feel.'

She leant towards him and her eyes blackened. 'Tell me your name.'

Even with her great power he was still reticent. Before he could speak, she put a finger to his lips and spoke softly. 'Whisper into my ear. I will never speak it nor tell anyone you said it. But, I would like to know the name of the man who shared my bed last night. The warrior who won me, the only one within these walls that will ever share my bed again.'

He brought his lips to her ear.

She smiled and shuddered at his hot breath. He lay back into the bed, a look of pride in his eyes. Mary climbed over and straddled him. She leant in and kissed him hard.

Sometime later, he made his exit from her chamber, and paused in the doorway. He turned and she inclined her head.

'My Lady, may I ask you something?'

'Of course.'

'When time permits, would you tell me something of the world you knew?'

Mary nodded. 'I will, provided you do the same.'

He bowed to her, and she watched his beautiful naked body as he disappeared out of her chamber. Mary sat again at her window and closed her eyes. There was a shift in the ambiance and she looked at her entranceway, and saw Neith standing there.

'May I enter?'

Mary jumped to the floor with a huge smile. 'Please.'

Neith swaggered in, running her hand over Mary's torn nightgown draped on the chair. 'I shall have to have more of these made for you.' There was a spark in her eyes. Neith sat on her bed. Mary came beside her.

'Child, your powers have grown and your use of them pleases me.'

Mary reddened but said nothing.

Neith gave a quizzical look. 'You are embarrassed?'

'A little.'

'Why?'

'I've ... well ... '

'Wait, stop. I will need my knife if long explanation requires ears be removed.'

They laughed. Then Neith smiled warmly at her.

'Mary, do not feel embarrassment. We are allowed pleasures in life. Your love for Albert is a bond, but you need not shackle yourself to your old world notions. I understand you, and I know your thoughts. Even when you sneak off to have secret meetings with sisters, I am aware.'

Mary laughed. 'I felt you were aware of Osiris's visit. She didn't see it.'

'Tell me of what she asked of you.'

'You already know.'

Neith nodded but wasn't instant with her reply. 'You made bargain with her, in exchange for my help?'

'I did.'

'Without consulting me upon subject?'

'That's right.'

'I see. I am to follow the desires of my student now? I, Goddess of old, am to be pushed and pulled like a lowly thing, all at a child's whim?'

Mary put a hand on her arm. 'I knew you'd understand.'

And Neith let out a laughed that everyone in the temple heard. 'You are a great warrior, Mary. I love you as a teacher should. Very well. What is it I am meant to do?'

'Bring your army to the Prison of Light.'

'And once there, I am to do what, exactly?'

'Kill anything in your path, I suspect.'

Neith looked at her. 'Why should I do this?'

'Why wouldn't you?'

Neith stood and moved to the window. 'My kin sit on one side of a wall, never taking any care to peek over. When the wall is broken they fight anything that comes through and then rebuild it. I am not like them. It is not my way.' She turned and there was darkness in her.

'Let me tell you something I have never spoken of before. I will not only peek over that wall but I will walk freely through enemy camps. I would get to know them, eat and drink with them, maybe take one or two to my bed. I am neither dark nor light, I see things through various ways incomprehensible to most. I am older and I have powers they do not understand. Beast, who sits in his temple ... he knows and fears me, but not the others. I do not like being coerced without understanding everything about why I should agree. Tell me, if I do this thing, what does Mary get in return?'

Mary came beside her. 'I didn't volunteer you without thinking through the reasons. I have a plan, you read something of it.'

'Yes, you keep it well hidden; I am unable to see much of it. It would seem that I have taught you a little too well, perhaps?'

Mary held her hand tight. 'I would have nothing hidden from you. Read me and see my thoughts. I have no barriers from you, I give you access to everything.'

Neith closed her eyes and her body shimmered. When everything had been read, she returned to earthly form. For the longest time she contemplated what was learnt, rubbing her lip, bright eyes unfocused. They shifted back to Mary. 'You still have these connections, I see.'

'Yes. When Osiris and I joined in mind, she steered me away from it, but ...'

'You want for us to join as she did with you, and for me to take you into this darkness in you?'

'Very much. Both of us could learn something. I know it's a selfish thing to ask, but–'

Neith held up a hand. 'Let us surf the darkness together. But Mary, I am compelled to say I read everything about you, including bargains and desires, but also things, perhaps, you may not have wanted me to.'

'Such as my plan for rescuing Albert?'

'Yes, my sister is trusting and you have steered her on a terrible path.'

'I know. That unconditional trust is what I'd hoped for.'

'She will not understand. It will seem like betrayal.'

'Yes, I know. Are you angry?'

'Angry? No, child. Surprised, perhaps, but then we both have a little darkness within us. But come, how do you plan to overcome power? It will not be an easy thing to accomplish. Not easily are we taken unaware.'

'That's where I need your help.'

Neith sighed. 'I suspected as much. Well, as I am now complicit in bold plans, I cannot refuse to participate till conclusion. Let us walk in the darkness of your mind, and then ready my army for battle.'

Mary and Neith stood facing each other hand in hand. They shifted into a coalescing blend of coloured mist. It swirled around them until their physical forms were no longer visible.

The Capitol of New Egypt - Giza

Palash and Dalyn were in deep conversation outside the king's assembly room. They had seen neither their king nor his Osirian servant Akhet for days, and they were worried.

'Palash, we can't keep hiding his disappearance. We have to tell them something.'

'I know, but what would you suggest? We have no ability to call Akhet, or the others of his kind. The business of government must still go ahead. Our people need leadership and they need to feel supported. We must do all we can to get this country back and up on its feet. The king would want that. I want that!'

Dalyn paced. 'You're not hearing me.'

'I heard everything you said. What you propose will cause fear and panic. That's the last thing these people need.'

'So, you'd lie to them instead?'

'For their well-being? Yes, I would.'

'Spoken like a politician of old,' he spat.

Palash opened his mouth and then closed it. 'God save us you're right. I ... I don't want to be that way.'

Dalyn softened his hard set face and put a hand on Palash's shoulder. 'I'm sorry, brother. That wasn't necessary.'

'Yes ... it was. I've been so overwhelmed since the king disappeared, I'm actually a little angry he didn't say anything before they just up and vanished.'

A voice behind them said, 'Sometimes a situation requires immediate response, Palash.'

They turned to see Ammon standing behind them, yet he wasn't quite real. He was glowing golden, clothed in white robe like an Osirian. They dropped to their knees.

'Stand, brothers. I have limited time, and would impart commands. Palash, you are as fair in mind as you are in character. I wish for you to hold stewardship over my land, until I come and reclaim title as King.'

Palash's eyes filled with tears. 'I hold you in my heart, my King. But without you, I am a broken man. I miss you, brother-king. I don't know if I can do what you ask. I fear to take on the responsibilities this stewardship will entail. I'm no leader of men.'

'Oh Palash, you are far more than you realise. You will know, soon enough, what power lies within you.'

King Ammon came forward and embraced him. Palash released his tears and wept openly into his shoulder. The ethereal Ammon gave comfort in whispered words. When they disengaged, Palash smiled, and bowed in new strength.

'Dalyn, come forth and receive me.' He did as was instructed. He and the king gripped forearms. Dalyn felt the warmth of power imbue him, his eyes glowed golden and his mind filled with knowledge.

'There, brother. You now have strength equal to Osirian and power to protect my steward, and my land. Build my army, and build them strong.'

They dropped to their knees and praised him.

'I do not know when I will return, but look for me when times seem hardest of all.'

With a whispered farewell he vanished.

The two men wept and comforted each other.

Nubia, the Prison of Song

The sun disappeared over the eastern wall and Akhet found his place at the path once more. His mind focused on the land. As the darkness crept around he felt them approaching, from all side. Slithering and sneaking in shadows. The fingers of the night again failed to grip him as he glowed ever brighter. Whispers and unnatural chatters emanated everywhere. With song, the Osirian called warrior guardians from hidden entrance. They marched out and formed ranks behind him, Captain Lethor at the front.

Akhet reached out with his senses. On the peaks above, he found the three guards, and he saw through their eyes. The shadow-dogs were close but they were no match for any of the warriors of the light. Akhet wasn't concerned with them. There was nothing new they could learn. It was to other things he turned his mind. They were close, a shadow and his men, and more behind. Not far, in the dark. Above him the moon disappeared, sheathed in cloud. The only light was his, and as bright as it was, they looked up at the disappearing moonlight, and they felt a heavy doom wash over them.

'I cannot see far enough ahead, but I feel sure they are close.'

Akhet had hardly spoken when a great rolling boom of noise came. A drum beat to a marching cadence. *Boom, Boom, Boom* it went.

The guard snapped ready.

'They are coming!' cried Lethor.

Eyes reappeared along the path, many pairs of eyes, disappearing at random. Deep they went back, many ranks. Akhet felt growing darkness. From their centre he saw a huge single eye and then it was gone.

'The dawn of darkness approaches. Men, be ready!' With quick movement Akhet stepped before the narrow pathway and thrust forward his great staff. There was a dazzling flash. It lit the road before him.

Hundreds of dog-like creatures filled it. In their centre sat Melrah. Good eye burning with fire, he gave long howl and his pack leapt forward in attack.

Akhet's great light hit them, but they circled around towards the guards. Lethor and company gave war cry of old, their staff-swords bit into flesh for the first time in thousands of years. Dog-creatures were cleaved and thrown, falling in pieces, the luckier ones limped away. They kept coming, a swarm, the sheer number surprised the Osirian. One of the guards was split off from the others, and the dogs overwhelmed him. He went down to a pack of forty, and yet still he fought, now with his curved blade. They bit at flesh and clawed his body, but they found no hold on him. With a great roar, he threw half of them into the air as he stood. A pile of them lay at his feet. Akhet recognised him as the one he'd admonished that morning and he smiled, turning back to the onslaught. His staff swinging in blur, disabling or destroying everything it touched.

A sharp bark filled the cavern and the pack retreated back into the dark.

Akhet breathed hard. Lethor came beside him.

'That was too easy.'

'It was never meant to succeed, but to keep our attention. Look.' Akhet pointed to the peak. Three guards were now fighting something neither could see nor recognise. The guards were well matched with it. Akhet lifted his staff and flashes of energy pulsed and fizzled outwards. The Shadow creature deflected them back with his blade of purple fire, and then continued his battle.

The Osirian felt fear surfacing, threatening to turn spirits.

Lethor made move to leave but Akhet stopped him.

'No, my friend. They have him contained. It is diversion. Always diversion.'

Then a great cry emanated from a loyal guard and he fell from the peak.

Lethor was with him in an instant. The guard coughed and spluttered, trying to raise himself. 'Stay, brother, we are here.'

'I ... failed ... '

'No not you, my brother. You will be well soon see, Akhet comes to give blessed healing.'

'He … he is … strong, as tough as … stone, our weapons did nothing, slipped through as if he was made of … smoke.'

Akhet was beside him Songs of Healing filled the air, his hands on the grievous wound to the guardian's torso. After a while Akhet fell back startled and exhausted.

'I'm sorry, it is no use. I cannot seal it.' The guardian grabbed each of them as tears fell from his canine eyes. He gave a piercing scream. Writhing in agony, he lifted from the ground and turned solid black and crumbled into ash between them.

'No!' Lethor cried.

Akhet stared at the remains in sorrow.

A cry alerted them, and they looked up in time to see the shadow behead another, and disembowel the last. Their bodies fell to the cavern, bursting into ash on impact.

'We are betrayed,' Lethor roared.

The shadow above was gone and Akhet felt they had time to recoup. He went to the other guard, tending them, using healing Songs to refresh them. Around the cavern floor, carcasses of the enemy lay in huge piles. Akhet waved his staff around his head and blue-fire burst outwards, disintegrating what was left behind.

He stood once again on the same spot and waited. This time Lethor stood beside him. His fury and sorrow threatening to overwhelm him.

The night wind blew chill up the valley path. Lethor prowled. Akhet remained calm. The guardians were now three down and Akhet was wracked with foreboding.

From out of the darkness more eyes came, this time taller and Akhet showered light on them. A row of dark powerful men, teeth as daggers, eyes black as night, advanced; behind a blackened hideous monster with fire for eyes. Its mighty form stood far taller than the rest; it smouldered and dripped liquid fire as it followed in slow thumps behind.

'Faulgoth,' Lethor growled.

Through their ranks came great shadow, in the middle of which was a dark man-shape form, its terrible power went before it. In its shadow hand a blade glowed with purple fire. There was a pause, and the weapon was lowered. Fire burst from Faulgoth mouth as it roared, and with a cry of war, the enemy came forward, swords meeting staff-sword.

Goddess Neith stood before the might of her grand army. Their golden armour shone under the eye of the sun. Mary watched from afar, taking in their majesty with a sense of pleasure at the historic wonder of them. Her eyes on one man in particular.

Neith's husband came before her.

'My Queen, in one day we will reach destination. What then are your commands?'

'We will hold until moment is ripe for our arrival.'

'And Mary? What of her? She has no skill with a sword. She should stay where it is safe.'

Neith shook her head. 'Mary has other skills.'

'Ah, final lesson then?'

'You read me too well, husband.'

'Aye, I know you.'

She kissed him.

'I have a request, husband.'

'Name it.'

'The one Mary takes to her chamber.'

'There is problem with him?'

'No, I would command him keep eyes upon her.'

The captain chuckled. 'I don't think command would be needed. See him now? His eyes are already upon her, when they should be facing you.'

She put a hand on his chest-plate and he took it in his. 'Another request I'd make of you, loyal captain of my heart. Be fierce, be unyielding, and be safe.'

'Always.' He lowered his head and then turned to issue commands.

Neith came beside Mary as the army marched away. 'You are apprehensive, child?'

'Yes, a little.'

'It is not uncommon. This is your first battle?'

She nodded.

'Your thoughts dwell on ... not Albert. For the warrior you ...'

'Yes—'

'He is fierce. He is also filled with love for Mary, who dominates him when she sees fit.' Neith's eyes followed her men as they approached the top of the dune and disappeared. She turned to see a tear fall from Mary's eye.

'Why do you cry?'

Mary looked into her face. 'I don't know. I suppose I'm worried about what will happen next.'

Neith put an arm around her. 'I too have this concern.'

'I thought you were fearless?'

She laughed and then shook her head. 'There is no such thing, child. Come, let us follow our brave men and sing happy tunes of old.'

Twenty-Five
The Osirian Last Stand

Nubia: The Battle for the Prison of Song

Swords swung and the melee went on. Men and guardians were evenly matched, each standing their ground, fighting hard. Akhet was lost in fierce skirmish with Prince of Shadow. He had come without pause. The Osirian had no time to take in the rest of the battle, as he fought off the relentless attacks of the dark prince. Sword struck staff over and over, and then the prince stepped back. A deadly, terrible voice within his shadow hood spoke.

'Old Osirian fool, your days are numbered. Look on my face and see your end.'

Akhet laughed. 'I would, Dark One, but it appears you have no face to look upon.'

'Filth, I have waited a long time for this.'

Akhet said, 'Naturally. I'm so sorry, in all the confusion I don't seem to recall your name?'

'Ha! You may call me Prince of Darkness, or Shadow Prince, if you prefer.'

'Prince, you say? To what royal line do you belong? I sense only the putrid plague of fell men in your blood.'

'Filth of Light, I would know the name of my enemy too, if he would but share it?'

'Certainly. Behold me, Shadow of Nothingness. I am Horus son of Osiris, daughter to Isis. And *my* face, as plain and old as it is, will be the very last thing you see.'

And Akhet swung his staff with such force the prince and Underblade were thrown into the rock behind.

*

Lethor ran for the Faulgoth and they battled hard. The dark monster's cumbersome blows missed their small target. It swung for him again but connected with sword-staff, which was deflected with triumphant howl. The warrior guard dodged the behemoth's roared flames and growled. They swung around each other and Lethor, as agile as a cat, ran up along the rock using it to pivot, so he flew high into the air landing on the flaming demon's back; his arm anchored around a thick neck, the other raining blow upon blow on the demon's head.

*

The man Aaron feared Lieutenant of the King's Guard, was locked in brutal battle with his Guardian of Light counterpart. They fought off, and traded blows. The guardian's sword-staff kept him at distance.

Aaron rolled and dodged then saw an opening and brought his sword up to cut through his staff. Guardian snarled and leapt aside losing the broken stumps, pulling a scimitar from his golden belt. Aaron leered as he circled. He flipped the sword in his hand by the hilt, pointing it at his enemy.

They came together in a series of fast, heavy blows. Swords clashed with ring and sparks. As they closed together, jackal warrior and man snarled at one another. The guardian backhanded Aaron and he spun a kick to his head, but Aaron ducked, punching upwards scoring a direct hit to his lower back. It knocked the guardian off balance. Wasting no time Aaron pivoted, planting his foot in the sand. He swung his sword to deliver the deathblow and found nothing to hit.

He recognised the danger too late.

Guardian sidestepped and swung and Lieutenant of the King's Guard fell headless to the ground.

*

The cavern floor ran red with blood. The giant Faulgoth and the captain continued their brawl. Men and guardians fought desperate battles. A gurgled scream to Akhet's left came from a guardian who fell, crashing to the ground, a deep wound to his shoulder. A pack of the dog-creatures howled and sprang from the dark. They set upon him with teeth and claw, ripping him to pieces. His screams had long since stopped as they dragged him in many parts back into the gloom.

Akhet took all this in whilst trading blow after blow with his enemy.

The Osirian held him off and Shadow soon realised melee would not be successful. The old Osirian, Horus, was more powerful than he'd realised. He lifted off in flight, drawing darkness to bolster his power. Akhet took opportunity and thrust staff upwards grabbing Sam in a ball of light, throwing him hard into the rock wall where he didn't get up.

The Osirian turned and looked upon the Faulgoth beast and there was Lethor, riding high upon its back, plunging his sword deep into its neck. The absurdity of it made him chuckle. The monster roared and bellowed but Lethor remain fixed. It threw itself into rock walls, cracking them on impact. It bashed and smashed against them, trying to dislodge the warrior, but the Captain of the Guardians of Light was too stubborn to let being squashed to death stop him.

He called out to Akhet far below.

'Old man! Are you going to watch me do this all night, or are you going to assist?'

Akhet called forth great song, thrusting his staff forward, but a missile of terrible blackness hit him left flank, and he was thrown high, his bolt of energy disappearing harmlessly into the night. He staggered up from the broken rock and turned to meet the foul Prince once more.

Light versus the dark battled for an age. Prince of Shadow used his hate and anger, drawing upon all the lessons his King taught, but the light slapped every attack back at him, without breaking sweat. The wrathful Prince called the flames of the living from around him, but the canny Osirian re-directed them to himself, it bolstered his power.

Shadow Prince was beaten back and he tired. The Osirian was an intelligent and fearsome warrior. Sam called upon hateful song and let forth a hideous screech, it enhanced the fears of everyone, and guardians howled, backing away in dread.

Shadow's men whooped and cheered. Their encouragement fuelled, they pressed attacks harder.

Akhet did not move or show any fear at the Shadow's Songs of Spite. He stood, bright white, resolute.

The Osirian recognised the strength of his enemy's power and where it came from. He also knew *his* was stronger. As old and worn as he now seemed, he'd had thousands of years to hone it, whereas he sensed the Shadow's was new. It was evident by the limitations of his dark reach, he hadn't drawn heavy upon it before this fight.

Akhet reached deep into the Prince of Shadow's mind, striking away the barriers he erected in his desperation to keep him out. Within his thoughts and memories, he saw many things. Journeys from dark lands; a man once, proud and worthy, forced into servitude and made shadow by the Lord of Darkness himself. The old man probed deeper. There in the core of his being, he found the weakness he'd been hoping for. The Osirian morphed into huge white spider, so large and so fearsome, the shadow shook in fear and dread. Within this dread he lost all power. Then Akhet tapped into the Songs of Light, became as he once was, and with calm voice said, 'Silence your foul tongue.'

He thrust the crystal end of his staff deep into the blackness where a head should have been. Light erupted and set the terrible Shadow ablaze. With an almighty cry, the Prince of Shadow burst apart, dropping Underblade, he fell to his back in earthly form.

Sam howled in rage and blinding agony. He writhed and held hands to his burnt face. His screams then increased as Akhet bathed him in a greater light. The man called Prince of Shadow, burst into bright flame. But Sam tapped into the pain and found enough strength within to roll away, the sand choking the fires out on his charred naked form. Blind, disfigured, and desperate, he dragged away in piercing cries and shrieks, crawling as far from the Osirian as strength would allow.

Akhet watched the disfigured, ruined, torched man crawling in the sand. He felt pity and stepped forward in mercy, to put an end to his screams. His staff lifted, its light grew in intensity. Akhet raised it higher locking eyes onto a burnt contorted face.

Peripheral movement caught his attention too late. Out of nowhere it leapt. Massive jaws found arm and staff, shattering both. The old Osirian staggered in surprise and pain. Melrah stood over the disfigured crawling wretch and growled. The two halves of Akhet's staff hit the ground and the crystal's light flickered, fizzled and snuffed out. It burst sending shockwave of energy, throwing them apart.

They stirred, but Melrah was quicker. Akhet stood, prepared for him. He saw the giant dog leap, but not at him. Melrah landed next to the prince, who cradling burnt flesh in whimpered moans. The hound of Hell kept his good eye on Akhet and howled warning. When the Osirian made no move forward, Melrah locked the prince in a gentle bite, backing away, tugging him to safety.

Captain Lethor had seen something of his friend's battle, and of the giant dog's attack, but since they flew apart he'd been unable to see what befell him. The monster reared and worry for Akhet slipped from mind as he carried on sparring with the deadly Faulgoth.

Unarmed, his sword broken, the blade embedded deep within the great monster's thick neck, he had nothing left to fight with. Strength waned, grip weakened. The Faulgoth felt it. It braced itself on massive front leg and threw his rider hard to the ground. Lethor landed with a thump on his back, the wind knocked from him.

The warrior groaned and looked into the monster's foul, fiery eyes. It threw its hideous head back in dreadful cry, lifting an enormous stump of a foot high.

Captain Lethor sighed in resignation.

'Ah, but what a battle? A fight worthy of song!'

He faced his death in rapturous cheer, which then turned to stunned silence as the giant creature threw its arms wide, shuddered, cracked, and with hideous trumpet-like rumble, burst into a mountain of ash. Lethor barely had time to cover his face before it buried him underneath.

The dark king's men fought with their all, but many fell, some horribly. Guardians too suffered grievous loss. The luckiest died instant death; the others fell first to sword then to rabid packs of shadow-dogs, who ripped them apart as they lay dying on the ground.

Those who were left protecting the Prison of Song retreated and regrouped.

Akhet raised himself from the ground supporting his ruined arm. Staggering back towards the entrance, he found his path blocked by yet another Shadow. They stared at each other for a time, the battle around them seeming to unfold in slow motion. This Shadow was different. Burning red eyes bore into him. King of Shadow's power was tenfold of the prince. He wore a large crown of jagged points upon no visible head. This, Akhet mused must be King of the Shadows Arnold.

They continued to stare and Akhet felt a hideous power reach for him. He threw up songs of protection, but through pain and weariness, his power diminished. King of Shadows raised hand and Akhet felt blackness stab through his shield. It gripped at his throat. An invisible hand choking and lifting him high, filling Akhet's mind with foul and vile images, smothering the light in terrible blackness he'd never undergone.

Shadow laughed. With a gesture he bashed the Osirian into rock walls. Over and over he slammed and smashed, until bones shattered and lifeblood fell from cracks and splits in earthly form. It was as though he was a marionette, the shadow pulling the strings.

Akhet found strength enough to call forth a Song of Energy. It knocked men, guardians, and dog-creatures away to the ground but not the Shadow King. He withstood it, hold unyielding. The Osirian used strength in reserve, but being too weak and exhausted to do any real damage. The king of the dark revelled in it.

Akhet had nothing left to fight with. The shadow, however, didn't know the son of the greatest King on Earth, as a consequence, he was not aware of the hidden, last resort, secret power he kept locked inside. But he would soon understand as the old Osirian looked inwards, calling it forth, knowing the power would end the fight and him along with it. A booming voice filled the air and he refrained from unleashing it, instead sent praise to Arrandori.

'Get your vile hands off my sister's son.'

Shadow King released his grip and Akhet fell to the ground. He spun to face the voice.

Swaggering in approach, the Goddess Neith came forward. Arnold-King expanded his shadow to envelope her but she swatted it away, as she would a fly, and the darkness ran to him and would not come back out. She stopped before him, hands on hips, a half smile playing across a majestic and beautiful gold-skinned face.

'So at last we meet, Darkness of the new world of men. You must be the one called Arnold?'

*

Akhet lifted himself from the ground and stumbled. His body was broken and he found no strength to call upon any of the old Songs to heal it. Neith's latent power now engaged the shadow, keeping attentions fixed on her. He lay there, unable to move, filled with regret. Then another came kneeling beside. A warm gentle feminine hand caressed his brow. Akhet gazed up into the eyes of Queen Isis, her beautiful face smiling, filling him with strength.

'Mother?'

'I am here, my beautiful son,' she said, cradling his head in her lap.

'My body is broken. I have no strength within me to fight.'

'Easy, my darling. There is no fight left for you this day. Rest a moment. I will help you regain some strength. I need you to hurry, there is still danger. You must do one last thing before I claim you and bring you into my bosom.'

'How are you here?'

'I never left you.'

'Ah, this is my inner-self's way of motivating me to struggle on?'

'If you see it that way I won't argue. Now stand, son. Stand, I say. Come forth with strength of your mother's call and father's rage.'

Akhet grit his teeth and took her hand, and she pulled him up onto his feet.

*

Shadow and Goddess stared each other down. Neither spoke. Then Neith felt Akhet limp away. Danger past, for Akhet at least, she engaged him and purred. 'What? You cannot speak in that form, Shadow?'

She prowled, he remained still. Shadow and death. She came to face him and then let loose a laughed that he felt in the core of his form.

'You do not have one ounce of strength, little man. Watch.' And she waved her hand and his shadow form shifted solid. He was unable to move. Arnold-King stood defiant and still refused to speak. It annoyed her.

'I would hear you speak before I cut your head off. Well?'

He stared.

'Have you nothing to say at all?'

Silence.

'Pity. Very well, little man. It is—'

'I am no longer a man,' he replied.

She beamed. 'At last, words are exchanged. If not a man, then answer, what are you?'

'Death and darkness.'

'Bold title. You answer well. Tell me. Do you see me?'

'I could hardly fail to, could I?'

'What am I?'

'Osirian filth. But a great warrior, no doubt.'

'Filth?'

She made a slight gesture with her hand, and he was knocked to the ground. The shadow staggered up spitting blood at her feet.

'Foolish answer. Let me tell you what I am. The greatest warrior you will ever face, at least today.'

Arnold-King chuckled. 'Certainly the most narcissistic and conceited.'

She angered. 'When you see your own body fall as your head goes in the opposite direction, perhaps you will think those words unwisely chosen?'

'Arrogant, too. Is it an Osirian trait, or just yours?'

She pondered. 'My own. But then I prefer straightforwardness. I say what I see, and in you I see something I would strip bare and flog until he begs forgiveness.'

'I bet you say that to all the boys?'

She gave a short exclaim. 'I admit your strength is attractive, where your form is not.'

'Sorry, Neith, I'm not into ancient whores.'

She struck him again. A gush of blood fell from his torn lip. 'I sense you enjoy pain. Answer poorly again and I will inflict it in a manner even you, dark thing, could never envision.'

She raised an eyebrow and he snarled but said nothing.

'It learns well. Before I end you, Arnold-King of the *Disjecta Membra* of your men, I would have you see something.' She moved to his side and pointed. 'Look, see? My army approaches, Lord.'

Arnold-King watched, unable to move or assist, as hundreds of golden warriors marched the path into the cavern. The feared Guard of the King outflanked, fought bravely, but their end came swift and unmerciful in the army of Neith's unrelenting execution. They made slow march. When they found enemy before them, in any form, they were cut down, slain and dismembered. Anything found already upon the ground was also treated thus. Her army of warriors left nothing alive.

Neith chuckled at his powerless rage.

*

Akhet staggered through hallways, corridors, and pathways, following the whispers of his mother who filled him with enough strength to carry on. He came now to the Shard and there found Lethor, bruised, injured, but breathing.

'You live,' Guardian Captain said, coming forward to assist the Osirian as he stumbled.

'Barely, help me to that rock.' Lethor took his weight and they limped together.

'You came to protect the Shard?' Akhet asked as Lethor fretted over him.

'I came to find you, my dear friend. I didn't see you when I escaped from the ash of that foul thing, so I assumed you'd come here. I've never seen you so broken.'

Akhet nodded and coughed a trickle of blood; it slipped from his mouth.

'You are bleeding inside?'

'I am dying. But I have enough power to remain while Neith finishes off everything else.'

Lethor looked shocked. 'Neith?'

Akhet smiled. 'Yes, she brought her army.'

'A little late!'

'Nevertheless. We have in her a fearsome protagonist, I may rest easy just knowing she is out there. Anything foolish enough to attempt fight will quickly wish they hadn't.'

'True, Neith is not known for mercy in battle. I hope she stays out there. '

Lethor put a hand on his shoulder.

Akhet patted it. 'It is well that it would be just the two of us, here. Like old times, eh?'

Lethor lowered his jackal mouth to the old Osirian's ear. 'If only you hadn't come, dear Horus, I say this to you now with great affection and sorrow, things would have been easier on my heart if you'd simply stayed outside to die.'

Before his words could be understood, Lethor slipped an amulet around his neck. The old Osirian frowned and then felt immobility take hold. Wide-eyed and confused he asked, 'Lethor, what is this?'

A deep growl emanating from the shadow cut off any further words. Akhet shifted his gaze as Melrah padded forth, fangs dripping in blood and saliva. The giant dog staring at the old man's ruined arm.

Neith slipped a knife from her belt and came forward.

'Now it is time I put you out of your great misery, shadow of the corpses of your men.' She brought the knife up to his neck. 'Have you any last words to say before I slay you?'

'Yes.'

She held her head close. 'Well? I am listening.'

'You are a foolish, vain woman, praise be for that.'

He grabbed her wrist. With a sharp jerk it snapped, and he threw her onto the ground. Her surprise was evident. Neith did not cry out despite the pain. In fact, she grinned as she brushed the sand from her. She approved of his newfound strength and audacity.

He continued, 'You did exactly as I predicted and went for the biggest prize. I knew you'd never look to smaller things; they're beneath the attention of someone like you. I played you, Goddess. Now your failure to recognise a simple ruse will cost everything you've fought for.'

Neith stood. She held her other hand over broken wrist, and healed it in a golden glow. She flexed and rotated it.

Arnold mocked her and Neith flashed him a wicked smile.

'If that was an attempt to court me, bold King, it will sadden you to learn, I am taken.'

She unsheathed a pair of beautiful short swords. 'You are not an impotent man as first sensed, and it is well. I do not know of what little things you speak too, but maybe you *are* worthy adversary after all? Come shadow, let us find out.'

With a warrior's cry, the Goddess leapt.

Arnold-King threw back head in deadly curse and burst into shadow.

*

Akhet's mind raced. The pieces of the puzzle fell into place. With horror and misery he understood things as they were, and he also realised why he had been blind to them. Lethor's betrayal had been long in the making. From the moment his heart was touched by evil, he'd been deep within the enemy's camp. As far back as the earliest times, he'd sowed the seed leading to this black day. It was how they knew where to come, the reason guard were overwhelmed. Lethor, Guardian of Light, friend for years beyond number stood bathed in darkness. It sickened his failing heart.

Lethor knelt beside him. He had the grace to appear remorseful.

'I'm sorry, friend. Wasn't it you who kept saying diversion, always diversion? You were right, as always. But it was never your day to win. I gave our enemy the tools needed to succeed. Everything went smoothly even Faulgoth played along. The fight … it was just enough to keep your mind occupied to real purpose. Do you know what else?'

Akhet could not move. 'It seems as though you're enjoying hearing your own voice. Why don't you tell me?'

Lethor chuckled. 'Let's just say the men of this time are not simple or weak, as they were back in ours. There is more than one enemy in the camp of men.'

'I am in no mood for riddles, Lethor. Speak plainly.'

'Look within for answers. I have said enough.'

'You have said much, yet very little at the same time. But then I expect that from foolish jackals.'

'Foolish? Foolish, you say?'

'Indeed. With ears that large, you could not fail to hear it. Lies and deceit, these are your ways now, once Champion of Ra. Whatever foulness drips from the hole in your head, I will never trust it, so save words for those who could bare to hear them. I pity and despise you.'

Lethor growled warning.

Akhet ignored it. 'Before I leave this world, friend, I would like to know what this thing is, around my neck, stopping movement.'

Lethor chuckled. 'Oh, that? I wanted to show you when we were here before, but you weren't interested, remember? It's pretty, isn't it?'

'I have never known anyone able to …'

'Ah, he sees now?'

'Yes, I see. This place has weapons fashioned to hold Osirian as it was meant to.'

'Indeed. The same one held Seth before he was locked in the Shard.'

'What did you do with Ammon?'

Lethor raised his hands. 'I did nothing. He disappeared of his own free will, fortunately for him.'

Melrah growled and Akhet read hideous purpose in his good eye.

Akhet shivered. 'I can't say I think much of your new companion, old friend.'

He felt movement to his right and turned eyes on another. Standing burnt, disfigured, blind and shrouded in a raging hate was Sam, Prince of Darkness. His blade held high.

'The crispy Prince of Shadows, too? My, my, what a party we're having.'

'Lethor,' Prince rasped. Captain stood and Sam threw him the crystal hammer.

Akhet's eyes widened. 'Betrayer! How did you find that? It was lost … lost in the darkest folds of the world.'

Lethor coughed. 'His memory is fragmented, my Prince, it's his age, you see.' He turned to the Osirian. 'Who was tasked with its burial?'

Akhet held him in sad eyes. 'You were.'

Sam cackled. 'Left guarded by a couple of old, fat, and very dead spiders.'

Lethor stepped towards Melrah and stroked him.

'There's new power in the world now, Horus. The old ways are gone. We join with it or we die. I like life better than oblivion.'

'And what life do you think you will see under the shadow of darkness, friend?'

'A better one than you, I'd wager.'

Akhet tried to call upon his hidden strength but the power holding him prevented it.

Sam said, 'Release our Lord's prize.' The shadow bent before him. 'I see with ruined eyes your face. I smell your musty odour, old man. Let this be the last thing *your* eyes see.'

Akhet cursed. 'No!'

Lethor swung the hammer at the Shard and a small crack appeared. It spider-webbed slow at first, then more appeared, extending out in short sharp bursts.

Akhet felt his life fading. He reached into his being. He felt desperately for the part of him giving link to Osiris, his father. But it was beyond his failed strength. He watched in despair as the Shard shattered, leaving a shower of diamond crystals in the sand.

Shadow came forward. 'Good night, old man.'

A purple fire spread along Underblade. He pulled it back, the tip touching the robe's cloth.

Lethor cast eyes downwards and flattened his ears.

Akhet faced the enemy in calm determination.

Prince of Shadow pushed Underblade in slow thrusts through the old man's chest. At first the Osirian did not cry out, but pain soon overwhelmed him. The sword pushed right through his earthly form, he shrieked in the agony, but felt no shame as tears flowed from his eyes.

Shadow Prince withdrew Underblade and cackled in glee, as the wound began to blacken into ash.

A hiss caught their attention, and smoky mist poured from the broken Shard. It flowed along the ground swirling and coalescing. In a flash of energy, a dark-skinned half man, half unknown animal, manifested into focus and stretched. He reached out long clawed hands. Amber eyes blinked a few times, glowing fierce. He took in long breath, blowing it out in a bellowed song everything Osirian on the planet could hear.

'Free at last. FREE!'

The fallen Osirian turned his form to black and red thunderous mist. Seth the God of Deserts and Storms lifted his arms and spun, bursting into a tightly confined whirlwind.

Lethor came forward and bowed. 'Great Lord, take me with you, so that I might worship your–'

'No,' a voice boomed. 'You are *not* worthy.'

Lethor beseeched him. 'But I am, truly. I have power, Lord. Great power. Let me serve your will!'

Whirlwind came forward. Lethor felt encouraged. 'I can become the captain of your warriors, Lord.'

'Be silent. Traitorous jackal. Keeper of the keys to misery and pain. I will keep counsel on who is or isn't worthy. Would he be tested? Would he seek to prove worth?'

'I would, my Lord Seth, please whatever quest I need do to show my worth, I will gladly undertake.'

'Very well, here is my quest for you. My sister Neith comes. I would be truly impressed if you were able to remain alive. Should you manage it, I may consider you worthy.'

Lethor looked alarmed. 'But Lord. Be reasonable. She will know. She will read it in me. I can't fight her!'

'No, you can't. Worse has not yet been heard, sneak. She will see you beside brother with grievous wound. I feel life leaving as we speak, and I grieve. But I have no pity for kin who punishes brother, leaving him to rot in void of nothingness.'

He came forward in earthly form once again. Seth placed a dark hand on his brother's head.

'Die well, my beloved brother. It is just I should come in time to witness your passing, and rejoice that the one who dealt it, also frees me from captivity.'

His eyes lingered on Horus, then with a sigh, he strode away coming to stand beside Prince of Shadows.

'Now I will leave this place before Neith comes to destroy us all. The prince of men shall ride with me. If you survive, traitor, I will seek you.' He gathered Sam into him and was once again a great storm. An evil laugh filled the air, and they melted away to nothing.

'The betrayer ... is himself ... betrayed.' Akhet's hoarse voice was quieter now.

*

Neith and the shadow battled. She countered his attacks, his power though great, was no match for hers. He came with flaming fist and she caught it, crushing its fire. He grabbed for her with his other arm and found it locked in a vice-like grip between bicep and forearm. She gave a sharp jolt and Arnold's arm splintered. He cried in agony.

Releasing him in a sigh, she gave him time to catch his breath. His form shimmered earthly for a moment then became blackened and deadly.

She prowled as she spoke.

'Disappointing, Great King of Darkness and Shadow. I had hoped I might see warrior of old in you, yet instead I find another weak man over-reached in desire. I pity your Lord if you are King of all his minions. I would beg for swift end before reporting failure.'

The Shadow snarled. 'My servants would skin you alive and bring your eviscerated body before him as a tasty gift.'

'It will not be a long or fair fight, if you are the best of them. How he has dulled to allow such weakness to be chief servant. If I felt so inclined, I could walk unhindered into his temple. And if that day comes, I would pull the whiskers from his fetid face and poked out his foolish eyes for appointing you as King of no challenge at all.'

He came at her with a rage, knocking her upon her back. She grinned and like a cat, sprang at him, pummelling him in an array of attacks he found no defence for. He shifted and weaved, tried to break away from her and flee. Each time he made escape, she pulled him back, continuing to lay hurt upon him, until he lay broken and whimpering on the floor.

She placed a foot on his neck, he grab at it.

'Pathetic worm; I will grind you to dust under my boot.'

She pushed hard and his head sunk into the sand.

He saw in her eyes, both fury and joy. He also saw his death reflected back at him. She was like nothing he had ever fought; her power was utterly beyond him. It was mixture of light *and* darkness. She wasn't Osirian, she was different, far stronger. He had never been prepared to face her.

Arnold saw no way out but death and stared at her, fear in his eyes, but resolute in his pride. She felt it and was pleased. 'Good. Hold you head high, King of Weakness. When I see light draining from your eyes, then you will have been worthy of my attention.'

A voice echoed across the land. It hit her hard.
FREE!

*

Deep within his temple, Beast heard the cry from the freed Osirian and knew his servants had succeeded. He roared pleasure in booming thunder across the world.

*

The words assaulted her senses and she stepped back, releasing him. The shadow crawled away and fell in a laugh.

'You foolish, clever thing. *You* released him?'

'Yes,' he croaked.

She was impressed. 'How did you do this?'

'By engaging you, knowing I would die doing so. You were the only one who could stop us. You're a warrior. Proud, powerful. All I had to do was keep you engaged. Keep your eyes focused on me, and nowhere else. That little thing we were talking about earlier? Surprise, it's free now. And guess what, mighty Goddess of old. I win.'

She chuckled. 'Shrewd. To use enemy's strengths and weaknesses to advantage, there is ingenuity in that. I respect you for it. I take back harsh words, Great Shadow King. It was unfulfilling fight without doubt, but you are not an unworthy opponent. I salute your strategy and you.' She leant forward. 'Now, because you have impressed, I will cut off your head, rather than beat the life from you, and deliver it to your master in person, where I shall tell him how his chief servant was not as feeble as I first thought.'

'Gracious of you,' he spat.

'You are welcome.'

She brought swords to bear but attention shifted and hesitation stayed her hand. Narrowed eyes found something in the distance. After a long pause, she sheathed her swords.

'It seems I have more pressing matters to attend to. You fought well, Arnold, but I will not end you this day, though you deserve nothing else. I expect you are tickled by pink to hear this?' She turned and left. He lay broken on the ground and he breathed a sigh.

Arnold rested for a moment, still unsure why he was alive. It didn't take long to make up his mind. With great pain he rose from the floor and limped away. Beaten, weak and bleeding, he could no longer take shadow form. His body shattered, each step wracked him in agony. He dropped to his knees taking shuddered breath. The exertion overwhelmed him and he toppled.

A shadow passed over him. Arnold feared the witch had returned to toy with him. He looked up, straight into the eyes of his beloved Mary, his relief evident.

Mary returned it and knelt behind him, reaching around to hold him up, to give him strength. He fell into her embrace. 'Mary, oh, my Mary, you returned to me. Help me to leave this place, my love.'

Mary kissed his cheek. 'Oh Arnold, I will help you to leave,' she said.

Arnold-King sighed and closed his eyes. Her warmth was intoxicating. He felt strength return just by their close proximity. Their heads pressed against each other. His body sagged against the arm holding him, and then stiffened.

He gave a sharp cough. It brought a trickle of blood to his lips.

Arnold looked down. In stunned confusion, he saw the tip of a golden sword protruding through his chest.

'Courtesy of Neith, my love.' Mary kissed his cheek. Then took hold of his neck hard and thrust the blade through till its hilt found resistance and would go no further. He gave a horrific gurgled cry and moaned as blood erupted, spraying from his mouth. With an agonal sigh, he fell limp.

She released him. Mary placed a foot on his back and pulled the sword free, then waited.

The wound pulsed and bubbled as thick dark viscous blood seeped out. Then the head of something vile immerged, slug-like, it wriggled to be free of the corpse. A tiny mouth opened and a mucus-filled gurgle emanated from it. Mary grabbed it and forced it into a small bag, and tied it off, before attaching it to her belt.

*

In the chamber once containing the Shard, Akhet had almost turned to ash. Only his will kept him solid and inner strength, though disconnected, kept him alive. He felt her coming. With considerable effort he muttered, 'Oblivion ... approaches.'

Lethor looked down the corridor and muttered in a tremble, 'Neith. ...'

Akhet rasped a chuckle then coughed.

Twenty-Six
A Guardian's Folly

Nubia: The Prison of Song

Neith came forward with great wrath and found Lethor standing beside the remains of the Shard. Eyes then fell upon Akhet, turning to ash before her, and she went wild with madness. Lethor swallowed back his fear, but he was unprepared for the terrible look she gave.

Neith read much, eyes golden, she took in everything.

'Traitor,' she snarled.

'Perhaps.' Lethor shrugged, licking nervous lips, mindful to remain outside of her reach.

She stepped forward, he backed away. He was a proud warrior. She respected that, but next to him laid her brother, dying or dead, and he'd offered no words of comfort. His hand now shook and it pleased her.

'Whatever you have done to my brother, Lethor traitor, you know I will pile upon you tenfold. Speak of what has happened and if you lie, I will cut out your tongue and force you to swallow it.'

Lethor held sword before him. 'Seth is freed, you are too late.'

'Arranged by you alone?'

'Nay, I was a pawn in the game, my Lady.'

'A pawn, you say? To this Arnold-King you now change allegiance?'

'Aye, he is my king now.'

Neith chuckled. 'Then I say to you commiserations, for your king is dead.'

Terror passed over Lethor's face. 'But I am not so easily taken, Warrior Goddess. I was a Champion of Ra, and have wrestled Faulgoth to death with my bare hands. I am imbued with power even Osirian would find difficult to best.'

She flashed him a terrible look. 'Yet you wet yourself in the sight of me. Good. Muscles are now warmed from last fight. Let us hope you prove better challenge.'

Then she heard a soft grunt. It came from a corridor in darkness to her right. She turned her head and golden eyes scanned the shadows. Another grunt came, followed by a low, soft growl. She turned to see a giant eye, blinking. Neith tilted her head and brought her swords forward.

She tensed muscle in preparations for whatever it was in the dark. Over her shoulder she said, 'You have a pet, I see?'

Melrah erupted from the tunnel in a lordly rumble and knocked her onto her back. Both swords were thrown as she wrestled him. His slavering jaws snapping at her. She was strong, but he pushed her back into the sand where she found no hold. Again the jaws snapped and she dodged them. Neith held the slavering head back with forearm to his neck, but the giant beast put great paw on her left flank and forced the arm away.

Melrah's giant teeth finally met flesh and he tore at her shoulder and neck, his back claws raking across exposed skin. Neith burst into golden light, howled in pain, and threw him off. The giant dog lord landed on paws and circled back to face her.

His posture was tight, ready. At any moment he could spring. His chest expanded and fell in the rhythm of his breathing; a great eye watched her every move.

Neith, on all fours, an ephemeral look of delight upon her face, kicked sand behind her and howled. Blood dripped from wounds he'd inflicted and red flaming welts covered her stomach and legs.

Melrah licked his blood-soaked mouth and globs of drool fell before him.

'At last,' she breathed, coming to stand, 'a worthy opponent.'

Neith ran a finger across her wounds and tasted her own blood.

Their eyes never left one another.

She observed the twitch in his muscled hind and readied for attack.

He came at her with a speed defying size. This time, she was ready.

Warrior Goddess stepped aside with the speed of the wind and laid punch so hard into his bulk, he flew from her. She followed it with movement faster than Melrah could see, punching him again. Before he landed, she blurred and hit him a third time, propelling into rock he hit so hard, his body smashed right through.

She bent down and collected her swords, staring into the gaping dust-filled hole. There was no movement. Neith turned and headed back to Lethor, but a grunt stopped her in midstride. Melrah was behind her in a flash, a snarl alerting to danger too late. Head low, he hit her and she flew into the wall, cracking it on impact. He jumped again but she flew into the air and rolled, standing behind him. They looked at each other. Melrah prowled, she mirrored.

They came together one last time, fighting like titans of old. Each caused wounds on the other. Neith bent her form to his right flank and kicked a hind leg. There was a sickening crack and Melrah howled. She stepped back breathing hard, blood seeping from fresh wounds.

She was predatory now, eyes sparkling, permanent grin etched on face, becoming ever terrible as the fight went on. He limped and put his weight on his good rear leg. She advanced, swords in each hand, swinging. He grabbed one and flung it aside, turned his great flank, and knocked her back.

She staggered and he charged.

He fell for feigned movement and she sidestepped, sword finding him deep, causing a grievous lethal wound.

Melrah yelped at its sting, and with a great whine that filled the cavern, he fell with heavy thump and rested, no longer able to stand or fight.

Neith dropped her sword and came beside him. She knelt down and stroked his massive head. She looked into his warrior eye and they communicated respect for one another. She sang to him while he panted, the rising and falling of his chest short and sharp. Her songs calmed him and she continued to comfort him as life slowly left him. Neith kept his eye open until his light faded. She cried as Melrah panted one last agonal breath and fell silent into the sand.

'Oh Great Warrior Dog of Darkness no more, I will sing songs of this battle, till voice is taken from me. Magnificent fiend, worthy adversary. Rest now, be at peace.'

She closed his open eye. 'I will see you in the halls of great songs someday. Farewell.'

Goddess Neith hugged him tight, then rose from him and turned with scowl to Lethor.

Again Neith recovered her swords, body covered and dripping in blood. Lethor's heart sunk, and he now saw he was doomed. The essence of wrath itself advanced, staring down sword edge, pointing directly at his head.

He trembled at her fury and looked for escape.

'What have you done to my brother, servant no longer? Speak, or I swear I will make your death ...'

Before she could reach him a flash of light burst into the room.

They shielded their eyes.

When light dimmed there standing in the middle of the room was the young man known as Ammon, High King of men, dressed in a white robe, glowing in golden hue.

Lethor whispered prayer and the boy faced him expressionless.

'So, my little king of cowards, you finally came out of your hide-hole, eh?'

Ammon looked on him with sad eyes. 'I see more than you could ever know, Lethor, holder of secrets now revealed. Did I not warn of consequences?' He bathed him in light. 'Feel the sting of your betrayal on those who would suffer in result of it.'

Lethor screamed as his mind was assaulted.

Neith grinned at the boy.

He passed Lethor who was holding his head in pain. He knelt beside Akhet who could no longer speak or see.

Lethor pushed through the agony and some of his former bravado returned. 'So the boy brings new power at battle's end? Where were you hiding?'

Ammon lifted the amulet off the old man's neck and dropped it to the floor. It turned to dust as it fell. 'Battles are often thought over when they are really just beginning.'

Lethor grew angry at the boy, who showed no sense and disrespect by keeping his back to him.

'Do not touch that feeble old fool. It is too late. He is already dead.'

Neith growled, and he turned eyes on her.

Ammon ignored him, stroking his old teacher's hair. 'I'm sorry I was gone too long to save you.'

Lethor snarled keeping the boy between him and Neith. 'Ignore me once more and you'll find you came back only to be found without head.' He raised his sword.

Neith gave warning but the boy did not look back.

Ammon raised his left hand and dropped it. A simple gesture, yet it made Lethor's sword turn to dust. The captain of the prison cursed. 'Osirian tricks won't save you. I need no blade to finish a boy.'

He rushed forward but Ammon threw his hand past his left ear, and the jackal captain flew into the wall, stunned.

Neith came beside the boy. 'What are you?'

'I am Ammon.' He stroked the old man's white beard. 'I am also the Light.'

Neith dropped to her knee.

Ammon smiled. 'Get up and help me.'

She complied and he looked at her. His eyes shone golden and her wounds healed.

'I could have done that myself, boy, but I thank you for your attentions nevertheless.'

Without warning, Lethor came again. Neith snarled in turn but the boy was far quicker. Moving to meet him at a speed even she was surprised by. He said one word. 'Stop.'

With wide eyes and no understanding, Captain Lethor stopped.

The boy reached out and said, 'I take back what was given as reward. Suitable punishment will find you soon enough.' The crystal amulet he wore fell to dust and his body glowed brief white, before returning to its normal hue.

Lethor, immobile, screamed in rage and pain at the loss of power, as he restructured into mortal man.

The boy found spark of life in his teacher's eyes. His body had turned almost brittle. Ammon stroked his hair and smiled through tears. Akhet could not speak, but a tear also fell from his eye, and then Ammon lost control and grieved hard.

For some time the boy cried uncontrollably. Neith in her own grief knelt beside and held him tight. They cried together, Goddess and King.

They shared memories. Neith sang sweet songs of remembrance and was surprised at how well Ammon complemented them. When they had both released enough grief, they stood. Ammon wiped tears away on his sleeve.

'You have power, Ammon. I feel it now. It is not like those of us, but greater.'

'Yes, I was made anew by Ardunadine. I am the first of my kind.'

Neith understood. 'Then you are father to me, not brother.'

Ammon lifted Akhet. The Osirian now blackened, brittle, and fragile. His wound had almost turned him entirely to ash, yet the great will of Akhet still battled. Ammon was careful as he lifted, for fear of his body crumbling.

Ammon turned. 'Be well, Neith.' He looked at Lethor then back at her. 'And be merciful.'

She bowed her head. 'What of, sister-son? Is there any hope?'

Ammon smiled as another tear fell.

'As Akhet once said, hope may be all we have left to cling to.'

Neith put a hand on Akhet's blackened face.

'Peace, my beautiful brother. Your strength and pride will remain part of me. I will mourn with such grief the darkness will tremble and find no place in its shadow to hide.'

She kissed him, tears flowing free once more, and then kissed Ammon.

'Farewell, father. I suspect we shall see one another again.'

Ammon nodded, turned and carried Akhet forward a few paces, then faded from view.

When the boy vanished, his control over Lethor broke, and he released with a drop robbed of strength and power. He saw her advance and skittered away. Begging, pleading, but she was relentless. When she got within striking distance he found himself on his feet. He fumbled for sword, but she knocked it from his trembling hands.

With a war cry she cut both his legs off in one great swipe.

He screamed and wept as he fell, the pain unbearable, he howled and cried, begging for mercy.

In a grief-stricken rage, Neith lifted her sword high and hesitated, as Ammon's voice whispered into her ear, *"... and be merciful"*.

Her shoulder dropped. Sheathing sword, she bent down.

'I promised the boy I would show mercy. Do not worry. I am not going to kill you, Lethor. I have ... a better use for you.'

'I will be dead from loss of blood before that time comes.'

The prison guardians entered the chamber. Neith sensed their confusion, but they read his betrayal soon enough, and it drove them wild with anger. They advanced on him but she stepped forward and commanded them to stop. Then with warmth in her voice she said, 'Lethor has doomed us and freed brother from confinement, but I command that no harm should befall him. There is much I would learn. Go now, be at peace, most loyal Guardians of Light. Wait for me outside.'

They swallowed anger and bowed. Obeying her orders, they left.

Lethor crawled slowly away, blood seeping from the stumps of his useless legs. 'I will tell you nothing.'

She turned and grabbed him by his belt, spinning him onto his back.

'Where were we?'

She raised a hand, and then bright blue-fire burst from it. He watched as her hand came closer to the bleeding end of a sheared off leg. He opened his eyes wide.

'Now, Lethor, this may sting. ...'

*

The guardians assisted Neith's army in piling the corpses of their enemy. The cavern littered with them, the sands were soaked in blood. Then a hideous piercing scream came from inside. The guardians looked concerned but not Neith's men.

Captain of Neith's army calmed their fears with a laugh and said, 'All is well. You will hear many of these sounds now battle has ended. Don't you know its name? They call it, "Neith's mercy cry".'

Men and guardian laughed.

Mary had stayed away from the battle for the most part, and now assisted in tending the wounded. Her eyes scanned the bodies of those who had fallen, and she was happy to note that there was none of Neith's army amongst them. Her eyes eventually found his. Wounded but only lightly, a smile crossed both their faces. Reassured, she turned back to her task.

The Goddess emerged from the prison dragging Lethor by his hair, his stumps cauterised. She dropped him and he coughed and whimpered.

The other guardians sneered but he did not meet their gaze.

Her captain came forward in greeting. 'My Lady, it is good you are well.'

'There was ever doubt?'

He put a hand to her face, and she took it in gratitude.

'Nay, but I won wager this time.'

She laughed. 'What was bet?'

'That you would come out with no wound.' He smiled, and she lowered her eyes.

'My Lady?'

'You lost this wager then, husband.' She put a hand on his breastplate and he saw sadness in her eyes as only he could. He frowned but she smiled in a way he knew, telling him to wait for explanations. 'Today my wounds run deeper than you know.' She turned and made for Mary, attending the wounded. Eyes followed her with deep concern.

Then he called after her, 'The guardians do not want this traitor's gaze to fall on them. Does it need eyes in your plans, Great Lady?'

'No,' she threw over her shoulder. 'You may put them out.'

Lethor struggled and screamed as they held him down and pulled his eyes from his head.

Neith came beside fallen guardian and healed his wound. She smiled as Mary employed similar techniques. When they had helped the worst, Neith took Mary to one side.

'Sweet child, you are well?'

'Yes, I think so.'

'You took care of our problem?'

'I did, thank you for giving me that. It was cathartic.' She handed her back the golden sword, but Neith put a hand up.

'No, she is yours, and no better hand would I place it in.'

Inclining her head, she said, 'A wondrous gift, I shall honour it.' Mary then took the bag from her belt. 'I have it.'

Neith's eyes studied the bag. 'It lives inside?'

'Yes, calling for its master.'

'There is only one place we can hide it.'

Mary looked over at the guardian she'd dragged from inside. 'You brought another enemy out?'

Neith sighed. 'Worse, a protector of Light bathed in darkness. He changed his allegiance and set Seth free. Then assisted in destroying my beloved brother.'

'Brother? Akhet? Oh no, I'm so sorry. I didn't think to ask.'

Neith let tears fall. Mary embraced her. 'Aye, a worse day has yet to come for me. I weary of battle. The boy-king may have healed my wounds, but I hold many more inside. I need rest and meditation.' She looked around her and sighed again. 'I would leave this place, would you come?'

'Of course.'

'Good, I need a strong companion.'

'What of Seth?'

Neith frowned. 'I do not know what his plans will be, but they are not likely to be kind.'

'Do you think he will give his loyalty to Beast?'

'For a time, until it suits him not to do so. My brother has loyalty only to himself. But we must not concern ourselves with what might be. For now, this battle is ended. I must give commands to my army, and husband. Then we may leave.'

Mary nodded and made her way to the man whose secret name only she knew. He inclined his head at her approach, went to kneel, but pain wracked him and he all but toppled into her. Mary saw blood seeping from underneath his armour and frowned. His wound was not light as had first been suspected.

'My Lady, forgive my weakness.' He grunted as the pain tore through him. Mary helped him to the ground.

'You are badly injured.' She was angry now. 'Why has no one tended this wound?'

Neith's captain came beside her. 'We tried, Great Mary, but he would not allow anyone to touch him.'

With great effort he stood to meet his captain. But his eyes lowered at the hard look received. Mary stood and unlatched the plate on his chest and saw the extent of his injury.

He said, 'Aye, that is the truth.'

She frowned. 'But why? Why would you suffer like this? It makes no sense.'

He said nothing.

Then the captain growled as realisation hit him. He put his head within inches of the warrior's face, and in whisper he said, 'You foolish boy, you gave her your name, didn't you?'

His eyes remained fixed on the ground, his knees buckled and he dropped to the sand, Mary beside him in support. She looked confused. 'I don't understand?'

The captain sighed and knelt, helping her remove his chest-plate. He put a hand on the warrior's naked shoulder.

'Didn't you know, Great Lady?' the captain's voice was low, 'when a warrior of the Goddess Neith gives his name, he is forever bonded. No one may touch him, unless she allows it to be so.'

Mary swallowed. 'I ... I see.'

The warrior felt shame rise in him and his face turned red, but the captain of Neith's army lifted his chin so eyes could meet, and those eyes were kind.

'Feel not ashamed, young warrior. I too gave this promise.' He eyed them both in turn. 'This knowledge must remain between us.'

They nodded and Mary thanked him.

'All is good.' He smiled. Squeezing the warrior's shoulder, he stood then marched away.

Mary stripped him down to his loin and tended his wound. When he was bandaged, she sat beside him in the sand.

'Darius, why didn't you say anything about this attachment ritual?'

He shifted his eyes away from her to the goddess.

'What was there to say? I didn't have choice, your power commanded it. My Lady, you are a studier of our history. I thought you would know.'

It was true, she should have known better, but base desires overrode academic learnings. She felt shame heat her. Mary bit her lip. She'd given him no choice but to comply.

'What does this mean, for you, I mean?'

He smiled and took her hand. 'I am bonded to you, my Lady. I understand this is not your way, and I know you cannot reciprocate my love. I will do as you command. I will please you when called for. If that is what you require of me?'

She retracted her hand. 'Require? Don't say it like that.'

He frowned. 'But you are bonded to another. I know this. How else should I say it?'

'You can never be ... with ... anyone else?'

He offered her a smile. 'Not while you or I live.'

'But that's ... why?'

'Because it is ...'

Mary put a hand to his lips. 'Forbidden?'

He nodded.

She dropped her hands. 'Oh Darius, what a mess I've made of things.'

And he took her face into his hands and kissed her with passion. For the longest time they locked eyes then he stood and helped her to her feet.

'My Lady, thank you for healing my wounds.' His smile tore at her soul. He lowered his head and she reached for him, but he turned and marched away.

Mary followed his back and felt sickened by her actions. But she also felt something more, and it concerned her deeply. Her heart beat hard in her chest. Confusion and mixed emotions coursed through her. She loved Albert. That had never been in question. But now, now things were more difficult, because she also had feelings for Darius, and he was clearly in love with her. She called on her power and commanded it to take away the pain, and it complied.

Neith felt her emotional conflict, watched the warrior limp away from her, and then Mary's power took control, and the conflict was gone. She narrowed her eyes, contemplating much.

*

Deep inside the chamber once containing the prison Shard, a dark mist swirled in slow pulses around the broken body of Melrah. It formed a bubble, collapsing him into nothing but a dent in the ground.

The Undying Lands

High in the mountain above the foul realm now known as The Black Lands of Beast, he sat surveying all, contemplating much. The fallen Osirian, commonly known by variations on Set, Seth, or Sutekh, came beside the Lord of the Darkness and stroked the fur of his colossal mane, with a long clawed hand. Huge luminous green eyes blinked at his touch.

He wore simple loincloth of black mixed with gold, adorned in the typical blue-gold symbols of the ancients. Unlike his brothers and sisters, he preferred to remain in a hybrid human-animal form, unless it suited his purpose not to do so. His upper torso an unknown animal with curved snout and long rectangular ears.

'I approve of this world you've created, my Lord.'

Beast gave contented purr.

'I am happy to hear you say so, although what servants like or dislike means little to me.'

Seth frowned. 'That is all I am to you? Servant?'

The great lion considered his response.

'You expected more? A reward perhaps?'

Seth removed his hand. 'Yes, and more beside, still … to be free of void of nothingness is in itself reward.'

'And if I was to grant one, in what form would that please you, Usurper of the Osirian?'

'Before I answer, let me pose question of you.'

Beast waited.

'Aside from the earth, which is now yours to rule as you will. What other prize does he seek, other than destruction of my hateful kin?'

Beast growled. *'There is only one other thing on this world I would take, but I am loathed to waste time on it. As to your kin? Their destruction I value highly, but you know they are protected, and as quickly as one is removed, so another claims name and title and continue on as though no change had occurred.'*

Seth said, 'I am high-born, as is Neith. Each time they conjoin or reform, they weaken. I have knowledge, but,' he sighed and looked to the horizon, 'as a lowly servant, I say, I am not in position to offer much, other than to cow to my new Lord and do his will, as payment for deeds done that led up to conversation.'

Beast laughed.

'I shall enjoy your company. What do you offer me?'

'Aside from my might and power?'

'Yes, I have that and more. You were born of my own brothers, I too have such abilities. I say, bring me ten men and I will make ten Dark Osirian to counter any light.'

'Ah yes, like your King of Darkness, Arnold? Neith crushed him like a bug.'

Beast growled warning, his eyes shone with mounting anger.

Seth turned to him and calmed him by touch. 'I do not say these things to annoy you. I know you could send me to oblivion in short order. But I am not some lackey either. I do not seek title, Lord. I already have many: God of the Desert of Storms and Disorder. That is how I was known, and I shall be known by them again. Tell me something. This thing you seek, would it give you more power over your enemy?'

'*No. But it would weaken spirits and connections.*'

'Ah.' Seth smiled wide. 'I sense it, the Destorian crystal is what you prize?'

Beast roared in laughter.

'*You are powerful, Seth. I was wrong to think of you as servant only. A mistake corrected, friend. Although I do not say equal.*'

'Never that. Friend? Yes. At least until I have power enough to take your kingdom from you of course.'

'*A glorious battle that would be, too.*'

Seth looked to the horizon. His vision zoomed forward, out of black wastes into stunning paradise. At its centre, a majestic palace of crystal. 'What is the place of light I see ahead of us?'

'*A gift from Arrandori, curse Him. For the people of this Earth.*'

Seth laughed. 'And He put it in the middle of your Kingdom? What a sense of humour He has.'

'*Nothing can penetrate it. Neither side can manifest within. Anything borne from darkness becomes ash within its light.*'

'What of the men of your lands?'

'*They too become ash.*'

'So the dark cannot enter and the light must travel through the dark to get to it?'

'*It is that way, yes.*'

'Well, my Lord. I thank you for my rescue. There is bond between us now and I ask him if payment for deeds done is satisfied?'

'*It is.*'

'Then I depart. I would seek to view this world and make choice upon where I would build my place on it. But before I leave, I have a gift for you. To solidify friendship, as two fallen sons should.'

'*What is this gift you offer?*'

Seth opened his hands and a shimmering light mist pulsed between them. When it finished, a huge jagged crystal appeared. Beast looked at him with deep respect.

'*You had it, all this time?*'

'Yes. It was in my prison chamber.'

'*You give this thing to me, willingly?*'

'What use is it to me? My power would not weaken by its loss, and I have no desire to travel to where we know it leads.'

Seth manifested a large pedestal and placed it on top. 'It is yours.'
Beast stood and sung. *'I will not forget what you have done this day.'*
'I hope you find use in it.'
'I would not use it. For now, it is not usable by Osirian either. We have taken their link. Lesser Servants of the Light will weaken and wither, unlike you and your sister.'
'Neith. She is a problem for us both.'
'Agreed. What would you suggest we do about her?'
'I will give it some thought.'
Seth turned into whirlwind and floated out into the world.

*

In his chamber, Sam felt burnt flesh with a mixture of horror and rage. Blind, at least of mortal sight, he knew his body must look hideous, but that didn't concern him. The inner eye of his shadow saw more and translated the shifting auras and ethereal flames into new vision. Seth had healed and imparted knowledge of what transpired in the battle after he was injured by Horus.

His King and brother lay dead at Neith's hand, along with all the King's Guard and Melrah, poor Melrah. The rage inside burned. Sam vowed to avenge them all, but knew if Arnold was no match for her, then new power and training would be necessary before vengeance could be satisfied.

He reached out for the amulet, a gift from Lethor. Through his shadow-eye he saw its alien beauty. Sam wondered if he could unlock its power and absorb it. For now, he placed it back on the small table and left the chamber. Sam needed answers and knowledge. The only one who could give these things, he feared.

Prince of Shadows emerged and called for his master, requesting audience. Beast heard and granted it.

They met in the observation cavern high in the mountain.

'I sense your approach, Sam-Prince. Come, be beside me and feel malice warm your heart. You are weary from battle and from loss.'
'Thank you, my Lord.'
'You have shown your courage and proven loyalty and love.'
'You will never have cause to question either, Lord of Darkness.'
'Spoken as your King once did, I see now why he brought you to me.'

'He was as a brother. Is there nothing that can be done to retrieve him?'

Beast turned a massive head. *He is dead, what use is his corpse to thee?*

Shadow Prince swallowed rage. 'I thought ...'

'You thought what? That my love for him would override sagacity? It is true I forged great connection with Arnold-King, who freed me from my prison, but Sam-Prince, he played his part and died in service. I will have songs sung in his honour, and then I will send you to crush those who put him into the dirt. But I do not seek to rescue a cadaver and nor should you. Are my words in your mind clear?

'Yes, my Lord.'

Beast stared at him for a moment and Sam felt his gaze penetrating deep into the fabric of his being. Then the eyes blinked. *Good. I have something for you, a gift, for your service. Perhaps it will aid you?*

There was a grunt in the darkness, and Sam turned and gave a cry as Melrah limped towards him. His body scarred, wounds from Neith still healing.

Sam turned back to earthly form and hugged the giant neck. 'Oh, I am so happy to see you alive.'

He gave a short bark. Sam smiled, and then he heard Melrah say, *Melrah overjoyed Prince also survives.*

Sam looked in astonishment. 'I can understand you?'

Beast chuckled. *'I granted Songs of Knowledge and Voice, Sam-Prince. There is more I would have you learn, but for now rest is earnt. You and this beast called Melrah did well, truly. I will call upon you both when suitable time has passed. Go now.'*

They bowed and left.

Beast turned his head back to the darkness around.

*

When he was alone and the night was at its darkest hour, Beast trilled slow melody and a great wall in the rock parted. A dais of obsidian crept forward. A form bent forward into ball, lay shackled at its centre.

Beast padded forward and gave soft growl.

'See my latest prize?'

The scarred figure unfolded, stood, and came to the edge of the dais where her shackles pulled taunt. Her cloak torn and ripped, soaked in blood and filth. The vile blackness of the land had penetrated deep into her earthly body. Around her neck swung amulet of crystal, it seemed to weigh her down. Older looking now, bent with no staff for support, Osiris known as Lady of Light found she was unable to sing.

She took in the sight of the great crystal and understood the meaning of it. Seth must have taken it from the prison. Their link to the Ardunadine now belonged to Beast. Osiris felt turmoil and rage at the betrayal. Beast sung tales that filled her with misery and grief. How Lethor had betrayed them all, and how he and Arnold-King ended the Osirian on Earth, how the boy-king Ammon had been murdered by those he wished to save, and how her beloved son Horus was nothing more than ash.

Osiris did not trust her voice so said nothing. She remained unblinking before him until his song had finished, and her spirit was destroyed.

'I shall enjoy watching you wither and suffer, Osirian hag.'

He lunged at her.

She did not cower.

He roared fury and hate.

She did not tremble.

'Leave my sight before I gorge myself on you.'

The dais melted back into shadow.

Osiris curled back into a ball.

In the darkness, cut off from songs and her kin, she cried soft tears.

Her thoughts on one thing alone: *Why had Mary and Neith betrayed her?*

Epilogue
The Choices of Man

The New World: A New Direction

The gathering occurred as it had in times past, but there was none of the usual joy within it. Kings and queens of men stood within the small group of Osirian. There was no celebrating this time.

One of the Osirian came forward. He had not been heavily involved in any of their previous gatherings, and most of the sovereigns of man had little contact with him. He put a hand up and they fell silent.

'I am Sobek, and it now falls to me to lead and protect, and I will do so, but I am no master of it.'

'What of Akhet?' a voice asked.

'What of Osiris?' said another.

Sobek came amongst them all. 'Akhet, my brother, is no longer amongst us, and we grieve for him. As to Osiris, we do not yet know what has befallen her. The light and songs are quiet yet we feel within us she is not gone but missing. There is still hope.'

Palash came forward and bowed. 'May I ask something of you? What of my King, Ammon?'

Sobek put a hand on Palash's shoulder. 'He lives and is now part of the Great Light. Neith witnessed his majesty. It was he who took Akhet away after Prince of Shadow pierced him with a vile blade.'

They were downcast and he felt the sorrow and despair.

'Listen to me, all of you. Have we been dealt vicious blow? Yes. Have we lost great warriors and loved ones? Certainly. Are we defeated by this?'

There was silence.

'I asked you, are we defeated?'

One by one they connected with each other and answered in unison. 'No.'

'Then let us continue as we were before. Each of you are building a society that is self-sufficient, and are becoming independent from our power, as your armies begin to develop. I will assist in the training, along with my other brothers, and we will build this society of man back to strength.

'Our enemy was also dealt a savage blow, too. His King of Darkness and all the men that followed him were destroyed. That is something to rejoice. Sister-Mother Neith has sent her great army into New Egypt so this land may be built under protection from things creeping along its border.

'We must also say welcome to Dalyn, King Ammon's gift to us all, who is now of Osirian strength.'

They greeted him and he bowed low.

'Let this not be a sorrowful gathering. We honour our fallen with song.'

Queen Elizabeth asked, 'What of Mary? I have not seen her in months. I would like to know that she is safe.'

Sobek nodded. 'Mary is with Neith, and her training is well in hand. They have become inseparable.'

'I see, well, should you speak with her. Tell her I miss her and would be glad to see her again.'

'I will do so, Elizabeth Queen.'

The discussions continued on topics affecting both man and their enemy. They questioned tasks and quests, which now seemed redundant or of no benefit. Sobek answered as much as he could, and then appealed for calm. He sung to them and they felt his peaceful grace. Then they connected to each other and began to formulate plans.

*

Goddess Neith and Mary sat at the top of the temple roof and bathed naked in the heat of the afternoon sun. They'd visited many places to assist Neith in breaking her grief. When they needed to, found monsters within darkness, and slew them together. Now they were content to enjoy the sun.

Neith sighed. Her eyes closed she said, 'Sobek has taken control of the Osirian Pantheon, now Osiris is no longer within their ranks.'

Mary looked downcast.

Neith glared at her. 'I hope you are not feeling remorseful?'

'I am a little concerned. I doubt she will fully understand.'

'No.' Neith looked to the horizon. 'She will consider such treachery unworthy of either of us.'

Mary looked hard at her. 'I don't regret the choice I made.'

'Nor would I have you do so. There are times selfish motives are necessary for greater goods yet to be revealed. Besides, she will understand in time, if she survives, of course.'

Mary nodded. 'I hope she does.'

'Survives? Or understands?'

'Both! But above all, survives.'

Neith nodded and lay back into her chair. 'We made a calculated decision. You were not alone in it, I too am culpable. When you first spoke your plan, I said what to you?'

'That it was sure to fail.'

'No. Not that.' Neith turned her head. 'I said it would be fun.'

Mary chuckled despite her guilt. 'Yes, you did say that.'

'Tell me something. Did you enjoy slaying that foul Arnold thing?'

She looked horrified. 'Enjoy it? No! I felt release and some satisfaction, I'll admit, but killing him was not enjoyable. I'm sorry if that displeases you.'

Neith looked happy. 'No, child, it would have giving great concern to me if you answered yes. To end a life with joy goes far into darkness, from which you might never return. Lessons are almost complete. You have only a few left to learn. One we will start soon.'

Mary nodded and closed her eyes.

Neith coughed. 'Would you not hear what that lesson is?'

'Absolutely.'

Neith gave wicked grin. 'I would teach you how to defend against sister's wrath. If she survives and does not understand reasons, at least you may give challenge before she swipes the head from you.'

Mary looked shocked. 'You think it might come to a fight between us?'

Neith frowned. 'I was making a joke. But you are not laughing so attempt was not successful.'

Then Mary did laugh and Neith was pleased.

'I adore you, Neith.'

'As you should. So what is our next move?'

'Our?'

'Why yes. Surely we are together in this deceit? I would not let prized pupil out of my sight. Now that she has discovered devious side and is willing to take men into her chamber, and dominate them like a true warrior.'

Mary said nothing.

'Admit it, Mary. You enjoyed the warrior I sent.'

'I did.'

Neith sighed. 'I know what you did, Mary, or at least I read something of it from loyal husband who has never once kept secrets from me before now.'

She felt shame break her.

'Do you love this warrior?'

'I don't know.'

Neith growled. 'This conversation feels like our first, when you would not speak plainly. You do know, child.'

'I'm sorry, I'm conflicted. I love Albert.'

Neith was quiet.

'But I also love Darius, too.'

'What will you do?'

'What I planned to do all along, rescue Albert. The rest I will take care of in my own way, in my own time.'

'I would release this bond, if you asked it of me.'

'Thank you, I will think about that.'

'He is a lucky warrior to have your love. You understand why I forbid them to speak their names?'

'Aside from bonding with unsuspecting fools like me? No, I meant to ask.'

Neith smiled. 'I forbid it for simple reason. I do not want to have lists of individuals who die in my service. It would be long and too hard for me to bear. Better they are known only as warrior or rank.'

'I understand. You're dehumanising them.'

Neith shrugged. 'Callous? Perhaps, but that is my way.'

Then Neith turned to her. 'Mary, may I ask something of you?'

'Of course.'

'Would you consent to becoming ... sister?'

'Consent? I'd be honoured to call you sister.'

'It is well then. We have destiny together, sister. I feel great bond with you.'

'And I you.'

Neith felt something from her. 'You wish to make your next move?'

'Yes, when I quiet the inner voices, I can hear him. I think I know where he is.'

'Well,' Neith said and closed her eyes. 'Let the sun warm us for a while, then perhaps we will go and find him.'

Mary looked up at the sun unblinking, her eyes black.

'Yes,' she said softly. 'Let's do that.'

*

Deep in the Undying Black Lands

It was dark. So dark nothing could be seen. From within, Mary whispered and dull golden light shone around. He came to her and they met in embrace.

'Finally we are together,' Albert-Nurrunadine breathed. They kissed. Mary held his face and her black-golden eyes met his.

'We have little time, Albert. Neith stands guard. I brought you something.' She handed him a black staff. 'It was his, now yours.'

He took it and power coursed through him. 'We have new strength now, Mary. I've waited so long to be this close to you; I don't want it to end.'

'Patience, Albert. Let us share this moment in passion rather than words.'

They fell pawing at each other in darkness and then her dull light extinguished.

From the depths of the Undying Black Lands, a mixture of strange unnatural sound intermixed with their own.

* * * *

Extract from the Book of Narrudeth–Appendix B

"... The realm known as Earth filled with grief at loss of great warriors on both sides. High in the mountains of the darkness, Beast set plans unfolding and remained as he had, locked away from the light in malice. His servant, Prince of Shadow, now sought quest to avenge his king's death and–for his Lord had made revelations-bring back the essence that still remained in the world of men. The Osirian found powers weakened and they knew not why. The loss of their great mystical link, stolen by Seth was known only to one, and she was now prisoner to the Lord of the Darkness.

And so it came to pass that Seth now reigned amongst all fallen men, who worshiped and despised him. They built fresh industries of war under his hateful shadow and the Lord Beast gave him what he needed and stayed above, where his power was supreme.

The coming days and nights found friendships and hardships on all sides, but above all, great sacrifices. And as light of love and peace washed away fears and shadows, or, shadows and malice washed away love and joy, they looked to new quests.

Ammon, High King of the Earth now elevated beyond Osirian, looked down with new eyes, and saw a plague of black transforming his once beautiful world. He knew what could be done to save it, but it meant walking a path not all were ready or willing to set upon. It would be some years before he would return to give voice to it.

Of the greatest Servants of Light, Horus known as Akhet, and Etheria once Osiris and Isis, not a whisper was heard. Goddess Neith remained outside the Osirian Pantheon, giving occasional appearance, but her mind centred upon her plans with Mary, although she kept an eye on the world and gave her army to stand in protection of all men.

And so, days went forward into years. The darkest chapters yet to been written. ..."

[Bonus Short Story]

The Last of Us

By Rob James

It's so dark out here, so very dark and so very quiet apart from the waves lapping at the side of my life pod. Sometimes I can hear the whitecaps breaking as they tumble inexorably back into the depths that carry them. *Am I flotsam? Or am I jetsam?* Being carried along on currents, taking me to where? I know where I came from. I know how I got here, memories are a wonderful thing. We were the last line, the final stand against the darkness enshrouding the system. We fell not in days, or hours, but minutes. We thought we had the measure of them. They were just toying with us until they grew bored. The greatest fleet ever assembled in our history–all nations uniting even the secessionist colonies joined–to make one final glorious stand. It was meant to be magnificent, it wasn't. It was ignominious. Thirty thousand ships from fighters to frigates, barges to capital ships, yachts and freighters. Gone … all gone. I don't know what they hit us with. It was as if the gates of Hell opened and rained fire upon everything before them.

We didn't stand a chance.

What about the folks back home? I pity them. They have no idea what's coming. Or perhaps they do? If the Unity Coalition is truthful with them, then maybe? I know what I would do, I'd bake the planet. If *we* can't have it then neither can they. It is our world. Our home. To do with as we wish. In the past, we came close to destroying it beyond repair, then we saw the light and changed our ways. All for what? For this? We should have ignored the warnings about global warming and climate change. We could have made it barren, then they would have left us in peace. They wanted fruitful lands and clean water, we saw that from the methods employed on other worlds, worlds cleansed of sentient life. That's all we knew about them, along with overwhelming firepower. I don't think anyone ever got to see one of them in the flesh. If they did, it was kept very quiet.

We tried to communicate. I remember hearing in the newscasts. They even broadcast a live subspace transmission off an emissary ship in an attempt to open communications, and that's when we saw what they could do.

That's when I knew we were going to become endangered, soon to be extinct.

Are they gods, or our God?

Or are they the Great Creators of the cosmos returning to view and judge their creations?

Did they find us wanting?

Is this Divine retribution on a universal scale?

Were they so disappointed with us and our past misdemeanours, they felt redemption was truly beyond us?

But we were redeemed. We wiped out poverty, hunger, and disease. We threw away misconceptions about greed and wealth. We learnt our lesson, in the most painful way, on the backs of billions of lives. We stepped from the brink and saw reason. We gained enlightenment. Maybe this was our undoing. In embracing reason and intelligence we turned from the old ways. Did we forget to worship our deities? Did that anger them? We replaced them with power, greed, and conflict … our world warned us and we didn't listen. We carried on a childlike and selfish drive, pushing us to gain more and more regardless of cost. But the cost was high … far too high, and we paid the price, our world rebelled … and we paid dearly. We repented, seeing for the first time the damage being done, and we stepped back from the brink. We grew up and the world gave us another chance. We repaired it, worked together to put things right, to undo the wrongs of one-hundred generations.

Here's an outlandish idea: We are vermin and they are the universal equivalent of interstellar pest control; coming to eradicate a contagion in this sector of the galaxy, with no negotiation, and no mercy.

We weren't worthy of their contemplation because to them, we were merely insects.

I can't feel my feet. Hypothermia probably.

How long have I been here? An hour? Two hours? More?

I didn't check the chronograph when I splashed down, and I am sure I've been dropping in and out of consciousness for some time. My head hurts like a bitch. I really should try to get my bearings, the pod is nearly dead. I'll have to do it the old-fashioned way.

The sky is clear. There's not a cloud I can make out. I see the vast majesty of the universe above me, a hundred billion stars in our galaxy alone. I wonder at its beauty. How many other systems out there have life? We have travelled through space for nearly two hundred years and we've yet to find any intelligent life. Until *they* appeared. Although *we* didn't find them, *they* found us. Is there someone out there at this very moment, like me, adrift on an ocean, looking towards the heavens and wondering as I do? Or are they gone too? Exterminated by unnamed goliaths from the deepest reaches of the aether?

My hands are numbing as I float on my little tin can, waiting for what or who? Godot? Hah! I'm slowly dying and my jokes are terminal.

I wonder how long I have left? I don't want to die like this. I want to go out on my own terms, but I don't think I can manage it now. My hands are just too numb to hold my weapon, let alone fire one, and the capsule? Well, if I can't hold my gun I certainly won't be able to open the suicide box. I guess I'll just have to wait for death to catch up to me, and I can join my brothers and sisters on the other side. Is there such a place? Can I really believe in something I cannot see or touch or smell? It's all a matter of faith. I lack it. Even as I look up at the celestial display and see the magnificence of it, I'm not convinced.

The years we spent studying it, proving it, disproving it, and still we don't know how it came to be. We theorise and explain it to a certain degree, but ask any physicist and they cannot tell you for certain what they propose is truth. Oh the irony in the myth, ask a physicist how it formed and eventually if you ask enough questions he'll reply, "God knows".

I stifle the yearning to laugh at this as the fluids are increasing in my chest causing me too much discomfort … I'm drowning in my own bodily juices whilst adrift on the sea.

The choices are a dilemma: Hypothermia, drowning, or starvation.

I wish my hands weren't so numb. I could make the choice for myself then, rather than the lottery I currently face.

The stars are fading, no, not fading, they're being blanked out. Slowly but surely they're being blanked out. I didn't notice, too busy wrapped up in my own thoughts. Here I lay, facing the night sky and I didn't notice the stars going out. Wait, it's far too uniform. A line being drawn across the heavens. One side stars the other nothing. Just blackness, empty, soulless and black. I've never seen that before. Back in history, it was said holy men were shut in the tombs of their kings when they died. As the final stone slid into place, and they witnessed that total blackness as they accompanied their king into the next life, did they watch the stars disappear too? Is this my tomb? Adrift on my pod watching the final stone slid into place, over humanity?

I'm not scared. I thought I would be, but I'm not. I was when we launched. I think we all knew it was a one-way trip. The fear palpable. It was sour, sickeningly so, and we could smell it, taste it, feel it. We hugged, saying our goodbyes, as the ships launched ... and then we died.

Did anyone survive the initial attack? I wonder.

Come to that, did anyone get a shot off?

And if they did, did it make a difference?

The stars are nearly gone now. I know what's causing them to disappear. It's them or rather one of them. Their ships are either the size of planets, or one is just a few metres above me. I can't tell because there's no noise. I have no comparisons to judge by, so I can only assume.

I can hardly breathe; my lungs are full of liquid. It's ironic that the life pod, which was supposed to save me, has probably killed me when it hit the water and dislodged conduits along the inner wall. The pain was excruciating. I don't remember much afterwards. I don't even remember pulling the sharp length out of my chest, probably not one of my better ideas in retrospect. I don't suppose it matters now. Here I am alone with my thoughts and I'm dying ... just dying.

I could be the last of my race. I don't even get to go out in a blaze of glory, something to let them know I was here, I stood for something, I mattered.

Gone, in the blink of an eye, an extinction level event.

Will they record our passing with reverence, or will we just be a footnote in the annals of their history?

Oh, my eyes. The light is so bright, blinding white enveloping me. Cold white as bright as a fusion bomb, and as painful as having them scooped out with a razor. I await the blast that strips my flesh from my bones before pummelling me into dust.

The blast never comes.

I feel lighter ... no, that's not right ... I *am* lighter.

I'm lifting ... rising ... up from the pod ... towards the light.

This isn't my doing. They're doing it!

I am being drawn upwards.

It must be a hatchway of some kind. They're bringing me aboard. Why? What do they want from me? Are they rescuing or capturing me?

No ... there's something *very* wrong here.

I am rising up, but I can see myself below. I look down at a lifeless broken body, *my* lifeless broken body!

I'm being drawn into their craft and I want to weep. I cross the threshold and sensed others there with me ... like me ... dispossessed of physical form. They're crying out for salvation. What is this place?

There's movement beside me. A shape of some kind? I can't make it out but it's there, only just, phasing in and out of my ethereal perception.

Is that an arm? It's reaching to me, touching me, stroking my psyche.

It hurts, oh it hurts!

No, it's not stroking me. It's taking a part of me and raising it to ... is that its head? Are those ears or horns?

It's ... oh my good God ... it's tasting me, nodding in approval ... tasting my *soul*.

For the love of all things holy.

We're not being invaded or eradicated ... *we never even contemplated this*.

We are being harvested. ...

* * *

About Rob James

I spend my time whilst not driving trains seeking creative inspiration, whether it is photography, music, writing, playing games on my computer or riding my Vespa. My qualifications were gained at the University of Life. I think I will graduate soon. I love to read and I always have at least two or three books on the go at any one time. I have no favourite genres, if it's well written then that's good enough for me. I live in Northamptonshire UK, and have done for many years with my beautiful and understanding wife Jude. We have 3 sons, 2 dogs and 2 cats, it's never quiet here. I've been working on a few short stories and I am also working on my first full length novel that I hope to have finished before I retire.

You can connect with Rob here:
www.facebook.com/authorrobjames

About Christopher D. Abbott

Christopher is a Reader's Favorite award winning author.

He has a background in human behavioural studies and psychology. Having worked in IT, communications, safety and health, and sales, he gained a good understanding of people and their behaviours. Abbott is a self-confessed avid reader of crime fiction, and he took creative writing courses, which fuelled his ambition to publish character driven stories. He loves quirky characters such as Rodney David Wingfield's Inspector "Jack" Frost, Agatha Christie's Poirot, and Sir Arthur Conan Doyle's Sherlock Holmes. The Idea for his sleuth, Dr Pieter Straay (Dutch Criminal Psychologist) came about by integrating the qualities he admires best in these characters.

Christopher's new series, Songs of the Osirian, is his first step into the sci-fi – fantasy genre.

You can connect with Christopher here:
www.cdanabbott.com
www.facebook.com/cdanabbott

Pop Culture Hero Coalition

Mission and History

Created by Chase Masterson with Heroism Experts Carrie Goldman &

Matt Langdon, The Pop Culture Hero Coalition is the first-ever organization that uses the universal appeal of comics, film & TV to create anti-bullying programs at pop culture events, and in schools and communities.

Founded in 2013, we are a 501(c)(3) non-profit that takes a stand against bullying, racism, misogyny, cyber-bullying, LGBT-bullying, and other forms of hate, using the phenomenal popularity of media to bring justice and healing.

The Coalition's work features global experts and advocates, including representatives from the United Nations, the Anti-Defamation League, the NOH8 Campaign, Justice League New York, and other major organizations; we also work with clinical psychologists who specialize in using pop culture stories in restorative justice and in therapy for victims of bullying and injustice.

Connect with the Pop Culture Hero Coalition here:
http://www.popculturehero.org/

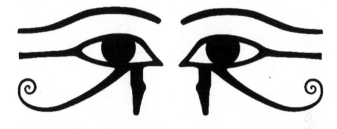

SONGS OF THE OSIRIAN

THE STORY CONTINUES IN BOOK 2

Made in the USA
Middletown, DE
15 October 2016